The Chalice of Immortals

The Chronicles of Ragnorak Book 2

A novel by

Christiano Prime
https://www.facebook.com/profile.php?id=1000333
01249234

Cover Art by Julie Tyslicky
https://www.facebook.com/profile.php?id=1000070
33579275

Foreword from the author:

This is a work of fiction. All the characters, organizations, and events portrayed in this novel are either products of the author's imagination or used fictitiously.

This book is dedicated to my eight wonderful sisters, for their eternal love and support! However fate brought us to be, I'm happy we all became family.

Chapter 1
Retreat

Retreat was a time for the fraternity to plan out goals and bond closer as a brotherhood. They were typically two to three days, twice a year in between semesters, with just the brothers. The Omegas had rented out a cabin almost two hours north of Bay City, going "up north" was a staple of Michigan culture. The Upsilon Delta Chapter of the Omegas left on a Friday afternoon, Virgil Pitcher was one of twenty brothers attending. Virgil rode with his pledge brothers Louie V, Dante, Troy, and Birdy who drove their group. They talked and sang along to the radio, their excitement reaching a fever pitch upon their arrival, at a luxurious three level home on a small lake outside of Mio. The brothers arrived a few hours before sunset, with plenty of time to enjoy the cabin on their first night. After the older brothers claimed the best sleeping arrangements, Friday night got crazy…fast! Everyone let loose, opening up, acting ridiculous to make others laugh, and sharing deep conversations. That night the men enjoyed for a small instant, the fleeting pleasure of youthful vigor.

It was winter in Michigan, thick heavy snow blanketed the land, making it too cold to do much outside for long. When you were with the brothers though, there was never a lack of entertainment. Virgil and his friends had four weeks off from school for winter break. All freshmen had to move out of the dorms for the break, but Virgil and his pledge brothers had just gone down the road to the Omega fraternity house. Virgil had gone to stay at his mom's house in Caseville for the week of Christmas. Afterwards he hurried back to campus to be with all his friends, missing the constant company, and endless options for fun and entertainment. Virgil's fraternity was different from the norm though. Unbeknownst to society, Nephilim, part human part Judge, lived among the general population. Fraternities like Virgil's were created in America hundreds of years ago to recruit young Nephilim to the Paladins, a Nephilim society that had existed long before the time of the pyramids. They were a military force, fighting to keep demons and other evil forces, from the Ever After, from taking control over the human world. After such a long break the guys were eager to get back to the structure and routine of college life.

The break had been needed by everyone, after the events that took place two months earlier. The Tear Drop incident, as Internationals was calling it, had forever changed the landscape of the world. The Arch Demon Abdanon had destroyed the Goddess' Tear Drop, and Virgil was the reason it had all happened. The Tear Drop sealed the Ever After off from the human world, a once enchanted realm inhabited by fairies, trolls, and other magical creatures, it was now the ethereal home to the demonic race and the Fallen Judges who led them. Since the Tear Drop incident, crime rates across the world had steadily begun to rise, the demons were coming over to the human world, with greater ease and in greater numbers. Virgil had naively given the Tear Drop to the Arch Demon in exchange for the lives of two of his friends. Abdanon snuffed out the lives of Virgil's pledge brothers Boyd and Darius. Abdanon almost killed Virgil and his brothers that night, and only by using his Devil Arms, Ragnorak, was he able to save everyone. Virgil also discovered he was the Redeemer, the Sixth Seraphim Nephilim, or Sixth Seraph. One of seven foretold beings of incredible power whose presence would bring about the end of the world or save it. He wanted to shrug it off and insist that he was just like the rest of his brothers, he knew though, inside, the truth of who he was.

Virgil had two Devil Arms symbols, a black scythe Chaos symbol on his left hand, and a white shooting star Creation glyph on his right. Devil Arms came in six colors each aligned with an element. When the name of the symbol is called, the soul weapon of that person materializes into a corporeal form. The same Devil Arms symbols could also create spells through sheer willpower, or Will, and the use of specific incantations. Virgil's white Devil Arms was Ragnorak, a mighty sword encased in a glowing golden aura. The most powerful weapon in existence, the Holy Blade was once carried by the Fallen Judge Raphael, revered as one of the wisest, kindest, and most powerful of the Judges. He sided with the Demon King, Diablos, and the weapon was taken from him. Virgil wasn't too keen on the idea of wielding such an infamous weapon, especially since Raphael was Virgil's father.

Virgil had never met Raphael, he had only known his name since November. Virgil had grown up in Caseville, in the rural Thumb of Michigan, living the American dream of freedom and the pursuit of happiness. He had been adopted by his parents and raised an only child. Growing up he had always felt different from the people around him. Most Nephilim's powers don't activate until their adults. Virgil was told that his mother had died giving birth to him, and they did not know who the father was. Virgil was shocked to learn the identity of his father. The ugly truth was hard to take in. Virgil was in the Omegas, a fraternity that belonged to the Paladin Order. The Paladins stood against the Fallen and the Death Dealers, and Virgil's father was one of the four Judges that led their forces. Virgil knew he'd end up running into his father someday, and he dreaded that moment. He doubted his dad would be happy to see him bonded with the weapon he'd wielded as a Judge for billions of years and fighting for the opposite side. To Virgil, John Pitcher, the man who had raised him for fourteen years, was his dad. Virgil wasn't about to turn his back on his family, friends, or country, for a man who'd abandoned him before birth. Virgil loved America and would be damned if demons and the Fallen would destroy it.

Saturday morning came early, and most of the brothers had to be forced awake for the meeting, some had only laid down a couple hours earlier. The brothers gathered in the large living room; the second floor had a spacious loft overlooking the living room. There were twenty brothers who had come on the trip including Gabriel, a handsome Italian and the Chapter's Epiprytanis or the vice president, with dark features, green eyes, and a commanding presence. Magnus the intelligent and condescending Prytanis, or president, had short blond hair that grew straight out from his head instead of lying flat with blue eyes that held a fierce intelligence. Vahn, had a head of light brown curly hair that he kept short. He was the Hegemon or New Membership educator, and Virgil's Big Brother in the fraternity. Vahn was humorous and sarcastic. Landon was a small, handsome guy with green eyes, who was in Lambda class with Magnus, Gabriel, and Vahn. Landon had a lot of spunk, was well liked, and had a deep passion for the fraternity. Jagger, also a Lambda pledge brother, was introverted and quiet. He was mixed Hispanic and Caucasian, with handsome dark features, and wore a soul patch on his chin. Abe was the fraternity's Histor or Historian, he was a good-natured brother. Lamar was a loud, entertaining brother, half African American and Caucasian, he had a medium complexion. Lamar was the co-Rush Chairman with Brody. Lamar was a brother that lived for the comradery of brotherhood. Zender was a quiet man whose calm exterior hid a complex and intelligent mind. He had black hair with handsome facial features, and intense blue eyes. Zender was the Pylortes, he had an abrasive personality. Tarek Jeter was the Hypophetes or Chaplain, and third in command. Tarek was the second oldest guy in the group at twenty-two, he was in Nu class with Abe, Lamar, and Zender, but was closest with Lambda, affectionately referred to as an 'adopted Lambda.' Tarek was the funny guy in the group, the person who was always trying to make others smile, and the guy everyone felt comfortable around. Doc was also in Nu Class, he was a shorter guy with dark buzzed hair and a larger than life personality.

Brody was one of the younger guys, a member of Xi class, he was the co-Rush Chair with Lamar. Brody was seldom serious, and the prankster of the group. Reece was Brody's best friend, they were pledge brothers in the three-person Xi pledge class. Jace a tall stout man with a green eye and a blue eye behind glasses, was also in Xi class. Jace was levelheaded, mature, and interested in the government, he had dozens of connections at the university that helped the fraternity. The rest were Virgil's pledge brothers, the men he had gone through the candidate process with just months ago. Nolan was the smart guy in the group, already a sophomore credit wise, he was a work alcoholic and seldom took time out of his planned schedule. Nolan had a love for video games, something he shared with Virgil. Nolan was one of the most selfless people Virgil had met. Dante had short auburn-hair, with a fiery personality. Dante had a macho attitude, and one of his favorite hobbies was body building. Birdy, whose real name was Alec, was Dante's roommate, and airheaded best friend. The two were constantly bickering, mostly Dante yelling at Birdy, who was so absent minded he often tuned out people, or maybe it was his hearing. Birdy wore hearing aids, to correct his dwindling hearing capacity, which only compounded the problem of him being an absentminded klutz. Birdy was sensitive, caring and polite, and was one of Virgil's closest friends. Louie was a big Asian guy whose dark hair was shaved on the sides with a Mohawk running down the center, Louie had died the middle blonde. Louie was a loving and friendly guy. Louie was so social his face was known campus wide. Louie was thoughtful, a great friend and brother. Troy was a short quiet guy with busy curly hair that covered his eyes. Troy was starting to come out of his shell more thanks to his growing close friendship with Doc, Lamar, and Abe. Hector was the oldest brother present at twenty-four. He was a nontraditional student and had taken off a few years after high school before coming back. Hector liked drinking and girls above all else. They had thirty active brothers, though at least six or seven of them didn't come around anymore.

The twenty guys focused with the help of Magnus. He sat in one of the rocking chairs, relaxed and quiet, yet still commanding the room. The E-Board were giving reports on their positions over two days, with eight Jeweled Officer positions, and four recognized chairman positions. Virgil had been appointed the Advertising Chairman by Magnus, the reelected Prytanis of the Chapter. After an hour and several officers had gone over their positions, Louie was next, he went to the center of the room. He reported proudly that he already had two mixers set up for the first two weeks, with two sororities on campus, the Sigs, and Blair's Nephilim sorority, the Alphas. Blair was one of Virgil's best friends, and one of the best warriors he knew. The brothers let out a chorus of approval at interactions with females, a few crude comments were exchanged, Virgil rolled his eyes.

Magnus hit the arm of his chair, "Let's keep it on topic boys." Magnus was cocky, arrogant, and extremely confident. He was one of the hardest people to read, you never knew what the guy was thinking, and as Prytanis, Virgil couldn't imagine anyone doing a better job.

"That was on topic!" Lamar chuckled at his own off-color remark with his typical deep booming laugh. He was the guy in the group always trying to have fun, even if it meant derailing the progress of meetings.

"Guys!" Gabriel cut in helping Magnus keep control of the room. "Next brother speaking out of turn will clean up the house after the meeting." The brothers sat up a little straighter and quieted down, everyone was tired, no one felt like tiding the train wreck of a house they had woken up to this morning. They left Vahn's Hegemon, and the Rush presentation for Sunday morning. After hours of sitting and listening, Magnus finally adjourned the meeting.

"All brothers clean up your sleeping areas, let's get this place back into shape before we all do our own things," Tarek Jeter, the Hypophetes and brother in charge of Retreat, called out to the group as people got up and stretched.

Virgil yawned heavily and retreated to the bedroom he shared with Nolan, Troy, and Louie. Virgil had slept on the floor with Troy the first night, they got the bed tonight, an agreement they'd come to in sharing the room. Nolan insisted on taking a shower. Troy was taking a nap in the bed, and Louie cracked a beer open and began to mingle. Virgil was feeling queasy from the previous night, drinking sounded like an awful idea.

Once Nolan had finished cleaning himself up, he went straight to the kitchen to begin making breakfast for the brothers. Pancakes, sausage, eggs, and toast, just the right sustenance needed by the men to recuperate from the wild night. Virgil was thankful to have someone like Nolan around taking care of them. Once the house was in order, everyone got a helping of breakfast, Nolan lightly sipped on a beer as he cooked, a goofy happy smile on his face. Nolan had a deep voice, and a perpetual five o'clock shadow on his masculine jaw line. He was fiercely intelligent, probably the second smartest guy in their Chapter, after Magnus.

"You're amazing Nolan," Gabriel praised, throwing away his plate. "Thank you for cooking breakfast for everyone, that really helped."

"I don't mind," Nolan shrugged, "I had to cook for myself and my Big anyway," he told Gabriel minimizing his part. Magnus was Nolan's Big Brother in the fraternity and a notoriously picky eater. He had Nolan make him special meals when he cooked for everyone else, which earned a few disgruntled complaints of envy, especially from Lamar who loved to 'bust people's balls' as he put it.

After everyone had breakfast the mood of the cabin became mellow. Half of the group passed out for a few hours more of sleep, the other half broke up into two groups; one playing a board game, the other getting in a circle to play some drinking card games. Virgil was in the first floor living room playing a round of Risk with Magnus, Nolan, Dante, Birdy, and Landon. The six of them were easily overpowered by the alliance created between Magnus and Nolan. Birdy was the first out, followed by Virgil. Dante was the last to be killed off, Magnus and Nolan agreed to split the world between them ending the game.

Several hours had passed, and it was well into the afternoon. The brothers who had napped were waking up, and the brothers who had been drinking were now rowdy. The two forces collided throwing the party into full swing. Virgil joined a new round of cards started in the dining room. Gabriel, Magnus, Vahn, Landon, Dante, Louie, Troy, and Virgil played President's and Assholes. After several rounds, Magnus was getting a little sloppy and abusive with his powers, only going down to vice once before going back to the top dog. Landon stood 5'7 with a thin frame, maybe 140lbs soaking wet. He had a bright smile with youthful features, even though he was twenty-one years old, he looked sixteen. Landon was the Asshole most rounds and kept getting more drinks because he took so long to clear the cards, he was hiccupping a lot and slurring his words.

"One!" the group counted. Landon was quicker this time, ready to be done with the position. "Two!" Landon threw all the cards face down and took his punishment. Vahn scooped up the cards and took the soft fuzzy Bay Valley mascot hat from Landon and placed it on his head. Vahn shuffled the cards and started passing them out to the group again.

"Alright Magnus take three drinks for being such a shitty president last round," Vahn commanded as he gave a card to him. "Gabriel take three drinks for suggesting we play this game with him," Vahn gave him a card. "And everyone else but Landon, take two drinks!"

"Hey why's he safe?" Louie complained, nodding his head towards Landon.

"Look at him!" Vahn quipped, gesturing his arm towards one of his best friends. "The poor guy doesn't need much more," he laughed. "Take a drink Louie," Vahn added giving Louie a look that said grow up.

"Yea," Landon hiccupped, "Yeah Louie!" he struggled to get out.

"Easy bud," Dante turned to Landon seated next to him. "You only stepped up to Beer Bitch this round, not much of a promotion, everyone but Vahn can still make you drink once the cards are passed out."

"You're," Landon hiccupped, "Alright in my book Louie," he said with a large grin, and a thumbs up, earning a few chuckles from the guys.

The cards had been dealt and Magnus spoke, "Vahn take six for thinking you can make the president do anything, Louie take two drinks," he spoke assertively.

"Why?" Louie asked.

"Louie take a drink," Gabriel added.

Louie guzzled his beer, "Bitch ass Lambdas," Louie said to himself.

"Add another on there," Magnus suggested.

"Damn!" Louie laughed.

After much more trash talking, as was the nature of the game, they switched it up. Nolan told the group that he'd make venison spaghetti for dinner, with salad, green beans, and freshly cut fruit. Everyone would have to fend for themselves for lunch. He'd bought food with the budget that everyone could share. Virgil took a break from the games and made some sandwiches and got out some veggies and chips. Everyone ate as they got hungry. There was always a group playing something, or watching something, or questing out into the snow to make forts and snowmen.

As the sun set most of the guys crashed to catch a second wind later in the evening. Virgil and Louie crashed in the bedroom they shared. Once Virgil awoke it was dark, the energy of the house had calmed down significantly. There were a few guys napping, some watching a movie, some up in the loft talking, others were hanging around in the back of the house outside. Virgil got his coat and gloves on and walked outside. Dante was out there with Birdy, Tarek Jeter, and Vahn, they were talking about going on a walk out on the frozen lake. Virgil joined his friends they walked down the slopping hill of the backyard, down to the house's dock.

"Its amazing out here!" Dante exclaimed staring at the vast starry night sky above. Out this far into the country, there was no light pollution, and the infinite expanse of the universe around Earth could be truly admired. They cautiously stepped onto the frozen lake and started a slow trek across the water, it was a beautiful night.

"This is my favorite part of Retreat," Tarek Jeter said his hands in his coat, his big rosy cheeks more fiercely red than usual. He was one of the taller brothers, with sandy light brown hair. He was charismatic and optimistic, and everyone always enjoyed his company.

"Going on walks?" Virgil asked Tarek.

"Just being part of nature," Tarek Jeter answered staring up. "Our lives are so busy we seldom take the time to just stop and look around."

The guys were getting cold, they could see their cabin lit up in the distance and turned back. Most of the houses on the lake looked dark, winter was not the easiest time living in Michigan. It was a 'tourist state' one that blossomed in the spring and summer. There was a house a little down the lake from where they were staying, it was lit up and looked like people were having a party. The bass of their music could be faintly heard across the snow-covered ice. A big smile came over Virgil's face, he felt so alive in that moment. The elements of nature were beating against him making him cold, the constellations above made him feel small, and his friends around him made him feel happy…life was good.

"You guys ever read The Perks of Being a Wallflower?" Virgil asked gazing at the sky.

Vahn nodded, a twinkle in his eye as he passionately said, "In this moment…we're infinite. That's a great book, I read it in a night."

"Yes!" Virgil laughed, that was the exact phrase that had come to mind.

They got to their house's backyard, Tarek shouted shrilly, "I'm freezing!"

"How was your walk!" Jagger called out from the back porch taking a piss.

"Great! You missed out," Dante yelled back.

Suddenly screams could be heard in the distance, faintly there were sounds of glass and other things breaking.

"What's that?" Virgil turned looking in the direction of the noise.

Magnus came onto the porch with Gabriel. A few other brothers were hanging close to the door, word was spreading around the house quickly that something was up. Everyone got quiet, listening, then came more screams, fire could be seen in the air from the direction of the house.

"Let's go," Magnus commanded, and the men assembled. Virgil and the others went into the house to warm their skin. Not everyone was prepared to go investigate, and they didn't want to make any one group too thin, safety in numbers. Magnus, Gabriel, Vahn, Tarek, Dante, Birdy and Virgil were at the door, none of them were drunk and they were willing to go.

"We'll stop in, assess the situation, and report back," Magnus told Zender, who stood with his arms crossed, his face set in a fierce scowl. Zender was in command of the house, as the Pylortes, with the top three Jeweled Officers going out. "If we're not back in twenty minutes, send some brothers to see what's keeping us," Magnus said to the group.

"I've got this place secured, get going," Zender said impatiently messing with his ball cap and glasses. "It could be nothing, but if it isn't, we don't have time to be dicking around."

"Louie why aren't you going?" Landon asked from his chair, nursing a headache, just as the group was about to step outside.

"Wha-what?" Louie asked as the room turned to face him. He'd been slinking towards the hallway off the living room, almost out of sight.

"Where are you sneaking off to?" Jace asked Louie in an incredulous and demanding tone.

"Uh, got the beer shits, really bad actually, headed to the bathroom," Louie said sheepishly with a lot of hand motion.

"Chicken shits is more like it," Landon said rolling his eyes.

"Louie, get your ass out there!" Jace admonished him. "Out of every brother in the group, you're the only one with a bow! You should be watching their backs!"

"It is alright," Gabriel said raising his hand in the air. "We have no need for cowards, he'll just slow us down."

"Be safe!" Louie called to them with a happy smile.

"Louie!" Dante snapped moving across the living room to be face to face with his good friend, "Get your panda ass bundled up and get out there! You really going to let dumbass over there, go 'check things out' without keeping a watchful eye on him," Dante asked exasperated, hamming it up. "We'll be short one Birdy! You know how much of an airhead he is. Is that how you want to lose one of your best friends?"

"Hey!" Birdy exclaimed, "He's talking about me, isn't he?" he asked Virgil.

"Alright, alright!" Louie shouted. "Damn whiny ass bitches can't do shit without Louie V," he mumbled heading down to the hall to grab his coat.

A loud explosion from nearby rocked the house. "We're going!" Magnus snapped, and he was out the door. Virgil followed close on Gabriel and Vahn's heels. They went out the front running down the snowy road, Dante and Louie coming last, running to keep up. Virgil's shoes became filled with snow within seconds it was so deep, these back roads did not get plowed regularly. A cold stinging wind picked up blowing the snow off the ground and into the men's faces. The smell of smoke was in the air, they approached the house, walking down the steep driveway. It was a two-story home, built into the hill like the house they were staying at. Magnus exchanged a look with the men, Gabriel and Tarek took point, Magnus moved to the back of the group, Vahn came to stand by Virgil in the middle.

"We stick together," Vahn said to Virgil. His Big Brother had become overly protective since the Tear Drop incident, and Virgil hadn't seen any action since. There'd been an opportunity to go on a mission, Vahn had shot Virgil down when he volunteered to go.

"I can handle myself," Virgil retorted. "I appreciate your concern Vahn, I really do. But I'm not going to sit back while you act as my living shield. If you recall, I'M the one who saved YOU from the Arch Demon, not the other way around," Virgil ended firmly.

"Don't get too big for your britches," Vahn snidely remarked. "You're still inexperienced and you're only eighteen! It's my job to look out for you."

"Ladies! Enough!" Gabriel's words cut sharp and they fell silent. They didn't burst through the front door, instead they crouched low to the ground, went around the side of the house looking through the windows accessing the situation. The house was on fire, though it had not spread enough to be a blazing inferno. It looked like multiple small fires had been created, as they came closer to the back of the house, they saw into the living room and Virgil swallowed hard. Large lizards with wings were inside the house, eating the inhabitants. They were dragging bodies to the backyard, it looked like they were getting ready to leave.

"Demons," Magnus whispered, "They look like wyverns," he said to the group.

"Dragons!" Dante exclaimed with a note of concern, oddly placed on his normally fearless face.

"Not true dragons, wyverns are less dangerous but still fearsome creatures," Magnus whispered.

"Why aren't we attacking?" Birdy asked. They'd come to a stop just near the edge of the home and the backyard. The scaled creatures with wings folded upon their backs walked on two legs, their wings were their arms and front legs in one. The creatures made their way out of the home, the back wall was destroyed and open to the elements. It was only thanks to the Dreamstone rings every brother wore, which cloaked their auras, that they hadn't been seen by the demons. If they made too much noise, the demons would be alerted to their presence.

"Wyverns are pack demons," Magnus spoke softly. "This is likely a scouting party, gathering food for the den. If there was anyone to rescue we'd slay them now. Sadly, it looks like they have killed all the people. We're better off following them to their lair, and taking out the nest, to prevent this from happening again," Magnus reasoned. He motioned for them to back up slowly away from the edge of the backyard.

"Magnus is right," Gabriel nodded. "We need to look at the bigger picture, killing this small group won't end the problem, we need to wipe them all out!"

"Gabriel and Tarek come with me. Vahn take the others back," Magnus ordered.

"What?" Dante sounded like he'd just been insulted. "I want in on this, I'm not going back to the cabin."

"We need to follow these things. We'll have to fly to keep up, and you don't have wings," Magnus said simply.

"Damn," Dante kicked the ground a pissed off scowl covering his face.

"We're going to find the den, then come back to the cabin for a raiding party, you're welcome to join then," Gabriel said placing a hand on Dante's shoulder.

Dante nodded, still disappointed. Every Nephilim was born with Devil Arms, the individual's soul weapon had its symbol branded on their hand. But only Nephilim who were pureblood, or very close to it, were gifted with wings. The Nephilim race was by biological makeup, a half breed, equal parts mortal and Judge. Pureblood Nephilim were exactly half and half. But pureblood Nephilim often married normal people and their children were born with three quarters human blood, a quarter Judge. As the generations passed on and sired more offspring, the celestial blood became more watered down with mortal DNA, most always resulting in a reduction of that Nephilim's powers. Most brothers didn't have wings, only the ones who had the most immortal blood in their veins were gifted with them. Virgil had wings, though he'd only used them twice in his life. Virgil's wings were an odd pair, his left was black, and his right was white, just like his Devil Arms.

Magnus, Gabriel, and Tarek gave themselves space, then groaned in pain as they produced their wings from their backs. The wings worked by using Will, mentally focusing on what the wings looked like, forcing them to appear with the mind. They were produced with magic and flesh, bursting from the backs of Nephilim. The pain was fleeting and ended by the time the wings were fully extended, but it was unpleasant to bring them out. The three men stood before the group, dazzling wings made of soft glistening white feathers extending from their backs.

"Another coat ruined," Tarek sighed unhappily looking around at the wings sprouting from his Columbia winter jacket. The demons took to the air and started flying away from the ruined cabin.

"Deal with it," Magnus said spreading his wings out. "We need to go, keep it tight on my flanks, I'll keep the wind warmed up in front of us." Magnus took the sky and Gabriel and Tarek followed him. The three men grew small as they pursued their adversaries.

When the rest of the group made it back, the brothers who had been left behind were a nervous wreck, crowding at the door the instant they approached.

"Where are the others?" Zender asked impatiently.

"There were demons," Vahn stated coming into the living room. "Wyvern demons, there were half a dozen raiding the house a few places down. There weren't any survivors, this breed of demon doesn't just feed off the emotional energy of people like normal, they consume their flesh. Magnus and the others followed the demons to their nest, so we can lead a team there to clean it out."

"How come the demons didn't come here, and attack us as well?" Birdy asked the group. "We would have been just as good of a target."

"We put up a barrier spell around the cabin," Zender said condescending to Birdy. "Its standard procedure, we go to a new place, we put up wards and other Illusion spells around it. It was the first thing Magnus and I did when we got here."

"The demons didn't attack us because they couldn't sense us here?" Louie asked relieved.

"Exactly," Vahn nodded. "And our rings help too. Though the barrier prevents them from even approaching."

"How big of a den are we talking?" Jace asked pushing his glasses up, his tone serious, his face concerned.

"We're not sure," Vahn shrugged.

Time grew slow, the whole house was tense, everyone's minds on the three brothers who were out in the cold winter night. If they didn't come back, they wouldn't even have an idea of where to start looking. Fifteen minutes the group sat in silence, pacing and moving around. Then the brothers landed on the deck behind the house, safe and unharmed. The tension dissipated, the group was visibly relieved. The three men came in the house, and the host of brothers turned their undivided attention to them.

"Well?" Landon yawned.

"It's bad," Gabriel shook his head looking down. "We're talking fifty at least, easily more."

"That sounds dangerous," Jace responded tightly. "We shouldn't take on a den of that magnitude."

"What else are we supposed to do?" Vahn retorted. "Party it up, wake up tomorrow and go home? If we wait, they could move dens. We need to take them out while we can before they make too big of an impact on the community, and it lands in the news."

"And risk the lives of our brothers?" Jace asked. "I'm all for taking down threats, but only when the benefits outweigh the risks. Most of our group is hungover, and we've all been drinking, we aren't in any shape to take on that many."

"I'm able to go," Tarek shrugged, a determined look on his face. "This is dangerous, I agree. However, there isn't a Paladin Chapter in this county, these demons will likely go unchecked for months. We leave these things be, we are leaving the people around here to die," Tarek said getting fired up.

"I'm not saying we leave them! I'm just saying we should be in peak performance, or we risk losing one of our brothers!" Jace's voice rising to match Tarek's.

"Fraters! Knock it off!" Magnus shouted silencing the room. Magnus never raised his voice or lost his cool, when he got loud people got quiet. "This is pointless, and it is getting us nowhere. I'm the Prytanis of this Chapter, it is my call to make."

"What are you thinking?" Gabriel asked crossing his arm, his eyebrows knitted together in deep thought. All eyes in the room landed on Magnus. Magnus looked his men in the eyes, knowing the decision, and consequences of that choice, fell onto him. Magnus paced for a moment, though Virgil suspected it was for show. Magnus' face was fierce looking, concentrated in thought, Magnus had already made his decision, he was just trying to act like it was taking him time to decide.

Magnus announced, "We'll take half our men to the demon's cave and do what we can.

Chapter 2
Redeemer of the Fallen

Virgil and nine brothers stood at the mouth of a cave, the presence of demons lingering on the air from within. Fresh blood was smeared on the floors and the walls as they walked cautiously inside. Dante and Birdy took point with Gabriel, Tarek, and Brody. Virgil was at the back with Louie, Magnus, and Nolan. Vahn was a few paces ahead of Virgil, staying close. Magnus' staff disappeared in a flash of amethyst light. The other brothers did the same, their Dreamstone rings could cloak their presence to a degree. Summoning a Devil Arms was something the ring couldn't conceal, akin to lighting up a firework display with an arrow pointing to one's location.

The cave was wide enough for three guys to walk side by side. They moved deeper into the cave moving deeper underground. The corridor began to widen out. They were approaching a large cavern, the claustrophobic tightness of the walls and ceiling, gave way to a tall open room, its top obscured in darkness. There were demons in the heart of the cavern, the same kind they had seen at the cabin. There were dozens of them on the floor of the cave, they were relaxing after a successful raid. The macabre scene of fresh kill and mutilated bodies was hard to take in.

The demons were wyverns, dragon like creatures with two legs and large wings for arms. Dangerous fangs for teeth, and razor claws on their feet. There were fires lit in the room from the creatures, illuminating the dark chamber. The demons had yet to notice their presence, some seemed groggy, and were falling asleep. Virgil and the other brothers had a prime opportunity for a pre-emptive strike. They backed out of the large cavern into the mouth of the cave they'd come from.

"We take on the one's closest to the mouth of the cave," Magnus softly instructed to everyone huddled tightly together. "Guys in the back don't fire your first spells until we've made contact. Brody stay at the back in case we need to send for reinforcements."

"We can't possibly take on all of them at once," Gabriel pointed out. "We'll be overwhelmed by sheer force."

"We can use the mouth of this cave for protection," Nolan suggested pointing to the tunnel as it opened into the main chamber. There was room for three men to wield their Devil Arms.

"Their numbers won't mean much when they can only fit so many into the tunnel," Magnus nodded. "Good idea Lil." They got into position, Dante, Birdy, Gabriel and Tarek getting into a runner's pose. Virgil and his friends stood just outside the tunnel ready to launch into action with supportive fire. Virgil was nervous, the cave's depths were undiscernible, there was no telling what else lurked in the shadows.

Magnus gave the signal, and the four brothers sprinted. They waited till the last possible moment, summoning their Devil Arms stabbing, and slashing them into the closest winged monsters. The creatures howled in pain, as they were cut down by the Omegas, they burst into ash, blood, and bone. The wyverns rounded on the intruders. The creatures' roars echoed in the cavern, sending shivers of fear into the brothers.

"Shiva's Bow!" Louie shouted. An icy breeze blew into existence through the air in front of Louie, in a burst of pale blue light, it solidified into a majestic bow of silver metal, and crystalline ice. Louie held his Devil Arms with his right hand, and pulled back along the string with his left, creating an arrow of light and ice. Louie's first arrow flew past Dante, it sank into a wyvern before it could tackle Dante to the ground. The four brothers were still fifteen yards away, racing back to the cave entrance. The demons were like a tidal wave, filling the room with overwhelming numbers, their friends were close to being overwhelmed!

Magnus summoned his staff to his hand, Nolan doing the same. Wind began to whip up around them, moving their hair about. They shot blasts of wind and electricity from their Devil Arms symbols at the horde of creatures attacking their brothers. Virgil whispered, "Soul Reaver," and a cloud of black smoke billowed out from his left hand. Winding like a snake, the smoke melted into a long ebony shaft, with a curved silver blade at the top, black flames perpetually covered the weapon. Virgil grabbed hold, the black flames crawled up his arm, the flames would burn through anyone's flesh and aura it touched, except for him.

Virgil focused his thoughts on the deadly flames of fire. He imagined a blast of energy erupting just behind Dante and Gabriel. He willed his thoughts to reality; the energy of his aura, the sphere of spiritual energy that surrounds all living beings, being burned up as the fuel. Virgil raised his right hand out in front of him. "Explosion!" Virgil screamed. A fiery boom erupted from the stone floor like a mushroom cloud, blasting the surrounding demons clean off their feet, setting some of the ones it had engulfed on fire. Virgil felt the cost of the spell take its toll, his aura's circumference shrank drawing in a little closer, weakening. Explosion was a second-tier spell, with four levels of casting for each branch of magic. A thunder of wyverns had taken to the air, flying as a swarming tight knit pack, they came to the mouth of the tunnel, looking to block Dante, Birdy, Gabriel and Tarek from joining the others.

A sphere of electricity began to gather in Magnus' palm his staff humming. "Shine Plasma!" Magnus shouted. A spell ripped from his Devil Arms with a flash of purple light. Thick bolts of electricity rained down from the ceiling. They moved at the speed of light, zapping the airborne demons sending them crashing to the floor. Bolts crashed down all around the entrance of the tunnel, as if a small thunderstorm had been generated inside the cave, raining down energy like a hailstorm. They ripped through the demons, frying everything in the spells path, corpses were left steaming.

The spell dissipated after several seconds, the brothers ran into the open cave entrance, dozens of wyverns still alive, hot on their heels. The brothers backed in quickly getting into formation. The creatures came in the cave crawling along the rock walls, the ceiling, and the floor. Louie concentrated on the ceiling of the tunnel, Nolan and Magnus blasted the demons off the walls with small bursts of wind and energy. The rest of the group fought fiercely at the front, battle cries echoing out as they attacked with their Devil Arms. Dante wielded a mighty double-bladed earth axe, Gaia's Wrath. Tarek had Stiria's Lance, a majestic polearm with a diamond like blade imbued with ice's power. Gabriel wielded one of the greatest Devil Arms Virgil had ever seen, LionsHeart, a powerful longsword aligned with earth. It had a golden handle and cross guard. Birdy's Devil Arms was Ixion's Glaive, a lance with electricity pulsing inside it. Virgil used his scythe like a boomerang, throwing it at demons, using his mind to control its movements.

Dante was at the front with Gabriel and Tarek, a wyvern charged him, knocking him down to the ground. Its jaws closed on his left arm biting fiercely, it began to shake its head, trying to tear the limb from his body. Dante bellowed out and swung his double-bladed axe, bringing it crashing down on the draconic creature's skull. The demon dissolved into black blood and bone.

"Dante!" Tarek called out spinning his ice polearm and slashing it across a demon that was in his way. He took the lance in his other hand and aimed his hand open palm at Dante. "Ply!" Tarek shouted. A pale blue light flowed from his hand and connected with Dante, spreading out to embrace him in a warm soft glow. The light speeding up the cellular growth rate of Dante's skin and muscle to superhuman levels, his wounds visibly began to diminish in size, mostly closing after several seconds. The spell dissipated, Dante got to his feet, to protect his friends once more.

The ten brothers were getting worn down. Their resolve to live was strong, they worked as a unit to defend themselves, and each other. They killed over twenty in the span of a few minutes, and the initial surge of their force had been intimidating. Since they were able to take care of crowd control, it seemed like less were at the mouth of the cave waiting to charge in. Where had the bulk of their force gone? Were they up to something, Virgil wondered? They hadn't seen the ceiling of the cavern as it had been too large and dark, perhaps these tunnels weren't the only entrance, and they were winged beasts after all. If there were any holes in the ceiling they could just fly in and out. And come back through the cave we came through, sealing off our escape Virgil thought. He turned around, the tunnel devoid of light, making it impossible to tell what lurked behind them.

Virgil drew his arm back and threw his scythe into the darkness, the flames that coated his weapon lighting up the tunnel as it went. The scythe sunk right into back of a wyvern as it slithered along the top of the ceiling coming towards Virgil and his brothers. The demon fell to the ground with the scythe spearing its middle. The entire tunnel behind them was covered with demons hastily crawling towards them with stealth, their sickly red eyes staring Virgil and his friends down. The demons would be upon them within the minute! Virgil summoned his scythe back to his hand from the demon's corpse.

"They're behind us!" Virgil screamed to his brothers. "They mean to pincer us in!" Magnus and Louie looked back in horror.

"Bolt!" Magnus shot a bolt of electricity into the darkness connecting with an approaching lizard, lighting up the area for a few seconds. "Gabriel push us forward!" Magnus demanded, powering up another spell.

Gabriel swung his longsword, LionsHeart, parrying a wyvern's claws, and thrusting the sword into the creature's chest. "We can't go further in!" Gabriel shouted back not taking his eyes off the battle before him.

"We must!" Magnus commanded. "We will not make it back up to the top! We cannot stay divided, fighting on both sides!" His staff sent another bolt of electricity into the cave taking down a demon that was sprinting at their flank.

"He's right!" Virgil suggested. "Let's get out and find a spot they can't flank us!"

"Sure, why don't you come up here and walk us through that bud?" Birdy snapped with a snarky tone, betraying the fatigue that was setting in. He leapt forward and pierced a lizard with his electrified lance.

"Virgil!" Gabriel called out, "Can you use your sword?" he asked. The whole group looked on Virgil, their eyes all holding the same hope…it made his blood run cold. There was such earnest confidence and trust in their faces, it hurt Virgil's heart. His friends trusted him with their lives. Virgil looked down at his right hand, the white symbol, like a shooting star was in its normal state. Virgil concentrated on its name, remembering how it had felt to hold onto the sword, its power was almost too much for him to wield.

"Ragnorak," Virgil commanded. Nothing happened. "It isn't working!" Virgil yelled frustrated. Gabriel grunted, and the group turned their focus back to the battle. Virgil felt so useless. He began spinning his scythe around in the same place, gathering flames in the air their volume steadily spreading from the scythe. "I'll blast us a path through, get back!" he told his brothers needing to help them.

"Virgil, allow me," Magnus told him just a few arm lengths across the tunnel. He moved his staff into his right hand, raising his Devil Arms hand palm up toward the entrance of the cavern. A faint glow of amethyst light began to glow from Magnus' glyph, his face fixed in concentration. "GET DOWN!" Magnus shouted. Gabriel dived to the side of the tunnel, his friend's following suit. Virgil took a deep stride forward and flung the scythe in the opposite direction that Magnus was aiming towards, the way they'd come in. Virgil dived to the edge of the tunnel as Magnus shouted, "Wind Tunnel!"

A vortex of wind was created from Magnus' hand, blasting everything in the tunnel ahead of them out with a tremendous force. The stone path was completely cleared of demons. Virgil's scythe had burned down anything that was too close behind them. He brought the scythe back to him with his mind as he got to his feet, running after the group. Virgil was impressed Magnus was casting spell after spell and still managing to move with agility. That last spell had cost him though, Virgil could sense Magnus' aura was weakened, its glow much dimmer than normal. Magnus couldn't cast a Master level spell like that again tonight.

"Where do we go?" Dante asked, with a note of panic entering his voice, as the group ran. His hands were steady on his battle axe. If they were to die, Virgil was confident Dante would be in competition for taking down the most demons before he fell.

"Run!" Magnus commanded, getting closer to the front of the group his athleticism coming through as he started passing the others. The den of wyverns was legion, they had underestimated their numbers, they swarmed towards them.

The group sprinted across the chamber seeking something, another tunnel or a defensive position they could fortify behind. Nothing was readily available; the horde was close on their heels. Brothers flung spells back, and Louie shot arrows at demons that got too close. If the brothers came to a stop they'd be swallowed up. Virgil didn't know what he could do to help, he was prepared to fight his way through with his friends, to death if need be. The Arch Demon had been worse right? He tried to joke to himself, though his heart pounded fiercely, threatening to burst up through his throat. Their perception was limited, on the fringes of their vision it seemed they were coming to the other side of the cave. As they neared the corner of the room, a humongous boulder loomed over them leaning against the wall. The closer they got the more detailed the rock became. Deep ridges outlined the features of a…wyvern! But not just any wyvern, a Wyvern Queen! This demon was fourteen feet long, it was resting on its hind legs its wings tucked behind it, obscured from view. The Wyvern Queen was emerald in color, her minions all a sickly shade of her magnificent green. She looked like a grander version, with the same red demonic eyes. She radiated power and was clearly the Alpha, every demon they'd fought in this cave was her offspring.

The Queen rumbled with laughter. "What a courteous treat, coming right to my hungry maw!" She mocked the brothers her voice rumbled low, mixed with the same demonic tone all demons shared. She was frightening. "You are the strongest meal my children have brought forth, after I devour your flesh my power will grow!" She said with delight.

"We're not on the menu!" Dante snapped back.

"Nonsense," the Wyvern Queen waved off Dante's comment with her left wing. "Judge spawn taste great! I will not let an opportunity such as this pass by."

"What are you doing here?" Louie V asked the demon. "This is the human world, you don't belong here!"

"Powerful things are stirring in the Ever After, twisted beings older than demons and Judges. Now that the barrier separating the Ever After is gone, there is no reason to stay," the Wyvern Queen boasted. "The Ever After is saturated with demons and Fallen, and this world has plenty of delicious meats for my young. I enjoy having fresh meat daily," the Wyvern Queen told them with a toothy smile, if giant flying reptilian monsters could smile. "These mortals are tastier than I am used too, I will not give that up!" she yelled angrily.

"That's awful!" Louie V spat out repulsed at the demon's casual attitude to feeding on innocent people. This demon was a serious threat, it couldn't be allowed to be left unchecked.

The wyvern younglings formed a perimeter at the brother's backs, their jaws snapping at them, just out of reach, not drawing closer, their Queen wanted to deal with them.

"Such is life," the Wyvern Queen said with pride. "The strong survive off the misfortune of the weak. I grow weary of this idle banter; you have killed enough of my hatchlings. I shall feast on your flesh and give life to a new and powerful clutch! You may eat what I rip off!" The Queen said to her subjects, earning a cry of excitement from the forty some remaining wyverns that were gathered around.

"This is bad, what the hell do we do!" Louie V shouted freaking out.

"Give me a minute," Magnus replied calmly in his same even tone.

"Guys?" Dante asked, "What the hell are we doing?"

"If we all had wings, we could just fly out of here, we can out pace this trash," Gabriel said looking at Birdy and Dante beside him. "This is why we only have brothers with wings on these kinds of missions!" he cursed stomping his foot.

"Whining isn't going to fix anything!" Vahn snapped. "Now man up and let's do this!"

The Wyvern Queen stretched out her form, her wings unfurling from her back, taking a step forward on her two powerful legs. "Flying away will do you no good, Judge spawn," humor dripping from her voice. "Dragons are the Elder race, we are lords of the sky," she said proudly. "None of you can out fly a dragon!"

"The wings of a Judge are more graceful than any dragon," Nolan quipped charging up a spell with his staff.

"You're no dragon!" Magnus taunted the large demon. "Just demonic filth!"

The Queen roared and spit a small burst of flames in front of her. The brothers dived into rolls to get out of the way, Birdy was unlucky. He tried to stumble out of the way, getting hit at the very edge of the blast. He got to his feet, revealing painful burns on his back from the fire.

"I'll get you patched up Birdman," Tarek reassured his brother.

The Queen beat her wings and lifted her form off the ground, she drew close to the brothers struggling back into formation. She let out a roar and gracefully dove into a backflip, her spiked ridged tail coming up like a wrecking ball knocking Gabriel and Dante backwards, lifting them into the air. She dove directly into another backflip, narrowly hitting Brody. She landed on the ground and turned towards the brothers.

"Her tail!" Gabriel stammered out getting back to his feet, the wind having been knocked out of him. "It's poisonous!" He warned with long scratch marks along his chest.

"Damn it!" Tarek cursed, "We need to get that treated before both Dante and you are dropping dead."

"No time!" Dante said swinging his axe around to face the approaching Queen.

She ran at their line, Dante and Gabriel charged her. Dante stepped out of her path pivoting on his heel and whirling his blade around to strike her as she passed him. Gabriel was knocked down, quickly getting up, he swung his long sword with grace cutting at her. Tarek and Birdy used their polearm's long reach to jab at the Queen's thick hide. Their attacks were working, though it was hard to pierce her armored scaled skin. She used her long fangs and snapped at Dante, rounding on the one who was getting the most damage in. An arrow of light shot true through the air, stabbing her in the neck seconds before her jaw closed around Dante. She recoiled, giving Dante a chance to reposition himself. The Queen regained her balance quickly, turning towards Louie V. Magnus shot a bolt of electricity at the Queen, it zapped her though spells were not as effective as normal. Nolan shot an Aero spell at her face, it didn't appear to slow her.

"Dragon skin is resistant to magic," the Queen laughed. She opened her maw and spat a line of flames, towards Virgil and Louie, lighting up the room. Virgil saw Louie was going to get hit full on before it happened. Virgil flung himself into Louie, shoving his friend out of the blast, and taking the hit himself. Virgil rolled around on the stone floor screaming in pain as his flesh and nerve endings fried in the heat of the flames. Virgil's connection with Soul Reaver snapped, unable to concentrate through the pain, the scythe disappeared from existence. The Queen launched herself into the air again, doing a backflip bringing her tail scraping along the ground almost impaling Tarek in the process.

Virgil struggled to his feet, steam rolling off his body, he was in so much pain he could barely focus. The smaller wyverns snarled at him, so close he could feel the warmth of their breath. They wouldn't last much longer like this. This demon was powerful, and they were all worn down from the waves of demons they'd fended off in the tunnels. I need to protect them! Virgil demanded of himself. If he had power, he would use it to protect his friends! He watched as the demon barreled over Gabriel and Tarek, knocking Gabriel down she snapped her fangs trying to scoop him into her mouth. I must save them! He concentrated on Ragnorak's symbol, please help me, he prayed silently. Please help me save my friends. The demon used its tail and slammed Birdy to the ground as he charged her trying to save Gabriel. The white glyph on his right-hand started glowing, coming to life. I need your help, Virgil thought, I cannot do this alone!

"Ragnorak!" Virgil shouted into the darkness of the cavern, raising his right hand into the air. From above their heads a bolt of white lightning crashed down into Virgil's hand. The light spread out becoming a blade. A sword of irrefutable beauty materialized once more into his right hand. The sword's handle gleamed with silver, the pummel adorned with a large flawless diamond. The blade was long and sharp, like ice it was completely see through. The entire sword had a golden aura visibly surrounding it, a humming sound came faintly from the blade, it was brimming with power. The golden aura enveloped Virgil once more, he looked at his arms and watched as the power of the blade began to heal the burns. The sword cast Regen and Veil, powerful supportive Creation spells, on whoever held it. Regen steadily healed physical wounds, while Veil was the golden aura, a type of shield that slowed down all attacks that entered, making many strikes miss that shouldn't. Normal spells ended after a period of time, while the Holy Blade's protective spells never ended.

Virgil sprinted towards the Wyvern Queen, lacking the superhuman speed from his Ascended state, his eyes went gold when the power of his inner judge was tapped. She was airborne hovering close to the group coming in for her next attack. She belched out a stream of flames at Virgil. Virgil concentrated his power into his sword, he felt it pulse, like a heartbeat, within his grasp. He swung it through the air in an arc and a wave of light, as tall as himself, swam from the blade. It went straight through her flames, destroying them instantly, and slammed into the Queen knocking her out of the air, down into a crumbled heap. The smell of burnt flesh hung in the air as steam rose up from her body. She clawed at the ground growling and screaming trying to regain her footing.

"Charge!" Gabriel screamed running towards her momentarily defenseless body. Gabriel, Vahn, Tarek, Dante, Birdy, Virgil and Brody hacked at her body with their weapons. Screaming with fierce determination they sought to do enough damage to keep her down. Magnus and Nolan shot spells at her long body, doing what they could. Virgil brought Ragnorak down on the wyvern, and it cut deep, the demon screaming in pain. She rolled back onto her legs after several precious seconds had passed of being slashed apart. She jumped to the air doing a backflip, raking her tail directly in front of her, and then gracefully went into another backflip, her tail catching Vahn this time. The poison was starting to affect Dante, he was ghost white, and slowing down, it looked like he could barely hold his axe up. Gabriel was holding up only slightly better and was looking deathly pale. The Queen's wings were badly tattered, she landed growling fiercely, raising herself to her fullest height to intimidate them.

"Let's finish this!" Virgil shouted. Virgil readied his sword and ran at her, she charged him aggressively. He leapt into the air and slashed the demon across its face with the sword, she snapped at him with her jaws, nearly ripping him from the air. An arrow shot forward saving Virgil from being skewered in her mouth. She growled menacingly; she was a fearsome warrior who'd fight until her last breath.

"There is no end to her!" Dante yelled frustrated.

"She tires," Magnus urged them.

"Even if you kill me," the Queen Wyvern spoke with malice, blood dripping from her muzzle, "You will not stop the mortals from being eaten for long. The Mother of Dragons stirs, and when she awakens not even Diablos could appease her thirst for destruction, she will devour this world!" she screamed.

"Begone from this realm, soul less spawn of Lilith!" A man shouted and leapt down upon her back. He wielded a long gleaming katana. In one swing of his sword, he cleaved the Queen's head from her neck, it flung across the room landing amongst her offspring. They dispersed in panic, not knowing how to react to the death of their Alpha, they cried out running blindly away.

The man leapt from the steaming corpse as it began to dissolve and moved to Virgil and his brothers. Everyone gathered close to Virgil, unsure if this was friend or foe. "I'm seeking the Redeemer," the man said to Virgil. He had long fair hair, it fell around his body like a cloak, coming down to his legs. He was immense in stature standing well over eight feet tall. His katana was sheathed at his side, the enormous sword too large for any man to wield. He wore a simple white robe. His skin was fair, his profile…breathtaking. His face was hard to take in, it was like a fog came over Virgil's memory or mind when he tried to recall what it looked like.

"My name is Virgil Pitcher, I don't like being referred to as the Redeemer, I'm a person not a title," he replied politely. "Thank you for helping us."

The man bowed slightly, "I am Ipos, once a Judge, now merely a shadow of my former self," he spoke humbly.

The group gasped taking a step back. Virgil had never met a Judge, Fallen or otherwise, no wonder it had been able to cut the demon's head off so easily.

"I mean no ill will, I can see that you suffer from your fight with the wyverns, heal your wounds. Virgil, may I speak to you privately once you are ready?" he asked politely.

"Not a chance in hell," Vahn said giving the Fallen an unkind glare.

The brothers took several healthy paces away, Tarek and Louie healed the brothers' wounds, Tarek knew a simple healing spell for poison but didn't know if it would work for the Wyvern Queen's poison. He tried it out on Dante, "Esuna!" A burst of green and purple light gently absorbed into Dante. Within seconds his color seemed to improve, and he said the pain had stopped. Tarek treated the others who had been hit by the tail. Magnus came up to Virgil, Ragnorak firmly in hand.

"Be careful," Magnus warned. "This is not a man we are dealing with, no matter what he appears to be," he whispered to Virgil. "Follow your instincts and do what you think is right."

"Thanks," Virgil nodded feeling nervous, he walked slowly up to Ipos, the Fallen. Everyone hung back within hearing range, they weren't going to let him out of their sight.

"How did you find me?" Virgil asked first.

"I was close by when I felt the presence of Ragnorak, when you call it to your side a surge of incredible power can be felt through the surrounding area," Ipos explained. His speech was soft, lyrical. He did not seem aggressive or threatening.

"You came here just to meet me?" Virgil asked suspiciously.

"Does that seem strange to you?" Ipos asked Virgil.

"I'm not sure," Virgil said honestly, "You're the first Judge, Fallen or not, that I've met."

Ipos was still, he turned from Virgil to look at his brothers standing not far from them. "You have no idea what you mean to us, what you represent to thousands," Ipos' words held a deep sadness. "Many of the Judges who turned on the Creator regretted their transgression. The promise of the Redeemer's birth helped us endure the millennia of penitence for our crimes," he said slowly as if the words held unspeakable pain. "You represent that the Creator has not turned its back on us completely," Ipos' words steel in their conviction.

Virgil felt an immense sadness from Ipos. "Where are your wings?" Virgil asked him.

"They were cut from my flesh, taken by the Creator for turning my back on my purpose," Ipos told him.

"But where are your black wings?" Virgil asked, always being told Fallen had black wings.

Ipos stared at Virgil intensely, his eyes were golden light, nothing else could be seen through the eye sockets. Virgil tried to meet the Judge's golden gaze but found it too overwhelming. He had to look away. "I've been wingless since my Fall. Black wings are gifts given to those loyal to Diablos."

"You never took them," Virgil said sadly, understanding.

"I would rather face oblivion than serve Diablos!" Ipos yelled his voice rising. Virgil's brothers grew tense behind him, edging closer. Ipos calmed and softly said, "After the Great Battle, the Fallen who still wished to follow Diablos did so, and were rewarded with new wings," Ipos told Virgil. "There were others, like myself, who no longer wished to follow the Dark god. The Fallen who refused to go into the Ever After with Diablos, were left in the mortal world, wingless and broken," Ipos finished sadly.

"I can't imagine what you have gone through," Virgil frowned shaking his head. "It sounds like you've suffered greatly. I didn't know Fallen like you existed in this world."

"Wingless Judges?" Ipos asked. Virgil nodded. "There are hundreds of Fallen like me roaming this world," he told Virgil. "All of them want to meet you, but only a few may be worthy of your gift," he warned.

"What do you want of me?" Virgil asked the Fallen. He felt his body shaking slightly, he was intrigued by this being, and fearful at the same time.

Ipos considered what Virgil had asked, there was a silence hanging in the air. Virgil was about to speak when Ipos finally said, "There is only one thing I want in this world. The only thing I have ever wanted since my Fall."

"I, I don't know," Virgil said hesitantly. "I've never done this before," he said honestly.

"You don't have to today, just meeting you was enough for now," Ipos smiled for the first time. "I have dreamed of this day for so long, it gives me hope for the future. You remind me of your father," Ipos said fondly. "Perhaps when you are ready, our paths could cross again," Ipos suggested. Virgil could feel an immense sadness from Ipos, he didn't sense darkness within him.

"I'm sorry, I wish I wasn't so clueless, maybe I can give it a shot though? Couldn't hurt to try right?" Virgil suggested smiling whole heartedly. Ipos demeanor changed, he became elated, his shoulders were shaking, and he had begun weeping.

"Virgil!" Gabriel yelled. "Are you nuts?" Gabriel barked walking up to Virgil. "Internationals forbade you from using your powers on ANY Fallen! You're not allowed to Redeem anyone!"

"Do you mean to stop me?" Virgil asked his old Hegemon. They stared into each other's eyes. Virgil had always looked up to Gabriel, he was the epitome of a man's man, and one of the best brother's in the fraternity. He respected Gabriel as much as he could any man, but in this moment, Virgil would not waver from his conviction. Gabriel saw this in his eyes and sighed shaking his head at him.

"This isn't a good idea," Gabriel told Virgil stepping back to the others.

"But it is his choice to make," Magnus said firmly.

"Internationals," Gabriel argued.

"Internationals wanted us to abandon you in the Ever After just two months ago," Magnus said turning to Gabriel. Gabriel had nothing else to say.

Virgil set his sword on the ground at his feet. Ragnorak's symbol glowed faintly. He wasn't sure what to do, he had been told he was the Sixth Seraph, the Redeemer, how did that work though? "I'm not sure how to do this," Virgil admitted to Ipos.

"That's alright," Ipos told him. "Relax, clear your mind. Concentrate on Ragnorak's symbol. You have the power inside you, you just have to use it."

Virgil looked down at the white symbol, taking a deep breath he closed his eyes. Please, let me help him, Virgil prayed. I want to help him, help me to do so. Virgil wished for an answer, for the ability to fulfill his purpose. Virgil opened his eyes, Ragnorak's symbol on his right hand was shining brightly. Virgil felt his eyes transform, their normal sapphire blue replaced with golden light like a Judges. Virgil felt the 'other' part of him come forth, its presence at the forefront of his mind, wanting to take control of his body. The other part of him, the part of him that was Judge, knew what to do. Virgil extended his right hand, two gold ribbons of light floated out from his symbol.

"All you need is the desire to use your power, and it is yours to command," Ipos told him.

The two golden ropes of light stretched out reaching for Ipos and gently touched him. Virgil's mind was flooded with the memories of the immortal. Ipos' existence from the moment of his creation began to play before Virgil's mind. Virgil saw through his memories the glory of Nirvana, home of the Judges. Ipos' mind was as foreign to Virgil as a god's mind would be to an ant's. It was hard to understand most things, as the Judge perceived the world in a different way than Virgil's mortal mind could comprehend. It felt like he was on a roller coaster, speeding along a track, Ipos' life streaming by him the whole time. So many memories flooded Virgil's head it was overwhelming, more time had passed by in Ipos life than Virgil's mind could hope to understand. They kept moving through his life getting closer to the end. Besides memories Virgil also felt emotions. Virgil saw flashes of the Battle of the Fallen, mere bits of information, then the Fall. It was hard to take it all in, but Virgil did understand one thing, pain. So much pain, and remorse. Ipos lamented his actions and spent his entire time on Earth roaming the land living with the regret for having turned his back on the Light. Virgil was seeing deep into Ipos' inner most self, even if Ipos had been lying to Virgil about being truly sorry for his past, Virgil now knew that he would be able to see through that. This power allowed him into the depths of another's very being, nothing was hidden from him. Time seemed to stretch on infinitely, and Virgil felt like he'd lived a thousand life times.

Virgil gasped and came to, looking wildly around. The golden ribbons of light still sprouted from Ragnorak's symbol, wrapped around Ipos. Ipos stared at Virgil silently watching and waiting.

"How long did that take?" Virgil whispered his head aching, feeling like an eternity had gone by.

"What do you mean, you just started," Louie V said from behind him.

"No, I didn't," Virgil said. "It feels like years have passed," he said breathlessly, "Decades," he said softly, the lifetime of the immortal consuming his mind. Tears stung at his eyes, and he realized that he had been crying. Virgil now had a choice to make, and he felt the power within him.

"What will you do, if I Redeem you?" Virgil asked him.

"I wish to return to Nirvana, and serve my Creator as a Judge once more," Ipos said with honest determination.

Virgil closed his eyes, he could remember Ipos' life, his thoughts while he experienced life, his true feelings and intentions, even leading up to when he met Virgil. Virgil realized if Ipos' memories had revealed him to be deceitful, unjust, and filled with hate, he would have known he was not meant for Redemption. The being's own life and thoughts showed Virgil the right thing to do.

"Ipos, I've seen into your heart, and it is not my place to decide your future, that is something you have already done, with the choices you have made. I Redeem you Ipos! Return to your proper place in this world!" Virgil said. Blasts of power erupted from Virgil's symbol traveling down the ribbons of light into Ipos. He rose in the air, golden light erupting from his body spreading throughout the cavern lighting it up completely. The light was so blinding, Virgil had to close his eyes and turn his head. Then the light diminished, Virgil looked back, the bands of light gone. The symbol of Ragnorak on his hand back to normal.

Ipos floated off the ground, dazzling white wings extended from his back. Happiness emanated from him, and Virgil felt glad for him. Despite any ramifications that came from this night, Virgil knew he could not regret bringing so much joy to one whose spirit had been so lost in turmoil and grief. Ipos landed on the ground and approached Virgil.

"I am in your debt," Ipos said softly to Virgil. "You have but to ask it of me, and I will grant any request within my power."

"I don't want anything of you," Virgil told him. "I am glad I could help you, you deserved Redemption."

"Virgil!" Louie V snapped. "Don't look a gift horse in the mouth!"

"You do not need to decide on this now," Ipos said. "Simply call my name when you are in need Virgil, and wherever you are, I will come to your aid."

"Thank you," Virgil nodded.

Ipos rose in the air and whispered, "No thank you, son of Raphael," and in a blast of light was gone.

Virgil picked up Ragnorak, he thanked the Holy Blade for coming to his aid, the sword disappeared in a flash of light. Virgil felt the inner power receding as well, the other presence in his mind fading back to the part of his unconscious mind where it dwelled, and Virgil's eyes lost their golden light.

"Well that was interesting," Dante said breaking the silence.

"None of you will speak a word of what happened with Virgil," Magnus spoke with an intimidating tone. "Not even our fellow brothers can know of this. No one will learn that Virgil Redeemed a Fallen."

"We need to hurry back to the cabin," Gabriel said sounding tired. "The brothers are probably worried sick." They walked out of the cavern, Magnus lighting the way with his staff. No one said much, Virgil was lost in his own thoughts. Ipos' memories were still fresh upon his mind, and he felt different. Seeing the world through the eyes of an immortal had changed Virgil's perception of the world and himself. He didn't feel young anymore, though his body was that of an eighteen-year-old man, his mind had experienced the lifetime of an immortal. That kind of pain leaves scars, and Virgil knew he'd carry Ipos' memories with him, till the end of his days.

Chapter 3
<u>Winter Semester</u>

Sunday night Virgil was sitting in the meeting room of the fraternity, on the second floor of the house at the top of the grand staircase. The Omega's fraternity house was located at the end of the section of forest that was reserved for Greek Housing. The complex had a fence gating off the entrance, with a well-maintained yard led down to a large mansion with an attached garage. The perimeter was surrounded by a brick wall at the front and on the sides, there was a spacious backyard that emptied out into the woods. The mansion, colored in cherry and grey, was six stories high, with the upper floor's used as residential levels for the brothers, and the lower levels for daily living and socializing.

Monday would be the start of the second week of the semester. Virgil was taking fifteen credits. Chemistry 111, the entry level class for students with a Chem major, it was twice a week on Monday and Wednesday afternoons. His companion Chem Lab was a separate class with its own credit. The Chem Lab was after Chemistry class on Wednesdays. His other three classes were just once a week, he wanted to try something different from last semester. He had Psych 100 on Tuesday nights from six to ten pm, Sociology 101 Wednesday nights from seven to ten pm, and Theater 132B Thursday nights from seven to ten pm.

Virgil's first week was easy, they'd had a mixer with the Alpha sisters, the all-female Greek Nephilim society belonging to the Paladins. The mixer had been a lot of fun, and Virgil had met many ladies he hadn't seen before. Virgil was seated next to Louie and Birdy, writing secretly to them on their notes for the meeting, which had gotten off track thirty minutes ago.

Lamar and Brody, the Rush Chairmen, had gone on a rant. Being two of the longest winded brothers, equaled a perfect storm.

"Rush is important guys!" Brody expressed feeling frustrated. "We have got to get through this," he said, turning their attention to the white board with all the Rush events laid out for next week.

"I just want to add something here," Lamar spoke dead serious, unnecessarily needing to add a pointless comment.

Kill me now, Louie V wrote as he rolled his eyes at the beginning of Lamar's next rant.

He means well, Birdy wrote defending his Big.

Rush felt different being a brother, Virgil was expected to recruit other guys to the fraternity and show up to events. It was simple, ten guys were less of a 'wow' factor than twenty. That made next week extremely busy, Virgil had written everything down in his planner, but he'd checked out from the meeting a while ago. He was planning what they were going to do afterwards with Birdy and Louie.

Did you text Blair? Virgil wrote to Birdy, who was ALWAYS on his phone.

Birdy wrote back, *Yeah her and Helene are already done with their meeting. They are at their dorm waiting for us.*

Shieeettt! Louie V wrote, *Let's get out of here already. Fake the shits or something.*

"Virgil what are you doing?" Brody asked catching Virgil unaware as he started laughing. Birdy and Louie leaned back in their chairs distancing themselves.

"About what?" Virgil asked blinking once, composing himself instantly.

"There are posters all over the halls from every organization, I don't see a single thing hanging up with Omega's name on it," Brody told him stretching his arms out as if to say 'what the hell man.'

"I'm sorry about that," Virgil apologized feeling himself getting warm with everyone in the room looking at him. It was embarrassing being called out like that, Virgil didn't know how else to respond so he said, "I'll go after the meeting to make some in Student Life."

"We need our name out there in order to get guys to come to our Rush events," Brody told him. "We can't start advertising for Rush the day of!"

"I'll get it done," Virgil nodded wanting the discussion to be over and the attention off him.

After the meeting was adjourned, thirty minutes later, Virgil and his friends got their coats on, and walked down the main staircase to the foyer.

"Hey douche bags wait up!" Dante called hurrying down the stairs.

"We're going to hang with Blair and Helene," Louie V said to him as he walked up alongside them.

"I know," Dante rolled his eyes.

"Louie will you help me make some posters to hang up?" Virgil asked as they left the warm comfort of the fraternity house and ventured into the cold January night out to Birdy's firebird.

Louie groaned, "I guess I can help," he sighed.

The four of them got in Birdy's car, Virgil buckled up and held on for dear life. Birdy whipped his vehicle onto the icy roads back to campus. Birdy was known for being a crazy driver, compounded by the fact that one hand was always on his phone.

"Birdy!" Dante, Louie, and Virgil yelled at the same time. The car was veering off the road and Dante reached across from the passenger seat to grab the wheel.

"I got this!" Birdy said waving Dante off.

"No, you don't!" Dante huffed at his roommate, "You're going to get us all killed! Put your fucking phone down for five seconds and watch the road," Dante demanded.

"Dude I'm scared back here!" Louie laughed nervously. "Maybe you should listen to Dante yo?" Birdy rolled his eyes but listened to his friends.

When they got to campus Dante and Birdy headed over to Blair's dorm while Virgil and Louie went to Student Life to make some posters. The fraternity had a running account and got some colored paper off the big rolls. Virgil tore off six sheets, he figured that was enough to put one in each of the main hallways.

"Dude this is a lot!" Louie complained. "I can't do all of these, you're going to have to do some," he told Virgil.

"I'm not artistic," Virgil groaned getting the markers out and starting to write. His handwriting was messy, it wasn't fancy, and he had to go slow to make sure it was halfway decent.

"Hey boys!" Virgil heard a familiar voice call to him a few minutes later. Virgil looked up to see his best friend Blair walking in with Helene, Dante, and Birdy. Blair had a personality larger than life. She was opinionated, talkative, loud, and not afraid to tell people what she thought. She didn't take crap from anyone and she was a HUGE shit talker. She was one of the guys, and the most fun person Virgil had ever met. She came over to Virgil and they gave each other a big hug. Blair was of average height for a woman, with dyed blond shoulder length hair, and brown eyes behind black glasses.

"What the hell dude?" Blair asked Virgil in her mildly raspy voice. "We were all excited for you guys to show up and Bird brain and Dante show up without you two!"

"Sorry," Virgil smiled sheepishly. "I'm the Advertising Chair and haven't put up any posters yet. I got chewed out a little at the meeting and just wanted to get it done."

"Ya dick!" Blair said giving Virgil a playful shove. "If you told us we would've came to help."

"I didn't want to bother you with this, it's not your responsibility," Virgil shrugged.

"Oh," Louie quipped in a snarky tone, setting his marker down. "I see how it is, don't mind making me do all the work, but won't ask HER!"

"Hey, you're my brother," Virgil said narrowing his eyes in a bored expression. "What's family for?" he asked.

"Let's all do one and we'll get it over faster," Dante said taking a sheet.

"I guess I'll help," Helene teased. She was a freshman like the rest of them, and Blair's friend since junior high school. Helene was the younger sister of frater Landon. They had very similar looks, they could've passed for twins, same eyes and hair color, even the same nose. She was a few inches taller than Blair and wore her hair up in a ponytail most of the time.

"Thanks everyone," Virgil said grateful he had such caring friends.

"Your meetings take forever!" Helene complained. "We'd been done for an hour by the time you got out."

"That damn Lamar," Dante said shifting from one foot to the other, the marker in his hand. "He just talks about the most random shit, loves to waste our time!"

"I like him," Helene giggled, "He's funny."

"He's alright," Dante begrudgingly agreed.

"What are you guys doing this week?" Blair asked them.

"Don't have any plans yet," Louie said, "Besides class, my schedule's pretty wide open."

"I was thinking we should have a get together," Blair suggested, "Nothing big, just a dozen or more people, drinking, smoking, hanging out," she said.

"Thirsty Thursday?" Dante suggested.

"Yes!" Louie cried out. "Sounds good, I'm done with classes by Thursday afternoon."

"I think Thiago is having Tuesday Boozeday at his place," Birdy said with one hand on his phone the other holding a marker barely making a mark on his poster. "He's trying to bring it back, used to be a big thing everyone did."

"Well we can definitely check it out," Blair said, "But I think we should have a get together Thursday with just our group, do something fun."

"Sounds great," Virgil nodded looking over to Blair and making eye contact. "We're all going to be so busy next week with Rush, we probably won't have much time to hang out."

"Right," Blair nodded.

After they'd finished, the six friends walked down the hall heading around campus to find open spots to place them. Louie's had turned out the best, they placed his at the place with the most foot traffic, everyone was impressed by the quality of work he'd done. It was a shame it was so hard to make it as an artist; Louie's parents forbade him from majoring in Art for fear he'd struggle financially though he had remarkable talent.

They walked to Blair's to play some video games, laughing about silly things they said to one another. The six of them had begun hanging out regularly, and they'd all become great friends. Soon it was after 1 am, and they parted ways with the ladies to get some rest. Virgil lived at the freshmen dorm directly next to Blair and Helene's, he had a short walk home. The others lived in the Zoo, the oldest dorm complex on campus. Virgil got to his dorm on the third floor of Living Center North, it was at the end of a hall near one of the stairwells in the building. The front opened into a modest living room with a small kitchen off to the right. There were four bedrooms and two bathrooms.

When Virgil had moved into the dorms in August, he'd gotten close with two of his dorm mates, Damian and Boyd. Boyd had joined the same fraternity as Virgil. Damian had joined Omega's rival fraternity, the Betas, who were also a Nephilim fraternity. The Betas had an elitist attitude and didn't like their men fraternizing with Omegas. Damian had distanced himself from Virgil going to great lengths to avoid contact. Damian's room was across the hall, though they seldom saw each other. Since Damian had started pledging, he'd been staying at the fraternity house. The Omegas had a pledge dorm at their fraternity house with beds that were always available should Virgil ever need it. Boyd had died during the Tear Drop incident. At first Virgil was numb, the pain of losing a good friend was hard to take. Virgil was doing okay now but, he tried not to think of his deceased friend as thoughts of Boyd usually made Virgil sad. Damian had softened up some sine Boyd's death, he spoke to Virgil when they saw each other. However, the intense rivalry between their two groups kept them from truly being friends.

Virgil lay in bed starring up at the ceiling unable to fall asleep. He had many thoughts keeping him up; his friends, the fraternity, and the threat that existed on the fringes of their modern-day college life. Demonic activity had steadily been increasing since the fall of the barrier, the Tear Drop had prevented the denizens of the Ever After from coming into the mortal world whenever they pleased. A group of brothers had gone out on a hunt since they'd been back from Retreat, to help clean up Bay City, but the demons kept coming. For every group they killed, there was a seemingly infinite supply to replace them. Virgil had felt different since returning from Retreat. He'd Redeemed his first Fallen, and in doing so had experienced every memory of the Judge. A mortal mind wasn't meant to handle that kind of information, much of what he'd seen was a blur, bits came through every so often with perfect clarity. Last week while he was sitting in Theatre 132B, which was mostly reading plays, then going to watch the play, Virgil slipped into a daydream, only the images were of Ipos' life. Ipos had been battling another Judge in the Battle of the fallen, in a field of ethereal flowers that were unlike anything that grew on Earth. Ipos had been stabbed by the warrior with white wings, and Virgil screamed feeling the pain as if it was his own. Virgil snapped out of the daydream to find his class staring at him like he was freak. Virgil hadn't said anything to his friends not wanting to worry them, but using his powers had changed him, changed his perception of the world around him. The universe was such a large place, and he'd come to realize how precarious the existence of mankind truly was.

Studying for tests and working on assignments was Virgil's priority, a close second was spending time with his friends and fraternity brothers. Chemistry was his hardest class, and since he was a Pre-Med major he needed to really learn and understand this material. Tuesday nights were always Brotherhood, a time when the brothers got together to bond and spend time as a family. This week's Brotherhood was casual, the brothers were getting together at the fraternity house to play cards, and games.

Virgil stopped by the fraternity house with Birdy, Dante, and Louie to make an appearance at brotherhood. The turnout was low, eight brothers were at the house, they were disappointed when Virgil and the others didn't want to jump into anything that would take a while. After a half hour, Blair was blowing up Virgil's phone demanding to know 'when he planned on getting his ass over to the party.' Virgil said goodbye to his brothers, and they got into Dante's small white car, he drove them the mile and half to Thiago's house. Thiago, one of the oldest active brothers in the Chapter, and the current Crysophlos or Treasurer, lived in a small duplex apartment down State Park Drive a mile from Bay Valley's campus. Thiago had moved out from the fraternity house for more privacy, not all the brothers chose to live at the fraternity house. He lived with Nasty Nate, another older brother in the fraternity. Thiago was having a party at his house, Tuesday Boozeday, with $5 cups for Shark Attack or Pink Pantie Droppers.

It was mid-January with permanent snow blanketing Michigan, there weren't many people outside Thiago's house, just the occasional smoker braving the icy air. Inside the house was wall to wall people, with close to two hundred students crammed into a small two-bedroom duplex apartment. There was a basement that was rather large and held the bulk of the people.

Virgil and his friends went right to Thiago to buy a cup. Thiago was latino with a dark complexion, and dark features. Thiago was of average height, with small eyes half covered by his always sleepy eyelids. It was hard to know what he was thinking because you never really could get full eye contact. He was glad to see Virgil, giving him a giant embrace. Virgil and Thiago had bonded during their interview. So much had happened, and Thiago had been a good friend to him, they had gained a respect for one another. Thiago was colder towards the other Omicron, but they were all brothers and therefore friends. Virgil took his cup and got a tall glass of Pink Panty Droppers, the first taste was sweet and delicious. Virgil took out a permanent marker he'd brought from his pocket and made a mark on his cup. He wanted to make tallies of how many drinks he had to help himself from over drinking, a trick he'd learned from Terra Peoples, Prytanis of the Alpha's sorority.

Virgil headed down to the basement where he ran into several brothers and Blair. There were several tables downstairs, one was being used for beer pong, the official game of college students everywhere, and the other was being used for flip cup. Virgil preferred flip cup, it was a game that could involve a lot more than four people. Two even teams were needed on opposite sides of the table, the first two people cheered their cups by tapping them together, and then one had to hit the bottom of the cup on the table before they could drink down their cup. Once the first person had emptied the cup, they had to flip it onto the table, so it landed open end down, then the next person could do the same. Blair was on a team with Vahn, Tarek, Gabriel, and TK, Gabriel's girlfriend. They were playing against people that were vaguely familiar to Virgil, people he'd seen around campus on other occasions. Blair and TK were in the same sorority.

Blair had just gotten in last semester and was pledge sisters with Raven, Omega's Sweetheart, and TK's Lil Sister in their sorority. TK was the reelected vice president of their Chapter. She was a striking beauty with a toned figure, long dark straight hair that she usually had done up in an intricate style, long curly lashes, and dazzling green eyes. She had a smile that made her eyes sparkle and turned heads wherever she went.

"Virgil!" Blair and TK called out to him. They both came up and gave him a hug. "It's been too long! How are you doing buddy?" TK asked Virgil.

"I'm doing well ladies," Virgil said with a smile, "Came here to have some fun!"

"Come on! You can join our team," Blair told Virgil leading him back to the table. Louie came down stairs and joined in on the other team to keep things even.

"Our team is on a winning streak so don't muck things up Pitcher," Tarek jested.

"Damn you guys got the dream team here!" Virgil commented. "Relax I'm actually not too bad at this game," he assured his teammates.

"Heck yeah, Virgil and I are an unbeatable team!" Blair said elbowing her friend. Virgil took a place next to her, and their team went on to win the next three rounds. After each win they'd come in as a group and cheer real loud. Virgil was having the time of his life! Vahn and Gabriel left to take a turn at the beer bong table, so Virgil started roaming the party, greeting other brothers and friends whom he hadn't visited with yet. Virgil ran into Troy, Doc, Lamar and Brody hanging out in one corner, sipping on their drinks and engaged in a conversation about a movie that had just come out in theaters. Most of Virgil's pledge brothers were present, except Hector. No one had seen him since Retreat, he hadn't been to any of the meetings, and Dante had quit Cheerleading, so he wasn't seeing Hector at practices and games anymore. Troy told Virgil he'd ran into Hector in the computer lab, and he had told Troy he was just too busy for Omega stuff. Virgil reached five tallies on his cup, and the night had become a little blurry, so he decided to stop drinking. Helene only had one drink and ended up driving all of them home that night. Virgil had a lot of fun socializing with his friends and brothers, so much so he didn't want the night to end.

The next night Virgil had his Sociology class Wednesday night at seven pm, the class met once a week which Virgil was learning to like better. On the first week Virgil had surprisingly run into Dante walking into the same classroom, they sat next to each other, and it made the class more enjoyable to attend. Dante was funny, and Virgil had a hard time staying focused as Dante would frequently crack jokes about what the professor had said or write messages to him on their notes. They were assigned a paper due in a few weeks, Dante suggested they hang out one night and hammer their papers out together. Virgil went with Dante back to his dorm to hang out with him and Birdy. They lived in the Zoo freshmen dorms with eight guys crammed into a space much smaller than what Virgil had.

Dante and Birdy's roommate Nevin visited with them. He had blond hair like Magnus that grew straight out, he kept it buzzed down as a result. Nevin was at Bay Valley on a Presidential scholarship like Virgil, Nevin was a math secondary education major. He was an intelligent young man, friendly and a little awkward, but good natured and fun to be around. Dante and Birdy told Virgil they had been talking to Nevin about the Omegas, and he was thinking of coming out to Rush. Virgil spent the rest of the night with Dante and Birdy hanging out.

On Thursday night Virgil found out Nolan was taking the same Theater class, just with a different professor. Now Virgil had someone to do his set building hours with for class, as well as someone to attend the performances with him. After Theater class, he went to Blair's dorm room. Blair and Helene had a few of their sisters over, Blair's Big Sister Margery was one of them. Tarek and Vahn had come together, Louie, Birdy and Dante also showed up. They played cards and made each other laugh. As night became morning, Blair's neighbor knocked on the door, to complain about the volume of the music and asking them to keep it down. Luckily no one complained to the RA, and they turned down the music and did their best to not be too loud.

Virgil didn't have anything going on that weekend, there was a large snowstorm on Friday that made the roads dangerous to traverse. He walked over to Blair and Helene's place to spend the day, after several hours they walked the short trip to the cafeteria when they got hungry. They ran into Louie there so he came back with them to play some Mario Kart when they were done.

Saturday, Virgil tried to get ahead on his classes for the upcoming week, knowing he wouldn't be spending a lot of time studying. He stayed in his room mostly, which helped him to relax and destress. He was on friendly terms with his roommates though none of them hung out or engaged in long conversations. Sunday was the third meeting of the semester. That week the Omegas and the other Greeks were having Rush, the most important event for fraternities. Recruitment is the lifeblood of any organization; if you are not growing you are dying. Men came and went, some through graduating, other men either transferred colleges or failed out. An Inactive was a brother who had joined the Omegas but was not paying dues or going to the school anymore. Also, brothers that could not handle the stress of being a Paladin could still be a part of the family by going Inactive. Omega was the fraternity for life, men of Valor,

Brotherhood, and Respect. A fraternity that recruited mortal men with Judge lineage in their veins.

Before the meeting on Sunday Virgil went to Student Life, he had bribed Louie into helping him make more posters for Rush week. Louie needed help with a paper for a class, so Virgil happily agreed to do some editing, so he'd get a good grade. The meetings were conducted using Parliamentary Procedure, with the Prytanis sitting at the head of the room acting as the chair running the meeting. Magnus was a good Prytanis, able to keep the rowdy group mostly under control. The main topic was Rush, which started tomorrow, though they'd been talking about nothing else over the past few weeks, so the topic felt exhausted.

The meeting lasted nearly two hours, afterwards Virgil headed back home to sleep. Monday was the start of Rush. Virgil made sure to wear letters, any clothing with the fraternity lettering on it, so he was a walking advertisement for the Omegas. That night all the fraternities on campus had a joint Rush event to kick things off. They had something like what Virgil had gone to last semester. Virgil walked around socializing as best he could with guys who weren't wearing any Greek Lettering, though he had a hard time talking to people he didn't know. Virgil's friends often teased him that he never shut up yet was quiet around strangers. There weren't that many guys at the event, it was the Winter Rush, and most people who were interested in going Greek had already done so. There were a few guys though, Dante's roommate Nevin had showed up. He looked nervous, dozens of guys were trying to talk to him, and he clearly wasn't used to having so much attention. Virgil spoke to Nevin briefly when he was momentarily free, and shook his hand using the hand with his fraternity ring. The blue Dreamstone on the ring reacted to Nevin's touch lightening up, signaling Nevin was Nephilim, the kind of guy Omegas recruited.

"So how is school going?" Virgil asked Nevin.

"School is going great," Nevin responded in his masculine voice. "I'm taking a few general education classes that are pretty boring, but I am taking two math classes so that makes it not so bad," he said with a smile.

"I thought I was a nerd," Virgil joked.

"Yeah I know I'm weird. I like math, normal people can't stand it," Nevin joked laughing.

"Eh you're not weird, just really intelligent, it is hard for regular people to relate," Virgil shrugged. "Dante seems to think you're cool so I'm sure you are. There are a lot of people to talk with here, and I'm over at your room all the time, so we'll have plenty of time to talk more I'm sure."

"Thanks Virgil, nice seeing you again," Nevin thanked Virgil talking to the next brother.

The week stayed busy for Virgil, keeping up with his classes took time, and Rush events every night took up his evenings. Virgil hung out with Louie, Birdy, and Dante after the Rush events, usually at Birdy and Dante's room. Nevin told the four of them that he liked the Omegas and was seriously considering it after the Rush Event on Tuesday. They played capture the flag inside the campus buildings, with each team getting a different building. Virgil had a great time running up and down the halls trying to avoid the other team while looking for their flag. Virgil's team won once and lost once, some guys wanted to play a third round to break the tie, it was getting late however, and more than a few guys had left, so they called it a night.

Wednesday was info night, the Rush event where the Omegas told prospective candidates about the fraternity, answering any questions the men might have. It was held in a big round room on campus, with windows looking out onto the grounds. It had the lowest turnout, as it wasn't a 'fun' event like the others. It was an informational event, and only the guys serious about joining attended. They had two guys show up, with fifteen brothers present. Nevin was one of the two guys, and most of the brothers had already had a chance to speak with him. The other guy was someone who hadn't been around yet, he was a few inches shorter than average height. He had an outgoing and bright personality, and seemed to be a one-upper, always having a story that outdid the story he just heard. He had dark hair and vibrant deep blue eyes. He was rather handsome with a masculine and attractive figure. His name was Rowan.

"This is the first event we've seen you at," Brody said to Rowan.

"When I got the Rush schedule in my email, I decided I wanted to come to this event, to show you guys that I'm serious about joining," Rowan replied impressing a few brothers.

"Tell us a little about yourself," Brody asked him with a smile, already liking him.

Rowan was in his first semester at Bay Valley. He was twenty-two years old and had just gotten out of the Navy. Rowan was high energy and enthusiastic. He loved women, his first and foremost passion, he also enjoyed music and partying. Rowan told the brothers that he'd been in the military and hadn't been able to really party, and now that he was out, he wanted to make up for lost time. Rowan told the brothers that he had enjoyed the comradery of the military and was looking for something to fill that void here at college.

"Well if you're looking for a group of guys to bond with like family you've come to the right place," Gabriel assured Rowan.

Brody went through a short PowerPoint presentation, then opened the room up to questions. It was very informal and laidback. Rowan and Nevin asked questions about the pledging process, what the fraternity stood for, what kinds of things the fraternity did, and how it could help them with finding employment after college. Brody and Lamar did most of the talking since they were Rush Chairmen, Gabriel stepped in when needed. Gabriel and Rowan seemed to hit it off right from the start, and as the event was winding down, Gabriel and Rowan were engaged in conversation like old friends, laughing and joking. Virgil was pretty sure Rowan was serious about joining. By Friday night, Rush was finally over, and the brothers were grateful that the busy week was behind them.

Friday night was the Rush Party at the Omega house, hundreds of students filled into the house for a night of fun. Virgil had signed up to be a Party Monitor, he was given a referee shirt to wear. The Party Monitors had to stay sober and watch for any sloppy drunks that needed to be cut off, or be given a ride home, as well as defuse any fights. There were Designated Drivers at the party as well, shuttling drunk people who had no ride back to campus to avoid having drunk drivers leaving their property. A group of brothers signed up for the cleanup crew, and in the morning, they were responsible for picking up the house. Every brother was responsible for working at least one party a semester. Virgil figured he'd get his out of the way now. It was fun walking around and watching all the drunk people make fools of themselves. Virgil knew many of the people present and spent the night walking the house and talking with his friends and brothers. Blair haggled him for not drinking, and as the night went on, she got tipsier. She kept coming back to Virgil and harassing him, getting more colorful with her remarks and humor. Virgil knew Blair was drunk when he felt someone grab his ass, causing him to yelp and quickly turn around.

"Hey bubble butt!" Blair said swaying slightly, a little of her drink spilled onto the floor. "Where have you been all night?"

"Blair!" Virgil laughed relieved that it was her and not a stranger who'd touched him. "I've been here girl, you've seen me. In fact, I'm sure we've talked like four times already."

"Oh yeah," Blair furrowed her brow, "You should be drinking!" She exclaimed for the third time.

"I know!" Virgil agreed chuckling. "I don't mind staying sober and helping to make sure the party goes smoothly tonight though, I can drink another time."

"Come dance with me," Blair grabbed him pulling Virgil along.

"Dance?" Virgil asked apprehensively. "Blair, I don't like dancing in front of people," his words falling on deaf ears.

"Nonsense," Blair said leading him to the dining area. The table had been pushed to the wall, a sound system had been set up to use the area as a dance floor. There were lots of drunk people dancing and talking. Blair brought them to a stop and attempted to dance seductively for Virgil, turning around and dancing down to the floor, she almost fell over trying to come back up.

"You're ridiculous," Virgil laughed grabbing her waist and steadying her from falling.

"Shut it," Blair quipped with a smirk. She turned to Virgil and smiled looking into his eyes, he smiled back. "You have the prettiest sapphire eyes," Blair sighed.

"Thank you," Virgil said looking down. "You're too sweet Blair," he said feeling a little embarrassed.

"Come here," Blair said pulling him closer as the tempo of the music transitioned to a slow song. They danced slowly, Blair resting her head against Virgil's chest. "I love hanging out with you," Blair sighed into his ref jersey.

Her comment cut deep, underneath was an ocean of unspoken thoughts and feelings. Virgil suddenly felt uncomfortable, an experience he'd never had with Blair, things with her were always so easy, so natural, it was like they'd been best friends forever. "I like spending time with you too," Virgil said choosing his words carefully.

"Aww!" Virgil heard someone coo at them. They turned and noticed Brody and his breathtakingly beautiful girlfriend, Selene, dancing close by. To say Selene was attractive was like saying the sun was a warm place, she was in a class of her own. Olive toned skin from being a quarter Native American, she had dark black hair that hung to her chest, with dark brown eyes and a dazzling white smile. Selene was a fiercely intelligent woman. Virgil felt dumb talking to her half the time, and he thought of himself as an educated man. Selene was confident, driven, and not afraid to say what she wanted, though she was a very classy and polite lady, doing so with tact. Selene was in the co-ed community service fraternity on campus and Virgil had looked at them before joining the Omegas. She had started dating Brody when Virgil was still a pledge. Virgil had spoken with her on several occasions, and besides TK she was his favorite of the brother's girlfriends.

"Hi Selene," Virgil smiled nodding to her.

"You guys make a cute couple," Selene said raising her eyebrows at Virgil.

"That's what I've been saying," TK chimed in from close by dancing with Gabriel.

"Knock it off!" Virgil demanded feeling his face grow flaming red.

"Yeah you bitches! Listen to the man," Blair said making herself giggle.

"What'd you say to me?" TK jokingly asked.

Blair let go of Virgil and turned to TK, "I didn't stutter! Need me to slow it down for you?" Blair said with sass shaking her head.

"I freaking love her!" TK said laughing at Blair. Gabriel sighed and rolled his eyes. The three brothers shared a look then turned their attention back to their dancing partners. Virgil finished the dance with Blair then told her he needed to continue walking the party and quickly made his exit from the room. Was I just imagining things or was Blair coming on to me? The thought made Virgil's heart race, he liked Blair, a lot, but he didn't know if it was in that way. They'd become close so quick, Blair was like family to him, he wasn't sure what his feelings were. Virgil tried to avoid Blair the rest of the night, which was easy. Her sisters were there looking out for her, eventually taking her back to the sorority house to pass out for the night. The party was a success and went down as one of the best the fraternity had ever thrown. Virgil went to sleep in his own bed back in the dorms that night. Blair was on his mind, his conflicted feelings making it hard for him to fall asleep.

Chapter 4
<u>Pi Class</u>

Sunday night was the Super Bowl, but the Omegas weren't watching it. This was one of the most important nights of the semester, after they had gone through officer reports, they moved onto reviewing the potentials. It was a lengthy process, the Rush Chairman introduced each guy, with a picture and information. Everyone wanted to voice their opinion on EVERY guy which dragged the process out, some even jumping into the discussion to speak a second time. Virgil was still gaining confidence in standing up at the meetings, and he tried to only speak when he had strong convictions to voice.

In the end, six of the ten guys they had voted on got bids. Once the meeting was done the brothers rallied and headed downstairs to the cars to head to campus. Virgil remembered the excitement and energy of the brothers back when he'd been one of the guys who'd been given bids. Virgil and the brothers got to campus and stormed the dorms, heading to the places where the guys lived. They pounded on the door and flooded the room when it opened, screaming out in triumph and excitement. Nevin was up first. When he saw the guys rush him in his living room he started laughing uncontrollably as he was lifted into the air by the brothers.

"Men of Omega, welcome Nevin!" Brody called out and there was a chorus of cheers. "This bid is an official invitation to the fraternity, you need to keep it in pristine condition, no water marks, creases or jizz stains, got it?"

Nevin's red face got redder, "What?!" he laughed clearly not ready for fraternity humor.

"Let's go!" Brody shouted and the group rambunctiously headed to the next room.

"Don't let Birdy anywhere near it," Dante advised Nevin, "Dumbass spilt water on my bid, and made me look like a fool on my first night," he recalled in a huff shaking his head at his other roommate.

"Got it," Nevin said putting on his coat and carefully placing it inside to protect it from the cold windy air. They'd gathered the six men from campus to the amphitheater behind the Bell Tower. Virgil followed the other brothers to the stone steps that overlooked the seal of the university, the six men with bids stood side by side looking up. Virgil had an overwhelming feeling of déjà vu.

Magnus and Gabriel gave short speeches and then everyone came down to shake hands with the six guys. Virgil had seen all of them, but the only two he was familiar with were Nevin and Rowan. He shook their hands congratulating them. After the ceremony concluded, Virgil went with Louie back to Birdy and Dante's dorm to hang out with Nevin. Nevin's room was right next to theirs. That night Nevin was in Birdy and Dante's room, still riding the high that he'd gotten from the excitement that came from being around the brothers.

"This is going to be awesome!" Nevin's tone more enthusiastic and excited than Virgil had ever seen. "I can't wait to start pledging and get to know all the brother."

Virgil shared a look with his friends, "Let's see if you'll be saying that after a few weeks, especially LIVING with two brothers, who often get LOTS of company!" Virgil pointed out. "You're never going to get any sleep," he realized in horror, shaking his head in pity for his friends' roommate and new potential.

"Shut up!" Dante said waving his hand at Virgil. "Yo Nev, can you go get me a water?" Dante asked. He turned his attention to his laptop and waited for his roommate to respond.

"Ahh do I have to?" Nev asked the group.

"No!" Louie and Virgil responded in unison agreement. "Not until after your first Education, then yeah," Virgil answered, Nevin frowned.

"It is only six weeks right," Nevin asked, "Then I'm a brother, I can handle that."

"This is going to be fun," Dante said leaning back in his chair with a shit eating grin, "I'm going to have a live-in pledge, sleeping right next door, can't ask for better than that," Dante boasted.

"Hey!" Nev laughed.

"Told ya," Virgil sighed.

Wednesday night the brothers gathered to see who would show up. When it was 10:20pm Vahn signaled the brothers to head over to the amphitheater with the candidates. There were four guys, Vahn had them approach one at a time. The first bid was a mess, the collective group let out a cry of disappoint. Several jokes came up from around the almost thirty brothers present, and Vahn handed the bid back to him.

"Go see if you can buff that out…or something," Vahn suggested. The potential looked like he might faint, or run, he took the bid and went to the brick wall, using the brick and a book from his bag he began smoothing out the stationary as best as he could.

Second came a stout Hispanic youth, Virgil's age or older. He had been a roommate of Doc's freshmen year. Agustin's bid was smooth and pristine, he was overly polite to the brothers.

"I'm impressed, Agustin take your place as first in line for Pi class," Vahn told him.

Rowan was the next guy in line. As good as Agustin's was, Rowan's bid seemed even crisper. There was a great debate among the brothers who had a better bid, and whether Rowan should have to go back to the end of the line.

"Brothers! Please!" Vahn said bringing the squabbling friends to silence. "This is my show, keep it down! Now, Rowan, take your place with your pledge brother Agustin," Vahn told him.

The last of the four was Nevin, but everyone was already calling him Nev. His bid came out of a book and in Virgil's opinion was the best of the four. Vahn agreed as well and he took his place as the third person in line for Pi class. The last was Josh, the guy with the messy bid who'd gone first, once he'd shown his bid again Vahn allowed him to take his place at the end of the line.

"Pi class!" Vahn said to the four men. "From this night forward, YOU are one pledge class. Success or failure is dependent on your ability to come together as a unit." They crossed campus on foot heading towards the bike path that circled the city and headed out to Midland. The woods that surrounded campus were just off the path and the brothers stepped to the side, Vahn had blindfolds for the candidates. It was time to lead them back to the stone temple that rested over a large gathering of ley lines for the area. It was a mile behind their fraternity house, protected by powerful spells and wards to keep it hidden from mortal eyes. Pi class got into formation.

"Listen to my voice Pi class!" Vahn yelled. "I'll be the one leading you through this! Let's go Agustin," he said walking in front of him, so he could grab onto his Hegemon. Vahn led them into the woods. The brothers had a trajectory towards a specific goal, the Oath of the Paladin was the candidate induction ceremony they held at their Nephilim temple.

They came to the edge of the clearing and Zender, the Pylortes, stayed with the candidates, while the brothers went on ahead. Virgil discovered that the chalice the Omegas had was filled from the original chalice given to the original Paladins, The Chalice of Immortals. The two cups were connected meaning the golden fluid that appeared came from the Chalice of Immortals, even as far away as it was. The ceremony was rather simplistic for the Paladins. By drinking just a swig of immortal blood it tapped into the latent powers that ran through any Nephilim's blood, no matter how small, bringing them fully online. There was also a glyph cast that helped them transition or Awaken into their power. The brothers entered the temple, invisible to any human who might be watching, and went to the bottom.

"Alright listen up!" Magnus shouted gathering everyone's attention. The ritual chest was open, and the brothers were taking out their silver robes for the ceremony. The Prytanis, Hegemon and Hypophetes were the three people who were robed and had speaking parts in the candidate induction ceremony. The ceremony was a history lesson of their race, and a brief introduction to the society of Paladins.

"Thank you," Vahn nodded to Magnus. "Now we have four great guys out there, so we need four Bigs, I've read over your Big Brother applications and I've decided on Bigs for the candidates," Vahn told them.

"I really want a Lil!" Doc called out to his friend.

"Agustin's Big is going to be Doc," Vahn announced and Doc nodded. "Rowan's Big is going to be frater Gabriel," Vahn told the group. Gabriel nodded and was excited and happy to hear it. "Nev's Big will be Landon, and Josh's Big is Jagger," Vahn finished telling the group. There were a few brothers who looked disappointed, there were a few more who looked like they might cry.

"Everyone who didn't get a Little Brother, I am sorry! Don't get upset over this or let it spoil the night! There are only four guys here and I need to make sure they match well with their Bigs. There is always the Fall semester, and Rho class which will have many more candidates, and we'll need a lot of Bigs," Vahn told the dejected brothers before leaving the temple to go get the candidates.

"Anyone who has wings may step out and fly around to scare the new guys," Magnus told them. He walked down from the center and briskly left out the northern entrance, running to the field to produce his white wings, in seconds taking flight soaring into the air. Landon, Jagger, Brody, and Tarek joined him. Flying into each other and purposefully trying to act up.

"You should go!" Louie whispered to Virgil elbowing him.

"No," Virgil said, "My wings are so different, I'll look weird."

"Whatever dawg, at least you have wings, don't know what your bitch ass is complaining about," Louie mumbled to himself.

"What was that?" Virgil asked.

"Leave him alone," Birdy told Louie. "If he doesn't want to show off, don't force him."

The candidates were led into the temple and up to the platform, their blindfolds had been removed when they were led across the clearing by their Hegemon. The brothers landed and reentered the temple. The three Jeweled Officers put their robes on and started the ceremony. At the end Vahn brought them each a Dreamstone to always wear, and lastly Magnus brought the Chalice around for them to drink from. Once they did and the glyph of Awakening was drawn onto their hands they began to react immediately. Their Bigs were called up behind them. The Bigs took their Oath and the ceremony was concluded. They turned around to be greeted by the Chapter, everyone cheering and celebrating on the addition of four potential new brothers. The Devil Arms revealed themselves and Pi class noticed their own symbols and those that all the brothers had on their own hands.

"What's going on?" Nev asked the group getting panicked, rubbing away at his amethyst symbol that had suddenly showed itself on his right hand.

"This is messed up!" Rowan exclaimed looking closely at the red Devil Arms symbol that was on his right hand. "What drug did you make us take?" he asked.

"We didn't give you any drugs!" Vahn said exasperated. "You're just seeing for the first time what you couldn't before."

"Everyone has one!" Nev asked looking around surprised. "I can't believe it, it is a lot to take in," he said nodding his head.

"The Devil Arms are gifts given to Nephilim, each one unique and a reflection of its warrior's spirit," Vahn told them. "Devil Arms instruction is part of the candidate process, our first Education is Sunday night, you MUST be there in order to start this process, or you walk away from this for good," Vahn warned. "Now let's get some food and chill!" he shouted.

The energy was high as the group of brothers and four candidates walked through the woods shouting and talking excitedly. There was nothing like new blood among the men to reinvigorate the love, and passion for the fraternity. Dante and Birdy were ecstatic Nev was joining, they raved about how they liked him, and he'd be a good fit for Omega. Rowan instantly fit in with the group. He had a loud personality, but in a good way, he was charismatic, friendly, and very outgoing. Agustin was shy but a nice guy. Josh was hard to read.

When they got to Denny's, right off the freeway in Saginaw, the group of over thirty men walked into the nearly empty restaurant. They had made reservations, and table was arranged that could accommodate most, with booths alongside the table to fit the rest. Agustin sat with his Big, Troy, Doc, and Abe. The five of them instantly clicked. Nev and Rowan sat with their Bigs, and all of Lambda sat together at the head of the long table in the center of the back room. Virgil sat at a booth a few down from Lambda with Louie, Dante and Birdy. Lamar started making bets wanting someone to do a maple syrup shot, Magnus was unable to resist, his betting nature taking over, negotiating like a lawyer.

"This is going to be fun!" Louie exclaimed, "Having pledges, I can't wait to mess with them."

"Oh yeah, real mature Louie V!" Brody remarked after over hearing Louie's comment. "You just got in so time to screw with the candidates, didn't you learn anything from Jace last semester?" he asked sarcastically.

"Yeah Louie!" Jace jumped in, "Guys, hey Pi class listen up!" Jace said to the four candidates. "If Louie starts giving you things to do, come to me, and I'll make sure he is put in his place," he told them politely.

"Hey screw you Jace!" Louie said getting upset. "I was just kidding, gosh!" he said to Brody and Jace. "I would never treat a candidate like you treated Omicron, you big bully. I want to be the brother that is there for candidates, not the one making them do bitch work, they'd dread being around me like we felt about you."

"Don't let him get to you," Virgil told Louie. The older brothers loved using Louie as the butt of a joke...Virgil liked joking with him too, everybody did! Virgil wouldn't want to embarrass his friend in the process though, when Virgil did it, it was out of love, and adoration for the ridiculousness that was Louie V.

"What are you guys doing after this?" Dante asked.

"You making plans over there?" Virgil asked.

Dante's faced sprawled in a cartoonish grin and he nodded gleefully placing his hands behind his head, his cell clutched in his left hand. "We're going to get crazy with Blair and a few Alpha girls when this is over!"

"I'm down," Birdy nodded with a pleased smiled.

"Where at?" Virgil asked.

"At the Omega house, they are bringing a few of their new girls over to meet some 'frat boys'," Dante quoted with his fingers, then batted his eyes devilishly with a large grin.

"You dirty mofo!" Louie laughed, "You just want to Mack on the ladies!"

"Uh huh!" Dante again nodded happily.

After enjoying a hearty late-night meal, the group made their way back to campus. Dante had invited the Alpha girls over. Blair brought six of her sisters, including TK and their Sweetheart Raven, along with their six new candidates. Pi class came back to the house as well, normalizing Devil Arms on everyone's hands, as the Alpha sorority girls also had them. It was a great opportunity for the two groups to meet each other, and everyone was laughing, and having a great time. Virgil and Blair got a game of flip cup going with water and formed an unbeatable team. Virgil was doted on by TK and Raven and he felt loved in his circle of friends.

At the beginning of Sunday's fraternity meeting, Magnus announced the Betas had five candidates they'd inducted this week. The brothers were pretty upset they had one more guy than the Omegas, but Magnus was able to keep them from getting out of control. Virgil thought Magnus looked like he wanted to throw the gavel at Brody to silence his bumbling jaw. Officer reports went first, as the Epiprytanis Gabriel told them he had set up fundraisers to help boost the fraternity. The Omegas would be working at the Detroit Tigers games and Cedar Point Amusement Park over the summer and fall to raise close to $20,000 for their Chapter budget. The fraternity was pleasantly stunned. Gabriel told the Chapter he did it for all of them and would continue to do things for the Chapter as its second in command. The other reports went fast, Vahn making a short announcement about the candidate process starting, and how everyone needed to be on their best behavior with the candidates.

Lastly, Magnus stood up and gave his report before the meeting could move to open. Magnus told them that there were a few assignments the Chapter Advisors had received. He asked that the brothers from last week's assignment give their reports. Brody stood up and told the group that Zender, Jace, Reece, Lamar, and Tarek had gone together and had been successful. There had been Greed demons milling about the local Walmart, obviously they were kept well fed by the constant supply of people. They'd wiped out the nest that had formed in the back of the store. Brody also worked in a funny story from their adventure, making everyone laugh at the expense of making the story five minutes longer. There was usually some kind of Paladin operation every meeting or every other that brothers could volunteer for. Virgil had tried volunteering, and the older brothers weren't going for it. They'd act like he had suddenly left the room when it came time for him to raise his hand to be put on the list.

"I volunteer!" Virgil said before anyone could get a word in.

"You have to raise your hand Virgil, and be put on the speaker's list," Magnus admonished him for speaking out of turn. "Aren't you the Parliamentary Procedure expert?

"Yeah but Landon never seems to write my name down!" Virgil said getting frustrated.

"Grammataues, can you please see to it that frater Pitcher is placed on the speaker's list?" Magnus asked Landon.

They shared a long knowing look and Landon made a face like 'what the hell?' and scribbled something down on the paper.

"Frater Tarek?" Landon called out recognizing him as next to speak.

Tarek stood up and said, "I'll volunteer to help out, what's going on?"

"We need a small group maybe five or six," Magnus said, "Something has been attacking teenagers at the skate park near the river. Professor Ramuh got a disturbing report from an Epsilon rank Paladin police officer, meaning he wasn't active in the Paladins but had a Devil Arms, who worked in the local police force. He asked if Professor Ramuh had some Paladins that could look into it," Magnus told them. "Routine cleanup operation, doubt there are more than a dozen," he added.

"Kay I'm in," Tarek nodded and sat down.

"Frater Jagger," Landon called out.

Jagger stood and shrugged saying, "Well I better go, or else you crazy bastards might get yourselves killed out there," making Virgil laugh. Jagger was a socially awkward guy, though he could be hilarious! As the Pylortes when Virgil was a pledge, Jagger had seemed intimidating and scary. Now Virgil saw Jagger as a friendly guy who just wanted to have fun, and break through his shyness with people to show the real him.

"Frater Pitcher," Landon called out looking up making eye contact with Virgil. Virgil rose to his feet.

"I volunteer to go on the assignment," Virgil told the Chapter.

"Request denied," Magnus said flatly, "Next speaker," Magnus told Landon.

"Frater Landon," Landon said earning a few light-hearted chuckles from the brothers.

"Wait a minute!" Virgil said not having sat down, "I asked to be put on that assignment!" he said feeling frustrated.

"And I'm telling you no," Magnus cut Virgil off, his tone suddenly filled with power leaving no room for defiance.

Virgil put his hands in his pockets and looked away from Magnus, "Why?" he asked rocking back on his heels.

"Because I am the Prytanis," he said simply, "if you want to speak out of turn again, I'll ask you to leave," Magnus replied sharply.

Virgil sighed and sat back down fuming the rest of the meeting. He knew his friends were trying to protect him by keeping him from fighting, but it made him angry, to think they didn't believe he could handle himself! Virgil kept quiet and coasted through the rest of the meeting. Afterwards to take his mind off the meeting, Virgil went to campus making two posters and hanging them in the halls thanking guys for coming to the Rush events. Once Virgil was done with Omega stuff for the night, he went back to his dorm to study for his Chemistry test he had Monday.

Tuesday night after having dinner at the cafeteria with a group of Omicron, Pi class, Blair and some of her girls, Virgil headed to his Psych 100 class. The class was only once a week from 6pm till 10pm. They had a quiz every week at the end of the class. They were supposed to read the chapter for the upcoming week and be prepared for the test. The professor lectured on the chapter before handing out the quiz. For the first few quizzes Virgil would read the chapter, then come to class in the hopes that the professor's lecture and the quizzes would have the same material. His reward was a fourteen out of twenty on his first quiz, and a thirteen on his second. His professor droned on and on about her life and career, going way off topic to talk about things she'd done as a Psychology Professor. She was polite, and educated, yet her quizzes were based solely on the book and had nothing to do with her lectures. Virgil quickly grew irritated having to listen to her talk for over three hours about things that did pertain to the quiz. He gave Nev a text asking that he bring Virgil earplugs before his class. He found some and brought them to Virgil at dinner. Virgil rewarded him with some merits to make him look good to Vahn.

Virgil got to his class and sat in the back behind a lot of people and sank into his seat. He got out the textbook and paper and put the earplugs in. While the professor went on a rant about things that she would never test them on, Virgil looked down and studied the chapter's material for the length of the class. He was confident when he got the quiz, having been drilling the chapter's material into his brain for three hours straight. Virgil decided that was going to be the best allocation of his precious time to study for that class from now on.

Brotherhood was at the Omegas house that night, so Virgil drove over after class. The guys were downstairs, some were in the kitchen eating a late dinner or snack, others were in the massive living room, playing pool, watching TV, and playing cards. Virgil mingled with the brothers sitting down next to Doc, and Landon, catching up with them.

"What's up Cherry?" Doc said slapping Virgil on the thigh.

"Oh no, not the nickname," Virgil sighed. "Please don't call me that."

"He's a Cherry," Landon said in a childish voice and burst out laughing.

Virgil rolled his eyes, "Yeah, yeah, get it all out of your system."

"So Virge the Virgin it is!" Doc laughed, "I'm happy with that being your new unofficial nickname."

"Why did I sit down here again?" Virgil asked moving to stand to go mingle with Abe, Jace, and Reece.

"Oh, come on princess! Don't get all upset! You're too easy to mess with," Doc said shoving Virgil playfully. Virgil sat back down.

Virgil rolled his eyes at Doc, "What is the Brotherhood for tonight?" he asked Landon.

"Telephone, Can, and then Devil Arms practice," Landon told them.

"There are bets going around on which candidate is going to summon their weapon to their hand first," Doc said.

"Did you place a bet?" Virgil asked.

"You bet I did!" Doc said happily. "And I'm going to win it too!"

"You're stupid," Landon said laughing. "Magnus is just going to take all the money, like he usually does."

"I'm going to beat him this time!" Doc said confidently. Virgil and Landon shared a look and chuckled.

True to form Magnus walked casually up to different groups asking if they had any thoughts on tonight's Brotherhood. Vahn called the brothers out to the back as the candidates were arriving. Zender gleefully got to his feet.

"I don't want the candidates talking at Brotherhood," Vahn said firmly. "They need to stand here heads down, waiting till we are ready," he told Zender.

"Oh, trust me," Zender said confidently cracking his knuckles, then his neck and rolling his shoulders, "I'm going to scare the piss out of these guys before this process is over," he grinned happily.

Pi class came as one to Brotherhood, all four guys showing up at the front door, greeted by a grumpy and hostile Zender. They came to stand in the foyer and waited quietly for their Hegemon to get them. It was February and the cold of winter was still heavy upon Michigan and would be for over another month. Virgil had on a thick winter coat with gloves. The path down to the backyard was cleared regularly by the brothers using spells, the task was simple but draining, so they all took turns. Virgil followed his brothers down to the backyard near the forest. It was cold out and the brothers were standing around, ready to get things started. Within minutes Vahn was leading Pi class down to the zig zag hill path from the patio to the flat long stretch of back yard that led to the edge of their property. Vahn started the Brotherhood promptly, and within minutes the same lessons Virgil had learned in the Fall were being instilled into the next generation of candidates. Once the lessons were completed, Vahn told them they'd be instructed on Devil Arms. Vahn and Gabriel gave Pi class a short demonstration.

"Furybrand!" Vahn shouted, fire blazed to life in his hand extending out becoming a short sword of celestial silver held firmly in his grip. Vahn swung it through the air, flames trailed the blade, dying down when it became stationary.

"LionsHeart!" Gabriel yelled, light pouring out from his Devil Arms symbol, transforming into his long sword. Gabriel was aligned with earth, his sword was one of the most majestic weapons Virgil had ever seen, with a gold handle and a topaz fitted on his pummel. His long metallic blade gleamed in the moonlight, polished to perfection. He wielded his sword with immense strength and precision, he was easily Omega's best warrior. Vahn was skilled and determined, he was more than a challenge for Gabriel.

"As Nephilim warriors it falls to us to stand against demons, Death Dealers, and the Fallen," Vahn told Pi class. "A demon is a malicious spirt, born of chaos. It embodies sin or negative emotion, and feeds on darker parts of mortal psyche, like rage, hunger, desire. A demon's strength and intelligence are dependent on the emotion or idea from which it feeds, so more complex emotions, make stronger demons."

"Devil Arms are our primary defense against these creatures," Gabriel explained.

"Gabriel and I will give you a little demonstration," Vahn said.

Vahn made the first move gathering flames in his hands he threw them at Gabriel, "Flame Wall!" he shouted and from his ruby symbol flowed red magic bursting into a fiery shield of flames that shoved past Gabriel. Gabriel lifted his long blade to deflect some of the flames, Vahn was there in an instant leaping into the air to strike at the off centered Gabriel. Gabriel was knocked to the ground, whispering to the snow-covered dirt, his Devil Arms symbol glowed and a pillar of earth shot up striking Vahn into the air. Vahn was flung back, snow spraying into the wind, the pillar loudly rumbling back into the ground from whence it came.

"This is awesome!" Rowan exclaimed, his eyes practically twinkling. He was hyped up, unable to stand still, pacing as he watched the two brothers spar, looking like he wanted to jump in the fray.

"What the hell!?" Nev exclaimed blown away, "Are you guys serious right now."

"Your Devil Arms is your source of power," Vahn breathed heavy getting to his feet. "Learning to harness its power is the first step of every Paladin, no, all Nephilim. It is what you'll use to slay demons, to protect yourselves, or more importantly, protect others," Vahn spoke with passion.

"Learning humility and respect is important for all warriors," Gabriel warned. "Do not allow the taste of power to be all corrupting."

"I want a cool sword!" Nev exclaimed letting out his inner nerd.

"Hate to break it to you," Landon told his Lil from across the field, "You have a staff like me!"

"What?!" Nev cried out, "Crap! I always get the-,"

"Short end of the stick?" Doc interrupeted before he could finish.

"Doc, please stop talking," Vahn retorted, "We're trying to have like a celebrity death match here," Vahn said sarcastically. "Now weren't we like fighting each other or something?" Vahn asked his pledge brother.

"Yeah I just knocked you down, so it is probably your turn to hit me," Gabriel suggested.

"Boo!" Magnus called out, "You guys are lame!"

"Yeah!" Lamar called out, "Someone throw a chair in there for 'em," he cried out making himself laugh.

"No, no," Vahn sighed, "Alright the moment is lost. What we were TRYING to demonstrate for you guys was a mock use of our abilities. Over the next six weeks you will be training with your Bigs, and myself, honing your individual skills. Everyone's fighting style is different because we all have different weapons. As you learn more about your weapon, and thereby yourself, given time, you will grow, and you will get better," Vahn beamed believing his words. "I'm sure everyone's cold, since there is only four of you, lets head to the garage. If you are not in Pi class or a Big, please do not feel the need to join," he added.

"Boo!" Magnus called out again.

"We want to watch!" Lamar complained.

"Fine," Vahn huffed. In a bored and dismissing manner, he told them, "Keep it down! Side chatter gets distracting, and you're out," he finished sternly.

Louie and Birdy were following Vahn so Virgil did as well. They used the empty half of the garage, since there were only four candidates there was plenty of room for them to practice. They struggled for the first half hour, mostly standing around getting warm, talking with their Bigs, it was getting boring fast.

"Let's go," Virgil suggested, "It is not even midnight, yet we have plenty of time to do something," he said.

"I want to see which pledge can produce a physical form of their Devil Arms first," Dante said excitedly.

"It's going to be Rowan," Virgil thought out loud surprising himself, it wasn't something he had thought, more like what his instincts were telling him.

"WHAT?!" Dante and Birdy said at the same time completely shocked. "Dude don't you want Nev to be the first, he's like part of our group," Birdy looked hurt.

"Why you gotta be hatin' dog?" Dante asked barely able to keep a straight face.

"Yeah," Louie said jumping on the hate train, "Nev's like an adopted Omicron!"

"Owww ahhh," Birdy and Dante reacted negatively turning to Louie. Dante shook his head, "Let's not push it too far man, he's still a candidate."

"My bad," Louie smiled sheepishly looking around with a nervous laugh.

Virgil watched Gabriel wrestling with Rowan. Gabriel was tall and leaner than Rowan, which helped him. Rowan was two years older and in great shape from the military, plus he was extremely competitive and liked showing off, it was an even match. Gabriel got pissed at getting a hit from Rowan and shouted out his soul weapon taking his longsword in hand. He used the

Dull spell to create a barrier around his blade, as to not kill upon striking a sparring partner. A spell created by the founder of the Paladins, Lady Diamond. Some of Rowan's bravado came undone, faced with Gabriel's powerful sword. Rowan's ruby Devil Arms on his right hand began to light up some, Gabriel started playfully swinging at Rowan, catching him on the ribs twice. Rowan became more agitated, his symbol glowing more, Rowan finally called out, "Crimson Edge!" A pillar of flames erupted from his Devil Arms symbol, and a katana came to life in Rowan's hands. It was the first sword of its kind Virgil had ever seen a Nephilim use, and he took interest as did the other brothers.

"Pay up!" Magnus called out.

Rowan rounded on Gabriel quickly feeling cocky and overconfident with his newfound power. Gabriel was careful, Rowan had not placed the ward on his blade, and the wrong move could gravely injure him. Gabriel's overwhelming skill was apparent, and he disarmed Rowan within two blows. Gabriel and Rowan eased things down after that, Rowan focused on testing out his new best friend. Nev didn't take long after that, "Loki's Rod!" a staff zapped into existence in his hands with the unmistakable sound of electricity. Nev's staff looked different from the others Virgil had seen. Nev had an amethyst Devil Arms, his staff was blue and at the top the wood twisted up into a cone. Inside the sphere cone of his staff it looked like a lightning storm had been captured within. Nev gripped the staff and a wave of purple energy flowed down his staff, he was shocked and impressed. It was the coolest looking staff Virgil had ever seen. The other two candidates couldn't figure out their Devil Arms and were disappointed, Virgil looked at them seeing himself when he was a pledge, reflected in their defected faces.

"Hey it'll be okay!" Virgil said going over to Agustin and Josh, "I remember my first practice I couldn't get my Devil Arms to work either," Virgil admitted moving his right hand around nervously, they looked at Ragnorak's symbol. "In fact, it wasn't until I was brother that I finally figured it out. And they gave ME a chair position," Virgil laughed at the sheer irresponsibility. "So, if I can make it, you can too," he said smiling wanting them to have belief in themselves.

"Thanks Virgil," Agustin said giving him a strong handshake, "I really appreciate that right now," he told Virgil and they headed in the house with the group.

Chapter 5
<u>The Good Witch</u>

Sunday at 7pm, Virgil was sitting in the fraternity conference room for the weekly meeting. As much as he enjoyed getting work done, his brothers sure knew how to filibuster and ruin a good thing. Virgil sat next to Louie who kept passing out and Nolan who was writing down detailed notes. Virgil felt somewhere in between. Vahn gave his report, and the room came alive. He gave a brief review of the candidate's first week, he felt they'd made good effort into getting to know the brothers, and they were working hard on their other requirements. Vahn opened it up to the brothers for comments.

"I don't like Josh," Landon said seriously.

"You're always hatin'," Brody laughed waving him off.

"No, I mean it, I don't think that kid is right for us," Landon asserted.

"Why don't you like him?" Magnus asked one hand on his temple.

"It isn't that," Landon shook his head.

"Then what is it?" Vahn asked his close friend.

"His heart isn't in this," Landon told them, "How many interviews did he have Vahn?"

"Two," Vahn shrugged, "Which is SOME effort for the first week. We have brothers here that only did one interview their first week," Vahn turned to glare at Louie V.

"I tried talking to the guy and he's just, abrasive, closed off," Landon sounded disgusted. "Maybe he'll change, I know it is only the first week, but still, there is something…off about him," Landon shrugged. "I say we keep him in one more week and tell him tonight at Education he was brought up for removal, see if it lights a fire under his ass."

"I'll tell him that, but if you aren't seeing something, you better be sure you tried to get to know the guy too. You can't form judgments of people without first interacting with them on more than one occasion," Vahn lectured him.

"I know!" Landon snapped defensively. "Did he produce his Devil Arms yet?" Landon asked.

"No, we have two Devil Arms practice this week. I'll personally work with him and see what we can do," Vahn offered.

"He needs to come around more," Jace brought up, agreeing with Landon. "I saw Agustin, Rowan, and Nevin around campus all week, and they came over to the house too. Josh needs to make a stronger effort," Jace asserted.

"Alright, I'll make that clear to him," Vahn said frustrated throwing his papers down. "Anyone else?" he asked sarcastically. No one replied. "Big Brothers are to have their Littles sleep over after Brotherhood Tuesday night," he announced.

"Sleep over where?" Gabriel asked furrowing his brow, "This is a huge house, they can crash anywhere or in the pledge dorms."

"No!" Vahn snapped, "That's not the point. There are plenty of fraternities that don't have fraternity houses. Since they don't have a central living and gathering area, and people live spread out, the brothers must work harder to be together. That type of effort when applied can create a strong bond. I was reading the Omega Hegemon guide and it suggested Big and Lil sleep overs!" Vahn spoke rapidly frustrated. "Look it is happening people, make a comfortable bed for them on the floor in your rooms. Hopefully at night as you gaze at the same ceiling, you can talk to each other in those last moments before you drift off, and share a heartwarming moment of dialogue before bed," he had a soft smile on his face, a dreamy look in his eyes.

Doc acted like he was throwing up, Zender couldn't keep a straight face and burst out laughing. Lamar concentrated furiously then let out a nasty fart, that got Brody laughing, and he farted too in response on accident.

Vahn rolled his eyes, "Why do I even try?" he asked himself sitting down.

The meeting came to the last of the officer reports. Magnus' statements were always well thought out, it made paying attention to him easy. He was smart and knew how to play to people's interests. Magnus wanted to start things off with a report over last week's Paladin assignment they'd been given to handle.

Tarek Jeter stood up addressing the room, "We went to the skateboard park, and we totally played around, I did an awesome trick! Then we came home because we got hungry, passing the story on to someone else," he laughed sitting back down.

"Okayyyy," Magnus rolled his eyes, "Didn't really shed any light on that situation, but colorful as usual. Anyone else care to step in and tell the Chapter what the heck happened with the demons at the skate park?" he chuckled nervously hoping there was more.

Gabriel sighed and stood up, "I'll talk because I guess no one else wants too," he said annoyed. "It was pretty basic, just some Rage demons with a few weaker solider demons, feeding on auras. We took them on as a team and they went down fast."

"That's what I said!" Tarek complained.

"Oh yeah, and we all goofed around, and Tarek totally did an awesome skateboard trick that made us all cheer. That is until the demons showed up and his board accidently got ruined in the fight," Gabriel laughed.

"Those bastards!" Tarek Jeter shouted out obnoxiously shaking his fist in the air.

"Moving on," Magnus said to the room. "I received a call from a business in downtown Bay City. A woman who owns a Boutique. I guess there are like plants, books, candles, and homemade herbal remedies for sale too. She heard about our Chapter and is asking for our assistance with a 'little problem' she has at her shop," Magnus explained then he went silent looking at the group, he had everyone's attention.

"Go on," Louie said blinking the sleep from his eyes.

"Finally joining us Louie V!" Magnus asked with an arched eyebrow clearly having seen him dozing off. "The local vampires have been restless lately; a Sloth demon has taken up residence in the old underground Prohibition tunnels that run under downtown Bay City. The local vampires live down there," Magnus explained.

"Vampires?" Birdy groaned, "That sounds gay!"

"Hey!" Louie V yelled getting angry, "Watch your language man, saying gay in a derogatory connotation like that implies being gay is a bad thing, which any educated person knows it's not. Let's work on NOT saying it that way, okay?" Louie asked annoyed.

"Sorry," Birdy said to Louie, "My point is, isn't that a little cliché and overdone?" he asked the Chapter.

"Vampires permeate society myths and stories because there is something all seductive and alluring about them," Vahn told the group. "Real vampires DO exist however, just like werewolves and witches, and NEPHILIM," Vahn emphasized, "not too far of a stretch here people."

"Real vampires are dangerous, even to Nephilim," Magnus warned the brothers. "If given the chance they would most likely feed on you as our blood is so powerful, the vampire would gain an immediate and permanent power boost. Keep contact with them to a minimum," he advised.

Louie looked a little sick, "Hell no! I ain't fighting no vampires!" he cried. "Arch demons should have been the line, damn it!" he said laughing nervously, looking around. "You know they'd want a little Asian persuasion. I'd be on the menu for sure!"

"We get it Louie, you'll be at the back looking to bolt at the first sign of danger as usual," Dante smirked.

"Whatever, I've never LEFT you guys…right?" Louie asked Virgil.

Virgil started to laugh and tried to swallow it down to meet Louie's eyes, "Right bro," he managed to get out.

"MOVING ON!" Magnus shouted, "Gosh we're almost done, stay on topic. The client wants us to take care of the problem before it drives the vampires out to new areas and feeding grounds. We'll need five guys to go sometime this week."

"Why does she care about vampire politics?" Zender asked deep in thought seated by the door, as was required by his Jeweled Officer position.

"She's a witch," Magnus shrugged, "They've traditionally been the neutral ground between vampires and lycans. She's trying to stop the vampires from fleeing north into the local wolf territory or south to the local rat territory."

"Sweet," Dante nodded, "I volunteer."

"Me too," Birdy said.

"Rats?" Louie asked looking sick.

"Wererats, you know, like werelions, and weretigers, and werebears," Nolan listed them off.

"Oh my!" Tarek Jeter said clasping his hands to his face in a high-pitched falsetto voice.

"Volunteers for the mission?" Magnus asked the meeting room, wanting to be done. Magnus looked around at the older brothers. Omicron hadn't seen action since Retreat and some of the older brothers had been taking on assignments almost weekly. Tarek looked like he needed a week off from saving everybody. "Okay we have Dante and Birdy so far," Magnus sighed.

"We'll take Louie," Birdy offered.

"Yeah that should count for at least half of a brother, we get Blair too, and we'll be three and a half," Dante said talking to Birdy.

"I'm not going so don't try to make me!" Louie cried out.

"We were just kidding Louie," Dante replied with attitude, "We know if we were struck down, unable to move, lying in pain, bleeding out…" Dante said theatrically hamming it up more as he kept going.

"Oh Lordie," Louie V moaned leaning back in his chair, a defeated look overcoming him.

"And dying, we would have our mighty Asian ice bow wielding archer, who would come to save us because he is the best friend ever," Dante said holding his hands folded up batting long eye lashes at his friend.

"What if I agree to come for the car ride?" Louie suggested like he was going out of his way to help them.

"Louie!" Magnus shouted.

"Alright, alright! Sign me up," Louie sighed leaning back into his chair seeming to pass out on the spot resuming his nap.

The room was quiet and soon Virgil found everyone looking to him.

"What?" he asked his friends suddenly feeling embarrassed.

"Do you want to go with your friends or not?" Magnus asked Virgil.

"Well yeah!" Virgil responded with enthusiasm. "Am I ALLOWED to go?"

"You can go," Magnus nodded. Virgil smiled and leaned back.

"On one condition," Magnus added, displeased groans coming from Dante and Birdy.

"I want you to take an older brother along," Magnus suggested.

"Aren't we getting a little big for training wheels?" Dante asked Magnus. "Give us a couple more Omicron and we'll be good," he waved him off.

"What youth's arrogance does not see, can be blinding," Magnus warned Dante.

"If they want to handle it on their own let 'em," Gabriel suggested throwing his hands up in the air. "Everyone is tired and needs a break, Omicron can handle this," he said with confidence. "They survived a trip to the Ever After and back," Gabriel recalled, "Not many can boast such a feat," Gabriel asserted.

"Alright!" Magnus contended. "Anyone else want to join them?"

"This is going to be a busy week for me," Nolan said, "or I would. I'll be there in a heartbeat if there is an emergency though."

"I'm good," Troy told them.

"Alright the four of you are to contact the client and arrange a meet this week," Magnus told them, "We'll be expecting a full report at next week's Chapter meeting."

Monday at dinner, the following night, Virgil was seated in the cafeteria, with Birdy, Dante, Louie, Nev, Blair, and Helene. They were talking about their plans for the week, Dante proudly brought up their mission to meet up with a witch. Blair and Helene were instantly interested.

"I've never met a witch before!" Blair groaned extremely jealous of them, "That's dumb, our sorority doesn't do cool Paladin missions. I want to go into the tunnels and maybe kick some vampire butt."

"Uhh," Louie said looking a little green.

"Then join us girl!" Birdy said to Blair.

"We were kind of counting on you coming with us," Dante admitted. "You see how Louie is!"

"I know, I just love the big guy," Blair said wrapping her arm around Louie and giving him a hug. "But yeah, the four of you wandering around in the dark tunnels by yourselves sounds like a disaster! I can just see it now!" Blair laughed.

Helene giggled and agreed with Blair.

As much as Virgil liked having Blair around, he worried about putting her in danger. She was useful in a fight, at the same skill level of Omicron or more. But Virgil didn't like the idea of having Blair thick in the fray, with the possibility of her never coming back…

"I called the lady," Dante informed the group, "her name is Ms. Morgan and she can have us over any day this week, in the morning or afternoon, preferably before dusk she added," he said that part lightly, Louie really took notice though, his pupils enlarging with fear.

"How about tomorrow afternoon?" Virgil suggested.

"I'm free then," Blair nodded. It was decided, they'd aim for 3pm giving them time to investigate and get Virgil back in time for class and done before dark. Virgil went with Blair back to her room to hang out and watch their favorite TV shows for the rest of the night.

Tuesday morning Virgil woke up and went to the gym to work out. He came home and got cleaned up for the day and decided he needed to reach out to the candidates. He'd seen Rowan and Nev around, but he hadn't had a chance to really spend much one on one time with any of them. Virgil started texting the candidates. Nev wanted to do an interview later in the week and Rowan was free today. Virgil told Rowan if he wanted to come over and hang out, they could talk and get to know each other. Rowan was over in thirty minutes, a drawstring bag with all his candidate materials present on his back. They went to Virgil's room, Rowan taking the desk chair with Virgil sitting on his bed.

"Gabriel said you give awesome interviews," Rowan commented getting his book out.

"I don't know about that," Virgil shrugged, "All we do is talk, nothing much else to it."

"I don't know," Rowan said to Virgil. "This is my second week and you're my, seventh interview, so I've had a little experience so far," he smiled confidently. "Some brothers are easier to talk to than others," he admitted. "Some are funny, some are shy, some are soft spoken, and some are really outgoing. There are so many personalities, no two interviews are the same, and every person has a unique story."

"Dang," Virgil said leaning back, "That's deep."

"Thanks," Rowan said smiling. "So, let's talk man, tell me what your favorite food is?" Rowan asked.

"Pizza, or pasta," Virgil said. "Yours?"

"I'm a meat and potatoes kind of guy," Rowan replied proudly, "I really like burgers too."

"What's your favorite TV show?" Virgil asked him.

"Right now, I'm really into this survival show, but I like watching those crime shows too," Rowan said. "Honestly, I'm not much of a TV guy, I like being active and outdoors. What's your favorite TV show?" he asked.

After they went over each other's list of favorites, Virgil told him about his childhood, in turn he asked Rowan to tell him about his. Rowan was very much an entertainer at heart, he liked showing off and being noticed. Rowan sounded like a spirited youth. He only had his dad in the picture, Rowan told Virgil he thought of his mom as an "egg donor." Rowan's face became tight when talking about her, and his usual plucky attitude was dampened. Rowan joined the Navy to help pay for college and said though it was hard he'd enjoyed the comradery with his fellow men. Rowan said that was the best part of the military. He had been his squad's medic, responsible for emergency medical care for thirty men. Rowan said the position gave him respect from his team and other squads, and the training he got counted as credits he transferred into the university from the military.

After a couple hours it was getting time to meet for his first Paladin assignment, they were so engaged in conversation Virgil hadn't noticed. "Tell me about your Devil Arms," Rowan suggested to Virgil.

"What about yours!" Virgil grinned. "A fire katana, I'm kind of jealous," he said honestly. "Such an awesome looking sword."

"Thanks," Rowan smiled brightly, and he actually blushed. "We should spar sometime," Rowan thought excitedly. "I hear you're a scrapper."

"What?" Virgil asked.

"Let's fight sometime," Rowan's grin growing. "If I can kick your ass, everyone will think I'm powerful!"

"What the heck are you talking about?!" Virgil laughed nervously.

"Gabriel told me to ask you the full story. Apparently, you saved his life from the Ever After? All the brothers say you killed an Arch Demon," Rowan's grin gone he stared intently at Virgil's face.

Virgil was quiet for a moment. He recognized the Chapter knew about that night, over half of them had been there. It wasn't something he liked to think about, and he was surprised to hear a pledge address the situation like everyone talked about it.

"Hey, it isn't a bad thing," Rowan said sounding concerned, "They aren't talking bad about you Virgil," Rowan assured him.

"Thanks," Virgil said nodding quiet for a few moments reflecting on his thoughts. "That night, I haven't really talked about it with anyone," he admitted to Rowan. "I've never felt so hopeless or frightened, watching helplessly as my brothers were killed and tortured around me. The Ever After, the demon realm that exists alongside our own, is a dangerous place. It was foolish for me to think I could go in and we'd all be safe."

"That's deep," Rowan nodded. "I can relate and I'm here for you man. We can rely on each other to get through those hard times. After the fighting dies down, the warrior still lives with the moments of battle."

Virgil was moved by Rowan, it was one of the best interviews he'd ever had. Rowan was a great guy, and any fool could tell that he was going to be an Omega and one of the greats. "The night of my eighteenth birthday, a bolt of light crashed into me, and I passed out," Virgil told Rowan. "The Paladins call it Awakening, my Devil Arms appeared branding me with their power as my soul weapons. A black sickle shaped symbol on my left hand, and a white shooting star on my left," Virgil recalled. "From that night on I knew that I was different, really different, and all I'd really wanted was to belong with everyone else."

Rowan looked at Virgil's hands brining his own next to them. "Your symbols are awesome man, you're the only one to have white or black ones in our Chapter, right?" he asked. "If I could choose colors, I would have chosen a white or black one," he admitted.

"Thanks," Virgil nodded. "They are aesthetically pleasing I guess," looking at them.

"I would love to see your weapons in action," Rowan's excitement coming back. "Especially your scythe, it sounds freaking sweet!" Rowan exclaimed excitedly.

"You like weapons, don't you?" Virgil laughed after he asked.

"I have a sword and dagger collection," Rowan admitted with a nod.

Virgil thought of something, "You know one of the best things about the Omegas, and all of this?" he asked Rowan. "It's about individuality, each of us is valued, and has something to offer the group. Reflected in our Devil Arms as well, I don't like to think of some as better than others, they are all unique with special gifts."

"Agreed," Rowan replied.

"Let me see your candidate binder, I'll sign off on our interview," Virgil said flipping through Rowan's pages seeing the different things brothers had written. Rowan handed him a pen, on Jace's page there was blue ink!

"Oh shucks," Virgil said, "That's going to hurt."

"Yeah Vahn already knows," Rowan said. "I got fifty demerits from Jace and ten from Vahn. I gave Jace my binder and not a pen, he used the pen he had in his hand, which just happened to be blue. From now on when people write on my shit, they are going to do it with MY pens!" Rowan exclaimed in frustration.

Virgil handed back Rowan's binder with some merits and his interview completed.

"Are you seeing anyone?" Rowan asked Virgil. They'd already established Rowan was fresh out of the military, and looking to play around, not be tied down.

"Not right now," Virgil shook his head.

"I thought you and Blair were a thing?" Rowan asked with a grin.

"WHAT?!" Virgil freaked utterly shocked. "Where did you get a crazy idea like that?" he asked.

"From the brothers, everyone knows she likes you!" Rowan grinned.

Virgil's brothers were worse gossips then a gaggle of school girls! Who knew grown ass men could be so clucky. "Please!" Virgil sighed. "We are friends! There is nothing more there," he argued.

"Does she know that?" Rowan asked. "Don't take too long making up your mind," he warned. "Another brother is likely to scoop her up if she stays single."

There was a heavy knock on the door, Rowan jumped up to answer it after a nod from Virgil. Dante, Birdy and Blair were at the door.

"We came to see what was keeping you!" Blair spoke first.

"I was just about to leave," Virgil said getting up and getting his things together.

"You guys having a little chat?" Dante asked them.

"Yup, one hundred and fifty minutes later!" Rowan teased.

"Whatever dude," Virgil retorted, "You were free to leave anytime."

"Where are you guys headed?" Rowan asked.

"To see a witch about a demon problem," Dante boasted proudly.

"COOL!" Rowan's eyes sparkled, "Can I come?" he asked.

"Hell no!" Birdy cried. "It is way too dangerous for a newb like you, how many practices have you had? Two and a half?"

"I wouldn't have to fight," Rowan protested, "I could just watch."

"The problem with just watching," Virgil explained, "Is the moment this world becomes visible to you, they know you are seeing them. There is no more watching, there is fighting or running, you are forced to action either way," Virgil's words held conviction. "This isn't a field trip, the only people going are Nephilim who are ready to fight."

"I'm ready," Rowan said packing up his bag and putting it on his back.

"Are we really doing this?" Birdy asked them. "Gabriel will kick our ass if he gets hurt!"

"Gabriel doesn't need to know, or a certain pledge's life will become a living nightmare! Courtesy of Omicron," Dante threatened.

"If you go, you stay back, and you do not engage unless provoked," Virgil sighed knowing Dante had made up his mind, and there was no arguing with him. "If we tell you to leave, you leave. You do not brag to your pledge brothers about what you see, and you do not tell any brothers that we let you come."

"Deal," Rowan nodded shaking Virgil's hand. They headed down to the faculty parking lot outside of the dorm. The science building was the closest to the four large freshmen dorms, and the parking area was small with some parking meters but mostly faculty only. Louie was sitting in the running vehicle, he was driving his SUV, it was cold out and the group walked fast.

"We don't have enough room," Virgil noticed.

"Nolan's coming too!" Dante said surprising Virgil. "Apparently he moved some stuff around, so he could join us."

Nolan pulled his car into the parking lot at that moment. "Hey guys!" he said pulling up.

"Rowan ride with Nolan there!" Virgil told him.

"Follow Louie!" Dante told Nolan who nodded. Everyone got in the cars and they were off.

"What's Rowan doing riding in Nolan's car?" Louie asked.

"He's coming to meet the witch," Dante said from the backseat, Blair had called shotgun.

"Are we allowed to take pledges with us?" Louie asked apprehensively. "Isn't that a little…irresponsible?"

"Don't worry about it!" Dante snapped. "He's not going to see any action, and we're strong enough to keep an eye on him. Wouldn't you have loved to go on a mission with the brothers when you were still a candidate? We'll totally be cool brothers to him and it'll further bond us together. Omicron and Pi class will form a powerful alliance going into the future," Dante said, "We could use Rowan and Nev on our side."

Blair cranked the music up, "Alright ladies, you done bickering?" Blair asked them. "Let's jam out before we get there and get our blood pumping!"

They arrived in downtown Bay City in fifteen minutes. There were many shops around this part of town that were only open during the morning and early afternoon. Ms. Morgan's Boutique was nestled on the corner of a block next to a breakfast diner. Louie and Nolan parked their vehicles, the group of seven went to the store, and walked inside.

Ms. Morgan's shop was a witch's dream destination. Herbs and potions of varying types were on display, along with a wide range of books. The shop also had a small café in the front, with the more eccentric stuff in the back. Stairs were at the very back, one leading down, the other leading up. Ms. Morgan came out and greeted them warmly. She was a tall woman standing 5'10 with strawberry blonde hair. She was in her early-thirties. She wore conservative clothing fit for the winter weather, her attire still accentuated her natural feminine beauty. Virgil's brothers' eyes got wide and their pulses picked up. Virgil could sense something 'other' about her, closing his eyes he centered himself calming his thoughts and opening his mind to the spirit energy surrounding the world. Virgil opened his eyes and was surprised. Ms. Morgan's aura was large and hued with an orange and dark green color, they were like ribbons of color fighting for dominance in her aura. Ms. Morgan looked to Virgil knowing he was seeing with more than just his eyes. He dropped his focus, letting his vision of the spiritual realm around them drop from his sight.

"Good afternoon!" Ms. Morgan welcomed them. "I am glad you were able to come on such short notice, this is something that needs to be dealt with swiftly."

"We are happy to help a lady as charming as yourself," Dante said bowing slightly with a goofy grin on his face. Birdy raised an eyebrow at him.

Ms. Morgan politely smiled, "I haven't had a Nephilim in my shop in ages," she told them, "I forget how powerful your auras are," she said her eyes lingering on Virgil.

"You can see them?" Louie asked.

"Oh yes," she nodded them, "And I can see your Devil Arms symbols as well."

"So, you're definitely not human then?" Louie asked.

"Louie!" Everyone shouted in annoyance.

"Sorry," Virgil said, "We were all kind of excited to meet you because none of us have met a witch before," he said with blunt honesty.

Ms. Morgan laughed loudly and genuinely, it was an intoxicating and beautiful sound. She spoke with a smirk, "I am a witch, but I am still mortal. My magic is different from yours. I have inherited my powers from a long blood line of witches. I rely heavily on herbs, potions, and incantations to utilize my powers. The powers of a Nephilim are that of creation itself, you simply will the elements to bend to your will and they do so," Ms. Morgan explained.

"I'd love to ask you some questions later about spells and wards," Nolan said always anxious to expand his mind.

Ms. Morgan was polite and friendly. Virgil could tell she was good people, a helpful good witch who ran a business that offered a unique service to a niche market, half regular people, and half were other witches in the community. Even the occasional lycan or vampire came through for a spell or potion.

"Tell us about this request," Blair asked after they'd been talking for a few minutes.

"Yes! Just let me close up and let's head to the back." Ms. Morgan waved her hand and the sign on the door flipped over and the lock bolted into place. Virgil, Birdy, Dante, Louie, Nolan, Rowan, and Blair looked at the door and then to the young and beautiful witch. She led them to the back, then closed the curtains so people from the street couldn't see them.

Chapter 6
<u>The Tunnels and the Sloth Demon</u>

Virgil and his friends were seated at a rectangle table in the back of Ms. Morgan's witch shop. She had offered them tea and cookies, non-spelled of course. Louie wanted to eat all she'd give. Virgil wished there was time to look around and maybe buy something. She explained that a costumer had come in on Saturday, it was after sunset, and she was planning on closing soon. He was bundled up from the cold weather, and she couldn't get a good look at his face. She asked him if he needed help, he only mumbled in reply. She was carrying some things to the back room, and was getting ready for her day off when suddenly the man in the cloak was behind her and attacked!

"The cloak opened up and a great form spilled forth," Ms. Morgan recounted the harrowing experience. "It was a demon disguised as a man. It must have been drawn to my aura."

"On my goodness!" Louie exclaimed getting scared. Dante rolled his eyes. "What did you do? How'd you survive?" Louie asked on the edge of his seat.

"I'm a witch," Ms. Morgan arched an eyebrow as if that explained everything, "It'll take more than a hungry Sloth demon to take me down," she said confidently.

"A Sloth demon?" Virgil asked.

"Yes, demons are typically classified by the emotion they feed off on. Rage demons are the weakest and the more complicated emotions, like pride, make the strongest demons. Sloth demons can be moderately strong," Ms. Morgan told them. "I blasted a powerful spell at the demon, then made a quick circle in salt and tapped a ley line, creating a barrier around myself. I was able to get it downstairs and seal off the basement," Ms. Morgan recalled. "When I went down there the next day it had escaped into the tunnels underneath this building. Most buildings along the stretch of the Saginaw River have entrances to the tunnels, either sealed off and decrypted, or semi-functional. Publicly they are known to be sealed and off limits to the populace. In truth they are the home to the local vampire coven. They have carved out an underground facility in the tunnels and run their domain with an iron fist. The Master vampire who rules in this area has an uneasy peace with the local witches and lycans. The demon is causing problems for them down there. Demons can't feed on vampires because vampires don't have auras, but they can kill them for sport," Ms. Morgan said.

"You requested our help before the demon pisses the local vamps off, and they lash out against innocent people out of frustration," Nolan pointed out.

"Yes," Ms. Morgan chuckled. "There is peace between our different groups, albeit a fragile one. It is best to keep it so. Demons are dangerous, and Nephilim are best suited to the task of defending us against them," Ms. Morgan smiled.

"We'll head down and see if we can slay this Sloth demon for you," Dante said with a more masculine tone to his voice then normal. Blair arched an eyebrow at him.

"I would appreciate it," Ms. Morgan beamed. "I would like to feel safe in my home once more."

"So, we're supposed to go into the dark tunnels, and go poking around for a demon?" Louie thought out loud. "I think it's best that Rowan stay behind, I'll wait out in the car with him," Louie offered gallantly. "A brother who is powerful enough should guard him."

"I want to go!" Rowan protested. "I may be a pledge, but I want to help this nice lady, and see you guys in action."

"I think Louie's trying to use you as an excuse to get himself out of this," Blair whispered loudly to Rowan.

"We're going to be in a lot of trouble if they find out we brought a candidate with us," Louie whined. "I'm just thinking of all our best interests here," he defended himself.

"You're coming with us, end of story," Dante said bluntly with a pissed off tone, leaving no room for arguing.

"Let me show you the way," Ms. Morgan said. She rose from her seat and led them over to the door leading to the basement. She moved her leg across the salt line in front of the door. Virgil saw a symbol hang in the air before the door, it quickly faded away, whatever seal she had placed on it, was now gone. They followed her down to the basement, which had dirt floor with a low ceiling, Birdy had to bend down so his head wouldn't hit the ceiling.

"That will lead you down," Ms. Morgan pointed to the cellar doors at the end of the room. They were surrounded by a salt circle. "All you have to do is break the circle of salt, saltwater breaks most spells, and the incantation keeping the cellar sealed with be lifted," she told them. "Be warned, Sloth demons are devious, he may try to talk his way out of things, lure you into letting your guard down before he attacks."

"Thanks, we'll be careful," Virgil nodded.

"Take this," Ms. Morgan said taking an amulet from her pocket. She pricked her finger with a small knife she produced from a sheath in the left sleeve of her dress. She had a few drops fall on the amulet, a light washed over it. "This is a locator amulet," she told them. "It will help you find your way back to the surface. If you get lost down there, use this to find an exit out of the tunnels before the sun sets. The vampires will rise around then, the stronger ones wake back up faster, and you don't want to be down there. Their living area is the entire southern end. Vampires aren't 'allowed' to feed on Paladins or risk being punished, but if given the chance the benefits they reap from your blood can prove too tempting to pass up," she warned.

"We'll be getting out before the sun sets," Dante assured her.

"Oh God! Please watch over us," Louie prayed out loud.

"We'll be fine!" Birdy shoved Louie slightly, "We've been through worse!"

"One of my goals in life isn't to see how close I can walk the line of death every month Birdtweed!" Louie shouted. "But I'll go I guess," he said with little confidence. Ms. Morgan brought forth a small glass of salt water and poured some on her circle. It fizzled, and a wall of energy pulsed in a cone in front of the entrance.

"Take this too," Ms. Morgan said taking out another amulet from her pocket. "Who wants to wear the light?"

"What do you mean?" Blair asked.

"This amulet has been spelled with a witch light, a wisp of light that hovers over the caster illuminating up to ten meters. Useful for places like these," she pointed out.

"I'll take it," Blair offered, "I'm usually in the middle of the pack, it is probably best to keep it centralized between all of us."

"Good idea," Virgil agreed. Ms. Morgan placed it on Blair's neck and spread some of her blood on the back of the pendant. A wisp of reddish orange light hovered in the air above Blair. "The spell is good for forty-eight hours, just take it off when you want the light to go out."

"Orange light?" Nolan asked.

"The light uses the aura around you as its energy, so it is colored with the same hue," Ms. Morgan explained. "Good luck down there, if you are in need of help, I will come for you," she assured them.

"We would never put a lady such as yourself in danger!" Dante said taking her hand reassuring her.

"Hey what about me!" Blair asked mockingly insulted.

"We can handle things, milady," Dante told Ms. Morgan in his most masculine macho tone.

"Aww you're a cute boy," Ms. Morgan said patting his hand. "Be safe."

"Let's go," Birdy said sounding annoyed steering Dante and himself towards the tunnel as the leads, Nolan handed Birdy a UV flashlight from a backpack he had on.

"I did some research after the meeting, I got to thinking about witches and vampires, and realized I couldn't let you guys hog all the excitement. Besides I figured you'd probably screw things up if I wasn't along," Nolan grinned, the only one who found that amusing.

"We would have been just fine without you," Dante shot him down.

"Did anyone bother thinking how you were going to see in the pitch-black tunnels?" Nolan asked.

"I have this amulet witch light!" Blair added with a smirk.

"Did any of you BRING a flashlight? More specifically a UV flashlight, that could actually burn vampires if we run into them?" Nolan asked them. Everyone went quiet.

"You got any more of them flashlights there Nolan?" Louie asked very serious causing everyone to laugh.

"I got two more Louie," Nolan grinned taking one out for Rowan and Louie.

"How are you going to use your bow and a flashlight Louie V?" Dante asked with an expression on his face that said 'come on'.

"Never mind!" Louie waved him off, "It's a work in progress, I'll figure it out as I go," Louie said optimistically staring down at the flashlight like it was a life preserver. The group became quiet and descended into the darkness...

Within minutes they were lost in the dark eerie earthen tunnels, Nolan brought out a compass from his backpack, and started acting as a navigator. They handed the locator amulet from the witch to him as well. Virgil was thinking maybe Nolan was right about them needing him on this trip. "Basically, we just have to wander around looking for the damn thing, just be careful not to go all the way south," Nolan recapped for them.

"Yes please!" Louie V shouted with feverish enthusiasm. He was at the very back. Rowan was between Nolan and Louie, and Virgil and Blair.

The UV lights and Blair's witch light were enough to really light up the dark tunnels. Virgil realized that they were announcing their presence to vampires and demons alike with such a bright light. The Sloth demon could ignore them if it wanted to with such a blatant give away. What else were they supposed to do? Doing this in the pitch dark was suicide. Damned if they did, damned if they didn't. Might as well see what's coming at you. Time started to drag, the tunnels were very disorienting, three times they came upon dead ends, and sealed off exits, and a couple times they found abandoned rooms, most likely for storage of spirits during Prohibition. They came across another dead end with a small open area with abandoned shelves and what looked like benches.

"What the hell are we looking for anyway?" Dante asked from the front as they tried to decide which way to head next. "Every demon has looked so different, what is a Sloth demon going to look like? A giant pile of garbage?" he asked making himself chuckle.

"I can imagine it being ugly," Birdy shivered.

"And lazy," Blair added smirking, "So it is probably overweight."

"It is probably really fat and slow," Louie chuckled.

There came a growl from behind them in the dark. Dante and Birdy reacted coming to the front of the group keeping the dead end to their backs.

"Do tell me, fat, little, mortal," a deep demonic voice called out from the darkness, dripping with anger. "Are you talking about yourself, or me?" it asked stepping just into the edge of the light ahead of Dante and Birdy, ten meters at most. Everyone grew tense, the figure was in the shape of a giant bear. It looked powerful and menacing, complete with red eyes, sharp claws and fangs. This demon had an intelligence in its eyes.

"Neither of us really," Louie said meekly from the back.

"You have come searching for me little Judge Spawn, well, here I am," it said simply.

When it was clear that the demon was waiting for them to speak Virgil asked, "Why haven't you left the tunnels?"

"Why?" the demon asked. "It is comfortable, down here in the dark," he admitted. The tunnels run underneath many homes and businesses, so many people, it was dangerous having a demon at their feet waiting to feed off their glutton, lazy energies, and auras.

"You seem like a nice guy, err…demon bear," Louie shrugged. "I say you agree to go home, we agree to go home, and no one needs to know."

"Hmm perhaps," the demon considered. "I could just eat all of you, or I could stay, or I could leave," it said.

"We want you gone back to the Ever After," Nolan stated.

"Three questions, if you get one wrong, I eat you," the bear said.

"If we get them all right, what happens?" Blair asked, "Because I can guarantee you that first option will end badly for you," her ruby Devil Arms symbol started to glow.

"If you get them all right, I will leave the caves, and these lands, but I will not stay away forever," the demon was firm on this.

"Why don't we try?" Louie suggested with his best diplomate's tone.

"We could," Nolan shrugged not worried.

"I say we just kill it," Dante said itching for his battle axe.

"Virgil," Blair asked, and he turned to his friend. "Is it really safe to just let it leave? What if it just comes back to a different part of the world, feeding on people who don't have Paladins nearby?"

Blair's comment cut deep, it rang with truth, an excellent point, yet Virgil couldn't ignore an option that solved the demon problem and guaranteed the safety of his friends.

"Give us the damn question already!" Dante snapped.

"The more you take away, the bigger I become, what am I?" the bear asked.

"Guys come here," Nolan said bringing in the group. "What are some ideas?"

Silence. No one met each other's gaze at first, "I've never liked riddles," Blair admitted.

"Me neither," sighed Rowan.

"It is something," Nolan said thinking hard, "Like debt, or land, or emptiness," he said thinking out loud.

"You're close," Virgil said thinking along those lines, he was sure there was the answer.

"A hole!" Birdy said. "It has to be," he laughed.

"What if it's wrong?" Louie yelled.

"Then we go with plan A!" Virgil told them.

"Yeah because what was plan B, letting it eat us?" Blair laughed at the ridiculous nature of the choice.

"Honey," Dante said jokingly as if he was admonishing a little child, "That was never an option."

"What is your answer?" the bear asked.

"Uh guys?" Dante asked.

"A hole," Virgil answered.

"Correct," the bear continued, "I have seas with no water, coast with no sand, towns without people, and mountains without land. What am I?"

"This one's harder," Blair said. "Crap come on think," she said. They threw out some ideas but nothing was sounding right.

Virgil felt much the same, this was a tricky riddle. It was something that had these things but not the real forms anyway, maybe just a picture of them. What would that look like though, what is that called? "A map," Virgil said with confidence knowing he'd discovered the answer, "Let's go with that guys."

"Agreed," Nolan nodded.

"A map," Dante told the bear.

"Correct," the bear replied, "Final question. No man has seen it, but all men know it. Lighter than air, sharper than a sword. Comes from nothing and will fell the mightiest of armies. Of what do I speak?"

Louie sighed, "I don't get it."

"Let me think for a minute," Nolan said.

"If we get this right, we win?" Birdy asked them.

"I'm waiting," the demon said impatiently after thirty seconds of silence among the friends.

"I think I got it, your hunger, right?" Nolan told the demon.

The demon in the form of a bear took a few steps back and gave a lazy yawn, "I shall be on my way," it said.

"You're leaving the tunnels?" Virgil asked. "And returning to the Ever After?"

"That is what we agreed upon," the demon nodded slinking back into the shadows its body no longer visible. They were alone once more...

"This is creepy," Blair said running her hands along her arms, "We should get out of here."

"Agreed," Virgil said.

"Is the situation resolved just like that?" Nolan asked uncertain. "Did we do the right thing? Should we kill every demon we see, or is it fair to negotiate with them for a peaceful resolution?"

"None of us got hurt, and the demon's back in the Ever After, right?" Dante wondered. "That sounds like a win."

Virgil checked his phone, they needed to get to the surface. "Nolan, get us out of here," Virgil told his friend. Nolan nodded and started paying attention to the locator amulet the witch had given him. They cautiously approached the tunnel they'd come down to get to the dead end. They had enough light to guide them, and the flashlights gave the group a small measure of confidence. They came to a large t-intersection, with the tunnel heading left and right.

"Which way?" Dante asked looking back to Nolan.

"We need to head right," Nolan replied. Birdy and Dante went to move forward, a shadow came across the right, something was ahead of them in the tunnel.

"What was that?" Louie asked his eyes sharp as a hawk.

"Not sure," Dante said keeping his voice low. The group cautiously moved forward. "Maybe we should head left man," Dante advised.

"No," Nolan said, "that will push us deeper into the tunnels, we NEED to head right," he said frustrated.

"Alright," Dante said, "Gaia's Wrath," he whispered, his Devil Arms symbol radiating light and materializing into a double-bladed battle axe. "Cover me Birdy," Dante told his roommate. Birdy nodded and summoned his lightning lance to hand, electricity running along its blade. Rowan kept the light on the men's backs, its beam of UV sweeping ahead.

They all made the turn without incident, coming down a main passage of the tunnels, multiple side passages were along their path on both sides, plenty of places for something to jump out, the group's eyes were constantly shifting, looking for something, hoping for nothing. They didn't make it far before the sound of a can being kicked across the floor echoed, then footsteps moving in the distance. Progress became painfully slow, their formation tightening, tension growing among them, they weren't sure what else was down here, and they weren't looking to find out.

"How much further," Birdy whispered to Nolan.

"I don't know, we should try to get back to Ms. Morgan's shop, we could spend hours trying to get through an exit that might be sealed off on the business side. I'm guessing it is going to take us ten, fifteen minutes? Thirty at the most, if we keep up this pace," Nolan estimated for the group. Nolan was working hard to stay confident but sweat was forming along his forehead, the stress and fear was starting to take its toll. After a minute the group's pace began to slowly pick up, their confidence returning. They came to another large junction, likely below a street. Suddenly the overwhelming sensation of being watched came over the group. The group came to a grinding halt just as they entered the larger area.

"Something's here," Dante said gripping his axe.

"I don't see anything, let's keep going!" Louie's voice rising, anxious to get to the surface.

"It'll cut us down," Dante warned, "It wants us to start running. It wants to separate us."

"What is it Dante?" Virgil asked ready to call Soul Reaver to his hand.

A laugh came out and the flashlights went towards it, shadows and movement were all they could catch.

"Would you mind turning out the flash lights, so we can talk?" a masculine voice called out to them.

Rowan and Nolan left their flashlights on but kept them pointed to the ground, Blair's witch light spell hung overhead, faintly giving them red-orange light. Two figures came from the south and west. They needed to keep heading north.

They approached with casual slow gaits, they were exaggerating their movements for the group to put them at ease, as these creatures could run faster than the eye could see. There was a man and a woman, the man looked to be in his mid-thirties, he wasn't altogether striking, rather plain and average. His female counterpart looked to be in her twenties, she was attractive but in a fierce way, her features were very angular. She gave off a cold and ruthless demeanor, it hardened her looks. Virgil had never seen a vampire before; they could pass for people in the right setting. They were slightly pale, paying homage to classical vampire lore. They had normal colored eyes as well, besides being pale there wasn't anything physically marking them as other. It was their presence that signaled they were something different. Virgil could feel the tension in the air, these two were killers, and Virgil immediately felt distrustful of them. Whatever their intentions were, Virgil knew these two were a danger to him and his friends.

"Allow us to introduce ourselves, I am Dan, this is Margaret. What brings you into the tunnels?" the vampire Dan asked them politely and with genuine curiosity.

"We came here to rid you of the Sloth demon," Dante answered calmly, he had nerves of steel, and was great under pressure. "We've just finished removing it and are now on our way back home."

"Aww, so the Paladins finally did come to clear it out, well done," Dan congratulated them. "I know our Master will be most pleased to hear that."

"It is getting late," Dante said awkwardly trying to be polite yet staying firm, "We really should be going."

"Are you sure?" Dan asked them. "We could take you to our Master, so he could thank you personally," Dan suggested. "I'm sure he'd be delighted to entertain you, we don't often have guests of your caliber down here," he flattered them.

"Listen lips," Blair cut in with a tone that left little room for bullshitting, "We came down here for a job, its completed, so now we'd like to go home. It was nice meeting both of you, we really can't stay. Please give your Master our regards."

The woman burst out laughing, she smiled at Blair, her eye teeth extending into fangs. "I like her, she has a lot of spunk!" the vampire Margaret giggled.

"We're just trying to be polite, no need to be pushy," Dan mussed.

"If you truly had pure intentions, you would have never approached us, or taken the hint and let us pass," Virgil said fiercely finding courage in the friends around him. "My friends and I do not wish for a fight, but I warn you, we will defend ourselves if forced too."

"My dear boy!" Dan cried out, "We do not wish for a conflict either!"

Margaret nodded, "We will be on our way." The two vampires walked slowly towards the southern entrance and then suddenly, vanished. Virgil knew they must have run, it happened so fast, like they blinked out of existence.

"Weird," Nolan said.

"You think they're gone?" Birdy asked.

"I don't trust it," Dante shook his head, "We need to get to the surface, now!" he barked. Nolan guided them towards the northern tunnel and the group hurried with renewed vigor. They moved at a jog, everyone was on edge, the tunnels reverberated sound greatly, even distant echoes made the hairs on their arms and necks stand up. They were getting closer, and things were starting to look familiar. Virgil knew that Ms. Morgan's shop was close.

Dante was flung back off his feet, it happened so quickly Virgil didn't have time to react, Dante slammed into a wall, falling to the dirty ground. Birdy was picked up by Dan, and flung backwards. Blair summoned her fire whipsword, Flametongue, to her hand in a burst of flames of light. Margaret was at her side in an instant, she savagely swung at Blair sending her spinning through the air. Blair landed on her stomach hard, her sword vanishing into ruby light moving back into the symbol on her hand.

"Shit!" Louie yelled, "Shiva's Bow!" he shouted his ice bow gracefully descending from an icy breeze of power into solid form.

Dan charged Louie, fangs barred, snarling. Rowan swung the beam of the flashlight at the vampire catching it full on. The vampire screamed as the light visibly burned his skin, sizzling as smoke rose from where it touched him. Nolan moved the flashlight's beam in his hands sweeping it back and forth on his friends trying to keep the creatures back.

"Shoot them!" Dante yelled at Louie.

"They're too fast!" Louie yelled back, "I'm not going to be able to get a shot in!"

Margaret was suddenly behind Nolan, he went to turn, and she grabbed his wrist, twisting it with a loud and sickening *snap!* He cried out in pain the flashlight dropping to the floor.

"Get off him!" Rowan yelled moving his flashlight beam towards her, she ran like a blur moving away from Nolan and dodging the UV light with ease.

Virgil's anger was boiling over, these creatures would not take his friends from him! Virgil noticed Soul Reaver's symbol blazing to life. Virgil didn't want to use Soul Reaver, in such a tight space, he would have a hard time using it properly, as it was likely he would hurt one of his friends with its fire on accident. Virgil silently prayed, asking Ragnorak for its protection. Virgil knew that he shouldn't be worthy of the Holy Blade. Virgil knew he had to act though, or they might never see daylight again. All Virgil wanted was to protect the people who meant the world to him! Ragnorak's symbol flared to life.

"Ragnorak!" Virgil called out raising his right hand and a bolt of white light crashed down from above striking his hand. The light formed into the sword, Ragnorak, the most breathtaking weapon Virgil had ever known. The gold aura of the sword quickly surrounded him.

Virgil felt the creature coming at him, he reacted raising Ragnorak up to strike. He dodged the incoming blow, to the left, then to the right, the creature Margaret snarled furiously at him, swinging with its hands, it clawed through the golden veil now surrounding him, but couldn't land a blow.

"That light is protecting him!" Margaret yelled out. "It is slowing me down as soon as I touch it, guiding my attacks away from him!" she told her partner. Margaret dropped back stopping her assault on Virgil.

"Their strength is in their weapons!" Dan yelled to his friend. "Remove the sword from his hand and he'll be as helpless as any other mortal! I'll enjoy draining you mortal!" Dan snarled at Virgil coming at him. Virgil swung Ragnorak, and he nimbly dodged the sword

Margaret picked up Blair and hungrily sank her fangs into her neck. Blair cried out in pain, and the vampire viciously ripped at her throat!

"BLAIR!" Virgil screamed true fear pumping into his system. Ragnorak pulsed within Virgil's hand, its power calling to him as it had before. Virgil knew what to do, he raised his sword above his head and swung it in an arc at the female vampire. From the blade a wave of light swam forth sounding like a sonic blast. The vampire didn't even have time to react, the wave of light blasted through her picking her up off her feet and carrying her back with its tremendous force. The vampire screamed in anguish falling to the ground as ash.

"Margie!" Dan howled. "You will pay!" he screamed his eyes going dark with bloodlust. Virgil went to use Ragnorak again, the vampire moved too quickly running at him with inhuman speed he shoved Virgil against the wall moving with him, pinning him in place. Dan sank his fangs into Virgil's flesh, ripping at his throat trying to cause as much damage as he could. Virgil's blood flowed freely from his neck, his concentration and vision beginning to fade.

Suddenly a fiery whip of flame and metal lashed around the creature's neck, it squeezed tight, Dan's head was cleaved from his shoulders, falling to the dirty ground. His head and body began to fade to ash. Blair retracted her fiery whip, the sections of blade coming back together until they were a sword once more. Virgil wanted to thank her, he fell to the floor, she looked bad, holding a hand to her neck to stem the flow of blood she moved to him.

"Virgil," she said with tears in her eyes as she took him in her arms.

"Blair," Virgil managed to whisper before he lost consciousness.

Chapter 7
<u>The Paladin Games</u>

Virgil awoke feeling tired and stiff, he thought he was in Ms. Morgan's shop, maybe the upstairs part, he'd never been up here before though. There were couches and a TV, a dining room, like any normal apartment, with a LOT of plants…everywhere.

Virgil groaned feeling his head ache as he sat up. "Eat these," Ms. Morgan said holding a plate of cookies out for him.

"Isn't there a saying about taking candy from a witch?" Virgil asked.

"Oh hush," Ms. Morgan said waving off his comment, "Like I'd dare poison the Redeemer, I don't need any angry Fallen Judges breaking in my front door," she said logically with a healthy amount of fear.

"You know?" Virgil asked sitting all the way up. "How am I alive? Blair!" Virgil yelled remembering the attack.

"Calm your tits, I'm right here," Blair said walking into Virgil's field of vison she sat down next to him. They gave each other a tight hug.

"I thought I was going to lose you," Virgil said as they broke apart.

"Me?" Blair laughed. "You fried that bitch before she got much blood from me. You however, that bloodsucker got you GOOD. You lost so much blood you were ghostly pale…," Blair said her eyes getting misty. "You'd managed to hold onto Ragnorak, so it continued to close your wounds even as you lay dying. Louie came over and immediately poured his energy into both of us healing our wounds, it took almost everything he had."

"Louie passed out from overuse of his aura," Ms. Morgan told them. "I was able to keep him safe until it was able to heal enough where he regained consciousness."

"Ms. Morgan came down right as you passed out," Blair told him.

"You came to help us?" Virgil guessed.

"Of course," Ms. Morgan said as if it was the most obvious choice, "I wouldn't send seven brave young Nephilim into danger, without being willing to go in after you. The witch light Blair held had a spell on it where I could monitor what was happening around it. When I sensed Blair being attacked through the amulet I came as fast as I could. Eat your cookie, it will help with your blood loss and fatigue," she said happily. Virgil shrugged and took a bite, chocolate chip and m&ms, it was incredible!

"Thank you!" Virgil said. They had a strange aftertaste, which he thought was the ingredient that was linked to the benefit or spell.

"She got us all back to her home safely and managed to contact Magnus. Magnus and Tarek came over within twenty minutes."

"Oh no," Virgil said an impending doom beginning to sink into him. He stuffed the last of his delicious cookie in his mouth and said, "I got to get out of here."

"They are downstairs waiting for you," Blair said with a grin spreading across her face.

"Is there a backway out of here?" Virgil asked Ms. Morgan.

"Okay, Louie!" Blair cried. "Go get yelled at so we can all go home," she joked.

"They care a lot about you," Ms. Morgan remarked sounding envious. "You are blessed to have so many friends. Most people go their whole lives without having had more than a handful of close friends."

"I know we screwed up, I just don't want to hear it from Magnus," Virgil said. "I'll feel like I disappointed him. At least with Tarek Jeter, he'll rag on me for a few hours then he'll get bored and we'll play some video games," Virgil thought.

"You're not what I imagined of the Redeemer," Ms. Morgan shook her head with a smirk.

"It's the generation!" Blair sighed.

"Hey!" Virgil said. "I'm still learning this stuff, I've only been a Paladin for four months," he said in his defense.

"No," Ms. Morgan shook her head. "I imagined the Redeemer to be a fearsome, frightening warrior," she told him. "The legends paint him as the Dark Knight of the Twin Reavers, or simply the Reaver, a warrior of darkness and death," Ms. Morgan said sadly.

Virgil's whole demeanor crashed instantly, Blair's quips and Ms. Morgan's addictive cookies fell away, and he felt like crap again. "Reaver?" Virgil asked.

"The Redeemer, or the Reaver," Ms. Morgan nodded sadly, "Your actions will ultimately lead you down one of the two paths, but you cannot be both," she said looking him straight in the eye. "I see the Reaver's shadow looming over you. He is angry, his destiny has been altered by someone who loves you dearly, and he wants control. You have a powerful aura," she spoke with a far-off look in her eyes seeing his spirit, his aura, reading him. "It calls to others, inspires those who follow you, be careful how you wield it," she warned. "Just because you can bend others to your will, does not give you the right to."

"I'm not like that!" Virgil said strongly not liking what he was hearing, "I decide who I am, not some legend, or a prophecy, or a witch. I'm an American college student, trying to get an education, and plan for my future. In between I'm juggling this Nephilim stuff. I don't consider myself above others, and I would never seek to harm someone unless I had too!" Virgil said getting angry. "I've never had to kill a person, and I pray I never will. It sickens me, the thought of taking a life. I am a solider, the modern equivalent of a warrior. I'm recruited to fight, my duty is to protect, and my job is to kill," Virgil said sadly. "I can only live each day as best as I can, and when faced with the choice between what is easy and wrong, or what is right and hard, I hope that I will continue to choose the path that makes me the man I strive to be."

"I think you have your head on straight," Ms. Morgan nodded getting up.

"Let's go," Blair laughed nervously, and they headed down the stairs to the back of the store. Virgil's heart sank lower with each step, he was glad Gabriel wasn't here, he didn't want to hear him give one of his famous guilt trips. Virgil came into the room and found his friends, in good health and spirits, which made him happy.

"Hey Buddy," Gabriel said very friendly from a chair at the long table. "We were waiting for you to wake up."

"Hey Hegemon, good to see you," Virgil lied with a bright smile.

"Getting deep in here," Louie muttered out of the side of his mouth to Birdy.

"You want to tell us how the hell you got your team attacked by two vampires?!" Gabriel asked Virgil all pretense of pleasantries gone. That was fast, Virgil thought.

"Listen, we got rid of the Sloth demon and were on our way back when we started being followed. We did everything we could to get out of there, but they came at us faster than we could react," Virgil said talking fast. "It could have happened to anyone, so how did I get my team attacked?" he asked his friends. "I didn't! We did everything we could to protect ourselves, you knew this mission involved the tunnels, and you all know the local vampires live there. If you want to get all huffy, point the finger at yourselves!" Virgil said getting angry.

"Hang on there," Gabriel said getting irritated with Virgil's fiery attitude. "In your self-righteous rant, you forgot to explain the reason for bringing Rowan, a candidate! Someone who hasn't had proper training as a Paladin, and therefore could not protect himself in the environment you exposed him to."

"I didn't get a scratch on me," Rowan said hands in the air, "They fought hard to make sure of it too," he said in their defense. "And I told them to take me, not the other way around."

"Yeah, yeah we heard you earlier," Tarek croaked at Rowan, "You don't have to repeat it again for Virgil."

Virgil went quiet, Gabriel wasn't denying they had no blame for being attacked, the reason they were mad was the brothers had endangered Rowan, a candidate. "I'm sorry," Virgil owned.

Gabriel nodded, "That's my Little Brother man, the kid is important to me," he told Virgil his face held anger, and disappointment, it hurt to have Gabriel look at him like that.

"I'm older than you!" Rowan said to Gabriel laughing.

"Quiet Lil! Big daddy is talking," Gabriel told Rowan making all the guys and ladies laugh.

"Okay, I get it," Virgil said. "I am sorry for bringing Rowan."

Gabriel sighed, "Just be more careful is all we're asking. Please! And don't bring candidates on Paladin missions!" Gabriel said getting angry. "Next time we'll bring you up on charges," he warned.

Virgil felt his face flush, "I'm sorry. I won't do it again," he promised Gabriel.

"Okay," Gabriel nodded and walked over to Virgil embracing him in a fierce hug. "I'm glad you're okay," he told Virgil.

"Alright enough of this," Magnus said. "Ms. Morgan we are sorry for any inconvenience," Magnus told her.

"You guys were no trouble at all!" Ms. Morgan's eyes glistened as she looked at Magnus. "Here let me pay you," she said going to get her purse.

"No mam!" Magnus said, "We cannot take payment from you."

"Why not?" Ms. Morgan asked looking sad. "You got rid of the Sloth demon as requested."

"With all the help you supplied to our people, we should be offering you money," Magnus told her.

"Well that's mighty kind of you," Ms. Morgan said blushing and batting her eyes at Magnus. Virgil's jaw dropped slightly, was it his imagination or was Ms. Morgan into Magnus?

"Any time you have need for us, just give me call," Magnus replied uncharacteristically soft and kind. "I am the Chapter President, I can make things happen," he promised her.

"Owww make it rain Prytanis!" Louie said from down the table making himself laugh.

"Louie, go away," Magnus told him without taking his eyes of Ms. Morgan.

"If I get any other referrals from the community, I will forward them along. A lot of people come here with problems looking for answers or solutions I may not always be able to offer," Ms. Morgan looked away shyly.

"That would be fantastic!" Magnus said genuinely excited. "We need to reach out into the community more. Omega is here to serve the Underworld community, and it's a Paladin's duty to keep peace between everyone."

"Consider it done," Ms. Morgan nodded happily.

"Wait!" Virgil said feeling at his neck. "I was bit, by a vampire, does that mean?" Virgil didn't want to have to ask.

"You're not going to turn into a vampire," Ms. Morgan assured him. "The process of turning is more purposeful. You must consume a large amount of blood from a vampire first, then be killed with the blood in your system. Your body reanimates within twenty-four hours, you have twenty-four hours to feed from a vampire or else you die permanently," she explained.

"So, we're going to be okay?" Virgil asked.

"Yes," Ms. Morgan nodded.

"Thank you," Virgil told the kind witch. She smiled at Virgil and his friends and they left her shop. Virgil realized it was almost seven pm, he'd missed an hour of his Psychology class! Virgil sighed not happy with the way the day had turned out, he couldn't go to class, the professor didn't allow people in past 6:15pm.

At Brotherhood that night, Josh didn't show, Vahn announced that he was dropping out. There were three men in Pi class. Virgil drifted through his week, not really feeling himself again until Friday morning. Magnus told them he'd received a call from the Master Vampire of the area. He'd been angry and short with Magnus, pissed off that Nephilim had been poking around in his tunnels without permission. He asked for the whereabouts of two of his people. Magnus explained that the Paladins had gone in to help the local vamps by removing the demon. On their way back they were attacked, unprovoked. Magnus told the Master Vampire that his men had defended themselves and killed the vampires in the process. The Master Vampire made a few threatening remarks, but Magnus didn't believe he'd try anything. Vampires were incredibly powerful, but they did not openly antagonize Paladin warriors, they had a healthy respect for the children of Judges.

Sunday night's meeting was the same as usual. During Vahn's officer report the brother's griped about the candidates not doing enough, Vahn did his best to support both sides of the argument. Everyone agreed Pi class could step up their game. This week's Brotherhood was the rock wall, one of everyone's favorites. Vahn stressed not to tell candidates secrets as to let them figure out the meanings themselves. When all the officers had gone it was Magnus' turn to speak, he asked for a report on the Paladin assignment that had been given at the last meeting. Virgil's friends looked to him to speak so he nodded and rose from his chair.

"We were asked to meet with a kindly witch, who seemed quite smitten with our Prytanis," Virgil pointed out.

"Hey!" Magnus exclaimed blushing for one of the first times in Virgil's memory. There was something there! "Keep your report on topic!" he commanded.

Virgil got a few laughs from the brothers and lewd questions hurled out from the audience. Virgil continued, "The witch told us she'd been attacked by a Sloth demon who had subsequently taken up residence in the tunnels beneath her shop that were once used in Prohibition. We went in and took care of the situation. On the way out, we were jumped by two vampires, luckily we managed to survive the encounter," Virgil summarized.

Magnus had another assignment for the Chapter that week, this one was north of Bay City near Standish. It didn't seem like it was going to be too dangerous, but Omicron were told right from the start they were sitting this one out. After briefly going over the mission and getting a group of guys to volunteer, Magnus' demeanor changed.

"I have something to tell the Chapter," Magnus said rather seriously. "This summer solstice in the Capital of Alexandros, the Paladin Games, or the Tournament of the Chalice will once again commence. Paladins from all over the world will be gathering for a weeklong of festivities and competitions culminating in a giant battle inside the Coliseum for the finalists. The winners of the Tournament are given the title of strongest Chapter in the world and become the protectors of the Chalice of Immortals. The Chapter Advisors want us to participate, and this will be the first time our Chapter has done so. As such we will all need to start getting into peak condition and practice with our Devil Arms, as a unit," Magnus told them.

"The Paladin Games are awesome!" Tarek cried out. "It is kind of like the Olympics for Nephilim. Nephilim from all over the world come to participate, and Alexandros is brimming with people from Paladin Chapters from places you've never heard of."

"It has been something the Paladins have done for thousands of years. Every fifth year the Tournament is held to bring together the Nephilim race for a friendly, competitive show of the best our race has to offer," Magnus explained. "The winners become the new Guardians of the Chalice and protect it for five years until the next Tournament. For us to even have a chance we'll have to work hard over the next few months to get prepared. If we're going to enter, I want us to do our best," Magnus said with passion.

"Only the best Paladins can enter and not embarrass themselves," Tarek warned, "The final day, is cut throat," he admitted. "The brutality of the Roman Coliseum inspired the Nephilim to build their own on a grander scale, and ours is still very much in use. It is the world's largest sport's arena."

"What?!" Louie said drawing out his response. "You're saying at the end of this competition a bunch of people battle it out for everyone to watch?"

"Pretty much," Magnus said. "The battles are legendary!"

"There is a tale about the Grand Prytanis," Tarek told them. "When he entered the tournament, he led his team to victory against all odds."

"That'd be fun to watch," Virgil said imagining the most unique looking weapons that had ever existed, gathering in one epic battle! All in good sport of course, the Dull spell was kept active in the battle to prevent lethal attacks.

"We will be having group practices," Gabriel told the group. "Once a week, until the semester is over, then increase it to three or more a week. That is what it is going to take people, to get ready for this thing."

"Why should we kill ourselves for this?" Lamar asked. "This is an Internationals event, but we don't HAVE to participate. We should go and just have fun," he told them.

"No one has to do this if they don't want to," Vahn pointed out. "So stop bitchin', things will go on as normal, we're all brothers and everyone can do the things they want to do here."

"Only a dozen men are allowed to enter from each group in the last stage of the competition," Tarek explained. "We can have more for the initial few days, in fact you need more in order to rank, then move to the higher categories, and ultimately the final event."

"We'll have our first practice after Spring Break," Magnus said, "Everyone interested can come to our first practice. Seems kind of foolish to do it now when Spring Break starts at the end of next week's classes," he suggested.

Monday night Virgil headed over to the Omega house after class and a quick meal at the food court. He needed some time to just unwind with friends. He was feeling stressed about his classes. Next week he had an exam, two papers, and his weekly quiz. He was going to spend this week working hard, so he wouldn't be so stressed out. Virgil came inside the house and walked to the first floor living room. Lamar, Abe, Doc, Reece, and Troy were watching TV. He said hello and headed upstairs. On the second floor no one was in the living room, but the doors to the library were wide open and Virgil walked inside. It was modest in size, stretching up to the third floor, taking up part of that floor as well, designed for practical use over lavish design. Vahn, Landon, Nevin, Birdy, Nolan, and Zender were sitting at the group of tables with their books out, not doing much studying. The room had no TVs, just several tables, and a few comfy chairs and couches. The books in the library were half college material, classical literature, with a fun YA section as well. The other half were books that you wouldn't find in a normal library. Books on Nephilim history, lore, battles, strategy, Devil Arms, more than Virgil had initially thought. No wonder Nolan knows so much, Virgil thought, he took the time to investigate this world they'd been thrust into. Virgil donated his books from last semester to the library, the campus' overpriced bookstore was offering nothing for them. Better someone else have access to the knowledge then give it back to greedy people like that.

Virgil pulled up a chair and joined in their conversation. They were talking about a good show everyone was into, every Sunday night while at the meetings, the only thing people really wanted to be doing was finding out what was happening to their characters on TV. Vahn and Zender were arguing about one character, and Nevin and Birdy were discussing the plot. Nolan was making some progress on his studies amongst the chatter.

"Virgil," Nevin, or Nev, said turning to face him, "How are you doing sir? I feel like we haven't had a chance to talk much yet," he said. "I've seen you a lot hanging out next door," he joked.

"Let's do something then," Virgil nodded. "My talk with Rowan went good, I'm looking forward to having one with you as well."

"Well, what about right now?" Nev asked.

"Well I did come here to hang out," Virgil said nodding, "We could go to the pledge dorm and talk."

Landon started packing up his things as well. "Where you going?" Vahn asked him.

"Over to Stephanie's place," Landon said.

"You whipped son of a bitch," Zender joked. "All you want to do is hang out with her nowadays."

"Well she's my girlfriend," Landon shrugged. "We can do things…I can't with all of you guys," he implied suggestively.

"Ew!" The group collectively let out a cry of repulsion.

"It's the truth," Landon laughed. "And we like spending time together," he said taking his stuff and leaving. Vahn seemed slightly peeved.

"What's up Big?" Virgil asked him.

"Landon, he gets so focused on his girl when he's dating, he sometimes sucks at juggling friends and his woman," Vahn said.

"He comes around," Virgil argued.

"He spends the night there most of the week, and usually only comes around for meetings and Brotherhoods," Vahn told him.

"Yeah, but it is his girlfriend," Virgil said, "That doesn't seem too strange."

"The thing is Virgil," Vahn said with a huffy sigh trying hard to get his point across without snapping at his Lil, "When any brother gets a girlfriend, they are going to be around less, and that's fine, that's to be expected! We all want that, it's a part of life. But a good friend is someone who doesn't make their relationship the only part of their life, still making time for their friends and family. Because what happens if the relationship ends?" Vahn pointed out.

"You make a good point I guess," Virgil shrugged. "A good friend needs to give time to their friends, away from their lover or partner."

"Landon is a great friend, he just hasn't been around a lot lately," Vahn said. "It sucks because we've been best friends for years."

"Sorry Big!" Virgil frowned.

"It's okay," Vahn nodded. "I actually like his girlfriend, I'm happy for him, I just miss my friend," he said nodding.

"Let's go Virgil," Nev said packing up his bag and getting up.

"Right, later guys!" Virgil said to his friends and walked with Nev down the hall and around the corner past the stairs and down the other hall. The pledge dorms were rather large, a big open room with lots of bunk beds, spare clothes, a few couches and chairs, and a big community bathroom. It was for candidates to stay at during the process, and for Paladin visitors, every Omega Chapter always had room for a brother in need. Nev had stayed here with Rowan and Agustin several nights, and he showed where they'd taken up residence in the room.

They sat in the back on the comfy couches, Nev got out his pledge binder and started asking Virgil questions. Nev was six months older than Virgil and had graduated from high school the same year. He was from Croswell, Michigan, just like Magnus, funny as Nev reminded Virgil of Magnus. Nev told Virgil that he hadn't really known Magnus or his siblings because they were older than him in school. Nev had a great family, with a kind and outspoken mother who was a leader in her work and the community. Nev had always been good at school and he liked it, he liked learning and teaching others new things. Nev had graduated top of his class and came to Bay Valley on a full ride. Even though Nev was the smart guy type, he was more masculine than most nerds. Nev loved watching and playing sports with the guys, especially football and followed it closely, fitting in with a good half of the fraternity. Nev was a leader, and Virgil quickly gained rapport with him.

Nev was intelligent like Nolan, yet more talkative and easy going like Birdy, without the absent-minded Birdy mannerisms that drove people mad. Louie had told Virgil he really liked Nev and was actually sorry he got thrown in a room with 'those two dumbasses', affectionately referring to their pledge brothers.

"So, what is the deal with your Devil Arms?" Nev asked not hiding his interest.

"What do you mean?" Virgil asked.

"Come on, you have two, and their white and black, different from everyone else. The brothers keep telling me to ask you about them," he said with a shrug. "From what I've read with Nolan's guidance in the Omega library, it is extremely rare for Nephilim to be born with two and never under Creation and Chaos."

"We're all unique," Virgil answered. "I don't know why my symbols are like this, I wish I only had one, at least then it wouldn't be so weird."

"What's the Chaos weapon?" Nev asked pointing towards the dark scythe symbol.

"Soul Reaver," Virgil told him. The black symbol came to life, like a demonic chuckle calling out, shadowy light dancing along its mark.

"Creepy," Nev said looking down at the Devil Arms.

"This one is a flaming scythe, its flames burn through auras causing physical and metaphysical damage," Virgil explained kind of excited. It wasn't often he got to talk about his weapon to someone else. "It is dangerous even when I'm practicing with brothers, kind of a hassle really."

Nev looked taken back, he nodded saying, "Note to self, never piss off Virgil," he laughed nervously.

Virgil rolled his eyes, "Whatever!"

Nev regained his composure, "Rowan said he saw you wield a sword," Nev said not making eye contact. "A sword so powerful, it pulsed with life almost like it spoke, and you waved it forward releasing a blast of power that destroyed everything in its path," Nev said.

Virgil sighed, "Kids these days! They like to blow everything out of proportion!"

"Dude, he's like four years older than you, I'm older than you!" Nev laughed.

"I know, I know," Virgil acknowledged, he was the youngest brother in the fraternity. Even if all three candidates got in, Virgil would still be the youngest. "What do you want me to say? Yeah, it's true what Rowan said. This Devil Arms is the Holy Blade Ragnorak, the almighty weapon that was once wielded by my father, a Judge, before his Fall. It isn't something that I really talk about, you know?" Virgil said looking off. "It is something I have to live with, day in and day out. It stops becoming a cool tattoo, more of a physical reminder of a heavy burden. We all have potential, unaccomplished destiny's waiting just in the horizon of time. Our Devil Arms are merely a reflection of our individual paths, a guide to our destinations. It is hard to be boastful of something so serious, and altogether alienating." Nev sat there stunned at Virgil's words. Virgil turned to stare at Nev looking him in the eye. "I'm proud to be a part of this fraternity. And I'm going to do my best for this group, I want to lead this Chapter someday, and I'm not daunted by the labor of leadership. The further you get in, the crazier things get, but the more time you spend with everyone, you begin to love the brotherhood, the guys, your family," Virgil admitted. Virgil raised his hands up and laughed, "The fraternity makes it all worth it, I couldn't imagine going through this alone."

They shifted topics, "So how is living with Birdy and Dante going?" Virgil asked.

"Sucks," Nev said flatly, "My room gets trashed daily. Brothers are always stopping by to see Birdy and Dante or me, the door never stops opening and slamming shut, it has pissed off our other dorm mates. The brothers have been razing me too, I'm doing well though. Honestly our class is strong, we get our stuff accomplished for each week and meet as often as we can," Nev told him.

"I agree," Virgil nodded. "I am impressed with you guys. You are my first pledge class, but it is easy to see how much effort you guys have been putting in. Some brothers like to complain, but it is only to make you guys show us you really want it, so we know you're not coasting through."

"There is nothing remotely near 'coasting' about this process," Nev said flatly.

Virgil chuckled, "Agreed!"

After several hours of asking questions, telling stories, and each of them taking time to get to know the other, Virgil realized he had just made another great friend. From that night forward, Nev was considered an adopted Omicron and became close with Virgil and his friends. Brotherhood that Tuesday was the Unclimbable Wall, Rowan became only the second brother in the group, besides Zender, to master it on his second attempt asking the brothers for help. Virgil was doing well in all his classes, two B's and three A's. Devil Arms training for Pi Class continued to go well, everyone had manifested their Devil Arms. Agustin wielded an earth mace, it had a long handle with a metal ball at the end with sharp spikes all over. Agustin had to keep the Dull spell on constantly when practicing or he risked maiming a brother on accident, lucky the spell stopped the spikes from penetrating flesh. The candidates' skills were coming along slowly but steadily, in a few weeks times they'd be ready to learn about auras and using their energy to cast spells of their aligned elements.

That weekend Virgil went home to see his mother, Sue, for the weekend in Caseville. He brought homework to study, and type papers, and made it a productive weekend, while also visiting with his mom. Even now his mother never noticed the marks on Virgil's hands, she was human through and through. Only witches, vampires, lycans, demons, Judges, fairies, and Nephilim could see them. Virgil was thankful for his normal, loving, human mother. She had instilled in him love and empathy, compassion for others, and the desire for understanding and peace over intolerance and conflict. Saturday night after his mother had gone to bed, Virgil took his Omega guide outside flipping to a section on Illusion spell casting. He found a symbol that was familiar, a symbol that he'd seen Magnus use, the Angelic ruin for protection, which was used in wards or barriers. He went around the entire house, drawing the glyph on the house, a white symbol hung in the air after each time. Once he'd made it all the way around, a golden circle linked the spells together and a thin veil of gold hung over the home. It would repel all

demons and vampires, masking it and creating a barrier from entry. A Nephilim or Judge could

destroy the spells if they were able to find the house, with Virgil's spell it would be invisible to

the celestial's vision. Human's had a harder time with magic, most unable to see it altogether.

Virgil went to bed that night feeling less worried about his mother, and the evil things that he

could accidentally lead to her home.

Chapter 8
Spring Break

It was the eighth week of the semester and the last week of classes before Spring Break. Tuesday night was Tradition, when the brothers took the candidates into the Ever After, the dimension that demons, Fallen Judges, and Death Dealers called home. It was dangerous, which is why they kept it low key. It was something the Chapter felt was important new members experience before coming into the group, to get a glimpse of this other realm so connected with their own. The reality of what was truly going on in the world, sank in a little deeper afterwards. After his psychology class, with an easy quiz thanks to his handy ear plugs giving him the entire lecture to tune the professor out and study, it was time for Brotherhood.

Pi class was starting to get burned out. Four weeks of pledging with just three guys meant they were getting a lot of calls, more than the few of them could handle. They were excited about Spring Break as well, hoping a week off would help them push through the final two weeks when they came back. Vahn was a great Hegemon, serious like Gabriel had been, stern and less playful. Vahn was a better teacher, but Gabriel was a stronger leader, the Hegemon position was a unique harmony of both. It was hard for Virgil to look at someone besides Gabriel as a Hegemon, his perspective colored by his own experience. Everyone had been told to be dressed warm. The snow was still deep, and the brothers had gone through to clear a semi passable path out to the ley line intersection in the woods, a stone temple had been built over the natural place of power. The candidates were blindfolded and led out to the fraternity's special meeting place. The going was rough and brothers did little in way of messing with the candidates, the natural elements were more than enough. The strong wind battered at the brothers, there was no snow falling, however the knee-high level of snow on the ground was whipped up stinging their faces.

Virgil walked close to Pi class occasionally sending out a wisp of flame from his Devil Arms into the air near them to warm them up. A few brothers gave him dirty looks, the brothers don't like people getting too "buddy buddy" with the candidates. Virgil shrugged and did it a few more times, keeping it as discreet as he could. It had taken minimal energy and Virgil got to the temple ahead of the group with Magnus. The temple was always clear of snow and debris, a magical barrier protecting it. Virgil followed Magnus inside and watched him create a portal through one of the many ley lines that ran beneath their feet, into to the Ever After.

"Do we always go to the same spot?" Virgil asked Magnus. "How does the spell work for different locations, how do you make it open up for us at just the right spot?"

"Slow down man," Magnus said as he worked, "I can't answer every question at once pal, and we'll need white boards and something to take notes for that explanation."

"Sorry, just curious to learn how to do this," Virgil said excitedly. "I like learning new things and that looks like complicated spell work."

"Yes, complicated," Magnus replied flatly. "Just watch for now, and I'll show you how to do it on your own sometime," he gave Virgil a quick smile. "The basic explanation is, we use the ley lines that run underneath the earth to jump from one point to another, kind of like a telephone line. The spellwork involved is VERY complex, too advanced to do without the help of this transporter. Most Paladins use similar structures for creating portals, otherwise you'd have to do the complicated spellwork every time you went to create a portal. Having this dais here skips us over that first step and helps us create portals as many times as we want, without having to do the complicated process. Honestly without this thing, I doubt if I'd be able to create a portal that I'd trust to go through and survive," Magnus explained.

"Thanks," Virgil nodded soaking up the knowledge, appreciating the explanation. "I'll help you create a perimeter when we get there," Virgil offered, "I did one around my mother's house this weekend."

"Is that right?" Magnus asked his tone stepping into that of the Prytanis. "You know spelling mortals houses without their permission is illegal right?" he asked in a cocky tone, arching an eyebrow such a judgmental look on his face. Virgil didn't know whether to burst out into nervous laughter or stay dead still, he chose the latter. "Just because we're friends and all, doesn't mean that I approve of you breaking Paladin law."

Virgil paused reflecting on what he'd said then answered, "After the whole vampire incident, I just needed to know she was safe in her home," Virgil said honestly with a heavy heart. "I was laying in my bed thinking of all the things that could be following me, and if they might find her. I was up and spelling her house within minutes," he admitted.

"If you did it right, no vampire would be able to enter, unless invited in," Magnus spoke casually. "And demons would outright be destroyed if they tried to pass the barrier. I'm sure your mom will be fine," Magnus looked at Virgil, his eyes were soft and kind. "Especially with such a devoted son."

He doesn't care that I did it, Virgil smiled to himself, Magnus was so hard to read on a good day. "I think I did it right," Virgil thought thinking back to what he'd done. "It was like when you created one in the Ever After at my Tradition, a golden line went through and I visibly saw the barrier wall extend around the house."

Magnus grew silent working the complex ley line portal. It involved a series of glyphs, specifically placed on the stone arch. Bright amethyst letters flowed from Magnus' Devil Arms symbol out of his finger into the air, hanging in place. Magnus concentrated, and a black portal began to spiral in the center. He nodded taking a step back, their path was open. The candidates came inside, their blind folds off, with the rest of the Chapter. The howling of the wind did not penetrate the inside of the roofless temple, it was strangely warm inside, the large stone basins at the center filled with fire, and so the brothers relaxed and caught their breath.

"Listen up!" Vahn said calling out. The Chapter's attention fell to him. "What you see and learn tonight, stays here! This is a Brotherhood that you will NOT talk about with anyone who is not present. We're going to be taking a little trip, safer than driving a car, we'll be there for ten minutes tops, then we're coming straight back. Stay close to your Bigs, no talking, or sudden movements. Let's roll!" Vahn commanded and Gabriel and Magnus headed through the portal first.

"I'll stay behind to keep it open," Jagger offered moving up to the arch way and placing his hand with a golden-brown Devil Arms against the stone. His symbol glowed holding onto the spell/portal.

Virgil went through with Vahn, stepping through the black swirling fog, Virgil felt his whole world enclose around him. It became impossible to breath, all of Virgil's senses were being muffled as his sense of being was battered about, then within the same moment his legs were moving on solid ground. The Ever After was a bleak, lifeless world, a constant cover of black stormy skies with a dying red sun. They were nestled up in a ridge of mountains, on a flat long shelf, the same place they'd come to when Virgil was a pledge. He figured they came here to minimize danger to their group. They were so isolated at this location in the Ever After, it was unlikely they'd be spotted by the many foul things lurking in this dangerous realm. It was Virgil's first time back here since the Tear Drop incident. He couldn't see the tall forest where'd they'd been, the Ever After was about the size of North America, landlocked at its borders, surrounded by an empty darkness that held naught beyond, just rolling clouds of nothingness.

"Virgil get started on the perimeter!" Magnus snapped getting to work.

Virgil nodded and walked to the edge raising his right hand to spell with. The angelic symbol for protection, Virgil traced it in the air concentrating and as he did his finger created a white glyph. He walked several paces and drew another, working his way in a circle to meet with Magnus who was doing the same. The brothers came through within minutes, and the circle was closed around them, protecting them from being seen. Vahn went into a speech about the Ever After, how it was the Paladins' duty to stand against the mighty threats that resided here. It was about that time Virgil heard the laughter of a woman. He looked up noticing a disgusting harmony of an extremely large rounded avian type of creature, with the upper half of a human body growing on its head. The humanoid part on top was feminine with saggy breasts, long gnarly hair, with bloodstained claws at her sides. Underneath the actual bird part had a large mouth and face in the large circular bird body. Virgil held his breath not sure if it had sensed or heard them. He noticed everyone had gone dead silent as well.

"Bird demons," Magnus explained to the group in a soft tone. "They live on the tops of these mountains. They are ranked as Lesser demons, above Cardinal and Soldier demons, but nowhere near the strength of an Arch demon. It is best if we leave as soon as possible," he advised the group. "These are pack demons, living in groups numbered in the hundreds. If one of them picks up on us the sky could be filled with them in moments. They are silent killers, swopping down with little noise."

The group quickly moved back to the portal, still held open by Jagger on the other side. Virgil kept his eyes in the sky, seeing another of the strange bird demons, this one had a similar large bird body with a big face in the middle, but had a male version sitting on top. Weird, Virgil thought, they were now down to just a few brothers.

"Let's go!" Vahn said ready to move through with Virgil. They stepped into the swirling vortex, traveling like a call on a telephone wire, on the life lines of energy that ran through the planet. They burst out through the stone archway back into the safety of their temple.

"Let the seriousness of what you've seen tonight weigh heavy on your hearts," Vahn told his pledge class when they had all gotten back safely. "This is what we are fighting for! To make sure that CRAP, doesn't end up in our world, and stays away from the people we care about."

Everyone was dismissed and headed back to the Omega house to hang out. When Spring Break started Friday, the candidates were no longer pledges for the duration of Spring Break. Giving the three pledges a solid week of vacation to do nothing, they didn't have to answer any brothers' calls and could just have fun. All three of Pi class were going to Florida, the place most people from their University went to for Spring Break. Virgil didn't have the money to go on a trip like that, he was going to enjoy the week off from classes and hang out at the Omega house. There was a solid group of guys who were staying behind, and they decided they were going to have fun and make the best of staying in cold, winter Michigan. It was March now, the temperature was slowly rising, and snow fall decreasing in likelihood, but plenty on the ground. Virgil and the guys who stayed behind threw a party Friday night, to kick off the start of Spring

Break. It was a small gathering, though they had almost a hundred people present, there were plenty of students not going on an expensive vacation. Blair had gone with Helene and a bunch of their sorority girls. Most of the older brothers had gone as well. Dante, Birdy, Nolan, Doc, Brody, and Zender, were a few of the guys left.

By Monday afternoon Virgil and the few brothers that were left at the house were bored out of their minds. They had partied hard over the weekend and chilled most of Sunday night, so by Monday afternoon Virgil was sitting in the first floor living room with Birdy and Doc watching TV. Virgil was playing his handheld video game system, grinding on a random Pokémon game that he'd beaten a couple times, those things were great time suckers, and so addicting.

"What do you guys want to do tonight?" Doc asked from the couch across the room.

Virgil shrugged his shoulders and grunted, more focused on his game. Birdy sighed, "We could go get some shit and drink or smoke," he suggested.

"I guess," Doc said, "Maybe we should plan one last get together before the week is over. Most people will be back Saturday and Sunday, maybe Thursday?" he asked.

"Put the word out let's see what day most people can come over," Dante asked walking in the room with Brody, they sat down in empty spots next to each other.

"Yeah, because we have to do something to spice things up," Brody said, "We can't have four more nights of this," he said gesturing around.

"We should pick up a little bit today," Virgil suggested. "Get the house back together for Thursday."

"Can't we wait till Thursday?" Dante sighed sinking into the couch.

"Virgil's right, this place is disgusting," Brody said laughing. "My girlfriend wouldn't like it like this."

Dante shrugged his shoulders, "Eh, that's not really my problem," he laughed not caring.

"How is Selene doing?" Virgil asked Brody with genuine interest.

"Really good!" Brody was happy to talk about her. "She's running for Student Government, or Student Association President. She stays active in her community service fraternity, and is working on her Master's program in Occupational Therapy. She also works part time and somehow has time for me in between," Brody laughed.

"She's awesome," Virgil sighed, "I don't know how you would find the time for all that."

"You don't play video games or watch TV," Brody laughed.

"I'm sure that'd help," Virgil nodded.

"Hey boys!" a friendly voice called out to them. Their Sweetheart Ariel walked into the living room. The first thing you noticed about her, was how short and cute she was. She had dyed red hair that was dark in tone, with eyes that just dazzled. She had the world's most friendly smile and loved people so compassionately you couldn't help but enjoy being around her. She came into the room and the guys quickly got up to greet her and get their hugs in.

"Hey Sunshine!" Ariel said to Virgil giving him a tight hug.

"It is so good to see you!" Virgil exclaimed. "I'm surprised you're not out of town!"

"Well this is my last semester of college," Ariel explained. "And I'm doing my student teaching and the little kids have a different spring break, closer to Easter, so that's when I'll get my Spring Break," she told him.

"That sucks!" Dante said plopping back down onto the couch laying down.

"Yeah," she sighed. "I got done with class and came over to see what you boozoes were doing," she said taking a seat next to Virgil.

"We were thinking of getting some dinner, maybe pick up the place," Virgil told her. "We might have a little get together Thursday or Friday night as well, we were discussing which day is best."

"Have it Friday night!" Ariel said excitedly. "I have class Friday morning, so if you have it Thursday, I'll have to leave before Midnight."

"We'll keep that in mind," Birdy told her. The group chatted with the Sweetheart then decided to clean the house up and cook dinner. Ariel helped them out, talking with them as they cleaned. They made a large helping of spaghetti, and sat down in the dining room, enjoying eating while they told stories. Virgil loved spending time with the Sweethearts, and Ariel was such a special gal, every guy who met her seemed smitten by her charm. She was like the best big sister you could ever hope for. As they were cleaning up their Chapter Advisor Ezekiel, Gabriel's older brother, showed up with Professor Ramuh.

"How is everyone doing?" Professor Ramuh asked them.

"Good, just cleaning up," Doc told him.

"Is something going on?" Brody asked them.

"Yes, we've received an urgent request," Professor Ezekiel told them. "Something that should be dealt with soon."

"A den of werebears is being attacked in the Huron National forest," Professor Ramuh explained with a somber tone. "They have an alliance with the werewolf pack to the north of us. We received a call from the head of the den, asking that we send a few Paladins in to investigate and resolve the matter."

"What would attack a bear?" Brody asked chuckling.

"A demon most likely," Professor Ezekiel said, "Death Dealer attacks do not leave survivors. Their youngest daughter was attacked, she is only ten and not able to change shape yet and therefore is more vulnerable," Professor Ramuh explained. "Werebears are one of the rarer species of lycan. You can't get infected with the disease like with a werewolf, it is a strain that you have to be born with."

"Some strains of lycan are more contagious than others," Professor Ezekiel added, "Like rat and wolf. Strains like leopard, tiger, and lion are harder to contract."

"Here is the address and the phone number," Professor Ramuh said giving it to Brody. "If a group of you are able to go there tomorrow or Wednesday by the latest. This family needs help," he stressed. "There were some reports of hunters going missing up north, could be demon activity, be careful out there."

"I can go with you guys!" Ariel offered.

"You?" Virgil asked surprised.

"Well of course silly," Ariel laughed. "Who else is going to take care of you green horns if you get hurt?" she asked. She had a point Virgil thought, looking at the men in the room, their Devil Arms were strong, yet none of them knew Restoration spells like Tarek or Louie. Ariel had a beautiful aquamarine Devil Arms on her right hand, it looked like a snake or a whip.

"You can cast Restoration spells?" Virgil asked. "You know how to fight with that thing?"

"Of course!" Ariel said incredulously. "I've been fighting demons for years kid! Don't be worried about me. I've been busy with the Education program, so I haven't been around as much recently. For a long time though I was going on missions with the brothers regularly," she asserted to Virgil. "Not all Sweethearts like to fight with the guys, but personally I can't stand thinking of my boys out there without me."

"We'd love to have you along!" Dante told Ariel happily, "An adventure with a Sweetheart isn't something we get handed every day!"

Gabriel's older brother gave Dante the information he could, and the Advisors left the fraternity house. The group decided they'd leave tomorrow from the Omega house by 3pm. This week wasn't a full moon which meant they'd be safe to go up there at any time. Lycans could transform at will, the only time they were forced into the change was on the night of the full moon. The next day Ariel finished at school and met them at the house for the three-hour car ride up to the forest. The werebears had their own small village up there, with over a dozen homes, one of them unoccupied, and a large building they used for social gatherings and special occasions. Some had jobs in the community, which helped them blend in as a normal family group even though some of them weren't related.

Everybody had to drive long distances to get to most places in Michigan, especially the further north you traveled. Having a reliable vehicle is a must for a road trip. Virgil's blazer was a piece of junk, and he 'babied' it good to prolong its life. No one wanted to ride in a car with Birdy as the driver, which left Dante volunteering his vehicle. But they had six people. Ariel volunteered her van, so everyone could ride together comfortably, the brothers filled up her gas tank in return and offered to buy her dinner. Everyone bought snacks and drinks for the long ride, and they set off. Dante drove, with Birdy riding shotgun. Ariel and Virgil sat next to each other in the middle with Brody and Doc in the back.

"Birdy did you get those rolled up?" Dante asked once they hit the freeway rolling down their windows.

"Yup," Birdy said getting out a rolled-up smoke lighting it, and taking a heavy drag. He passed it to Dante, who took a hit. The smell was strong and instantly recognizable.

"What the hell are you boys doing!" Ariel said. "I don't want you smoking that shit in my van."

"We brought an air freshener don't worry," Dante said holding his breath after taking a hit.

"That's not the point!" Ariel said. "I'm going to be a teacher I can't be doing that stuff!"

"Oh, lighten up Lil Ariel," Dante said blowing the smoke out the window. He passed it to her. "Take a hit," he offered.

"We're going on a dangerous mission and you two want to catch a buzz?" Ariel sighed.

"If you're not going to hit that, I will," Brody said. He took a few hits and offered to Doc.

"Naw I'm good," Doc declined.

"Virge," Dante said playfully, "You want some?" he asked looking in his rearview mirror making eye contact with Virgil.

"I've only smoked hookah one time, and it wasn't anything special," Virgil shrugged. "I'm good."

"Dude, this is nothing like smoking out of a hookah, its way better," Dante said with a cocky grin. "Trust me. It is safer than any alcohol you've ever gotten drunk on. Thousands of people attempt suicide via alcohol poisoning and end up through hospital ER's. Subsequently they get sent to a medical floor or psychiatric hospital. Not one person has ever been able to suicide while smoking. There are consequences on your lungs if you vape and smoke every day over years, it's no worse and far better than cigarettes," Dante told him passionately.

"Enough with the speeches already, we all know you think it is better than alcohol," Ariel said. "Cops could arrest us for smoking and driving, that's illegal you know."

"It's true what Dante said though," Brody added from the back seat.

"If Virgil doesn't want to smoke, he doesn't have to," Ariel retorted. Dante nodded and passed it back to Birdy.

"You know Blair thinks you're a stiff right?" Dante asked Virgil looking back at him through the rearview mirror.

"What?" Virgil asked completely surprised. "I'm not boring! Wait does she think I'm lame guys?" he asked them. The car went silent. "Well!" Virgil asked, and they all laughed.

"Dude!" Birdy said laughing, "Calm your shit down brother. Blair's your best friend, of course she thinks your fun."

Dante grunted with an exaggerated eye roll Virgil caught in the mirror, "Why else would one of the coolest chicks on campus constantly want to be around a bookworm like you?" Dante asked rhetorically.

"Does Blair smoke?" Virgil asked them. The van went silent once more. "Guys!" Virgil snapped.

"Of course, she does," Dante said while holding his breath, then let out a big breath. "It isn't a big deal. It isn't like she is some criminal. It is no different than cracking open a beer, which in some social settings one could argue it would be out of the norm to NOT be drinking when everyone else is," he argued. "Alcohol is socially acceptable," Dante shrugged. "And this is safer than alcohol. So, don't think badly of Blair," Dante added in her defense.

"I don't," Virgil said. "I don't think it is a big deal, as long as you are able to maintain work and your responsibilities, doing it recreationally isn't bad, moderation is the key in all things. I think it is okay to drink, just not every night." Birdy passed it to Brody who leaned over the seat to take it. "Maybe I'll try some?" Virgil asked.

"Sure bud," Brody said surprised passing it to him.

Virgil took a heave drag, the smoke burned his lungs, and it tasted awful to him. It had a distinctive, strong, pungent aroma. He coughed heavily, gave it to Brody, and then took a sip of his drink.

"Oh no, you guys corrupted him," Ariel sighed.

"Lighten up, little Cherry's just growing some hair on his chest!" Doc laughed.

"We did not corrupt him!" Dante protested. "We have three hours still till we get to this place, at most it lasts two hours. Virgil is going to be fine, I doubt he'll feel anything off it his first time anyways."

"I don't feel anything," Virgil nodded. "I'll be fine."

The car ride was fun. They talked and laughed nonstop, Virgil felt more giggly than usual, and there weren't a lot of dry spells in conversation with his friends. Dante and Virgil were both talkative and Brody was a conversationalist, friendly and goofy. The guys discovered Lil Ariel, as the older brothers called her because she was so short, was a firecracker. She had such sharp wit, she was good at razing the group. She was so pure, and kindhearted, it was clear that she had a lot of love and compassion for other people. She was filled with funny stories, and Virgil learned a lot about older brothers from her. They stopped in the last small town right before the back roads they'd have to take the last half hour. A local diner was open, and they stopped in for dinner. Giving local mom and pop places your business, always felt good to the Omegas, like they appreciated it more, and he liked that his friends thought the same.

After dinner Dante stepped out to call Xiphias, the head of the werebear den to let him know they were a half hour from arriving. They got back in the van and made it to their den just as the sun was setting. The houses were lit up, large two-story homes that could house families of up to eight people. The large gathering hall at the end of the small cul-de-sac was lit up with people inside, they parked the van, and walked in as a group. There were a few men and one woman inside the large meeting hall. They were talking softly, gathered in a circle. A large burly man turned towards the college kids with open arms and shouted, "Welcome!" He towered over even Birdy, close to seven feet tall with a thick beard and dark thick body hair. He was bundled up like everyone else, winter was receding though still present. "Well look at you small fries, we asked for the Paladins help and they send us a bunch of kids!"

"Easy now!" Dante said taking it in stride. "We may look young, but we have experience, you want help with your demon problem or not? We know what we are doing, and we won't be talked down to. We wouldn't have come unless we were confident, we could handle your problem," he spoke confidently to Xiphias, who towered over Dante by several feet!

Xiphias let out a booming laugh, "You've got guts kid," he told Dante looking down at him with pride. "I sense the spirit of a mighty warrior within you."

Despite Xiphias' large and daunting appearance he was a friendly man. He and his fellow lycans were a peaceful group of people, and one of only two werebear dens in Michigan. Not all strains of lycanthrope were the same. They tried to stick together to keep their numbers up, a problem the nearby werewolf pack did not have. People were infected with the disease from werewolves every year and joined their ranks. Xiphias' people were guarded to outsiders, but polite and welcoming to Virgil and his friends nonetheless. They had encountered demons before, they reported a growing presence of them in the area. Their numbers were low, so to lose even a few people would be devastating to their population.

Tabby was the only woman present. She was tall and muscled with a natural feminine beauty. It was her daughter who had been attacked. "She was out playing with her brother, when they rose up from the shadows," Tabby told them. "Large gelatin like creatures with giant mouths filled with razor teeth, no visible eyes and two large arms on either side that had sharp claws."

"Sounds like a Rage demon," Ariel said, "The lowest class of the Cardinal demons," she explained.

"They were able to escape, not before getting a few scraps," Tabby said.

"Where was this at?" Virgil asked.

"Not far behind our settlement, there is an old hunter's shack and cabin, it has been abandoned for some time, the children used to use it as a playhouse," Tabby explained. "Humans sometimes stumble across it and use it for a short time."

"We'll take a look," Virgil told them confidently.

"We'd greatly appreciate your help in resolving this matter," Xiphias spoke with genuine concern. "Our people have been fearful to step out of their homes, we need to feel safe once more."

They followed Xiphias outside, Lil Ariel retrieved a UV flashlight from the van. Xiphias went running and leapt into the air, transforming into an enormous bear mid leap, causing everyone to jump. Xiphias could still talk in his bear form and laughed at the Omegas reaction, Virgil had never seen a bear laugh, if Xiphias wasn't so friendly he'd have been scared. Xiphias was twice as large as a normal bear, he ran through the snow with ease, barreling through a path in the snow. He led them to the log cabin, almost a mile from their homestead. When it came into view, Xiphias wouldn't go further. Virgil looked ahead, a dark presence loomed in the peripherals of his vision, there were demons here, and it was unsettling how quiet the woods had suddenly become.

Xiphias changed forms becoming a man once more. "I'll be waiting for you," Xiphias told them, "Good luck kids, I hope you know what you're doing," he said with apprehension and paused looking down at the young people, like he didn't want to let them go. Virgil could tell the man had a kind and loving heart.

Virgil noticed Xiphias' trepidation and he smiled kindly at the large man, "Sir," Virgil said gaining his gaze. "Thank you for your concern, I can tell you are good people. We will be fine here. I promise we'll resolve this issue so your families can be safe," Virgil said confidently. "My friends, I will guard them with my life. Do not worry for us."

Xiphias looked at Virgil staring intently into his eyes as if he was suddenly seeing more of Virgil than he first had. Virgil did not know if werebears could see auras, but something about the way Xiphias almost studied him made Virgil think they could. Xiphias then laughed to himself, "I would've guessed the short one was your leader from his attitude and physique!"

"Hey!" Dante yelled in response, he was sensitive about his height.

Xiphias continued uninterrupted, "It's clear that you are the leader of your people. A true leader of men is not chosen for the strength of his arm or the sharpness of his mind, but by the compassion in his heart." Xiphias nodded, his doubt fading from his face, "I did not see it at first, because you are not boastful of your power, but a stronger Nephilim I've never seen." Virgil felt his already cold red cheeks flush darker, he looked away from the man's gaze embarrassed. "Take care of your friends, young warrior," Xiphias told him with a kindness and a big smile. Virgil looked back up at the large man, grateful to have crossed paths with someone he might not have otherwise.

They were alone now, just the five brothers and their fraternity Sweetheart. Birdy quickly put the Protect spell on everyone. It was an Alteration spell that created a metaphysical invisible force field around the person that became visible upon striking it. It only lasted for so long and had to be reapplied but could be the difference between a broken rib and a Devil Arms blade through your lung. Ahead of them was a rundown shack, and just beyond was an old log cabin, "Do you guys feel that?" Brody asked them.

"Yes," Ariel said staring at the shack with an intense gaze, "There is a foul presence here," she warned. "This malevolence is stronger than a Rage demon."

Dante and Birdy took point, Ariel close to Virgil's side in the middle, he kept her to his right, not wanting the flames of Soul Reaver anywhere near her when he summoned it. Thankfully there was no wind, the cold seeped into their bodies, the closer they approached their destination the more adrenaline and tension warmed them. They approached the cabin, with a small shack nearby, the shacks front door was slightly ajar; the windows had been broken and boarded up long ago.

Dante approached the shack cautiously and opened it gently, Birdy stepping through first. Virgil was quick on Dante's heels, looking around the condemned building, it was strange that children would play in such a place. The six of them entered the building, there was no one present, just an old desk and cupboards with junk littered around. They walked the short distance inside and turned back. The door slammed shut, as did the shutters. In the darkness three figures rose up from the cervices. They were just as Tabby had described, rising to five feet in height, they moved at the pace of a brisk walk, fast for creatures with no visible legs. They were like fiery blobs with a big mouth and claws, but no discernable eyes. The Rage demons roared and charged forth.

"Scythalla's Whip!" Ariel shouted, and a coiled blue whip came into her hand, she spun it above her head and cracked it down hard on the closest demon. It bellowed in pain slumping forward ceasing its advance for a moment, buying precious time.

Virgil's scythe snaked into his hand and he threw it at the demon closest to him. It cut through the demon, the scythe whirled forward then came back on an arc and sliced through it again. The demon dissolved onto the floor as ash, the scythe returned to his hand, flames crawling along his left arm. Brody wielded an earth halberd Devil Arms, Doc wielded an earth throwing axe Devil Arms. Dante, Birdy, Doc, and Brody got the two demons that were left. Ariel kept the flashlight on the creatures, and even lashed one again before they were defeated.

"Are you boys alright?" Ariel asked looking the guys over with concern.

"I think we're good," Dante nodded enthusiastically. "That wasn't so hard."

"Those were just the lookouts," Ariel said. "There are more up ahead."

"In that cabin," Virgil said to Ariel, "I can sense it too." The group quickly got the front door open and walked outside. Everyone kept their weapons drawn, they circled around the small building to the house. This cabin had been here for years, at least since the early 1900s. As they came closer to the side of the house, they noticed a collection of vehicles, mostly trucks and some cars. Most of them looked new, like they hadn't been sitting there for long.

"What's going on up here?" Dante asked, "Are these demons taking out passing hunters?"

They approached the front door, opening it cautiously. The door opened into a small foyer, with a living room on the right, and stairs on the left, a hallway ran down in between. Once the six of them came inside, the door slammed shut. A demonic voice spoke to them seemingly from all around them with no specific location, "Why do you disturb this house?" it asked them in the now familiar deep demonic tone that all demons had.

"Begone from here!" Virgil shouted back to the demon. They looked around, there was nothing in sight.

"This is my domain, you are trespassers here," it told them growing silent.

"What do we do?" Birdy asked them.

"Look around and kick some ass," Dante replied.

"Don't fall flat on your face trying to impress the Sweetheart," Doc warned from the back, his small earth throwing axe in hand.

"Doc, shut up," Dante replied annoyed not bothering to look back.

The first floor was empty, they walked down the hall to a dining room and kitchen. They decided to look upstairs, there were two small bedrooms and a bathroom on the second floor, the floor was empty. The top floor was a large room with just a decayed bed, and an old dresser. On the dresser sat a bottle, with a black substance swirling around inside.

"What is going on here," Doc whispered clearly creeped out. "The whole place is just...empty? I don't buy it," he told them. "Let's get out of here."

"We haven't accomplished anything yet," Virgil shook his head. "We can't leave something like this so close to those innocent people!"

"They are freaking werebears man!" Doc cried out. "I think they can handle themselves. I say let's just burn it down, and kill off everything in it," Doc suggested.

The house shook, and a demonic roar echoed throughout the dark structure...whatever was here didn't care for that idea. Virgil wasn't feeling too confident, the unknown was far more frightening then the known. He wanted to see what was stalking them and be done with it. Virgil was closer to the dresser than the others, the eerie bottle was like a lava lamp, black smoke rolling around inside. He felt a strong presence coming from it, an aura of Chaos. Virgil moved the bottle with his scythe, it rolled across the dresser heading to the edge, he went to make a grab for it and missed, it fell crashing to the floor. The black smoke rose and there was a menacing growl. The smoke solidified into the powerful form of a Wrath demon, a tall slender black shadow with ceremonial armor over its chest and torso, a dark blade hung in its hand. Seven Rage demons came up from the shadows in the room circling the group.

"You will die here," the Wrath demon told them.

"You first!" Virgil yelled charging forward swinging his scythe. The demon's sword swung out to meet it, the two blades slammed against each other. Virgil strained against the demon's tremendous strength; he'd never fought one who wielded a weapon before.

"Wateraga!" Ariel cried out and a massive deluge of water materialized powered from her Devil Arms. Half the room was engulfed in water, it surged to the ground and then blasted upwards with extreme force, harming the demons, and outright killing two of them. Ariel was breathtaking in her fierceness, and she wielded her whip with astounding precision and fought as hard as the rest of them. Virgil saw she was as experienced a warrior as Lambda class, maybe more so, this being her fifth year in the fraternity, it showed in the way she handled herself.

"You!" the Wrath demon yelled at Ariel, shoving Virgil to the floor with a forceful blow, its shadowy figure floated over the floor to attack her.

Virgil jumped to his feet spinning his scythe around in an angry flurry. He shouted at the demon, "You're not through with me yet!" Virgil threw the scythe at the charging Wrath demon, then raised his hand and shouted, "Fire Lance!" two arrows of flame appearing before his hand firing off after the scythe. The cost of the spell took its toll immediately on his aura. He had gotten enough practice that a few simple spells didn't wipe him out anymore.

The Wrath demon spun around, slashing his sword forward deflecting the scythe's blade. The spell came on its heels not giving the shadow time to deflect it, the arrows of fire pierced its chest causing it to wail in pain. It regained its composure and charged Ariel, who stood within several meters of it.

"Ariel!" Virgil screamed.

Ariel's whip cracked against a Rage demon, who desperately clung to the water whip for its master. Ariel turned in fear struggling to grab free her weapon from the demon's grasp, to see the shadowy figure approach, raising its blade. She turned her hand towards him, "Torrent!" she commanded, and the demon was thrown back with a jet stream of water with such force it slammed into the wall causing large cracks to run up the sides. The powerful spells took their toll, she swayed looking like she might faint, her strength waning.

"Get around Ariel guys!" Dante commanded seeing she was ready to pass out. There were only two Rage demons left, Virgil's brothers having cut down the rest. The guys surrounded their Sweetheart protectively while they fought the last of the Wrath demon's minions.

Virgil's scythe was once more in his hand, he sprinted at the Wrath demon, ready to end it. The Wrath demon sprung back quickly, though severely injured, its strength had not faltered, the benefit of not being contained in a physical mortal body. Virgil's scythe slashed out, slamming once more into the demon's sword. Virgil viciously worked the sickle blade, whirling and slashing with newfound determination, driving the creature back. Virgil had it on the defensive, the demon didn't have time for anything but blocking Virgil's incoming blows as it was pushed back. Finally, it glided back just a little too far, Virgil took the opportunity and lounged into his next swing with tremendous momentum. The demon's black blade strained against the blow, and it was flung from the demon's grasp. Virgil's scythe spun around, and he screamed slashing it through the demon's form, it dissolved into black sludge, its dark blade slowly deteriorating from existence.

Chapter 9
New Beginnings

Xiphias and his den of werebears were grateful to Virgil and his friends for solving their demon problem. They tried offering payment, but Ariel wouldn't hear of it. "We came because we wanted to help, and had the ability to help, you shouldn't need payment for that," Ariel explained. Xiphias and his kin were grateful, he told them he would let others know that the Omegas could be trusted to help handle a crisis when it developed. They were tired and hit the road after saying their goodbyes. On the long drive home most of them passed out, with Dante vigilantly at the wheel, safely getting them back. Virgil was glad he had gone, helping others, and getting a glimpse into the lives of people living in the same world as him, yet so different from his own. It had been a rewarding experience.

Virgil went back to his hometown the next day to spend a few days of his vacation with his mom, getting caught up on homework and spending time with her. Spring Break was over quickly. They had a get together on Friday night, close to a hundred people showed up. Mu and Lilly came, and Lilly brought a variety of wonderful party food for the guests. She was the star of the night, and all the brothers present were talking to her frequently wanting her to come around more and showering her with praise. Everyone got back from Spring Break with dozens of stories, tales of adventures and conquests, mostly the guys talked about partying and the thousands of hot people everywhere. Brothers were exhausted from their vacation, there was no time to recuperate from Spring Break however, classes started back up on Monday. At Sunday's meeting Dante gave a report on the mission they'd been sent on, telling them how Sweetheart Ariel was amazing and everyone should spend time with her as she'd be graduating soon.

Vahn announced that the White Carnation Ball was coming up and had taken it upon himself to plan it for the brotherhood. The fraternity voted on a date for the event, mid-April won out, five weeks away, and two weeks before classes were over. The WCB was the Omegas formal, the dance at the end of the year to celebrate all their achievements as a Brotherhood. Vahn told them he'd make the reservations at a hotel in Houghton Lake. They'd gone to Houghton Lake a few years in a row. It had a small indoor water park and swimming pool that they left open later for the brothers, really going out of their way to make it a good experience for the fraternity. The brothers could bring one guest each and could invite their parents if they wished. Formal was the topic of everyone's side conversations for the rest of the meeting, especially for Omicron since this was their first formal.

Brody brought up the topic of a 5-K Run, the Omegas hadn't done this before, and one of their philanthropies was Alzheimer's. Brody pushed for the fraternity to get this event going as they needed to do more community service events in the public eye. Brody volunteered to oversee the event. Brody told them he'd reserve the large gym at the University for the Philanthropy Event. He stressed they'd need to get the word out to sponsors, so they could order t-shirts and start setting up tables around campus. Mu stood up telling the group his girlfriend Lilly's mom worked at a shop where they could order the shirts, and she could get them a discount. Gabriel, Jagger, Nolan, and Virgil volunteered to be on the committee with Brody and they met after the meeting. They decided they'd break off into pairs and look for sponsors, as they'd only have two weeks to collect sponsors before they had to get the shirt order in.

Things were getting busy on campus, as the weather was warming up people gathered more, classes were getting stressful, and the semester was ending. After classes on Monday, Nolan and Virgil went out to a few businesses in town, one's Nolan had already set up contacts with, a local restaurant and car dealership. They made their appointments and Nolan was able to seal deals with both places. Invigorated with their success they hit up a few more places but didn't get anything else accomplished, leaving their information for a few bosses who were out for the day. Lilly had become a part of the group; over a few short months she'd become a good friend to most of the guys who came around. Lilly had gotten a sponsor who also donated huge signs for the event and bought advertising space on the back of their shirts.

They scheduled a meeting for the 5-K Run Wednesday night, they had a lot of work to do before then. Pi class came to the meeting as well. Their philanthropy event for their class was going to be the 5-K as helping put it on was more than enough work for them. Virgil spent the meeting having a side conversation with Nev for entertainment when things got boring, writing back and forth to each other on a piece of paper. Virgil really enjoyed his company since Nev had become a part of Virgil's inner circle of friends.

Virgil was struggling to maintain A's, he doubted he'd make the 3.5 GPA required for his scholarship, he was hoping to be above a 3.0 at least. The problem was he was pulling a B in Psychology which was four of his fifteen credits, so it was more heavily weighted than the other classes. He signed up for classes next semester, registering for Anatomy and Physiology, a General Ed History class, the next Chemistry Class above his current one, and a General Ed Communication class. It was only 13 credits, but Anatomy was going to be the hardest class he'd ever had, he needed a light class load. A few of the older brothers warned him that people often changed their majors after that class.

Thursday, Virgil went to a flower shop in Bay City and bought a single white carnation, then drove back to campus. He text Blair, *Hey Girl! What cha up to? I am bored and was wondering if you wanted to chill?*

She text back, *Hey Virge, I'm hanging out at my room, looking at apartments online. Come over if you want!*

He text, *Cool I'll get heading over.* He walked over to her dorm and knocked on her door. Blair answered dressed casually, her hair a mess, looking tired and stressed, her sharp wit and bright smile ever present.

"Hey you!" She said letting him walk in, she then closed the door, and turned to give him a hug. "What's that?" She asked a surprised look on her face.

Virgil was filled with anxiety and racing thoughts, he blurted out, "My fraternity has formal next month, and it is called the White Carnation Ball. We're allowed to invite a guest and when I thought of who I should take, I thought I'd have the best time if I went with you," he smiled looking away shyly. "This is an invitation to the White Carnation Ball," he said giving her the flower.

"Oh Virgil," she said taking the flower, her eyes crinkled with a genuinely real smile. "You are so sweet," Blair said twirling the flower in her hand.

"You can think about it and let me know," Virgil mumbled not knowing what to say, "I mean unless you don't want to, or another brother already asked you."

"Actually, Nasty Nate asked me to go with him," Blair said looking down not meeting his gaze.

"Oh!" Virgil nodded in surprise. Nate was a brother from a pledge class several years ahead of Omicron in their Chapter. He lived with Thiago and went to Delta now. He was a good guy, kind and giving, someone Virgil liked and respected.

"I told him to let me think about it, because…I was kind of hoping you'd ask me to go," Blair said uncharacteristically shy meeting Virgil's gaze hesitantly.

"Of course, I'd ask you!" Virgil laughed. "You're my best friend, we'd have the best time together," he said.

"I agree!" Blair laughed, and they hugged. They sat down and played a video game while they caught up.

"Why are you apartment shopping?" Virgil asked her. "Can't you just move into the Alpha's sorority house?"

"Yeah, if I wanted to, but I don't," Blair said simply. "They have strict rules for the girls who live there. Who can come over, when they can come over, rules on who is allowed to stay the night, no boys, and even rules about what we can, and can't have, in our room. Can you see me following a bunch of uptight rules?" Blair asked him.

Virgil thought about it, Blair wouldn't last a week living in that sorority house. She was popular, her place had a constant flow of brothers and sisters dropping by for a visit. Blair liked to have a good time and could get rowdy, or rather she was usually rowdy. "Yeah, I guess you're right, you're better off living in a place that is your own where people aren't telling you how to live your life," Virgil told her.

"I love those ladies, don't get me wrong. But this chick won't be tamed by anyone!" Blair said confidently earning a laugh from Virgil. Whoever was brave enough to try, Virgil thought they'd be a lucky guy.

"What about Helene?" Virgil asked.

"What about her?" Blair asked. "She's coming with me, we're going to stay roommates," Blair said fondly. Blair liked picking on Helene but, Virgil knew she loved Helene more than any of her other friends.

"I already have a dress," Blair told Virgil.

"You own a dress?" Virgil asked shocked. He'd never even seen her in a skirt.

Blair smirked, "Shut it! Maybe we could go tie hunting and get something to closely match?" she suggested. She showed Virgil what she had, it was a lovely teal dress with a black bodice and thin straps. Virgil thought she'd look beautiful in a dress, though he'd never seen her in one. Blair didn't do girly, she never wore skirts or dresses in her everyday attire.

Blair suggested they go have dinner. They shut down the gaming system and headed to the cafeteria. On the way, Virgil decided to find a brother to split a room with, he didn't want to give anybody the wrong impression by getting a room with just Blair. It would be more fun sharing with Louie or Birdy anyways.

At the cafeteria Louie, Birdy, Dante, and Nev were already there and waved at them catching their attention. Virgil and Blair grabbed what they were in the mood for and sat with their friends. Virgil wanted to casually ask Louie about sharing a room, he waited a few minutes into sitting down before he popped the question.

"Heeyyyy Louie," Virgil said with a big smile and his best poker face.

"Hey," Louie said giving him a funny look then looking around at the others. He laughed nervously, "What schemes do you have cooking up over there?" Louie asked him.

"Schemes?" Virgil asked surprised. "I was just wondering how my best buddy was doing, no harm in that, is there?" he wondered innocently.

"Uh huh," Louie said not buying it. "You're terrible at hiding your emotions Virgil, what do you want homie?" he asked.

"Would you like to room with Blair and me at WCB?" Virgil asked him.

"Ohh shieeet!" Louie exclaimed, "So you finally asked her huh?" he said. "About damn time! Blair was bugging the hell out of us wondering if we knew if you were going to ask her or not," he said. Blair got a peeved look on her face and swiftly kicked Louie from under the table. "Ow!" Louie cried out. "So angry!" Louie exclaimed to Blair in a high-pitched humorous voice, Virgil grinned.

"I would love to room with you two love birds," Louie told them.

"Louie!" Blair and Virgil yelled at him.

Louie continued as if they'd never responded. "But I can't because I'm getting my own room," Louie told them with a shy smirk and a head bob.

"Who are you taking Louie?" Nev asked Louie.

"Rachel," Louie said proudly, "I just asked her to be my girlfriend last night."

"Congratulations!" Virgil told his friend a bright smile overcoming his face feeling genuinely happy for Louie.

"Details!" Birdy barked.

"She's in a sorority on campus," Louie told them, "We hung out together a lot on Spring Break, and things just seem right between us," he explained.

"In other words, you guys banged all Spring Break, and now you want to make it a regular thing?" Birdy asked crassly.

"Birdy!" Virgil yelled at his friend appalled by his tactless way of handling their best friend's big news.

"When can we meet her?" Dante asked.

"You fools?" Louie asked incredulously his eyebrows rocketing up into the air. "Never! You'll scare her away!" Louie motioned to Birdy, "You heard what he said, can you imagine if Rachel had been sitting here and heard that? She would have died of embarrassment and probably would never show her face around you guys again," he said nervously. "Let's give it some time before I introduce her to the family," he told them shaking his head at his friends, returning to his meal. "You bitches are too much to handle all at once for someone new."

"Aww," Blair whined, "I want to meet her. I'll be good! I'll even cut the cursing down to a minimum," she added sweetly.

Dante laughed, "Blair you curse like a sailor, and you couldn't last five minutes without dropping a dirty word."

"I can too you fucker!" Blair retorted with a sassy attitude earning chuckles.

"She's a cool chick," Nev added, "Louie and I were in the same suite, so I saw her a lot over Spring Break. She was over every night," he added teasing Louie, drawing out every night emphasizing it heavily. "I could hear them through the walls, 'Oh Louie,'" Nev made his voice high pitched, poorly imitating Louie's girlfriend. "Oh Louie, give me that Asian chode, yes! There!" Nev cried out. Virgil burst out laughing so hard he spit out the food that was in his mouth all over the table. Everyone else joined in unable to stop laughing as Louie's face got red and Nev completely lost it, slamming his hand down on the table, his face beat red, he was laughing so hard he could barely breath.

"Yeah, yeah," Louie sighed, "I'm sure you had your ear pressed to the wall jerking yourself off with some tweezers you were so excited," he told Nev.

Once they had regained their composure Birdy turned to Virgil, "I'll room with you bud," he told him.

"Awesome!" Virgil said happily. "Who are you taking?" he asked his friend.

Birdy shrugged, "Just a girl that I've been talking to."

"Do I know her?" Virgil asked.

"No, we haven't been talking long," Birdy shrugged.

"Trust me, Birdy doesn't do much talking when he brings her over to hang out on the top bunk," Dante butted in, "Which is RIGHT above my head Birdy," Dante said with a less than pleased tone.

The group ragged on Louie for the rest of their meal egging him on for more details. Louie had a giant smile on his face, his friends' good-natured jabs only making him beam brighter. They could tell Louie cared about this girl, and they were all very happy for their friend.

After theater class later that night Virgil was free for the weekend. He went over to Birdy and Dante's dorm to hang out. Nev and Louie were there and the five of them spent the night watching movies and making jokes. That weekend was stressful for the candidates, they were approaching their final week of pledging and everyone in the fraternity was coming down hard on them. Nev was stressed out, he confided in Virgil that he was getting a C in one of his classes, and it was freaking him out. Nev was also on the Presidential Scholarship, if his GPA dropped too low, he could lose it. Virgil did his best to listen to his friend, validating his feelings and concerns. Virgil told Nev that after the final week, he'd have several weeks left to push hard and bring his grade up. Virgil suggested that there was always the final exam that could help his grade if he did well. Virgil told Nev he was just as smart as Nolan, and that he could get his grade up if he worked his ass off. Nev had calmed down some after venting and he looked less worked up. Virgil told him he'd always be there if he needed to talk.

Friday night was the fraternity's first practice for the Paladin Tournament, coming up in the summer. The Omegas had decided that they'd start practicing once a week from now until classes ended in May, then start working harder once they all had more time to dedicate to practice. Their first practice didn't go so smoothly. They mostly goofed around, making jokes and acting silly, using their Devil Arms more to make each other laugh than practicing. About a half hour into the practice Magnus got pissed and started yelling, demanding they shape up immediately or he would withdraw their entry.

"I will not be made a fool of," Magnus said passionately eyes blazing, "If we are going to compete, then we are going to be competitors. If we go into this, we go to win. The Paladins training at Alpha Chapter, at the Academy in Alexandros are cutthroat, the best our race has to offer. If we don't buckle down now, and start putting in some serious effort, we are going to look like fools to the world!" Everyone got serious after that and they started practicing for real. They worked hard for a solid hour and a half, then everyone was too tired to work anymore. Virgil was drenched in sweat and his body was sore from getting hit by his sparring partners. Virgil had practiced some spells, the only way to strengthen his aura so he could use more magic without exhausting himself, was to practice. Their auras were like a muscle, they had to be used in order to grow, only auras grew very slowly and for some the results were almost nonexistent even after weeks and months of training. Virgil was determined to get better, and he pushed himself hard.

Saturday night Virgil hung out at the Omega house, he'd spent the day with Blair shopping for a tie that matched her dress. Virgil went with Blair and Helene to check out a few apartments near campus. Spending time with Blair made the time race forward, his day had slipped by seemingly in an instant. The guys were having a game night, most of the fraternity was present, including the three Pi class pledges. Virgil was playing cards, at one of the small tables that had been set up, with Jace, Zender, Lamar, Mu and Buck. He didn't hang out with these brothers as much, and he was quieter around them then his close friends. He enjoyed their company though and tried to insert himself in the conversation. Virgil liked Jace and Zender a lot. Jace could be opinionated and off-putting with his blunt attitude, though he was thoughtful, and one of the more dedicated Omegas. Jace was always representing their fraternity well on campus, and his passion and love for the Omegas were among the highest in the group. Zender had outright scared Virgil in the beginning. Now that he was a brother, Zender treated Virgil with the utmost respect and kindness. Zender was fiercely intelligent, and Virgil was beginning to see that translated into some awkward social graces as a negative payoff, like Nolan. Zender was a sweet guy, underneath his need to have everyone think he was a badass. Virgil would never tell him that out loud, he was fearful Zender would treat him like he had as a pledge as punishment. Zender still liked to give some of Omicron a hard time, especially Louie.

Zender and Jace found out Louie had a girlfriend and the two of them wouldn't stop ragging on Louie, only their teasing felt meaner than when Virgil, Dante, Birdy, Blair, and Nev did it. After a solid fifteen minutes of them teasing Louie mercilessly, Virgil felt they'd gone too far when they brought up the topic of Louie's 'chode' which made Louie visibly upset and hurt. Louie tried to make them stop once, that only egged them on more, and most of the room started laughing at the joke as they kept bringing it up in unique, and hurtful ways. If there was one thing Virgil couldn't stand, it was a bully.

"Hey!" Virgil shouted to his brothers seated at his table, interrupting them on their most recent jest, surprising himself. The guys at his table gave Virgil a questioning look, Zender and Jace arched their eyebrows wondering what was up. "Knock it off!" Virgil's words were steel. "You've had Louie on blast enough for one night, ease up," Virgil demanded.

"They are just kidding," Buck said clearly irritated at Virgil for having said anything. "Calm down," he added.

"Yeah, it is what guys do!" Mu pointed out laughing a little.

"Yes, just kidding," Virgil mussed his blood beginning to boil, "But joking with friends should have an edge of good will and kindness along with the hurtful words, or else it is just being mean, to be mean," Virgil pointed out. "I've never found bully humor to be funny."

"Is this a sorority or a fraternity?" Buck asked.

"We weren't being serious," Zender said defending himself.

"That may be, but Louie's had enough," Virgil wasn't backing down, "Please just stop, okay?" he asked them politely his face getting a little red. He liked teasing Louie too, but EVERYONE in the fraternity liked to do it. Louie never really said anything, though Virgil knew it hurt him sometimes, ALWAYS being the butt of the joke. Louie was one of the best friends Virgil had ever had, and it stirred up something very primal deep inside him, having to watch his friend have that hurt look in his eyes. Virgil would do anything to protect the people he loved and making himself feel a little embarrassed, was the least he could do.

"We'll stop," Jace sighed playing a card. "Sorry Louie!" he called over to Louie waving.

"Sorry Panda," Zender said in his usual mean tone he reserved for brothers he wasn't fond of. Buck rolled his eyes and just shook his head. Virgil had found through his time with the fraternity, and his psychology professor, most men were just as sensitive as women. Society cultured men to be more reserved and less forward, to be 'manlier', not the healthiest way to handle one's feelings. Louie shared a look with Virgil, Louie's eyes sparkled with moisture and he had a small smile, Louie knew Virgil had his back, and Virgil always would.

Sunday's meeting felt like it went on forever. Omega's formal was quickly approaching, and they voted on WCB awards that would be handed out then. This was the final week for Pi class as candidates. Nev, Rowan, and Agustin were starting to feel the pressure. Vahn announced the schedule for the week; Tuesday was their final brotherhood, Wednesday was the Last Supper, Thursday was their Final Test, and Friday was the initiation and party following.

"This is their last week boys," Vahn told the room, "I do NOT want them thinking they are guaranteed entry into this fraternity. They need to feel that until they sign the scroll, any minute could be their last. I want the brothers to step up their game and really call these guys. Their phones should be blowing up all day long with requests to hang out from you guys," Vahn said. "I'm expecting you guys to scare them, they are worried about their Final Test, I told them that we had one class fail before, so they think that it is possible. DON'T tell them anything to the contrary or you'll be having a very unfriendly talk with me soon thereafter," Vahn warned.

Pi class was a great pledge class, Virgil thought, the three of them were very united, they were close, and often together. Virgil was closest with Nev, and he had bonded with Rowan. He didn't know Agustin very well, though Virgil knew he'd become best friends with Troy. At the Last Supper on Wednesday Virgil went and bought a bunch of fruit to bring to the dinner. The night was about the candidates relaxing and letting the brothers wait on them for a change. Rowan had a big grin on his face which lit up his breathtaking blue eyes.

"I could get used to this," Rowan said with his hands behind his head as Gabriel, his Big, made his plate for him.

"Don't," Gabriel called across the room to his Lil earning a few chuckles from the guys. Gabriel brought his and Rowan's plate over and the two ate and talked. Gabriel and Rowan had grown close over the six weeks and were easily one of the closer Big and Lil pairs in the whole fraternity. Virgil decided once Pi class was initiated, he'd try to see Vahn more. Vahn was so funny and snarky, it was hard not to laugh the whole time Virgil was with him. After dinner the candidates retired to the Pledge dorms to study the night away with their Hegemon. Louie and a few of the Omicron brothers wanted to join as they were the most recent pledge class in.

"Sorry guys, just the candidates will be studying tonight," Vahn told them.

"Ahhh," Louie whined, "Gabriel let Xi class come to our study night."

"When Gabriel was the Hegemon, he called the shots, I'm saying no one else is welcome to come. You will only serve as a distraction. We need to stay focused on studying," Vahn said harshly and left with his pledge class. Vahn could be brash with his presentation, Louie looked disappointed, Virgil knew what he said came from a good place.

Thursday, Pi class was freaking out. They were running on little sleep and none of them felt prepared for the Final Test. Virgil came across poor Nev asleep with his face on the Omega guide in the food court when he stopped by for lunch. Virgil went over to his friend.

"Nev," Virgil said nudging him. Nev came to, his eyes were bright red, and he looked like crap. "Hey bud, why don't you go home for a bit? Lay down and take a nap," Virgil suggested.

"I can't, I need to study," Nev said blinking slowly, he put his elbows on the table, propping his head up on his hand his eyes drooping lazily.

"Nev, I am a brother of this fraternity, and I am telling you to go home and get some sleep. Are you going to disobey a direct request from a brother?" Virgil asked in feigned anger. "Do you think your Hegemon would like to see that you got demirts from his Lil from talking back, on the day of your Final Test?"

Nev got a big smile and stared up at Virgil with a goofy expression from sleep deprivation, "Thanks Virgil," he said getting his things together and zipping up his bag. "You're a good friend," Nev said. They shared a bro hug and Nev headed home. Virgil prayed he didn't happen across brothers on his way there, they'd nick that nap in the butt. Virgil laughed out loud imagining Nev trying to explain to Jace or Lamar that he was going home to take a nap, they'd bust his chops for sure!

Virgil was excited for the Final Test, it was the first time he'd get to see it from the brothers' perspective. That night Virgil met his brothers at the Omega house, Vahn asked the brothers to go to the waiting place ahead of the candidates. Virgil walked with the group through the woods to the small cave with a waterfall, they came to the back side where the waterfall fell into a small pond that trickled off into a small creek. It was late March, Michigan breaking away from the clutches of winter weather, it was cold out, the pond wasn't frozen though. Virgil couldn't imagine the water being very warm. Virgil went up to the pond and cast a few balls of fire from his ruby Devil Arms into the water to warm it up for the candidates. After a few minutes Virgil cast a fire spell into the water, not wanting the candidates to get sick.

"Alright cupcakes listen up!" Doc called out to them. "Show's about to get started, don't come out until they swim to the edge of the pond," he instructed.

Virgil hid near Dante and Gabriel. Gabriel had Rowan's clothes in his hands, he had bought his Lil a lot, more than the average Big. Virgil had been spoiled by Vahn as well, not all Bigs went all out for their Lils.

"Are you excited?" Virgil asked Gabriel his breath was visible in the air.

"Hell yeah!" Gabriel responded a contained grin turning up the corners of his mouth. "This is my first Lil, I'm so proud of that mother fucker!"

"You got a great Lil," Virgil said proudly, "Rowan's a powerful Nephilim, and a great friend."

"Everyone shush!" Jace called out as several people had started whispering.

"You shush!" Gabriel called back to his past pledge.

Agustin was first, they saw him come to the mouth of the cave looking out over the pond, a look of incredible fear overcame his features, he did NOT want to jump into the water below and Virgil did not blame him. Virgil remembered what it had been like standing at the edge not seeing anyone in sight, looking down at the murky water fearing what might be lurking inside its unseen depths. Agustin took a deep breath and leapt into the water. He surfaced, panic in his eyes. He quickly swam to the edge shivering. Gabriel turned to Dante and Virgil and nodded, the group came out from hiding to embrace him as their own. Agustin's Big gave him his letters and a towel and Agustin quickly dried and got dressed. They repeated the process for Nev and Rowan. Landon gave Nev his letters and Gabriel gave Rowan his. After they'd finished the group walked back to the Omega house, spirits were high, and everyone was happy.

Friday was initiation, they had a formal ceremony like Omicron had, Virgil had been so overwhelmed he hadn't taken it all in the first time. The initiation party was epic, Virgil had a great time with his friends celebrating Pi class. Virgil saw lots of familiar faces and worked his way around the party catching up with everyone. TK and Selene were talking with Raven and Terra Peoples, the Alpha sorority's President. Terra was short like Raven, with short blond hair. Terra was a charismatic, intelligent, and straight-laced leader. She had a serious personality and ferociously loved her sisters. She was a responsible woman, a good example for her sorority sisters. Virgil joined them in their conversation about the upcoming elections for student government President, happy to see some of his favorite ladies.

"I'm voting for you in the election for President!" Virgil said happily to Selene.

"Aww you're such a sweetheart," Selene told Virgil giving him a hug.

"He really is," TK said with a large smile.

"What are we talking about ladies?" Virgil asked them.

"Oh, not much," TK told Virgil catching him up, "We were just talking about our sorority and the upcoming Paladin tournament. We are debating if we want to enter or not."

"You ladies should!" Virgil said. "It would be much better with all of you there!"

They shared looks and some laughs.

"I hear you asked Blair to the Omega formal with a white carnation," TK said to Virgil with a sly smile on her face.

"Yeah," he said feeling a little warmer.

"Aww!" The ladies responded.

"That was sweet!" Raven said looking at Virgil with a renewed liking.

"I love that girl," Terra said with a fierce look on her face, her tone stern and serious. "Break her heart and I'll break your neck, got it?" she asked him.

"Wow, wow, wow," Virgil said backing up some. "I care about Blair too! She's my best friend!" Virgil said defensively.

"Well, she's my best friend too!" Terra snapped. "And she is really excited to go with you, just treat her right, will you?" she asked him her tone softening some. Virgil looked in her eyes seeing true concern in the elder sister's face. Terra was just being a protective older sister, Blair was lucky to be loved by such a good friend.

"Terra don't worry," TK told her sister, "Virgil is one of the good ones. He's not going to hurt her."

"Do you like her?" Raven asked him.

"WHAT!?" Virgil asked not liking where this conversation was headed.

"Do you like Blair?" Raven asked again, "Like more than friends?"

"Where is this coming from?" Virgil asked his words slurring slightly. "We are just friends," he said wanting to walk over to a different group of people, he started looking around for an exit from this train wreck.

"Does Blair see it like that?" Terra asked him.

Virgil hung his head, Blair knew they were just friends, right? Virgil looked up at TK, he trusted her second only to Blair of the women he knew on campus. "TK," Virgil asked, "Does Blair want to be more than friends?"

TK stared deep into Virgil's eyes not responding right away, her look was all the answer Virgil needed. He nodded and waved goodbye to the ladies wandering through the party his mind a blurry mess, things were getting complicated.

Chapter 10
White Carnation Ball

The next few weeks were fun and stressful, the end of the semester was drawing near, which meant exams and big papers. It was the most happening time of the Winter semester at Universities, the weather was starting to get warm again which brought renewed energy to the people. It was April, most snow was gone, the people of Michigan gave one collective sigh of relief. This brought everyone out, tired of being cooped up all winter. The First Annual Omega 5-K Run for Alzheimer's was quickly approaching. Pi class had really stepped up after becoming brothers, they were family, and all of them had an attitude of wanting to contribute to the fraternity. Nev became one of the main organizers for the actual event. Lilly also put in a surprising amount of effort to help with the 5-K. Brothers were starting to talk about her, like she was becoming a part of the family.

Virgil went with Blair to her sorority formal. The Alphas were a great group of women, but it was still strange seeing all of them dressed up so fancy, with Devil Arms upon their hands. They seldom joined the Omegas in the field, and Virgil hadn't seen most of them materialized into their physical forms, the girls' symbols went largely unused. Their formal was held down the road from campus at a VFW hall. Their group had a hard time agreeing on things, and the more conservative members did NOT want the formal to be out of the city, as then the sisters would have to rent rooms…with dates. Not the kind of thing their sorority went for, they were serious about keeping a good reputation as a sorority. Over a dozen Omegas were there, some were dating Alpha sisters, others were just guys who had been asked so a sister had a date to escort her. Virgil sat at a table with Blair and many of his brothers, it was an enjoyable evening that was out of the norm. Seldom did everyone have a chance to get dressed up. The Alphas were strict on not allowing minors to drink at their function, Virgil and his friends didn't need alcohol. They danced, ate, talked, and laughed the night away into the early hours of the morning.

The White Carnation Ball was the following weekend, the two formals were punctuated by a long drawn out week of classes. Selene won the election for Student Association President. At the E-Board meeting on Wednesday night, Virgil sat with the Jeweled Officers of Omega going over their reports for Sunday's meeting. Virgil got bored and started daydreaming. He saw a pack of sorority girls walking by, recognizing TK, Terra, Helene, and…Selene?

"Is your girl joining the Alphas?" Gabriel asked interrupting the meeting and everyone stared out the glass windows and doors, to see the group of thirty some sorority sisters and potential candidates. Selene was easily recognizable, with her raven black thick hair, always gracefully styled, and her big friendly smile and kind eyes. Virgil sighed, she'd probably rule the world someday…

"Who knows!" Brody laughed. "I don't know how she does it all. She is the most motivated human being I have ever met. When she puts her mind to something, she is determined, and she makes it big, no matter if it's a can food drive or a freaking cancer event!" Brody exclaimed and received a chorus of nods among the brothers. "She has been talking about joining the Alphas for a while. Selene is a freaking Pureblood Nephilim, like her parents and little brother. She's destined to be one of us, she just wanted to do it on her own terms, when she was ready to," Brody said proudly.

Virgil rode up to Houghton Lake for the formal with Birdy, his date, and Blair. It was an hour and twenty-minute drive, North West of Bay City towards the center of the lower peninsula.

Things had been as good as ever with his friend Blair, the great thing about her was, she was a cool chick. Even if Blair did have feelings for him, she wouldn't show it or make things weird for them. Virgil knew they were going to have this conversation sooner or later, maybe tonight, maybe in a few months, either way he wasn't worried. They were friends, first and foremost, and he cherished what they had.

They checked into their room on the second floor, the entire second, and third floor were reserved for their fraternity. Virgil and the others changed into formal wear and the party began. They went to Gabriel and TK's room, they had a suite on the 3rd floor. Tarek, Vahn, Landon, Jagger, Brody and Dante were already there with their dates. Virgil and Blair joined them having a drink before dinner. TK, Raven, Selene, and Landon's girlfriend Stephanie were mostly congregated in the bathroom with the other dates, finishing hair and makeup. Blair was chilling out in the room with the guys, she looked incredible for having spent so little time getting ready. Her blond hair was done up, with two curled pieces hanging down. The teal dress she had on emphasized her femininity, she was striking, and the other guys noticed it as well. Blair usually down played her looks, tonight she was playing to her strengths. Her makeup was conservative, enough to accentuate her eyes, cheeks and lips. She had on small dangling earrings and a silver necklace that matched. Blair was already causing mischief wandering around and giving the brothers grief, a drink held firmly in one hand, decreasing in volume by the minute.

"Blair is that you talking shit out there?" TK asked in her best mom voice, coming out of the bathroom with her hands on her hips.

"He started it!" Blair laughed pointing at Vahn.

"Vahn, knock it off or we'll have to ask you to leave our room," TK said playfully.

Vahn laughed, "Oh yeah, like I'm the one causing trouble. We all know who the rowdy one out here is," he said. All the guys shared a synchronized laugh including Virgil, Blair glared at him, and all he could do was shrug his shoulders smiling sheepishly.

"Just what in the hell does that mean?" Blair asked looking around at the brothers with narrowed eyes taking a large gulp of her drink.

"How many drinks have you had little lady?" Gabriel laughed half watching a football game with Dante and Jagger. The other guys in the room didn't care for football.

"This is only my second one!" Blair insisted.

"You're second?" Virgil asked surprised.

"I might have had one while I was getting ready," Blair said with her shoulders hunched up, and her eyes squinting slightly as she spoke, like she was a kid in trouble.

"Dude, you know I don't care how much you have. Have fun!" Virgil insisted to her.

"I am," Blair nodded happily.

"We're heading to dinner!" Selene announced to the group looking as stunning as ever, and the room slowly cleared out, everyone heading to the third floor where the banquet hall was located. The room was filled with tables around a dance floor, with a small podium that had been set aside for announcements including the awards they'd voted on earlier in the semester. At the back of the room was a large balcony, people were going out to take pictures with the lake and setting sun as a background. Houghton Lake was Michigan's largest inland lake, a warm but somewhat shallow lake, it is about 7.5 miles long, north to south, and 4.5 miles at its widest. Houghton Lake, the town, was situated at its south western shoreline. The lake was a large tourist attraction, though this was still in the off season, one of the reasons they'd been able to get the hotel so cheap.

"Dude!" Louie came up to Virgil and embraced him firmly upon entering the banquet hall. "All of Omicron needs to get a picture, right now!" he told Virgil. "Come on Dante!"

"I heard ya!" Dante replied in a huff, sounding annoyed. "Let me grab a good seat first!"

Virgil and Blair grabbed a table with Dante, his date was a friendly brunette from a sorority at Bay Valley, and Birdy, his date a ditzy, tipsy loud mess. Along with Louie and his new girlfriend Rachel, and Nev and Nolan with their respective dates. Troy their only pledge brother not sitting with them, was seated with his best friend and newly initiated brother, Agustin. They'd know each other before college, something Virgil hadn't known, their bond strengthened by their old acquaintanceship. Virgil and his pledge brothers went to the balcony to take some photos, and Blair came with her phone to take some as well. There were technically seven Omicron left, but Hector had stopped coming around since the start of the semester. The six of them standing together, this felt like Omicron to Virgil. He smiled a big toothy grin, feeling elated standing next to some of his best friends at the celebration of the year for the Omegas.

"We need our honorary female Omicron in here!" Dante barked. "Blair get your small butt in here quick!"

"What?!" Blair laughed. "No! I'm not bringing my butt anywhere near you!"

"Now Blair!" Selene and TK insisted. "Get in there!" They were also out on the balcony taking pictures, EVERY pledge class started taking group pictures, each class wanting to outdo the rest. Lambda kept making claims they were the best class of the Omegas. Blair reluctantly ran into the group getting in the middle and making goofy faces.

"Come on, give us a good one!" Selene insisted bossily tapping her foot slightly. The group quickly did as they were told.

After a few takes the group disbursed and walked inside where it was warmer. Soon everyone was called to their seats, and dinner started. Tarek went to the podium to give a prayer as he was the Chapter's Hypophetes.

Tarek bowed his head and closed his eyes and began, "Dear Lord, and Heavenly Creator. We gather tonight under your grace to reflect and celebrate on a successful year as a Chapter. Please bless this food which we are about to consume, and watch over everyone tonight and keep us safe, in the Creator's name we pray, Amen," Tarek opened his eyes and began to walk away from the podium, then quickly came back to add. "Please remember to wrap it…before you tap it, thank you," he said with a shit eating grin walking back to his table with Vahn, Gabriel, Landon, and Brody, trying hard not to laugh. Virgil, and the friends at his table found it funny, though the more conservative people present were slightly put off.

The tables with the oldest brothers got to go first, Tarek took it upon himself to help mediate letting tables go up to get their plates. They had a fine selection of chicken which was Virgil's favorite, and beef with plenty of healthy greens and vegetarian options for everyone who was present. Virgil gossiped with his friends enjoying dinner and their company. They spent almost every day together as a group, conversation was comfortable and hilarious, never a dull moment, Virgil smiled to himself. Dante and Louie bickered over something, and Blair was making the rest of the table smirk with her usual antics and loud off-color humor.

After dinner Vahn took the podium to start the awards. The first award was the James G Royle award, in honor of their Chapter's first Chapter Advisor. It was awarded to the brother the Chapter felt most exemplified the aspects of scholastic achievement, someone who went to class, got good grades and generally encouraged the other brothers to strive in their educations.

"This year the award goes to…Nolan Goll!" Vahn announced. Everyone cheered and clapped as Nolan got up from Virgil's table to accept the plaque. Virgil knew he'd win it; Virgil had voted for him and had spoken on his behalf to win it. Magnus had been his main rival, but Magnus had spoken up as well stating he'd won it two years in a row and wanted someone else to get it. Magnus told the Chapter his Lil, Nolan, deserved it more than anyone and if they couldn't see that then they obviously didn't come around much.

The Michelle Raider award was a community service award, named for one of Upsilon Delta Chapter's legendary Alumni, Raider was a member of Beta class. His mom had passed shortly after him joining, the fraternity really came together for him and his father. Raider's father was also part Nephilim, though he'd never Awakened into his power. Raider's father was initiated into Omega as an honorary member, even signing the scroll of their Chapter. He'd gotten his own Devil Arms symbol after he'd gone through the Oath of the Paladin and became a part of the Upsilon Delta family. Jagger got the award hands down, he was truly passionate about community service, and making sure their Chapter put in effort to give back to the community.

The Diamond in the Rough award was for most improved brother. They guy who'd made a 180 turn in the past year and someone who'd shown a lot of effort into the brotherhood, and bettering himself. Abe, the Chapter's Histor, won the award. He started crying when he took the award and his brothers cheered him on. Everyone had seen how dedicated he was to their brotherhood, Virgil couldn't have been happier for his friend. The Brother in the Bond award was for the brother everyone felt closest to, the guy who most exemplified what it meant to be a brother and a friend.

"This award goes to a very close personal friend," Vahn hinted looking down at the shiny plaque in his hands. "There isn't a more deserving man in this room, he's the guy everyone loves and the brother everyone looks up to, Gabriel Galea!" Vahn announced. Virgil cheered for his Hegemon, as Gabriel got the loudest chorus of cheers and applause by far. He was slightly red in the face, an uncharacteristically shy Gabriel took the award from Vahn, and gave a short wave and bow to his friends. Hurrying back to his seat and a beaming TK who hugged him warmly upon his arrival. Gabriel was truly humbled by the award, tears were in the corners of his eyes.

The last award was Omega of the Year, the brother who had done the most for the fraternity, the Omega who represented the Omegas the best, was seen the most, did the most. Basically, the brother everyone thought helped the fraternity succeed over for the course of the year.

"This last award is for a man who has a somewhat inflated ego," Vahn dropped a large hint. "He is incredibly gifted and intelligent, a fact which he'll vocally let you know upon meeting him. He's a smart ass and a know it all. He is also one of the greatest leaders our Chapter has ever had. He has earned the respect of every brother in this room, with his confident and unflinching leadership. I know there isn't a man here who could do the job he does with as cool a head and steady a hand. The one and only, our Chapter Prytanis, Magnus Trewhella!" Vahn announced and the Chapter cheered for their Prytanis. Magnus walked up giving Vahn a slightly narrowed glare, he clearly hadn't enjoyed the first part of Vahn's speech. They embraced and Vahn handed their Prytanis his plaque.

Gabriel took the podium next. "If I could have everyone's attention for a moment, I have one last announcement for the evening," Gabriel said to the room. Once everyone had quieted down, he continued. "It doesn't happen often, but every once in a while, a special someone comes along that manages to touch the hearts of us all. It has been a while since we've added a new one to our family, and someone has come along that everyone feels is a natural fit for us. This person is kind, generous, loving, and is never too busy to lend a helping hand to a brother in need. Lilly, could you come up here for a minute?" Gabriel asked.

Lilly was seated next to Mu and she looked completely shocked, turning to her boyfriend not really understanding what was going on. Mu helped her to her feet and walked with her to the front of the room. Gabriel brought out a bag, Lilly pulled out a sweatshirt from it. The sweatshirt was green with dark letters on the front that were the same letters as the fraternity, in cursive writing underneath it said, Sweetheart. The men of the fraternity got up from the seats and went to the dance floor kneeling before the podium and Lilly. Jace presented her with a bouquet of flowers. All the men of the fraternity knelt in front of her and began singing, horribly off key, but mostly in unison. The fraternity ended their singing and Lilly was in tears.

"Everyone please welcome, Upsilon Delta Chapter's Sweetheart Number Five, Lilly!" Gabriel shouted out and the men rose to their feet and cheered. Everyone quickly got in line to hug Lilly and congratulate her. Raven and Ariel cut to the front to congratulate their fellow Sweetheart. Jace had suggested inducting Lilly as a Sweetheart a few weeks ago at an E-Board meeting he'd attended for that specific purpose, it passed through E-Board, and was brought up at the following Chapter meeting. After an hour long and heated debate, the brothers finally agreed with a close majority vote that Lilly would be their next honorary female member. Lilly was taken by complete surprise and was overwhelmed with emotion. Virgil finally got his chance to congratulate her and she hugged him fiercely and with love. She kissed him on the cheek, her flaming red hair looking dazzling in her green dress which made her green eyes dance.

After the guys had finished announcing Lilly's new place in their family the dinner portion of WCB had ended, the rest of the night was open for everyone to do as they pleased. Music shifted from low volume classical set as background ambience, to louder more modern tunes from new and recent recording artists. The pool and indoor water area were also open, the group shifted from the hall to their rooms to change. Some people gathered in a few brothers' rooms, to drink, smoke a little bit, and hang out. Some headed to swim and others to dance. A few couples snuck off to their rooms, passion consuming them.

Tarek came over to their table and said to Dante and Blair, "If you guys want to come over to my room and chill, Vahn and I are heading there now," Tarek told them. "Birdy and Virgil can come," Tarek nodded to Virgil and Birdy who were still seated at the table, Nev and Nolan had already gone to their rooms.

"Sweet! We'll be right there," Blair said excitedly, and the group got up. Virgil and Blair went with Birdy and his date back to their room to change. Virgil changed into some swimming shorts with a t-shirt. They went over to Tarek's room and talked about dinner and quickly got lost in conversation.

Virgil left Tarek's room after a bit and headed to the pool on the opposite end from the dining hall. The water park area was large and as tall as the hotel. It was only open to the fraternity now. There were over a dozen people there, Virgil got into the water and visited with Zender and Doc who were there with their dates. After a few times down the water slide, Virgil ran into Selene and TK who were heading down the lazy river, Virgil joined them grabbing a large floating ring to sit in. They exchanged small talk, Virgil knew them well by now and had hung out with TK many times, though Selene had really started coming around more this past semester as she grew closer to Brody.

"This is so much fun!" Virgil shouted out laughing as they drifted past a small waterfall that sprayed them all.

"We have to hang out more Virgil!" TK told him, "I always have so much fun when you're around."

"Thanks, I like you too TK," Virgil said with a big smile.

"I wish you were Gabriel's best friend, instead of Dante," TK made an off handed remark.

"What?" Virgil asked.

"Gabriel and I were arguing the other day. He doesn't like one of my best friends, Stephanie? Landon's girlfriend? And I don't really care for one of his best friends, Dante. We both told each other to try working on liking them more, I don't think I want to," TK sighed.

Virgil was surprised at TK, she was such an open minded, quirky, loving person. Dante was hilarious, so it should seem like they'd hit it off no problem, Virgil wasn't sure what she meant. "Why don't you like Dante?" Virgil asked her calmly, he wasn't mad she didn't like his friend, just was curious.

"I don't know," she said looking around, scrunching up her face near the corner of her mouth. "He's so damn pushy. He thinks that whatever he believes is the absolute best view point and shuts you down if you try to explain otherwise," TK swiveled her tube around to face Virgil. TK looked him in the eyes, "He's stubborn, egotistical, loud, a know-it-all, and he likes to talk a lot of shit about sluts…I don't like that kind of talk Virgil," TK said being raw and honest. Virgil nodded, those were the same reasons why Virgil hadn't become friends with him right away.

Selene had been quiet, and she took a moment to speak her piece. "I don't know Dante all that well, I don't think he is a bad guy, I just think he is young and immature," Selene pointed out.

"Dante is one of my best friends," Virgil told them. "I can see how Dante comes across as brass and arrogant sometimes. To tell you the truth, I didn't like him much at first either. He seemed like a stuck-up preppy jock type. Underneath his loud, look at me attitude, he's compassionate, loyal and adventurous. I don't think you're giving him the benefit of the doubt. You've had interactions with him and clearly perceive him to be a certain way," Virgil pointed out. "Our own perceptions become reality. If you are to ever truly give Dante a chance, you need to look past your own biases of him to see underneath," Virgil said passionately wanting to defend his friend's honor. "Dante is a little rough around the edges, sure, but if you hang out, I think you'll like him. Dante is really funny."

"You know, maybe you're right. I can give him a chance," TK said cheerfully. "For you! Because I like you that much, I'm going to do it," she said playfully splashing him.

They'd circled once around then they decided to get out. Gabriel and Brody were sitting near the pool with solo cups, talking and sipping. Dante was with them. TK went and sat down next to Dante and struck up a conversation with him, seeming genuinely interested in him, Dante responded warmly pouring on his usual bravado. Virgil toweled himself dry and went to change into dry clothes. He went to the banquet room and ran into Lilly, there were over a dozen people dancing and several more milling about in conversations. She was rather tipsy, being a person who almost never drank, a few had her feeling great.

"Virgil Pitcher!" Lilly yelled at him. "Get your butt over here and give your Sweetheart a hug!" she shouted out. She'd changed into jeans and her new Sweetheart sweatshirt. Virgil hugged her and sat next to her and her friend who'd come as one of the brother's dates. Mu was on the dance floor, acting silly, generally how Mu behaved.

"I'm happy to have you in our family," Virgil grinned at Lilly. "Are you having fun?" he asked.

"I am having so much fun!" She laughed. "I had no idea you guys were going to make me a Sweetheart," she insisted. "I am so honored, I love you boys so much," she said getting teary eyed. "I can't wait to buy a bunch of Omega stuff, get more shirts, this is so exciting."

"You'll be able to come to our Brotherhoods and secret stuff," Virgil whispered to Lilly with a smile. "You're one of us now," he told her proudly.

"I'm going to make you boys proud!" Lilly told him. Virgil joined Lilly on the dance floor at her insistence. Ariel was dancing as well, and Virgil paired off with her after dancing with Lilly for a song, dancing with her for some time. He migrated back to his room to grab another drink. When he got inside, he noticed Blair right away. She was making herself a drink, she had red squinty eyes, like she'd been partying a good amount.

"Hey you!" Virgil called to her.

"There you are!" Blair replied loudly. "I've been looking all over for you!" Blair proclaimed excitedly coming up to him and hugging him. "Thanks for bringing me, I'm having a lot of fun!" Blair told him.

"I'm glad Blair, I am too," Virgil grinned.

"Want me to make you a drink?" she asked him.

"That would be lovely, milady," Virgil said handing her his cup and sitting down on the bed.

"I feel bad we haven't got to hang out much," Blair told him as she made their drinks.

"Girl, stop," Virgil laughed, "I'm not your babysitter. I came with you because I knew you'd have no problem fitting in and having fun with everyone. Some of the dates that came were sitting in the banquet hall, bored and miserable," Virgil said remembering back ten minutes to when he was dancing with all three Active Sweethearts, when Raven made her appearance to the dance floor.

"Okay, I just want to make sure you're having a fun time," Blair said handing him his drink and sitting next to him. "Where'd you just come from?" she asked him.

"The dance floor," Virgil said still feeling a little hot and sweaty.

"Figures," Blair laughed, "You're a great dancer."

"What?" Virgil shook his head nervously, "No I'm not."

"You got some moves," Blair nodded, "You just don't like being watched."

"Yeah that's true," Virgil laughed taking a sip of his drink.

"So I," Blair started saying while Virgil said, "So what do you want to do?" they both laughed.

"You want to go find some of the guys?" Virgil suggested getting up. He offered her his hand. She took it and when she got to her feet she tripped and fell into Virgil. Both their drinks got spilt, they laughed and set them down cleaning themselves up. They were both in the bathroom, Blair was wiping her skin off, Virgil stood there smiling, he had drink on his shirt and face. Blair turned to him and wiped his cheek, the white towel turning dark from the pop and alcohol. She stared into his eyes, Virgil's smile fell slowly. Blair leaned into Virgil and Virgil leaned into her…their lips met slowly and hesitantly. Her lips felt soft and warm, she kissed him slowly at first, then she pushed back more passionately, but still gently exploring. The kiss ended shortly thereafter, with Virgil pulling away first. He walked out of the bathroom and stared into the mirror in the bedroom. Blair came out and sat down on the bed, Virgil sat down next to her.

Neither spoke, Virgil looked to Blair who had been avoiding his gaze just as surely as he was avoiding hers. "Blair?" he called to her softly. She turned her eyes on him, and they stared into each other's depths. Virgil wanted to tell her how he felt, explain all the emotions that were running through him, he didn't want to hurt her…

"Blair I," Virgil started but Blair held up a hand and stopped him.

"I like you Virgil," Blair said looking down, "You're a great guy, you're charming, polite, funny, and so damn loyal it hurts. You're also super cute," she said which made Virgil chuckle and get a little red in the cheeks. "But you're also my best friend," Blair pushed on bravely. "I have such strong feelings for you I didn't know what they really were. But when we kissed...I wanted to feel something, I thought I would," she told him looking up.

"But you didn't?" Virgil asked wondering if she felt the same.

"No," she said honestly. "And truthfully, I'm glad. I don't want to spoil things between us, friends who become couples and break up, never end well, and it hurts ALL their shared friends. I can't imagine never hanging out with Dante, Birdy, Louie, and you again because we tried something, and it didn't work out," she explained. "We're more like best friends or siblings."

"Exactly!" Virgil agreed with a large grin. He was so relieved to hear everything she was saying, it resonated with his own thoughts and feelings. "We are such great friends, a relationship would only spoil that. I didn't have anyone in my life except my mom before I joined my fraternity. Now I have so many friends it is hard to even talk to them all enough, out of everyone I know, you are one of the people who means the most to me," Virgil told Blair taking her hand. "You're like family. I want you around for years to come," he said. "Through boyfriends and girlfriends, and everything in between, I don't want this to change," he smiled.

"Through girlfriends and all," Blair nodded looking like she wanted to say more. "We'll always be friends Virgil." They hugged each other warmly. The rest of the night coasted on a strong high note, Virgil was happy that he had resolved things with Blair, and they came out closer in the end.

Sunday morning at check out, the group of brothers and friends leaving was a much more mellow bunch then they were seven hours earlier. Virgil napped most of the day. That Sunday after their meeting, they went with Lilly to the Paladin temple behind the Omega house and inducted Lilly into the Paladins. Raven and Ariel had come to watch and show their support. After Lilly drank from the chalice filled with golden fluid, the blood of the Judges, her powers came online. Lilly Awakened and her Devil Arms formed on her hand. A breathtaking amethyst Devil Arms in the design of a staff or rod. Mu gave Lilly her Dreamstone ring that would cloak her aura and presence from demons, Magnus stressed the importance of always wearing it. Lilly looked at the brothers with newfound respect as Gabriel and Magnus explained the reality of demons, Nephilim, and Judges in the modern world. Lilly checked out the brother's symbols, asking questions. She was shocked to know that everyone had the symbols the whole time she'd known them, having previously been completely invisible to her. She was most fascinated with Mu's symbol and her own. She'd held hands with her boyfriend for months and had never seen the golden-brown symbol on his right hand. Mu promised to train her, and Gabriel invited Lilly to train with the fraternity for the upcoming Tournament at the Paladin Capital, Alexandros.

It was an exciting night for everyone. A new Sweetheart was different from a new brother's initiation. New brothers happened twice a year and there were many of them. A new Sweetheart came only once every so many years. With Ariel graduating at the end of the semester and possibly moving away, there would be a huge hole in the fraternity. Ariel was deeply loved by ALL the brothers. Ariel had told Virgil at WCB that she was graduating with a teaching degree and she wasn't confident she'd find work in Michigan. She was thinking of moving to Florida where there were many opportunities for her to find work all over the state. Raven was a great Sweetheart, she had been in the fraternity for over two years. She came around but was busy with her sorority and Alpha sisters as well. Really the bottom line was, it was best to have more than one Sweetheart! Lilly was the perfect addition to their group! She was a very different personality from Raven and they got along good which was important to everyone.

There were just two weeks of classes left, with finals being the last week, all freshmen were required to move out from the dorms within 24 hours of their last exam. Virgil had already decided to move into the Omega manor. They were rearranging rooms Friday of finals week, the day that everyone would get their room assignments from Nolan, who had been placed in that officer position. Some brothers were failing out of college and thus moving out of the Omega house, some brothers would be aging in the Chapter and would be upgrading to better rooms, while the newer members would take over the rooms on the third floor. Virgil went to bed that night with racing thoughts, tossing and turning. There was so much to be done in such a short period of time, he could scarcely calm his mind.

Chapter 11
<u>Finals</u>

Every college student will agree, the last two weeks of the semester are some of the most stressful of any student's life. The second to last week was sometimes even more stressful then finals week. The week before finals was usually chalk full of papers and exams, followed by a week of final exams that covered material from the entire semester. Virgil had seen some of his classmates looking like they were on the verge of a mental breakdown from all the stress. Every waking moment of Virgil's life, the last two weeks, was consumed with studying. He had his sixth Chemistry exam the week before finals and then the Chem final the following week. Virgil also had a Psychology final to study for, a Sociology final, and they had a paper due the week before finals in Sociology. Virgil regretted not getting a head start on his studies. Virgil bombed his Chemistry exam and managed to get a decent score on his last Psychology quiz. Wednesday night Virgil was finishing his paper due in Sociology minutes before class started. They'd watched Guns, Germs, and Steel a few weeks ago in class, and the paper was an analysis of the information. Virgil managed to hit the minimum requirement of four pages, quickly printed out the paper, making it to class just as the professor started talking. Virgil shared that class with Dante, he took his usual seat next to his pledge brother.

Thursday night there weren't any assignments due in his Theater class, their final paper was due next week. After class Virgil retreated to his dorm and turned off his phone. Virgil kept himself locked in his room the remainder of the weekend. With three finals to study for and a paper to write, he didn't have any time to spare. By Saturday night Virgil's brain was feeling fried, he turned on his phone and had dozens of missed messages. There was a party going on tonight? Virgil read over the message again, his fraternity brother Thiago was having a finals party at his house for anyone who wanted to hangout and relax from the stress of finals. Blair, Dante and Birdy had all text him asking if he wanted to go. Virgil responded back to his friends letting them know he had to study all weekend. Virgil shook his head, how could people party when there were exams to prep for? Things had been good with Blair, granted they hadn't spent much time together since formal, yet he felt their friendship was as strong as ever. The rest of his weekend was spent pouring over the study guides he'd created, switching subjects every so often when his brain felt overwhelmed. Virgil made sure to take the occasional break to eat and listen to music but kept his breaks short.

After his Chemistry final Monday, Virgil went back to his dorm to study some before going to dinner. Damian was inside his room packing his things. Virgil paused at his door, Damian was playing some Avenged Sevenfold softly while he packed, one of Virgil's favorites. Virgil turned around and walked to his doorway.

"You need any help?" Virgil offered Damian. Damian looked up surprised to see Virgil. They'd only seen each other a handful of times since their other roommate, Boyd, had died in November. Virgil thought they'd mended things between them, at least to the point where they could be friendly.

"I'm mostly done packing," Damian told Virgil, "Just have to carry stuff out to my car to take over to the Beta house," he said.

"I can help with that," Virgil shrugged with a friendly smile. Despite being in rival Paladin fraternities, Virgil liked Damian, and he wasn't going to stop trying to be his friend.

Damian shrugged, "Sure, it would make it go quicker for me," he said, "Thanks Virgil."

"Of course, man," Virgil nodded coming into the room a few paces. "So how have you been?" Virgil asked. "I haven't seen you or any Betas around lately," he told him.

"I've been good, just busy with classes and the fraternity. We are training hard for the Paladin Tournament in June, so I haven't had much free time the past month," Damian explained.

"That's cool man. We are too though it doesn't seem like we've put as much practice in as you guys. How many guys did you initiate this semester?" Virgil asked him

"Just two, don't worry about the Tournament though, with you on the Omegas team, I'm sure you guys don't have much to be worried about," Damian said.

"What do you mean?" Virgil asked not understanding what Damian was getting at.

"Virgil, come on, you don't need to pretend to be humble, I fought against you in the Fall remember?" Virgil felt awkward, he didn't know what to do with his hands. Damian stopped working and stood up looking straight into Virgil's eyes. "I've seen the kind of power that's inside you, your body was covered in black flames, and your scythe was glowing with dark energy. I knew at that moment that you weren't normal, even by Nephilim standards. Malachi told all of us you are one of the Seven Seraphs, the Nephilim who are supposed to herald the end the world. You're the Redeemer, right?" Damian asked.

Virgil looked down unable to maintain Damian's gaze. It was sometimes easy to forget with the normal routine of going to college and classes, that Virgil was part of a legendary prophecy foretelling the end of the world, he wished it wasn't true. "I'm still me," Virgil said wishing his voice sounded more confident.

Damian's expression was unexpected, he looked concerned, Damian saw the uncertainty and fear within Virgil. Damian came over and gave Virgil a hug, Virgil wasn't expecting it and felt taken back. The hug was brief, Damian sensed Virgil was tense, he stepped back. "There is so much good in you Virgil," Damian said with heart.

Virgil shook his head, "There is darkness within me," he said admitting it out loud, it made it feel more real. "I feel it sometimes, the call to power, the call to Chaos. You saw me that night, how can I be good, with so much evil in my heart?" A question that had been plaguing Virgil's mind for months, he didn't like to talk about it, especially to his brothers. He already got treated different from the rest, he didn't want to alienate his friends by admitting his own fears to them. Soul Reaver was like a visible curse upon his hand, forever reminding him of his affiliation with Chaos. Virgil looked at Damian's hands, he had two white Devil Arms symbols one on each hand. Damian was aligned with Creation, his Devil Arms were a pair of gauntlets, powerful metal gloves that turned him into a deadly warrior. Virgil wished he had only a Creation symbol, he yearned to be rid of the black Chaos Devil Arms.

"Virgil, listen to me, you have a kind heart. I tried not liking you, the Betas don't know that I still talk to you, I'm not really supposed to. But I don't care what they say, even when I tried pushing you away, you never once stopped caring. You're a friend to me Virgil. No matter what happens between the Betas and the Omegas, remember that. I believe in you, if anyone can be trusted with that kind power, it is you," Damian said his tone indicating he believed it.

"How do you know that?" Virgil laughed. "We barely know each other anymore," Virgil's words came out bitter, he hadn't meant for it to sound that way.

"Because I can feel it," Damian told Virgil closing his eyes. Damian was aligned with Creation, so he was more sensitive to the 'other' than regular Nephilim. "The light, it surrounds you, Virgil. I can see your aura when I concentrate, auras aren't something people can fake. Your aura is so warm and gentle, you've so much power, yet you remain empathetic and compassionate to others. Even now I see a gold light, not darkness coming from your spirit," Damian opened his eyes and smiled warmly at his roommate. "I believe in you Virgil," Damian spoke with conviction "You have to believe too."

"Thanks man," Virgil said feeling a little emotional he took a deep breath willing himself to calm down.

"Anytime bud," Damian told him. "You want to help me carry my stuff down?" he asked.

"Of course!" Virgil nodded. Virgil and Damian carried his things down, Damian's car had been parked illegally in the faculty parking lot next to their dorm. Luckily, he hadn't been ticketed. They talked about their plans for summer and kept the conversation lite. After Virgil had finished helping him clear his room out, they said goodbye. Virgil spent the rest of his night studying, his conversation with Damian weighing heavy on his mind.

Wednesday Virgil finished his Chem Lab exam and left feeling exhausted, Virgil still had his Sociology exam that evening and a paper due tomorrow night. Virgil had put off the paper in favor of studying for his exams, he figured he had all day Thursday to type the paper as it was due at 7pm. Virgil texted Dante and asked if he wanted to study together for a few hours, Dante told him to come over. Virgil arrived at Dante's dorm room, Birdy and Dante were in their room along with Louie.

"Hey what's up Cherry?" Louie called out to Virgil.

"Please don't call me that," Virgil sighed.

"It is your fraternity nickname," Louie pointed out.

"What are you fools doing?" Virgil asked leaning against the door frame.

"Just hanging out," Dante said looking up. "You ready for this exam?"

"I think so, but I need to study for a couple hours more," Virgil told him. "How are all of your exams going?" he asked the room.

"Horrible," Louie complained falling back on Dante's bed, "I wish this week was over!" he whined.

"I'm all done," Birdy told them. "I even have most of my grades back," he said.

"Lucky!" Virgil exclaimed. "How'd you do?" he asked.

"I got a 3.8 GPA this semester," Birdy said a big grin spreading across his face.

"Congrats Birdy!" Nolan said walking into the room, bumping past Virgil.

"Holy shit Birdy!" Louie said sitting up, "You're one of the smart guys in the group!"

"Who knew?!" Dante, Louie, and Nolan said at the same time.

"Hey! What's that supposed to mean?" Birdy said sounding genuinely offended.

"Well," Virgil said choosing his words carefully as Birdy was one of his best friends, "You are kind of absent minded," Virgil responded softly.

"And a klutz," Louie added.

"You walk around constantly bumping into stuff," Nolan said.

"Probably cause he's always on his phone!" Virgil smirked.

"And in general, you act like a dumbass," Dante added curtly with a winning smile.

"Okay, okay," Birdy said holding up his hands, "Please, don't feel the need to keep going."

"I could list things for hours," Dante laughed. "You're messy as hell and live like a slob, it's a wonder you're able to be so organized with school."

"Oh yeah, how are your classes going Dante?" Birdy said getting a little angry. Dante shut up and stared at his computer going silent. Did I miss something, Virgil wondered?

"Anyways," Nolan said breaking the awkward silence, "Congrats again Birdy on doing well this semester, it is good to hear. I just finished having lunch with my Big," Nolan told them.

"How is Magnus doing?" Virgil asked him.

"Great, we actually had a long talk about the fraternity. Magnus thinks that we're going to be handed the fraternity within the next year or two," Nolan said beaming proudly.

"What do you mean?" Virgil asked curiously.

"Magnus told me that once the sun has set on Lambda's time in the fraternity, it will be Omicron's turn to lead this Chapter," Nolan was excited, talking in a way Virgil rarely saw him, enthused and energetic. He usually had such a monotone voice, his tone was always deep, rarely this excited. "Magnus told me he believes our pledge class will be the next leaders."

"Shittttt!" Louie said drawing out the word. "I'm not ready to lead this fraternitty!" Louie laughed.

"Neither am I," Dante shook his head. "I'll be the new chair of ass kicking."

"We're still Freshmen dawg! I just want to have some fun!" Louie joked.

"Louie you already ARE leading the fraternity," Virgil pointed out. "We've both been on E-Board for a semester now."

"Oh, your right man," Louie laughed, "I'm always doing stuff for this fraternity! I'm like a walking billboard for Omega, wearing my letters and representing."

"It isn't happening today," Nolan sighed "I'm talking about when Lambdas are all graduated, Omicron will be the leaders of the Chapter," Nolan said with confidence.

"Magnus had said something similar once," Virgil recalled, "During our interview, I remember him saying he felt our class had a lot of potential."

"There are a lot of classes between Lambda and Omicron," Louie pointed out, "Shouldn't it be their turn first?" he asked.

"Do you see Nu class leading us?" Nolan asked the group. Everyone went quiet then they burst out laughing. Nu class was alright, Tarek was one of the best brothers, but they weren't the most unified. The five of them looked at one another, and a sense of pride came over them. They'd come a long way since being pledges, hard to imagine that it was already seven months since they'd started their pledging process.

"Good point," Dante nodded feeling excited himself, "Well if you ask me, I think we'll make damn good leaders," he told them proudly. "Omicron's pretty cool."

"We're aw'ight," Louie said dusting off his shoulders.

"I was just stopping in to say hi," Nolan said placing his hands together in front of him. "I have to get to work and then an exam afterwards, so I'll see you guys for your rooming assignments Friday?"

"You gotta hook Omicron up!" Louie cried out comically.

"Of course," Nolan said with a large smile. "I'm most loyal to my Big and my pledge brothers."

"Good deal," Virgil nodded, "If I don't see you around, I'll see you Friday," Virgil was thankful they had a guy like Nolan looking out for them.

"See you guys later," Nolan waved cheerfully, off on his own once more.

The group was quiet for a moment, of course Louie broke the silence first. "Anyone else hungry?" he asked.

"Starving!" Birdy replied.

"Do you still want to study together?" Virgil asked Dante.

"Sure," Dante told him, "Let's grab an early dinner and then study till class."

"Alright," Virgil agreed happily, it was near impossible to concentrate on an empty stomach.

After a late lunch, Virgil and Dante went to their final class. "How are you feeling?" Virgil asked Dante as they walked to class together. Virgil had his study guide in his hands, wanting to look over his notes every second, he could.

"I'm confident, I don't think it'll be that hard, this professor is pretty easy," Dante told Virgil.

Dante was right, the final was the easiest one he'd had. Virgil worked on packing up his room that night, it was a little sad taking down his posters, and packing his clothes. He'd moved in at the end of August, since then his life had changed dramatically. His room had always been a haven for him, a place where he could be alone, escape from the world when he needed. Living in the Omega house, it was hard to imagine getting much alone time.

Friday morning Virgil showered and changed, then packed everything he had in his dorm. It took him five trips to get everything to his blazer. Virgil said goodbye to his home, feeling incredibly sad as he turned in his key at the front desk. Virgil drove the short drive across campus to the Omega house, his new home. The front gates to the Omega manor were wide open as Virgil drove up to the house, excitement started to bubble within him. He'd visited the Omega house many times since he'd first started pledging, and even more since he'd become a brother. Moving in though, it was going to take things to a whole other level.

Virgil left his stuff out in his blazer heading inside. The house was lively, everyone from campus had just migrated over, adding nine more brothers than there were previously living there. The living room was full of people, everyone called out to Virgil as he walked in and a smile came over his face, it felt good to be with people who cared about you. He took a seat on the floor next to Troy and Agustin and caught up with them while he waited for things to quiet down. Troy was his usual friendly, quiet self. Agustin was in a depressed mood, he was thinking he'd had a bad semester, grade wise, it was weighing heavy on him. Nolan rounded the brothers up shortly thereafter giving everyone their rooming assignments. Magnus had helped him he'd told everyone 'so no complaining' he ended on. Virgil took his key when his name was called and quickly went over to the grand staircase off the foyer up to the third floor. Virgil's room was in the west wing, he was at the very back at a dead-end corner. There were four rooms and one large community bathroom for them to share at this section of the house. The upper classmen rooms had their own bathrooms. Virgil opened his room and walked in getting acquainted. It was the same size as most of the brothers, he'd been in their rooms many times before, especially when he was pledging. It was about the same size as his dorm had been. Virgil walked back out to the hall.

"Nev!" Virgil laughed. Nev was the room right next to his, closest to the hallway leading to the other rooms in the west wing.

"Good, I'm glad I'm near people I like," Nev said.

Louie and Nolan came out of the other rooms and the four of them came together.

"The four of us are sharing a hallway and a bathroom," Louie nodded. "We're like dorm mates. Good choice Nolan," Louie approved patting him on the back.

"I wanted to be by guys I trusted," Nolan said simply. "Hope you guys don't mind being at the end of the hall. I kind of like this spot because it is like we have our own little area," he said walking up and down the hall.

"Don't mind at all, I'm happy with this!" Virgil said smiling like an idiot. He was so pumped up with excitement. "It feels like the first day of college all over again."

"I know what you mean!" Louie nodded. "Chatting with the new roomies, getting your room settled in, walking around exploring. Only this is better already because now I got my own room. I can finally jack off in peace without worrying my roommate's going to barge through the door," he said nonchalant sounding like it had happened more than once.

Nolan's face went blank and Virgil rolled his eyes, good 'ol Louie.

"Let's check out this bathroom," Nev said walking to the very end of the hall and the other three followed. The bathroom had two sinks so more than one person could brush their teeth or get ready in the mirror. There was only one toilet, but it was behind a privacy wall, in case someone came in while it was being used. The shower was back in a corner, so you couldn't see unless you walked back, giving the user privacy. The lock on the bathroom worked though, and they all agreed they could lock the bathroom if they were using the toilet or taking a shower, otherwise they'd leave it open to let others know it was unoccupied.

Virgil headed outside to grab his things and began the slow process of moving into his new home. The older brothers came milling around the hallways, wanting to see where everyone had landed and where to find whom.

"Virge!" Vahn called out coming into the room. He looked around admiring Virgil's stuff.

"I have to get some things to finish it," Virgil admitted looking around taking notice of a few things he needed, maybe another chair or a small sofa. He had his TV and Playstation hooked up but nothing to sit in while he played.

"It's fine, you just moved in," Vahn told him pulling out his desk chair and sitting down. "I have an old computer chair you can have if you want it, so you can have more seating room," he offered.

"That would be awesome!" Virgil told him. "Thanks, Big."

"We're going to let everyone finish unpacking, and in a little bit we're going to make some food, and get some games started," Vahn said.

"That sounds fun," Virgil nodded. "How did your semester go?" he asked him.

"Okay, glad it's over," Vahn laughed. "Nervous about next semester," Vahn sighed. "Fall pledge classes are twice as stressful as winter ones. Rho class is going to be HUGE," Vahn said proudly.

"Damn," Virgil said realizing he was right. "How are you going to handle all of those guys? Keep 'em all in line," he asked.

"Put the fear of God into them," Vahn said getting a crack out of Virgil. "Lay down the law. Being Hegemon is all about attitude, if you walk in there with confidence and authority, that is how the process is run. The Hegemon sets the tone for the process," Vahn explained. "If the Hegemon is lax and laidback with his candidates, they develop a laidback attitude about the process. Which is the quickest way to piss off the Chapter."

"Gabriel and you are good Hegemons," Virgil said nodding.

"What position do you want?" Vahn asked. "It has been forever since we did your pledge goals," he said.

"Let me pull out my old pledge binder," Virgil said smiling rustling through his box of class textbooks and fraternity stuff. Virgil found it and flipped it open. "My fraternity goals are to improve community service, be a Big Brother, and have the Jeweled Officer position of Hypopthetes," Virgil read out loud.

"Everyone wants that one," Vahn laughed.

"You wanted it?" Virgil asked.

"Of course!" Vahn laughed. "Hypopthetes and Hegemon are my two favorite positions. At the first election Lambda could run, Gabriel wanted Hegemon, and Magnus was dead set on Hypopthetes, so it made sense for me to run for Epiprytanis," Vahn recalled. "And this past election I wouldn't have minded being the Hypo, but when I saw everyone that was running for it, I figured I'd just go for Hegemon. I knew I could do the job our Chapter needed of a Hegemon, and Porter wasn't ready," Vahn said. "He was the only real candidate besides me," Vahn said. Brody Porter, most brothers called him Porter, Virgil had always stuck to calling him Brody.

"So how was your semester?" Vahn asked.

"I'm not sure, I haven't checked my grades online yet," Virgil admitted.

"How do you think you did?" Vahn asked.

"I'm thinking I did well, I might be below a 3.5," Virgil shrugged.

"Well if you get put on probation, you'll still have your scholarship for next semester. You just get above a 3.5 semester GPA next time to keep it," Vahn sighed. "I lost mine in my second year."

"If I lose it, I lose it," Virgil decided. "Having loans is just a part of going to school."

"Yeah, the new poor man's tax," Vahn poignantly pointed out.

They sat there talking until Gabriel and Tarek came looking for Vahn.

"Here's the little guy's room," Gabriel said to Virgil with a small smirk.

"Hey guys!" Tarek called out loud and obnoxiously. His rosy cheeks were spread in a shit eating grin, he got a kick out of being over the top sometimes.

"Nice room," Gabriel nodded. "This used to be my room," he told Virgil fondly.

"Really?" Virgil asked surprised.

"Yup, second year," Gabriel said. "Shared the hall with Magnus, Vahn, and Landon. It's the best second year rooms, kind of cool having that small hall here."

"Sweet," Virgil nodded.

"Which is why Magnus recommended I reserve it for myself," Nolan smiled walking in. "Hello everyone."

"Hey Nolan," everyone greeted him.

"Just letting you guys know, I'm going down to start dinner. I'll let you all know when it is ready," Nolan said.

"Thanks!" they said in unison and Nolan left.

"That guy is a life saver," Gabriel smiled shaking his head. "This house is going to be so much better with him living here."

"We'll just get fatter," Vahn said flatly.

"Yay!" Tarek cheered.

"You guys want to race some Mario Kart?" Gabriel asked them.

"Heck yeah!" Virgil replied excitedly.

"Let's head to my room," Gabriel said. The guys left Virgil's room, walking with a bounce in their step, to the fifth floor, where the oldest brothers of fraternity lived. Their rooms were larger and had their own bathrooms. The Chapter Advisors offices were on the top floor.

They entered Gabriel's room which had been decorated to reflect his personality. "TK bought me that," Gabriel said motioning to a cardboard cutout of his favorite hockey player in the corner.

They sat down in Gabriel's room and started a round. Magnus, Brody, Birdy, Louie, and Rowan wondered in, they traded off the lowest two places after every race, giving everyone a chance to play. It wasn't long before dinner was finished, and the house sat down as one. There were twenty-six brothers present, they sat at the large dining room table off the kitchen. Virgil was happy with how things felt, it was like…being home. He'd been here so many times before, the only difference is now he slept here. Virgil had become so comfortable with his brothers, without realizing it, being around them had become like being around his mom.

Chapter 12
<u>Summer Vacation</u>

Virgil woke up the next morning disoriented, he looked around noticing he'd made it to his room and passed out on the floor next to his bed. Virgil showered and got ready for the day, feeling much better, laying on his bed with the door open. He thought of breakfast…hopefully Nolan is around he smiled wickedly, Creator they took advantage of that poor guy. Nolan loved to be of service, he was an amazing brother and person, it was part of who he was, taking care of others. Dante chose that moment to walk in, he pulled up the awesome chair Vahn had given him last night. They'd taken turns pushing each other on it down the hall in the early hours of the morning, Louie almost broke the dang thing.

"What's up buddy," Dante said with a large grin, he looked like crap.

"I'm still drunk I think," Virgil told him. "I don't know whether to start drinking again or pass back out."

"We should go check out Blair's new place, then go get breakfast," Dante suggested.

"Oh yeah!" Virgil exclaimed.

"I wanted to talk with you before we go over there though," Dante looked shy.

"Why what's up?" Virgil said becoming more alert, putting his feet on the floor facing towards Dante, and mirroring his body language.

"I'm not moving in here with all of you," Dante said looking down.

"What?!" Virgil asked not understanding.

"I looked at my grades this morning, I failed out of Bay Valley, or at least I can't use FASFA here," Dante admitted shocking Virgil mute. Dante stared Virgil down. "I'm telling you this because you're my friend. I have to go to a community college, get good grades, and then apply to transfer back…if I even come back," Dante said breaking eye contact looking off. "I don't know what I want to do. I have my car packed, I'm moving back in with my folks in Clio. I'll probably head back after breakfast."

Virgil grappled for a reply. "I didn't know you were struggling with grades…I'm sorry, we should have studied more together," Virgil sighed feeling part guilty, they'd shared a class together.

"Dude, stop right there, I can read your guilty face, there is nothing anyone could have done differently to have changed this, I did this," Dante told Virgil throwing his hands up in the air. "Everyone is responsible for their own education. I obviously didn't put in the effort. That doesn't mean I'm dumb, bad grades don't equate low intelligence," Dante said getting defensive.

"I agree," Virgil nodded. They were quiet. "No wonder I didn't get to see your room." Last night they'd wandered around the Omega mansion, getting acquainted with where people were now living. "Dante, I want you to know that just because you're not going to Bay Valley anymore, doesn't mean you're not a brother, or any less a part of this brotherhood than the rest of us," Virgil told him.

Dante nodded his serious stoic face cracking, letting out…relief, and regret. "Thanks Virgil, you don't know how much it means to hear that from you."

"I want you to get back here by next fall," Virgil told Dante. "Omega won't be the same without you around."

"Oh, I'll be around," Dante laughed. "I'm not going to be one of those brothers who just disappears because they don't go here anymore," he told Virgil. "Clio is only thirty-five, forty minutes away, I'm going to be coming up most weekends, and for the important brotherhoods," Dante smiled. "I'm an Omega, I don't give a shit about Inactive, Active, Alumni status," he told Virgil.

Virgil's phone buzzed a message from Blair. *Yo, where you at slut? Just got a new place, you should come over!*

"You want to go over to Blair's?" Virgil asked.

"Let's grab our Asian and our Birdy," Dante nodded getting up and heading into the hall.

Virgil knew it was hard for Dante to say that. The easy thing to do would have to been to get in his car and drive off, avoiding the confrontation altogether, leaving everyone to find out by word of mouth. Dante was a man of honor, Virgil respected the hell out of him. The four of them headed to Blair's. Virgil rode with Dante, Birdy following behind. Blair's new apartment was just a mile down the road, into Kawkawlin where plots of land had been turned into college student apartments. Blair had a two-bedroom place with Helene that was three floors, the basement was the length of the house, they set it up as the party area. The group got a tour of their new home, Helene was excited to show them around, and Blair made fun of her along the way. They had the essentials in place, but there was still more work to be done before they were fully unpacked. Everyone got caught up sharing a giant relief that finals were over, and now everyone could go back to normal stress levels. Blair was her usual animated self, listening to her was better than TV any day.

Louie asked Dante why his car was full of his stuff, Dante announced he was moving home, and they all shared in the grief of not having one of their best friends around for the following school year. Everyone was supportive, and Dante looked happy, he knew his friends cared about him. The six of them headed out to breakfast with high spirits, with the clowns in their group it was hard to stay sullen for long. That hour at the diner, could have lasted a lifetime. They were all so happy together, laughing constantly, with such strong rapport they had their own inside jokes, and stories, they could almost start and finish each other's thoughts they were getting so close. Virgil had never had this before, such a strong bond to other people that weren't his parents. This was what humanity should be like for everyone, he wished. Love, intimacy, compassion, trust, loyalty. Virgil could have lived in that moment forever and would have always known happiness.

Once the bills came, everyone was full and sleepy, less talkative. Louie had eaten enough for two or three, he had almost passed out at the table. Louie graciously picked up Dante's tab when he reached for it, he was cool like that sometimes. After breakfast they went their separate ways, Virgil was still tired, and Blair had to do more unpacking. Virgil rode home with Birdy, Louie was passed out in the back seat. They got back to the Omega house and Virgil made his way up to his room to check his grades. Virgil had gotten a 3.1 GPA, which was good, though his scholarship required he keep a 3.5 GPA. Virgil sighed, he'd be put on probation now and if he didn't do better next semester, he'd lose his scholarship. Virgil crawled back into his warm bed and fell asleep.

Virgil awoke to someone shaking him, he sat up startled…it was Nev.

"Hey Virgil, we're all gathering down on the first floor, it is time for training," Nev told him.

"I slept that long?" Virgil asked stretching and getting up, still fully dressed. "I might need some green tea or something before I work out," Virgil said feeling a little groggy still.

"Green tea?" Nev asked him, "Not coffee?"

"I don't like coffee," Virgil admitted getting up, "And green tea boosts metabolism, good before working out, after or before eating, helps to stay in shape. Why do you think the Japanese have one of the lowest obesity rates in the world?" he asked his friend.

"I didn't know that," Nev said, "Maybe I'll start drinking tea," he laughed.

After Virgil had some tea, a few brothers joined in as well, and everyone was ready, they had a short meeting about what their goal was for these next seven weeks: To train harder than they had ever before and to prepare themselves so they could compete with one hundred percent maximum effort. Some brothers were not present, at this time it was made evident which brothers had failed out of Bay Valley. There were going to be twenty-three Active Brothers going into the Fall semester, the same as when Virgil had pledged. He realized that they hadn't grown at all this past year, they'd just maintained, gained enough new blood to replace those that left, graduated, or failed out. Some of the older brothers that never came around had graduated. Buck, Benson, and Thiago were now the only brothers older than Lambda. Landon was the fourth oldest, scroll wise. Doc and Reece had failed out of Bay Valley in addition to Dante. Upon learning Doc would no longer be living at the Omega house Virgil's mood dropped. Doc was one of his favorite brothers, sure he was a little colorful at times, but that just made him even more likeable, he had personality. Reece, he was one of the three Xi class members, he was Brody's best friend, Brody was less animated than usual.

"There are only twenty-three Active brothers in Upsilon Delta Chapter," Magnus said, "Look around the room gentlemen, THESE, are the brothers of our Chapter now. We must unite as a group and move forward with focus, and determination," Magnus' voice was enigmatic, deep and moving. He could captivate a room, and at that moment all eyes were on him, everyone was silent, taking in what their leader was saying.

After Magnus' speech, which was concise lasting a few minutes, they cheered and headed outside pumped up and ready to work hard. Training for the Tournament became a full-time job for all the brothers living in the house. Magnus and Gabriel, their Prytanis and Epiprytanis, evolved into drill instructors, making the brothers hit practice with maximum effort working to improve their endurance, skill, and experience. There were many categories of the Paladin games held over the course of several days: A strength Devil Arms competition, an endurance test, a long-range Devil Arms shooting competition, and sparring among many others. Not every team was even able to compete in all the events because they didn't have enough varied Devil Arms among their members.

Summer Vacation lasted until the end of August, the last weekend was when the Freshmen moved in and the weeks that followed were the busiest for the fraternity. It was the first week of May, they had seventeen weeks off until the Fall semester began, but only seven weeks to prepare for the Tournament. The Tournament of the Chalice was held in the Floating City of Alexandros, the Nephilim Capital. The competition lasted four days, with the final event being held on the Summer Solstice. They'd had practice once a week since Spring Break, now things kicked into high gear. After a three-hour practice that first Saturday, Virgil spent a little time each day training in the back of the Omega house on his own. A new attitude had started to sink into the brothers. As the days started to go by, a drive overcame the men, to work harder, to push themselves further. No one was expecting to place first, but they wanted the world to take notice of the Upsilon Delta Chapter of the Paladins. Lambda class pushed themselves the hardest. They were the group's strongest members on the field, and they knew it. They had an obligation to the others, to watch over them, guide them, and protect them. Being your brother's keeper in the Omegas meant more than making sure your brother got good grades. It meant fighting with your Devil Arms, doing your best to keep the guy next to you alive and breathing.

Every brother had their own Devil Arms, unique to them, and they found strength and inspiration from that. Everyone wanted to sharpen their skills with their Devil Arms, even the three Sweethearts started coming to practices. Ariel, Sweetheart #2, was the eldest of the three and the most experienced. Ariel was aligned with water and her Devil Arms was a whip. Virgil had seen her in action and had gained a deep respect for her when she came on a mission with them on Spring Break, over two months ago. Ariel told the fraternity the sad news that she'd be moving to Florida in August for a teaching job, the brothers were devastated. Raven, Sweetheart #4, was aligned with earth and had a dagger for her Devil Arms. Lilly, Sweetheart #5, and the newest member of the fraternity was aligned with wind, her amethyst Devil Arms materialized into a rod, a smaller version of a staff with an emerald adorned on the top. The moment Lilly called out her Devil Arms's name the rod came into her hand. When Lilly gripped it the wind around her began to dance stirring her fire red hair in the breeze, her abilities were like Magnus and Nolan, and she was a quick study. After only her second practice she'd gotten two spells down well enough to fire them in quick succession. Mu was knocked down multiple times, they eventually switched out and Nolan practiced with her. A mage was more suited to battle another mage, Nolan had a much easier time deflecting her spells without getting harmed. Lilly was winded, sweaty, and exhausted…with a grin across her face.

"I love hanging out with you boys," Lilly told the brothers as they walked up to the house to clean up and get some food. "If any demon tries to hurt one of my guys, I'll blast it with Valefor's Rod," she elbowed Virgil with a wink.

Virgil laughed and nodded, he was glad to see her confidence was high, training had put everyone in a good mood, and helped the group bond. Everyone had such different interests, hobbies, and past times, that different cliques formed out of people who liked doing the same stuff. One thing that unified them was their Nephilim blood. Pi class was already one with the group, to Virgil it felt like they'd always been there. Nev wielded his lightning staff like he'd been training as long as Nolan. Agustin was deadly with his large earth mace. Rowan had quickly distinguished himself as one of the best warriors of their Chapter, he was skilled with his fire katana, and he wielded his blade like he'd been using it for years. Virgil struggled when sparring against him as if he were one of the Lambdas. Rowan was one of the older brothers at twenty-two years old, the same age as Tarek and Benson. All the Lambda's had turned twenty-one over this past year, Gabriel's birthday had been a week before finals. Nev had already turned nineteen, and Agustin was twenty. Most of Omicron had turned nineteen over the school year, only Birdy and Virgil were still eighteen, Birdy's birthday in July and Virgil's was the last day of September.

A few weeks into summer vacation things started to get serious, Magnus called a meeting on a Tuesday afternoon. That day at 4pm inside the meeting room, they had twenty guys in attendance. Malachi had reached out to Magnus telling him they welcomed the competition at the upcoming games and hoped to move forward with better relations. Everyone had a healthy dose of skepticism at the Betas sudden interest in repairing relations.

Virgil remembered his conversation with Damian, and he spoke up to the room. "I spoke with Damian and he had mentioned they had been training hard ALL semester," he recalled to them.

"What else did he tell you?" Vahn asked Virgil.

"He was moving out and I offered to help him carry his things, we didn't really talk about Beta or Omega, we were friends before that," Virgil said with attitude.

"No one is questioning your loyalty!" Vahn snapped back, "Maybe you know something, and you don't realize it," he suggested. "Can you tell us anything else?" he prodded.

Virgil sighed and took a deep breath remembering back to what they had talked about. Damian had been comforting to Virgil, he believed there was light in him, something he needed to hear. "We talked about me being the Redeemer, and the burden it weighed on me. Harmony and Order, or Chaos and Discord, both pull at me," Virgil told his brothers. "Sometimes I don't know which side of me is stronger, I feel a pull to Chaos, to power. I feel like I don't do enough to fight it. I need to be more than I am," Virgil said vocalizing feelings that he'd been having for some time.

"We are all here for you brother, any time you need one of us," Gabriel told Virgil. "Just pick up the phone and give me call bud, I was your Hegemon. You know I will help you if I can. Everyone here cares about you, we all know that you've been given a responsibility that is more than anyone has the right to ask of you," Gabriel came close to Virgil looking more emotional than he'd ever seen him. "But you're still you. Virgil Pitcher, scroll #123, and we're still your brothers. We're Omegas. You," Gabriel pointed his finger at Virgil's chest, "Are the fraternity," Gabriel's words were reverberated through Virgil's soul, "Remember that," Gabriel told him lowering his hand and walking slowly in a circle in the meeting room. "You decide who Virgil is going to be, no one else. We have no control over our environments, and that is something every mortal must accept. BUT, we do have control over our REACTIONS to our environments, or our behaviors. We have to take responsibility for the good and bad we do each day," Gabriel told the men. "And each new day, try to do a little better than the day before," Gabriel turned to Virgil locking eyes with him. Gabriel's eyes spoke volumes Virgil smiled softly fighting back emotions that started bubbling up.

"Thanks Gabriel," Virgil said overcome by Gabriel's strong reaction to what he'd said.

"I'm always available day or night, if you need to talk brother," Gabriel told Virgil.

"So am I," Magnus told Virgil.

"Here if you need me," Tarek called from the back of the room.

"You can also count on me homes," Louie said seated next to Virgil slugging him in the shoulder.

"We all are here for you," Vahn told Virgil.

"And this brings up a good point for everyone," Magnus said turning it a teaching moment. "If any brother is hurting, feeling overwhelmed, upset, or afraid, please reach out. That is why we are here people. I know we sometimes get caught up in all the macho ego bullshit, and don't want to let that wall we put up crack, because we want to be tough, but we are brothers, and we can talk to each other, and help one another. If any of you see a brother, who isn't doing so well, or they're more withdrawn, let them know you care, or else, what is the point of all this?" he asked them throwing his hands in the air exasperated.

The room was quiet, the brothers reflected on what Magnus had said.

"Virgil you did mention something important," Vahn said, "Going back to the earlier topic," he laughed awkwardly.

"What did I say?" Virgil asked him.

"The very first thing you said," Vahn told him, "It immediately stood out to me. You said you talked about being one of the Seven Seraphs, right?" Vahn asked Virgil. The room went quiet, everyone turned to look at Virgil.

"Umm," Virgil looked down, his palms became sweaty, his heart was racing. He hadn't told Damian, he wouldn't have revealed something like that. He was a Beta after all, they could be friends and have Virgil's secret NOT be known. No, Damian had said Malachi told all of them he was a Seraph, they all knew. "They all know," Virgil said out loud realizing Vahn was right, he had known something, unknowingly.

"They all know?" Magnus asked Virgil, very interested, his face in deep concentration.

"They know I'm a Seraph," Virgil sighed. "Damian told me Malachi had told their Chapter."

"How does Malachi know?" Vahn asked.

"I don't like this," Landon said speaking up. "Smells like bullshit to me."

"Or Death," Tarek said speaking up from the back of the room seated next to Brody, Benson, Rowan, and Jagger.

"Death?" Lamar asked. "What the hell you talking about?"

"Death Dealers," Nolan sighed.

"It could be someone from the Capital," Tarek shrugged. "It is a hub for gossip and knowledge. If the wrong person in the Capital knows, it could have leaked back to the Betas."

"Or Malachi is on talking terms with the Commander of the Death Dealers," Vahn said.

The room was quiet, "We don't have proof of that," Landon said.

"Just postulating of course," Vahn nodded. "But Virgil did see Betas kidnap Louie and attempt to take him. Then the next time we saw Louie he was with the Harbinger and the Gatekeeper," Vahn recalled.

"I saw Malachi talking to that Death Dealer guy!" Louie cried out. "I just now remembered cause you guys brought it up," he said.

"What did they talk about?" Magnus asked Louie.

"I didn't catch much, by the time I was coming to, Malachi was pretty much leaving with his big muscle friend, Jamal," Louie said. "It sounded like they knew each other or something though."

"Knew each other?" Lamar asked skeptically. "Are you sure you're not just saying that because of what a brother said a minute ago?" he laughed, and a few brothers nodded, Lamar had a good point.

"No," Louie protested, "I remember Malachi told him this time they'd got the right one," he said.

"Interesting," Magnus stood there deep in thought, "It doesn't prove anything, but we can benefit from communication with them as they are still Paladins," he said in his best diplomatic voice, which was so convincing it almost sounded like he was chastising them. "We must all be on our guard when they are around however," his tone darkened, betraying his real thoughts, "It is highly plausible they are covertly involved with the Death Dealers. Which means at any time, they could turn on us and attack, we must be ready for that day," Magnus said solemnly, "Whether it be tomorrow, or in a few months, in my term as Prytanis, or under a future Prytanis of the Chapter. If it happens, we need to be ready to take them out," Magnus' words cut through the room striking his point home.

"We're ready," Agustin said smashing one fist into the palm of his other hand.

"Easy newbie," Lamar told Agustin with a laugh and the room laughed a little too.

Magnus had laughed as well, Lamar was funny, and he had great timing with his comments. Magnus collected himself and his face became almost mean, "We will NOT start anything with the Betas," Magnus said very stern. "It bears repeating, if any of you are found to have started a fight with a Beta, I will personally bring you up on charges," Magnus told them dead serious.

The group's laughing and smiles fell flat, and the room was silent. Everyone understood.

"If there is to be a fight between us, it will not start with an Omega," Magnus said ending the conversation.

Magnus steered the rest of the meeting to talk about the schedule from then until the Tournament. It was going to cost each brother, two hundred and fifty dollars to attend the competition. That paid for the hotel for the stay, two meals a day at the hotel, and thirty dollars in Capital money. Gabriel plotted out the training schedule for the rest of their time. He announced they'd have a game of capture the flag with brothers, Sweethearts, and a few Alpha sisters who wanted to join. It was to help in preparation for the Tournament. The game would be similar to what some people called, LARP, Live Action Role Play, only they were using their Devil Arms with Dull spells to prevent them from killing each other on accident. The game was going to be roughly a week before the event.

Time went by in a lovely blur, spring and summer was a time when Michigan came alive. The state blossomed into a beautiful, recreational land, with lakes and rivers all over, and almost limitless forests and woods still untouched by man. There were many summer activities that could be enjoyed, and the State was truly in its prime during the warmer months. Everyone was outside as much as possible, playing volleyball, golfing, swimming, playing football, and having BBQ's. The Omegas had one get together a week after their meeting, roasting up a ton of food and inviting anyone from Bay Valley who was still around to come. They had a couple dozen people they didn't know show up from a few of the other clubs on campus. They had some sorority and fraternity people come, and the Alpha girls showed up. It was a fun party, with a long beautiful sunny day with high seventies weather, the Omega's backyard could finally reach its full potential for company.

Of course, every day was filled with exercise and training for Virgil. Spell casting was something Virgil was trying to improve on by himself, it took a lot of energy to practice, but it was worth exhausting himself. Each time he tried to push a little further, and he felt like he could, his gold aura seeming only centimeters different, but it stretched further the same. He practiced calling Soul Reaver to his hand, practicing his footing and techniques, attacking an opponent, and blocking. They did a lot of sparring, Virgil was careful not to harm his brothers, but got into his training. Virgil felt he'd come a long way since he'd first started. He was no longer afraid to cross blades with Tarek or Gabriel. Virgil had grown more confident in his skills, he knew if he faced a Death Dealer that he had more than a fighting chance. Through all his practicing however Virgil never could use Ragnorak. He'd tried but the Holy Blade wouldn't respond to his calls. He felt silly at practice, everyone wanted to see this 'legendary' Devil Arms, not everyone in the Chapter had seen it. And those that hadn't seemed almost…offended they hadn't. The Sweethearts were interested, but polite and encouraging. Lamar openly teased Virgil about not using his Creation Devil Arms, and Virgil wasn't sure where his animosity came from. Vahn was always nearby though, barking at anyone who started picking on Virgil, Virgil couldn't have asked for a more loving and protective Big. Out of Omicron Virgil had gotten the best Big hands down.

Dante came up to the Omega house after the first few weeks and was around most days after that. He'd gotten a job in Birch Run at the Outlet Mall, which was close to his home. He'd also signed up for classes in the Fall semester at Mott Community College which had a branch in Clio, with its main base in Flint. Dante told Virgil three of his classes were at the Clio location, and once a week he had to go to Flint for a class. Dante kept his Dreamstone ring on at all times, Flint had one of the highest concentrations of demonic activity in Michigan. The high crime rates reflected the Chaos from the demons, they drove humans mad and pushed them to do things their inhibitions would normally ward against. All in all Dante was positive, he told everyone he was going to focus on building himself, mind and body. Dante wanted to be in the Tournament, and after much debating among the Jeweled Officers it was decided that he should be allowed to attend. Because of this Thiago had insisted they open up the option to Doc and Reece as they had also been Active in the Winter semester. In the end Doc and Dante were going with them to Alexandros.

Virgil and his friends spent their free time having as much fun as they could while Michigan was in its most glorious state. Virgil applied for a few jobs but had no real prior work experience and didn't have any luck. He decided to try to enjoy the summer and spent his time with his brothers, and Blair and Helene, frequently visiting their house to hang out. June came and after a few weeks of training it was the day they had planned on playing capture the flag. Everyone who was interested in playing gathered behind the Omega house.

There were forty people who had shown up, the twenty-three Active brothers for the Fall semester, and Dante and Doc, plus the three Sweethearts. Twelve Alphas came, TK, Blair, Helene, Terra, and Selene, along with girls who were starting to get more familiar to Virgil. They had forty people, two teams of twenty. Gabriel and Terra were the team captains, and starting with Terra they began picking from the large group who they wanted. Terra picked Magnus to start with, Gabriel chose Tarek, Terra took Jagger, she stumbled over his name…a little too eager to have him on her team. This did not go unnoticed by Jagger as he blushed slightly, visible even with his Latino complexion. Jagger came to stand by Terra, who had a happy look on her face. What's going on there, Virgil wondered silently with a raised eyebrow.

They continued taking turns until the teams of twenty were made. Each team was given a flag. They divided the woods up, Terra's team had near the Nephilim temple as a base and Gabriel's team was stationed across the woods near the Omegas home. The Dull spell was to remain on everyone's Devil Arms symbol at all times, if anyone removed it they were immediately disqualified from the game. If someone got hit two times in the same limb, they were supposed to pretend that limb fell off and stop using it, eventually having to sit down and stop moving for ten minutes, unless someone who could use Restoration magic came along and healed them. This was to protect people from getting beat on. Even with the Dull spell people could get broken limbs. Thankfully they had people who could heal present, but there weren't a lot. Tarek and Louie could, Ariel and Raven could, Lilly was still learning and had not mastered the art of Restoration spells. Virgil had at first thought only people aligned with water could use healing magic, but he'd discovered people aligned with any element could learn how to do it. But not every person could master it. It took more power and energy to heal and create, than it did to harm and destroy. The Alphas had a few sisters who could heal, Terra was one of them. She had an amethyst Devil Arms that looked like a sword with lightning snaking around it. Virgil was chosen by Terra to be on her team, he looked at her Devil Arms with curious interest, there was a reason this woman was the President of their sorority. Virgil was willing to bet she'd be a formidable opponent.

Virgil followed his team into the woods. They spent ten minutes choosing the perfect spot that was well hidden. Virgil volunteered to defend the flag, defense had always been his best position in baseball and soccer. Selene was on his team, and she volunteered to stay behind with Virgil. Rowan, Nev, and Troy were told to join them. Magnus looked at his phone, the time was up, Magnus raised his staff to the sky and shot a ball of electricity up, it crackled in the sky like a firework. The game had begun!

Chapter 13
<u>Capture the Flag</u>

"Let's move out!" Terra commanded holding a sharp saber with electricity running along its blade. She led the group away from the flag, towards the other team's location. Virgil stayed behind with Selene, Nev, Rowan, and Troy to guard the flag. Everyone had cast the Dull spell on their Devil Arms. Selene held a long slender polearm in her right hand, the long shaft of the lance had a red tint to it leading up to a ruby embedded in the metal near the shaft of the blade, when she did practice thrusts flames blazed to life along the weapon's peripherals.

"I've never seen your Devil Arms in its corporeal form before," Virgil said to Selene. "It looks beautiful."

"You're sweet," Selene told Virgil with her dazzling smile. "I've been training hard with TK for the Tournament. I'm excited to actually get to use it."

"Are you and TK close?" Virgil asked.

"Well yeah!" Selene laughed, "She's my Big!"

"Oh!" Virgil laughed. Raven and Selene were both TK's Little Sisters in their sorority. TK must be loved by her group to get two great Lil's, Virgil thought.

"The Alphas have been practicing more because of the games in Alexandros," Selene told Virgil. "There were a few of us who pushed to get the girls involved."

"Guys get ready! They could be coming through at any minute," Rowan said excitedly moving constantly looking like he was trying to hold his bladder.

"Calm down!" Nev laughed. "You're so damn loud you'll give away our position. We're not supposed to lead them to the flag," Nev pointed out.

"Right," Rowan nodded his demeanor instantly changing, his Navy Medic training kicking in. He started to whisper, "Let's move down a bit, give the flag some space," Rowan advised.

"Agreed," Virgil nodded, and they moved further into the trees, though there was plenty of room. It was early afternoon, much better on the eyes to fight opponents, most of their real battles WERE in the dark.

"I'll guard your back if you guard mine," Virgil offered Selene. He wanted to make sure she didn't get knocked out by his overzealous brothers, the guys could get a little out of hand *especially* when it came to competition, assertion of dominance bull crap.

"Aww of course!" Selene beamed at him with her dazzling smile and chocolate eyes. "We'll look out for each other, promise," she winked.

"I won't let anyone get you," Virgil said smiling turning his eyes to look at the woods. They'd been waiting for ten minutes, but that wasn't long enough for someone to make it to their location, too many bodies in between. Then they heard it, the sounds of battle not far into the woods, spells and Devil Arms clashing. The tension began to build, the inevitable knowledge that soon there would be people coming into their view, people looking to get past them…

Virgil saw him first, Mu moving at a steady gait, his large earth club held high and resting on his shoulder when he came to a pause in the large clearing with the temple. Their flag was within his grasp, he just didn't see it yet. Coming up behind him were Jace with his fire mace, Doc with his earth throwing axe, and Lamar with his giant earth hammer. Not the people Virgil had expected, but perhaps the strongest warriors had clashed he thought, which left people from either side to slip through in the process. Still these brothers were all older and more experienced than Virgil's team, they weren't to be underestimated.

"There they are!" Lamar pointed out their group.

"Get em!" Rowan said charging forward with his flame katana, eager for battle.

Nev followed behind, staying at a distance, a staff wielder's optimal position was in the back of the group. Troy charged Doc, his wind rapier stabbing swiftly, almost too much for Doc's small axe to handle. Rowan crossed paths with Lamar and Mu and both used their heavy weapons to try smashing him down. Rowan was nimble and dodged their weapons, rolling on the ground, he narrowly missed having his spine cracked.

"Look out!" Virgil said to Selene as they reached the fight, Jace was closing in fast, and Abe had just come onto the field, he was on the other team as well. He started running for the fight to help his team take them out.

"Yeehhhaaa!" Selene shouted as she ran at full speed. She stabbed her lance into the ground, and like a pole-vaulter catapulted herself into the air, she leapt gracefully her legs tight together, her body like a missile. Selene landed almost on top of Jace, stabbing her lance into the ground as she came down with a tremendous force. Fire erupted around her like an explosion, Jace was literally flung, full body into the air, clean off his feet. He rolled across the ground, his deadly flame mace dematerializing, and his ruby symbol going quiet, he was down for the ten minutes at least.

Abe had reached them, Virgil got his scythe ready, Selene was too quick though, she sprinted at Abe spinning her lance around. They were within striking distance of each other, Selene struck out her lance in a series of swift forceful jabs. Abe was taken off balance, he could barely parry her blows with his small wind sword. Selene struck at him with a fierceness that startled him. Virgil was standing there with his mouth hanging open, she'd given him precious little to do besides watch her kick ass.

Selene looked over at Virgil after planting a kick to Abe's chest that sent him onto his back. "Virgil behind you!" Selene warned her eyes fearful.

Virgil turned to see Lamar raising his giant hammer to crush Virgil. Selene came running, she raised her hand into the air her Devil Arms symbol blazing with life, "Fuming Dragon!" Selene shouted. From her symbol rose the form of a flaming dragon. It arched in a parabola, crashing down into Lamar within seconds. The spell was so powerful it brought Lamar down to his knees breathing heavy. Lamar got back up with surprising stamina and swung his arm towards Virgil, Virgil moved back easily escaping the lazy swing. Lamar got both hands on his weapon, his determination and concentration coming back into focus. He charged Virgil, Virgil swung Soul Reaver at the hammer, the metal scythe sending sparks as it collided with the giant hammer, and then again. Lamar had enormous strength, and each time Virgil clashed weapons it felt like his arms were going to buckle and give out against him.

Virgil backed up from Lamar bouncing on the tips of his feet, he needed space to end this. Virgil got his body into position, readying to throw his scythe, his stepped forward and swung Soul Reaver as hard as he could letting go of it sending it at Lamar. The scythe spun into him with so much force it knocked him to the ground. Lamar conceited defeat and began timing his ten minutes until he could get back up. Nev had helped Rowan and Troy handle Mu and Doc. Troy had gotten hit too many times, and was now sitting down. Selene had finished Abe, who was also counting his time till he could stand back up. They were down to four defenders, they gave the brothers some space, and their group reformed.

"About earlier," Virgil said to Selene, "I feel like a dumbass, you don't need anyone protecting you," he mumbled feeling embarrassed.

Selene giggled, and they shared a look. "Well thank you Virgil for saying that. I don't want people to think that because I'm a woman, I can't do all the same great things that a man can do."

"You can do anything you set your mind to!" Virgil affirmed. "I'd say you're capable of more than most men, easy!"

"I feel sorry for the guy who tries to push you around," Nev laughed.

"No kidding!" Rowan said sharing in the laughter. Selene was an incredible warrior!

"Okay boys!" Selene said rolling her eyes at the guys, blushing.

Gabriel came into the clearing at that moment, along with Vahn, Landon, and TK...the Bigs of every person in Virgil's group. Vahn and Virgil both began to shake their heads at the irony of the situation, and then started laughing when they noticed they were both doing the same thing.

"Take your Lils," Gabriel commanded, "You take down your Lil, help the person struggling with theirs."

"Crap!" Nev's face flushed red with anxiety. "I'm so screwed."

"I'm going to kick your butt Nevin!" Landon taunted his Lil laughing as he did so, finding it hard to be mean and keep a straight face.

Virgil tightened his grip on Soul Reaver the flames running along his left arm growing slightly. "I don't care if they are our Bigs, we push them back like anyone else!" Virgil did his best to encourage his teammates.

"Easy for you to say, you're not going up against Gabriel," Rowan said with a nervous laugh.

"Big Show," Virgil said to Rowan holding his arms out, "This is your moment to shine! You want to be the best in the fraternity, taking down Gabriel earns bragging rights," Virgil encouraged him. Rowan seemed to like that idea, readying his katana he charged Gabriel. LionsHeart was one of the greatest Devil Arms Virgil had ever seen. Gabriel's longsword was regal, it had been crafted for immortal hands. Gabriel playfully swatted Rowan's first few attacks, he was enjoying his Lil's fierce determination to triumph.

Vahn's Furybrand came hammering at him within seconds. Virgil had trained the most with his Big and knew his moves better than any brother. Virgil defended the first few hits, wanting Vahn to leap into his attack. Vahn had a tell for when he was about to step into a swing with full momentum. Virgil had practiced enough to see it in his eyes, subtle body language, and he planned to use it against him. Vahn gave the signal, he hit Virgil hard, and when he backed up to regain his footing, he was getting ready to finish Virgil.

Vahn lunged forward, and Virgil dodged to the right, Vahn had anticipated this, hitting Virgil hard knocking Soul Reaver out of his hand, and Virgil to the ground. Vahn rounded on Virgil ready to tap him on the shoulders a few times to begin his timeout. Anger licked at

Virgil's thoughts, his Big had tricked him, he'd read his thoughts and played him like a fiddle. Why should they deserve to win? Because they are the Bigs? Virgil's brow furrowed with darker thoughts, he didn't want his Big to think himself superior simply because he was the Big. Virgil snapped his fingers and flames began to gather in his palm. Virgil didn't have a spell in mind as Vahn came at him, he held the fire in his hand controlling it on pure emotion. Vahn was upon Virgil, his sword coming to finish him. Virgil swung his hand out and desired the fire to grow. The flames rocketed out of Virgil's hand blasting forward with such force it blew Vahn into the air. He landed on the ground coughing and rolling. He had natural resistance to fire as he was aligned with it, and Furybrand had got the brunt of the blast. Virgil felt surprisingly well after using the flames, in fact it didn't feel like that had pulled from his aura at all! It had felt like the fire was responding to Virgil, Virgil willed it, and the fire responded of its own volition.

Virgil got to his feet, his black Devil Arms symbol glowing, Soul Reaver vanished from existence where it lay across the grass from him, and in a black fiery cloud of smoke it reappeared in his left hand. Nev and Landon were evenly matched and still struggled, sending spells at each other. Selene had out maneuvered TK and had gotten three solid hits on her, while getting one herself. TK admitted defeat and went to sit by the group who had moved out of the way to avoid being hurt in the fighting. Rowan fell in defeat from Gabriel, Gabriel was breathing hard and sweat had gathered on his forehead, his Lil had made him work for his victory. Selene and Virgil locked eyes, together they'd have to take on Gabriel.

Gabriel gave them both a sultry glance and beckoned them with a hand to make their move. Virgil and Selene quickly moved across the clearing approaching Gabriel carefully. Gabriel was fast, if they worked in tandem, they could out maneuver him, barely. It was hard to keep pace against his attacks, he was relentless, his stamina and effort never seeming to waiver a moment. It was what made him such a great warrior and leader, he had something fueling him that couldn't be taught...passion and heart. So much heart that he could take himself past his breaking point, on sheer willpower alone.

Selene made the first move, stepping into a powerful jab, Gabriel swung his sword down deflecting her lance into the ground. Virgil swung his scythe in response. Gabriel was like a dancer, his feet elegantly repositioning himself with fluid grace, LionsHeart deflected Soul Reaver with ease. Selene and Virgil worked as best they could to get past Gabriel's guard, after two attempts, Gabriel went on the offensive. Gabriel brought his sword down with immense force hitting Selene so hard when she blocked his attack it knocked her off balance. Virgil came in raising his scythe, Gabriel shot a leg out kicking Virgil in the abdomen, causing him to back up sucking at air as the wind had been knocked out of him.

Selene was able to block Gabriel's next blow, she didn't look like she could take much more from LionsHeart. Virgil caught his breath and charged Gabriel. Gabriel slammed a fist to the ground, the earth around Virgil began to shift thrusting straight up throwing Virgil into the air, he landed hard on his back. Virgil watched dazed as Gabriel managed to knock Selene back, then lightly rapped her on the shoulder, she nodded in defeat. Virgil struggled to his feet, Gabriel hadn't forced Virgil down yet.

"Just you and me bud," Gabriel said to Virgil twirling his sword around by the hilt as he slowly walked closer.

"You're not getting past me," Virgil defiantly told Gabriel, Soul Reaver firmly in his hands.

"Who do you think you are, talking to me like that?" Gabriel asked him confidently, running forward and lunging at Virgil with Lionsheart.

Virgil was nearly overwhelmed, Gabriel was a masterful warrior, and he had gained harmony with his Devil Arms. Their blades became locked and Virgil strained against Gabriel's strength. Gabriel roared fiercely, and his fist came out to connect with Virgil's jaw. Virgil went down, losing his balance, he fell back into the grass.

"Stay down!" Gabriel commanded as he walked past Virgil. "I see their flag!" Gabriel called excitedly to his group receiving a cheer from the growing group that were sitting down.

Virgil took a deep breath and got to his feet.

"Gabriel!" Lamar called out.

Gabriel turned to see Virgil on his feet, scythe in hand. "You still haven't had enough?" he asked Virgil with a cocky and irritated attitude.

"You think you're better than everyone Gabriel?" Virgil asked his Hegemon. "I'm not someone you can just push over. I will never, Stay, Down!" Virgil screamed the black flames along his scythe and arm growing from their small stature just above the flesh to tall angry columns.

"You want a fight Virgil?" Gabriel asked him, his cocky demeanor morphing to anger of his own. "You were MY pledge! No matter how powerful you become, I will never fear you!" Gabriel yelled.

Virgil charged Gabriel attacking him ferociously with his scythe, Gabriel blocked his attacks, Virgil drove him back with each slash. Virgil was a madman, something deep inside him having incurred injury, the fuel of hate, hubris of man…his pride. Virgil knew what he was

worth, as arrogant as that was, he was cognizant of his place in the world. He had slain an Arch

Demon with Ragnorak, something he wasn't entirely confident he could duplicate. Virgil felt he

could take Gabriel down if he wanted to, if he really wanted to. Virgil fought hard against his

teacher, his anger and rage boiling inside him. Gabriel slipped past Virgil's reach and hit him

hard on the side, Virgil's ribs bruising, his lungs feeling like they couldn't get air. Gabriel

stabbed Virgil's chest and Virgil was knocked down, his body aching as he struggled for breath.

Lionsheart hadn't pierced his flesh, though the attack had still caused damage, Virgil's chest

already bruising beneath his clothing.

"Just because you are a Seraph, doesn't make you better than the rest of us," Gabriel spat

at Virgil. "You're still mortal, like any other Nephilim."

Virgil started getting up, Gabriel hit him hard across the chest with his sword, "Stay

down!" Gabriel commanded.

"Knock it off Gabriel," Selene called out angry.

"Stay out of this!" Gabriel shouted.

"You're only making things worse!" Selene yelled. "Be the bigger person," she pleaded

with Gabriel.

"This little fucker wants to take me on, let him!" Gabriel yelled his temper having flared.

Men were competitive, the alphas more than the rest.

"Back off!" Virgil told Gabriel his instincts telling him to fight.

"Virgil, you're technically out because you got hit at least three times," Jace called out from across the field. "Start counting your ten minutes and get comfortable, let Gabriel grab your flag already."

"You had enough?" Gabriel asked Virgil.

Virgil glided to his feet. He flung Soul Reaver at Gabriel, moving it with his mind like he was still holding it. Gabriel blocked the scythe, only to have it fly back for another attack. Virgil's fists were clenched, he was standing still, all his concentration was with Soul Reaver, it had taken months of practice to become this efficient, and he still wasn't perfect.

Gabriel became enraged as his attacks were nowhere close to striking Virgil, the scythe keeping him back at a safe distance. He shouted, "Scatter Shot!" Energy flowed from his Devil Arms forming into spear shaped rocks that sprayed at Virgil. His scythe was knocked to the ground, Gabriel ran at him, he jabbed a left hook. Virgil blocked the blow, and Gabriel kicked him quickly in the ribs causing him to stumble back, he needed Soul Reaver! Virgil commanded Soul Reaver to return to his hand, and the scythe levitated off the ground, and came spinning back.

Gabriel did a round house kick on Virgil that connected hard with his face, he was lifted off his feet, and fell to the ground hard. His vision spotted, pain thrived along every nerve ending, his brain so rattled the world swam, and he tasted blood. Soul Reaver came to his hand on the ground, though the flames along his flesh were greatly diminished. Virgil thought he should close his eyes and just relax for ten minutes, he was beaten up. Then Soul Reaver's glow intensified, Virgil opened his eyes and looked down at the scythe. It flames began to dance, Virgil stared into the fire, whispers caressed his mind, from his soul weapon. Soul Reaver's fire extended all the way up his arm. Soul Reaver did not want to stop, it wanted to fight. Anger…it was so full of rage, a wellspring of fiery hatred. Virgil had only to open himself fully to its limitless power. Virgil was frustrated at how easily Gabriel had defeated him. Virgil wanted to show him…show them all, that he was someone who wouldn't be pushed around. Soul Reaver's flames screamed and washed over his flesh, the black flames covering his entire body, he got to his feet, his determination renewed.

Gabriel had their flag in his hands he came back into the clearing on his way back to his team's base to complete the game. Gabriel's green eyes met Virgil's pure black ones, Gabriel started running, Virgil's wings burst from his back. Virgil jumped into the air, his wings beat hard, he raced ahead of Gabriel coming to land directly in his path.

"Is this how you want it to be? Is winning that important to you?" Gabriel asked Virgil.

"I'm just playing the game, same as you," Virgil told Gabriel his voice…sounded like a demon's.

"You've stepped past that," Gabriel shook his head. "You've let Soul Reaver take control of your mind."

"I'm still in control," Virgil insisted, "Drop the flag," he demanded.

"No," Gabriel said stuffing the flag in his pocket and readying Lionsheart.

Virgil charged Gabriel, fighting with a strength and speed that Gabriel could barely contain. Virgil felt his scythe brimming with power, he knew what to do. "Soul Stealer!" Virgil shouted and swung Soul Reaver in an arc at Gabriel. A wave of dark energy swam from his scythe in an arc, it blasted through Gabriel, consuming him in its fiery embrace. Gabriel was flung to the ground, Lionsheart vanished from existence, he wasn't moving. A wicked grin covered Virgil's face, he'd beaten him.

"Gabriel!" Selene screamed, everyone ran over to him.

"Is he breathing?" someone asked.

"His aura is barely visible," someone else pointed out.

Virgil's brow furrowed, he concentrated, and everyone's auras became visible. Gabriel's normally strong and vibrant aura was so weak, it barely hung above his flesh. Virgil's anger began to recede, the black flames along his skin dying down. Virgil moved towards Gabriel, he hadn't wanted to really hurt him, just show him up.

Immediately several brothers moved forward, Rowan wore a look of disgust and revulsion, coming to stand in front of his Big barring Virgil's path. They are protecting him from me, Virgil thought, horrified at the way everyone was looking at him…like he was a monster. Virgil sent Soul Reaver away and opened his wings, he leapt into the air and beat his wings taking flight. Virgil had taken things too far, let his anger control his actions. Virgil felt guilty and deeply regretted his actions. He flew over the forest reaching the Omega house in less than a minute, he came down to the ground and sheathed his wings. He went inside and upstairs to his room closing the door behind him, he laid on his bed and stared at the ceiling. Virgil prayed there was nothing wrong with Gabriel, he didn't know what he'd do if there was. How would everyone react to that? Virgil would probably be blacklisted from the fraternity, Gabriel was the golden boy of their group, the guy everyone loved. Virgil rolled over, he was just the freak, the brother everyone probably regretted joining. Virgil's stomach felt acidic, he was racked with guilt and anxiety, his mind raced with hateful thoughts, aimed at himself. He lay there tearing himself apart in his mind for who knows how long, when a knock came at his door. Virgil didn't move or respond, he didn't feel like getting yelled at, he didn't feel like talking with anyone.

Vahn came into his room and pulled the chair up next to the bed. "You okay?" Vahn asked him. Virgil didn't answer, he was facing the wall, his back to his Big. "Gabriel's going to be alright, he's a little weak, should be fine by tomorrow," Vahn informed him. Relief washed over Virgil, some of the tension that he'd been holding subsided. "I figured you'd want to know that. I also guessed you'd be beating yourself up, I know how self-critical you are."

"I'm so stupid," Virgil said feeling tears come to his eyes.

"No, you're not," Vahn said angry, "You're one of the smartest guys I've ever known."

"I fucked up," Virgil sobbed.

"Well that's a more accurate statement," Vahn admitted making Virgil laugh nervously. "Come on bud, look at me," Vahn said shaking Virgil slightly using a gentle tone, "I'm worried about you."

Virgil rolled over meeting Vahn's gaze, his Big looked sad, Virgil looked down ashamed of himself.

"Gabriel's not mad at you," Vahn assured him, and Virgil met his gaze once more. "He cares a lot about you, you know. A couple brothers were making comments about you, and he shut them all up. Saying you had a heart of gold and would fight to the death to save anyone of them," Vahn believed those words. Virgil's heart broke and the tears finally slipped out falling down his face, Gabriel was defending him even after what he'd done?

"Don't cry Virgil," Vahn said softly.

"I don't deserve any of you as friends," Virgil said closing his eyes. "I'm evil."

"Will you knock that crap off already?" Vahn demanded kicking Virgil's bed causing him to open his eyes. "Anyone who really knows you, would tell you that's a load of bull. You love so deeply Virgil, you're so compassionate about others...you inspire people, did you know that?" he asked him.

Virgil laughed rolling his eyes, "I'm a freak Vahn," Virgil's words were bitter.

"The great ones are always different from the crowd," Vahn defended his Lil, "You should never be ashamed of who you are. Take pride in yourself, I do. I was proud as hell to brag to Pi class you were my Lil. You're Virgil Pitcher, a brother of the Omegas, smart as hell, funny, kind, overly critical of yourself," Vahn sighed, "and everyone else. But you know something else?" he asked him.

"What?" Virgil asked his brow furrowing.

"You're my Little Brother, and no matter what goes down, you always will be. Which means I'm always going to be in your corner, fighting for you, even when you've stopped fighting for yourself, and you know why?" Vahn asked him his voice becoming thick with emotion.

"Why?" Virgil whispered his vision blurred with tears.

"Because I believe in you kid, and I love you," Vahn told him. Virgil started crying he got up from his bed, and Vahn embraced him.

Virgil cried as his Big held him, "I'm so sorry," Virgil said, "I didn't mean to, I can't believe I hurt him," he said letting go of the pain inside.

"I know," Vahn nodded. "I know you'd never want to hurt Gabriel. You idiots let your egos get the best of you. Gabriel knows it wasn't all you. You pushed him, and Gabriel being the competitive guy he is took things too far," Vahn shrugged. "You were both at fault."

Virgil withdrew from Vahn taking a few deep breaths to steady himself. "Thanks, Vahn," Virgil was so thankful. "I don't deserve a Big like you."

"Shut up," Vahn clipped, "I don't like hearing you knock yourself down."

A knock came at the door, Gabriel stood in the doorway. "Can I come in?" he asked. Virgil nodded.

"Come hang out with us when you're done," Vahn told Virgil. "Blair, Dante, and a group of us are going over to her place soon to chill, we'll be waiting for you," Vahn left the room closing the door.

Gabriel stood there awkwardly neither really knew what to say. "I'm sorry Hegemon," Virgil said staring down at the floor, too embarrassed to meet his gaze. "I'm so ashamed of myself, I could have really hurt you. I hope you know that you mean the world to me, you were my Hegemon, and I look up to you. I feel like shit…forgive me," he rambled nervously.

"I forgive you," Gabriel said simply, and Virgil looked up meeting Gabriel's powerful gaze. "I'm sorry too," Gabriel nodded. "I'm the older brother, I shouldn't have let things go as far as they did. You just, pushed my buttons. It's not often I'm challenged by someone who can actually beat me, and I don't like losing," he shrugged. "I'm not mad, we were practicing for the big games coming up, things got a little out of hand, but I'm fine," he assured Virgil. "And I don't want you sulking like you did something wrong, I already told the rest of the brothers not to bring it up to you, what happened was between you and me, it is no else's business. And I'm telling you, it is over. Water under the bridge."

Virgil nodded trying not to cry, "Thanks Gabriel," he said.

"Anytime bud," Gabriel smiled, "Now come here and give me hug already," he laughed opening his arms.

Virgil laughed and shook his head, "No its okay."

"You dick, I wasn't asking," Gabriel said and walked forward grabbing Virgil in a bear hug that crushed him. "I care about you kiddo," Gabriel's voice was emotional. "Don't ever forget that alright?"

"Alright," Virgil nodded.

"Are we good?" Gabriel asked ending the hug and holding him at arm's length looking into Virgil's eyes.

Virgil smiled, he didn't deserve friends like this, "We're good," he replied.

Chapter 14
<u>The Paladin Capital, Alexandros</u>

The day had finally arrived, the Omegas were headed to the Paladin Capital, Alexandros. Magnus had been grumpy, short with the brothers, demanding everyone go to bed early. Virgil had a large duffle bag, filled with clothes and the essentials. The brothers gathered in the living room, the Alpha sisters showed up, and the energy of the house spiked. Everyone was excited, only a couple of people present had ever seen the Capital, the idea of traveling to a floating landmass above Lake Michigan was exhilarating. Once everyone was accounted for, Magnus reminded them to leave their cell phones behind, they didn't work in Alexandros. The group left the Omega manor, walking to the temple in the woods behind the house. They entered the stone structure, taking seats while Magnus created a portal at the stone archway on the center dais. When he was finished a familiar swirling vortex of black and blue energy hovered in the air.

"All aboard!" Magnus bellowed in a deeper than normal voice.

They stepped into the portal, the disorienting feeling of being compressed began. Pressure bombarded Virgil from all sides, and a nauseating spell of vertigo kicked in. When it started to feel unbearable, they came through the other side their feet touching down on firm ground.

"WOW!" Virgil heard Blair exclaim next to him, Virgil's mouth dropped open. They stood inside a stone structure, and what lay before them was more magnificent a sight than any they'd seen before. The metropolis of Alexandros stretched out to the north, the city was massive in size, easily matching one of America's largest cities. A single mountain peak rested at the northern end of the floating landmass towering over everything. The city itself gradually rose in elevation as it stretched to the mountain's base. A castle could be seen far in the distance, at the very edge of the city, built into the mountain. The castle was like something out of a movie or a story, and its splendor had no equal in the human world below. There was a large grassy plain that formed a semi-circle on the outskirts of the city, there were several temples, with a steady stream of people flashing into existence within them. The edges of the land weren't far behind the temples, a part of Virgil wanted to walk over to the edge and look down. He could see the blue of Lake Michigan stretching in every direction like a giant sea. The entrance to the city had a make shift check point with several silver garbed Paladins as security, white wings on their backs. Blair and Virgil left the temple, following their friends down the path to the entrance of the city to get in line.

"This is incredible!" Dante was so giddy he was almost jumping up and down. "I want to go exploring!"

"Me too!" Blair agreed. "Let's ditch the group," she suggested with a grin.

"I'm in!" Virgil grinned looking anxiously around, his excitement beginning to build.

"I don't think so, ghetto Nedeau!" One of Blair's sisters called out from behind rhyming her last name. "We are all checking into the hotel as a group before anyone goes anywhere!"

"Oh merr!" Blair retorted; her earlier elation dampened.

As they approached the city's massive front gate the security's procedure was made clear. Chapters of Paladins were checking in, with their members already preregistered. The security checked each member of the group over individually, recording their Devil Arms, making certain they presented no threat to the city. Professor Ramuh walked with some Paladins past the Omegas.

"Gentlemen!" Professor Ramuh beamed warmly to his fellow fraters. "Once we get our Chapter through the gate, I will escort all of you to Good Neighbor, the hotel we will be staying at."

Professor Ramuh came up to Virgil, "Might I have a word with you Mr. Pitcher?" He asked. Virgil nodded a little surprised. Professor Ramuh wandered off from the crowd of people towards the large open plain outside the city.

"There something you needed sir?" Virgil asked Professor Ramuh after having followed him in silence for a full minute.

Professor Ramuh stopped and turned to face Virgil, he produced a white glove with a glyph on the top, a few feathers were tied near the entrance were a hand would fit. "This is for you," Professor Ramuh told Virgil. "It is a gift from the Grand Prytanis. Wear it over Ragnorak," Professor Ramuh suggested.

Virgil took the glove, it felt soft and expensive. The glyph was obviously magic of some kind. Virgil did as he was told, placing the glove over his right hand. It was comfortable, and stylish.

"Amazing," Professor Ramuh said in surprise.

"What now?" Virgil asked looking up at his fraternity advisor.

"Ragnorak, your Devil Arms…its completely vanished," Professor Ramuh told him.

"It is just covered up by the glove," Virgil said plainly not seeing what was so special about a glove covering his Devil Arms symbol.

"No, you don't understand. I can't see the glove at all, now that you put it on. It looks like you just have an ordinary plain right hand, with no Devil Arms" Professor Ramuh told him.

"What?" Virgil asked looking down at the white glove.

"Grand Prytanis Aseril, the Second Seraph, made that himself. It has a very powerful glamour spell, meant to conceal your Creation Devil Arms while you're here. None of the guards spell detectors will respond to it."

"People aren't supposed to know I'm the Redeemer," Virgil guessed as to the purpose.

"When it's the right time, I am sure the Grand Prytanis will help you, he's the Oracle you know. You'll be free to wander the city in the safety of amenity. If people knew who you were, you'd have mobs of onlookers following you everywhere, staring you down, asking you questions, wanting intimate personal details of your life."

"Sounds like paparazzi, more of a celebrity's problem don't you think?" Virgil asked.

"The Seven Seraphs ARE celebrities of our race. Each is powerful enough to slay hundreds on their own, good or bad, they are respected and feared. Paladin legend and myths have spoken of the Seven Seraphs since before our founding," Professor Ramuh explained.

Virgil's group was next in line at the gate. He wanted to explore the city with Blair, Birdy, Louie, and Dante. He imagined what it would be like if EVERYONE knew his secret, following him around, pestering him constantly, Virgil shuttered. "Maybe this is for the best." Virgil followed Professor Ramuh back to the group.

A Capital Paladin guard ushered the Omegas forward. "Chapter ID," he asked.

Magnus, Gabriel, and Tarek were at the front of the group. "We are the Upsilon Delta Chapter, members of the Omega fraternity," Magnus told him.

The guards went down the list and briefly met with each of the registered members. When it was Virgil's turn the guard asked him, "Name."

"Virgil Pitcher," Virgil told him.

"Devil Arms?" he asked looking to examine Virgil's symbol.

"Soul Reaver," Virgil told him.

The guard did a double take, "What did you say?" he asked Virgil.

"Soul Reaver," Virgil said again trying to keep his face from growing red.

"Like the first Death Dealer's Devil Arms? That Soul Reaver?" the guard asked and another guard who had overheard game to over to them.

"Is there a problem?" he asked them.

"This…Paladin, has a Chaos Devil Arms, he says it's named Soul Reaver," he told his coworker.

"What the?" he looked at Virgil's symbol and took a device that was magicite and spoke into it like a walkie talkie. "We're going to need back up at the main city gate," the magicite glowed when he talked.

"Roger that," a voice called through the other end.

"I don't believe that will be necessary," Professor Ramuh said approaching Virgil and the guard. "The boy has done no wrong."

"He wields Soul Reaver!" the first guard yelled his mood elevating as his tone shifted, he was on edge. "That's the Devil Arms Loiken, Son of Lucifer, used to almost enslave our entire race!"

"Now it has fallen into the hands of a much more noble heart," Professor Ramuh told them. "The Grand Prytanis is aware of his impending arrival, as is the Grand Pylortes, Master Rasler. I am sure neither would appreciate you discriminating against a fully initiated Paladin," Professor Ramuh spoke quickly with a dangerous edge to his words. The guards went quiet sharing a look.

"Virgil Pitcher, Upsilon Delta Chapter, Devil Arms Soul Reaver, aligned with Chaos," the guard made note of on his records unhappily.

"Actually, I'm aligned with spirit," Virgil corrected the guard.

"Hmph," the guard huffed at Virgil his nostrils flaring looking down at his black Devil Arms in disgust. "You're aligned with Chaos," the guard corrected him firmly.

"Spirit is both Creation and Chaos, they are two parts of the same whole," Virgil tried to explain. The guard did not care walking onto the next person.

"I am sorry you had to go through that Virgil," Professor Ramuh said as they walked through the gate into a wide city street that emptied into a massive circle several blocks in. "Unfortunately, you just had a taste of one of Alexandros' most prominent and seldom discussed social problems," Professor Ramuh told him.

"What do you mean?" Virgil asked. "I thought this was the Nephilim Capital of the world, a bastion of culture, knowledge, and safety for our kind."

"Over time spanning thousands of years isolated from humans, this city has its own customs and culture. The people who live here, have developed an air of superiority. They think of people, human and Nephilim alike, who live on the Earth below as lesser. Racism runs heavily within our people, something most Omegas aren't exposed to living in the human world," Professor Ramuh said sadly.

"Racism?" Virgil asked unhappy. Nephilim were just as petty and hateful as humans.

"Nephilim with wings are considered superior," Professor Ramuh put it plainly, admitting it for what it was. "Be cautious as you explore," Professor Ramuh warned Virgil. "A common misconception of the people here is all Nephilim who wield Chaos Devil Arms are tainted, and inherently evil. A fear born from hatred and suffering at the hands of Death Dealers," Professor Ramuh's words hit Virgil like walking into a brick wall. "You may encounter some hostility, just be polite, and remove yourself from their ignorant presence."

"I won't start anything," Virgil nodded acknowledging his warning.

"Good lad," Professor Ramuh clapped him on the shoulder. Ramuh led the Omegas to the busy town circle, shops and people were both in abundance. The locals seemed somewhat perturbed with the tourists, they remained cordial nonetheless in their interactions. The people of Alexandros wore their wings on their backs, and wore fancy robes of white, blue, silver, and gold. The circle branched off north, east, and west, the city expanding out for miles. The large Coliseum that Virgil had heard about was on the eastern side of the city, with the castle all the way to the north. Professor Ramuh led them west down a wide main road. They passed bars, restaurants, and businesses of all kinds, one shop dealt exclusively in magicite, crystalized magical energy, for more purposes than could be listed. Virgil had never known there were so many colors and that they served so many functions. Another shop dealt in potions and herbal remedies like the witch, Ms. Morgan.

Virgil and his friends were constantly looking around, their walk was a stroll through a foreign land, there was so much to take in, it was overwhelming, in the most exhilarating sense. The people were just as interesting as the shops. Virgil had never seen so many Nephilim, most had wings, it was incredible there were this many of their kind. It was comforting, Virgil felt elated, a feverish excitement racing through his veins. After ten minutes of walking they came to a very lively road running perpendicular to the one they were on. Large buildings filled the street, and Professor Ramuh led them to a particularly charming building, with a sign reading, Good Neighbor. The hotel was like any other Virgil had seen, except everything seemed to be powered by magicite. The glass elevators appeared to float in midair, magicite propelling them without cables. Virgil was on the third floor, sharing a room with Louie, Birdy and Dante. The four were happy with their room assignment. There were two beds, Dante refused to sleep in the same one as Birdy, Virgil agreed to sleep next to Birdy. Once they were settled, they walked down to the lobby to meet with the group. Tarek was waiting, along with Magnus.

"Alright guys listen up!" Magnus called out to them. "There is a city-wide curfew at midnight for participants, no exceptions. The city guards find you wandering around after hours intoxicated you could be singled out and expelled from the games. The hotel serves breakfast and dinner daily. I recommend everyone try to utilize the food here as you'll have to pay for your meals in the city. Alexandros uses a different currency then the American dollar. Tarek has fifty silver for everyone as part of your payment for the trip. If you need more money, you'll have to visit one of the banks and exchange to Paladin currency," Magnus explained.

"Let's grab our money and go get Blair," Dante suggested.

"Money here should be easy to remember, one hundred copper equal one silver, and one hundred silver equal one gold," Tarek explained.

They were handed three attached key rings, one for each type of coin. After they took their money, and a map, the four friends left the hotel, and walked across to the street to the hotel the Alphas were at. They ran into Blair, TK, Selene, Raven, Helene and a few familiar faces in the lobby.

"What are you clowns up to?" Blair asked.

"Coming to find you," Dante told her.

"I'm actually going to hang with my sisters for a while," Blair looked guilty. "Selene is taking us on a little tour through the city ending at her parent's home in the northern district."

"Oh yeah, I forgot you're from here," Louie remarked.

"It's been a while since I lived here, though I come visit my parents every break," Selene happily said. "We're heading out boys, see you around soon!" Selene led the girls outside. Virgil and his friends left as well, Virgil started opening the map he'd taken, but Dante quickly grabbed it, and folded it back up.

"We don't want to stick out!" Dante sighed as if admonishing a child. "We have to play it cool. Let's just wander around and explore. That's the best way to see a city," excitement in his voice and a spring in his step.

"I want to do some shopping homes!" Louie told them as they walked past a string of bars and restaurants. "I need to buy some souvenirs for my folks."

"We could check out a shop, look for one that has some cool stuff in it," Birdy said.

"We have all week to go shopping, don't spend all your money on the first day," Virgil advised. "Let's explore!"

"Virgil gets it," Dante nodded. The four friends began to wander the western side of the city. It was the college and entertainment district. The Academy, the Paladins version of college, renowned the world, over had a large campus that took up the western most part of the city. This part of town had a lot of young people establishments, lots of clubs, bars, tea shops, comedy clubs, gyms, parks, libraries, restaurants, and small businesses. The people around these parts were easy going, more welcoming to outsiders.

After an hour of walking around the western part of the city, Dante led the group north, the architecture became more elegant, stunning even, as buildings got closer to the castle. Some were works of art more than houses. Virgil wished he had a camera, pictures like these would be known the world over. Louie still hadn't bought anything and started complaining. They wandered in a shop run by an older woman, she had long grey hair and wore a deep purple dress that looked more like robes. She had an amethyst Devil Arms on her right hand in the shape of a small wand. She had two large white wings on her back.

"Can I help you lads find anything?" she asked them.

"Just looking around," Dante replied with a large grin.

There were potions, and solvents that looked like they were for cleaning, different dried herbs and plants were available. Virgil wandered over to a large display of different colored stones, he started reading what some of them were for. He picked up an opal colored gem, it was no bigger than a small rock

"You are perceptive, that is a very powerful piece of magicite," the woman explained with a smile.

"What does it do?" Virgil asked her.

"That is Optimum one of the rarest kinds of magicite. The gems are capable of holding aura energy," she told him.

"What does that mean?" Virgil asked not understanding.

"Every Nephilim has an aura, over time they can grow or even diminish, and our capacity for spells is limited. Someone with a gem of Optimum, can siphon energy from their auras INTO the Optimum," the store owner explained, "storing and building it up for later. That small piece of Optimum can probably hold tenfold the energy in your aura," she estimated.

"That's incredible!" Virgil exclaimed. "I'd never heard of anything like that before."

"There are many kinds of magicite," she smiled enjoying teaching him. "I have some that can give momentary anti-gravity effects, heightened sight or smell, change your appearance, or even help you find something that is lost."

"Cool," Virgil nodded. "How much for this?" he asked holding up the Optimum.

"That is three gold coins, and I can have it fitted on a bracelet or necklace," the kind woman offered.

"I think I'll pass today," Virgil said putting it back disappointed.

The woman saw Virgil's Devil Arms for the first time as he did. She became panicked and backed up with a shout almost knocking a display over.

"Mam?" Virgil asked wondering what was going on.

"Get out!" She yelled, "Get out of my store freak!" she shouted.

"What?" Virgil asked astonished at what he was hearing. Was this because of Soul Reaver?

"What's going on?" Dante asked quickly coming over to them, Birdy and Louie hot on his heels.

"Virgil what did you do?" Louie asked like a parent admonishing a child.

"I didn't do anything!" Virgil exclaimed. "She saw my Devil Arms symbol and freaked out."

"Take your Death Dealer friend and leave my shop!" the woman yelled at Dante.

"Excuse me?" Virgil asked his pride making him angry.

"Virgil is one the best damn Paladins there is! And I don't want to be in a shop where the owner is a judgmental, prejudice, intolerant, old bat!" Dante shouted back.

"OUT!" She shouted.

They quickly left the shop, a few men in their forties with wings on their back were out on the sidewalk, and they approached the Omegas. "You guys causing trouble for Lady Tori?"

one of the men asked. "We heard her shouting. She's run business in this part of town for over forty years. We don't need no trouble from Lambs like yourselves," he spoke harshly.

"We didn't do anything wrong," Virgil said defensively, "We were just leaving, excuse us," he motioned to his friends to follow him.

The men stepped forward almost like they didn't want to let them through, this could get ugly Virgil thought.

"Is there a problem, gentlemen?" A woman asked quickly coming into the center. She was in her fifties and tall for a woman, with graying sandy blond hair, dazzling white wings, and a bold beautiful blue Devil Arms symbol on her hand. She exuded class, elegance, and authority. The men's demeanor instantly shifted; they were no longer hostile but apologetic to this woman.

"Lady Jeter, these boys were causing trouble for Ms. Tori and," the man explained.

"These boys are clearly from out of town, they don't know our customs and shouldn't be shunned for their ignorance," Lady Jeter admonished.

"Wait Lady Jeter," Virgil thought out loud, "Do you know a Tarek Jeter?" he asked her.

"Of course!" she smiled brightly, "He is my son."

"We're Tarek's brothers!" Louie exclaimed almost jumping into her arms, as if crying out to be saved. Dante rolled his eyes at his Asian friend, as if to say, grow some damn balls.

"Omegas!" Lady Jeter cried out. "Come back to my home, Tarek is there with a few others, I'll take you there," she offered them. They followed Tarek's mother, she was very friendly, and Dante hogged the conversation the entire walk, a few minutes further north into the city. Lady Jeter's manor was four stories high, not very wide but long, with a small iron wrought fence enclosing a small front landing with a few flower beds and some grass. Buildings were packed densely together.

Inside there were seven brothers, Tarek, Gabriel, Vahn, Magnus, Lamar, Jagger, and Rowan. They greeted the others warmly and everyone took a seat in Lady Jeter's living room. Tarek's mother had a strong presence, with an iron determination, sharp mind, and deep sense of justice. Virgil remembered from Tarek's interview his family was one of the well-known noble blood lines in the city. And apparently Selene's family was just as high up, surprising that such powerful families had children who chose to live on Earth with humans.

"Those guys really changed their tune when you showed up," Louie laughed. "They went from tough guy bullies to whimpering sissies!" Lady Jeter blushed slightly and tried to hide a smile.

"They were probably scared of her," Tarek laughed. "My mom's legendary among the Paladins," he told them.

"Tarek!" Lady Jeter snapped. "Please don't embellish," she said obviously downplaying herself, Virgil liked her already. "The Jeter family is one of the older more respected houses, that's all it was," she told the boys wanting to keep up her innocent mom appearance. Underneath Virgil was betting she was a fierce warrior, like mother like son.

"That was ridiculous!" Louie said breaking the silence of everyone drinking, eating and reflecting on what had just happened. "Are people up here racist or something? We're Omegas which means we're Paladins right?" Louie asked the group.

"It is more complicated than that," Tarek sighed. "People who live here think your importance is based on one thing."

"Purebloods and Pureborns are considered the elite," Lady Jeter said simply sitting down in the red chair centered at the head of the room, her chair. She set her tea down. "Being half human and half Judge fully, insures you all the privileges and amenities available in this fine city. As you know many Nephilim, especially the ones who join Paladin fraternities and sororities, are not. They may have an eighth Judge blood in their veins, if their grandparent was a Pureblood. Someone like that would have little chance of having wings and may not even produce a Devil Arms without the Oath of the Paladin. Those Nephilim are looked at as weaker. This distinction is made clearly apparent by the ability to manifest wings," Lady Jeter pointed out.

"Wings are everything," Gabriel agreed, "That's like the unspoken rule of our race."

"All Pureblood Nephilim have wings and Devil Arms," Lady Jeter said.

Virgil remembered walking the streets of the city, so many people were walking around with their wings on their back, out in the open. There were no humans here, no reason to hide who they were.

"All who live here wear their wings permanently throughout the day," Lady Jeter explained. "It is a sign of nobility, as those citizens without wings are clearly low born and not Pureblood," She had wings Virgil took notice. He thought she must wear them permanently like the others here. That made Virgil wonder if Tarek wore his permanently when he lived here too. Virgil looked over, Tarek's wings were not out, still hidden, like a Devil Arms that was in a dormant state.

"I didn't realize this was such a big deal," Virgil said surprised. "Having wings, being Pureblood, it is not something the brothers ever talk about," he admitted.

"Omegas are sheltered from what life is like living solely among your own kind," Lady Jeter said with a smile. "Most of your brothers grow up in the human world, most of you are more human than Judge, more a part of their world than this one," she spoke with a soft tone and a dreamy look. "That's why I encouraged Tarek to study at a University in America, so he could see another side to our people. One not so…steeped in bloodlines, tradition, and hierarchy," Lady Jeter said.

Virgil laughed. The guys and Lady Jeter looked to Virgil, "Oh sorry," Virgil said, "It's just, that sounds like our fraternity to a tee, tradition, and bloodlines. We have that stuff in Omega."

"Yes, with brotherly love, in this city you get crushed if you don't play by the rules," Lady Jeter said firmly.

"Wow," Louie exclaimed.

"Mom, come on, it's not that bad," Tarek sighed. "Don't freak my friends out. Things have been getting better," he pointed out.

"What's changed?" Gabriel asked with genuine interest.

"Lady Diamond," Lady Jeter said proudly. "We have great leaders, who truly try above and beyond to lead our people into the future, yet so many want to keep things the way they have been. It is hard to let go of the past for some families."

"Who is that?" Dante asked rolling his eyes as none of the Omegas knew who that was.

"One of the Grand Officers," Tarek told Dante. "She's the Grand Hypophetes."

"She is dedicated, to the people," Lady Jeter said with pride, she admired this woman. "Lady Diamond would come into the city and just wander the streets, healing the sick, praying with the hopeless, guiding the helpless. People started following her in droves looking forward to her visit each day, they truly love her. Too many of the high nobles went in an uproar, felt she was trying to seduce the minds of the people, making them worship her and perhaps ensure her ascension to the throne of Alexandros. All nonsense of course," Lady Jeter sighed with an eye roll. "Petty words from men of power, with inflated egos, who wish to stay in power. It turned into an ugly mess for a short time, in the end she stopped helping the citizens as much. She still comes around every so often, to help a truly needy family, or solve a dispute before it escalated into something irreparable."

"Mom and Lady Diamond," Tarek said rolling his eyes. "She can do no wrong where you're concerned."

"She's been a trustworthy friend in a sea of liars and fakes," Lady Jeter nodded. "More than that, I feel she is the leader our people deserve. Enough about Alexandros' politics and its leaders tonight!" she cried. "Tomorrow the Tournament begins, and things will get serious for everyone. I want to hear some fun stories about my boy!" she laughed.

"Where should we begin," Gabriel started laughing sharing a look with Vahn, the room quickly filled with laughter. They told Tarek's mother all the horrible shenanigan's her son got himself into, it felt good to reminiscence with people who cared about each other. After several stories Lady Jeter began to make dinner for the boys, they looked around the Jeter Manor which had been in the family for over ten generations. It made Virgil's childhood home look like a one room loft. Virgil was fascinated by how different life was up here, it was reflected in the home as well.

Dante suggested their group take off and head back to the hotel for dinner, as there were already eleven brothers there. Virgil left with Louie, Birdy, and Dante and they walked the streets of Alexandros once more. It was late afternoon with sunset a few hours away. A couple blocks from Tarek's home Virgil realized he forgot the pouch with his silver coins at Tarek's.

"Guys hold up I forgot my money back at Tarek's," Virgil said.

"Want us to wait for you?" Birdy asked him.

"I'm starrrrrving yo!" Louie complained.

"Virgil, do you mind if we take this hungry panda back to the hotel? He'll whine the whole time if we don't," Dante sighed.

"Sure," Virgil said with a big smile, "Go ahead, I'll catch up."

"Thanks!" Louie yelled, and his three friends continued the walk back to their hotel. Virgil turned around and went back the way they'd came; the Jeter manor was towards the middle of the northern district. Virgil kept his pace quick and made sure not to make eye contact with people, he still enjoyed looking around all the same, a smile plastered across his face like a grinning fool. Even if there were problems here, it still felt great to be around other Nephilim.

"Look at the little Lamb, crying! Get up little Lamb!" Virgil heard cruel taunting drifting down a small side alley. With it came the sounds of fighting, or at least, someone getting beat on. Virgil was walking down the alley before he'd even had time to decide if he should. Something inside him felt scared, concerned for whoever was on the other end of that hate, and it shook a primal force in him, something animalistic. People who purposefully slung hateful speech to inflict pain, people like that needed to be put in their place.

Virgil came around the corner to see a small four-way crossroads in the sidewalk, there was a bench and a lamppost, a small set of stairs led down to a home or a business back entrance, the street continued east, north, and west from where Virgil emerged. There was a boy on the ground, he was around fifteen years old, and didn't have a Devil Arms yet. A group of men surrounded him, they looked to be the same age as the Omegas, ranging from eighteen to early twenties all with wings, all of them had Devil Arms. The leader of the group was a tall and well-built man, with looks that rivaled Gabriel's. He had a strong jawline and piercing eyes that betrayed a deep intelligence. The handsome man went to kick the boy, Virgil yelled out, "Knock it off!"

"Who the hell are you?" the leader asked with a smirk on his face finding Virgil's interruption humorous.

"Leave this guy alone, and be on your way," Virgil told them doing his best to keep his voice even and sound confident, as the five guys quickly turned their attention to him. Nerves were beginning to take over, his earlier adrenaline rush crashing hard, his hands and breathing began to betray his anxiousness.

"Some little Lamb from the surface coming to protect one from our city!" He cried out getting a laugh from his collection of friends.

"Look at his Devil Arms, this guy's aligned with Chaos!" one of the cronies commented.

"You invite some Death Dealer scum into our city to protect your worthless hide," another of the men asked the boy.

"I could hear you beating on him from the street!" Virgil yelled in the leader's face. "If there is one thing I won't tolerate, it's a bully," his words strong with anger, his confidence coming back to him.

"Its fine," the boy on the ground said meekly looking Virgil in the eyes, "Walk away." Virgil saw pain, sadness, and the will to fight having been beaten out of him long ago…the hell he would!

"I'm not going anywhere," Virgil said walking to stand in front of the guy who still hadn't gotten himself off the ground. "Get up," he told the boy.

"Stay down!" the bully commanded.

"He doesn't get to decide who you are," Virgil told the boy who looked like he was about to have a heart attack. "Only you get to choose who you will become. Can you lay down and accept this as your life? Filled with taking their hateful words of poison like a daily supplement, or will you rise up, take control, and let it be known you'll not swallow one more day of this abuse!" Virgil felt his pulse racing staring the boy down. He looked up at Virgil and nodded, he got to his feet.

"You obviously don't know how things are done around here," the man's tone was dangerous. "This boy is from the orphanage, no parents, no bloodlines, maybe no wings. He is a nobody. I'm going to give you three seconds to get out of my sight, before I kick your ass off Alexandros, back down to the muddy slop of dirt you call home, filthy Lamb!" he said the word like Virgil's blood was dirty. The bully had a Creation Devil Arms, the white sword symbol pulsed with light, responding to its master's emotion. Virgil clenched his fists at his side Soul Reaver beginning to blaze with black light.

"Axion Whitefeather!" a feminine voice rang out into the alley. "I am ashamed at what I've heard!" she said walking into view coming down the north part of the intersection. She was a gorgeous teenage girl, a few inches shorter than Virgil, with waist length golden blond hair, white wings resting on her back, and striking sapphire blue eyes. She had a Creation Devil Arms symbol on her right hand, hers was in the shape of a long spear with curved blades on both ends.

"Alexa!" Axion said sounding very surprised.

"You're picking on Verchiel again, I told you to leave him be!" she yelled walking over to the boy standing beside Virgil. "Are you alright?" she asked him.

"I'm fine mi'lady, please, don't bother yourself with me," Verchiel bowed to Alexa.

"Nonsense!" Alexa waved off his concerns, "We're friends. Now, go home alright? And try to avoid trouble on the way, I'll see you around soon! If ANYONE, is rude to you between now and then, I'll pay a visit to them personally," she spoke with such a forceful tone, Virgil thought she could give Selene a run for her money. Verchiel hurried out the way Virgil had come.

"I've come by your home to call upon you, you're never available to go out," Axion said to Alexa pouring on the charm. He was stunningly attractive, with a dazzling smile, if Virgil hadn't seen him impersonating a slimy serpent moments before, he might have believed the show.

Alexa locked eyes with Axion, she was not someone who could be pushed around. "I'm not interested Axion," her words were sharp, brimming with emotion, almost yelling. "And I never will be! Stop asking my grandfather for permission to court me, because IT ISN'T HAPPENING!" she yelled at him.

"You've never even given me a chance," he told her his upper lip curling in annoyance.

"If ever I was interested, listening to how you spoke to Verchiel and this foreigner, it was enough to sicken me to my very core. You're handsome, intelligent, and powerful," Alexa noted looking Axion over. "You're also a spoiled brat, who values power and rank above all else. I could never love someone like you," she shook her head in disgust.

"Let's go!" Axion told his friends and the group left. Axion stared Virgil down as he left, Virgil had a bad feeling he'd be seeing the jerk in the Tournament, he'd felt incredible power from Axion's Devil Arms.

"I'm sorry about that," Alexa beamed at Virgil, "Thank you for defending Verchiel. He's a great guy, just shy. He gets bullied because he doesn't have a house name, most Nephilim in the city like that don't get wings," she said embarrassed.

"It was nothing," Virgil felt himself grow red. "I heard some commotion, and before I realized it, I was halfway down the alley."

"I'm Alexa," she said extending her hand.

"Virgil," he said smiling taking her hand.

"So where are you from Virgil?" she asked him.

"Michigan, in the United States," Virgil explained.

"Oh, so not too far away," Alexa nodded. "You're here to compete in the games I take it?" she asked.

Virgil nodded. "I'm an Omega. I'm here with my fraternity brothers, first time in this city. It's an amazing place," he said looking around.

"It is beautiful," Alexa commented as if the statement were to the contrary. Virgil gave her a puzzled look. Alex shook her head, "Alexandros truly is a marvelous city. Sometimes I stare at the world below however, thinking of all the people down there, and wish I could see it for myself."

"You've never been out of the city?" Virgil asked surprised.

"No," Alexa said sadly.

"There is an entire world out there, to see and discover!" Virgil exclaimed. "You have to explore it someday."

"Have you seen it?" she asked him. "The world?"

Virgil laughed, "Truthfully I haven't seen much outside of Michigan. My parents took me to Florida a couple times. and we went to Canada one weekend, that's about it."

"There is an entire world out there," Alexa said to Virgil mocking him, "What are you waiting for?" she asked laughing.

They sat down on the bench and began talking, about everything and nothing. Alexa was so easy to talk with; Virgil hadn't felt an instantaneous connection like this since when he'd first made friends with Blair. Virgil strangely felt so…comfortable around Alexa, like they'd known each other their whole lives. Alexa was sixteen years old, still a student in the equivalent of

Alexandros high school. She was entering her final year of school in the fall when she turned seventeen. They liked a lot of the same things, and she knew a surprising amount about video games, a topic that Virgil could talk about for days. Apparently she'd gotten a gaming system smuggled into her home, she was crafty and kind. They were good at making each other laugh, and the time slipped beneath their notice until the dying light of the sun began to streak the sky.

"Oh no, my friends!" Virgil remembered he was supposed to have met his friends. "I was supposed to be at the hotel hours ago. I better get going," he said getting to his feet.

"Dinner is long over by now," Alexa broke the bad news to him. "You'll have to go to a restaurant in the city," she advised.

Virgil sighed, he didn't even have his money on him, let alone know which place he wouldn't get thrown out of. "Got any suggestions?" Virgil sighed feeling a little defeated his stomach rumbling with the beginnings of hunger pain.

"Why don't you come back to my house for dinner?" Alexa volunteered. "I don't have guests over often, I'm sure my mother would love to meet you! I can already tell she'd like you," Alexa giggled.

"Why is that?" Virgil asked.

"You're so sweet and polite, you're kind Virgil, it is part of who you are," Alexa said.

Virgil laughed, "We barely know each other! How could you possibly know me well? I could be dangerous," he warned her. "Just look at my Chaos Devil Arms. I was already thrown out of one shop today. It's not good to be too trusting of strangers."

"You're a better person than Axion, obviously the color of one's Devil Arms isn't a reflection of everything inside," Alexa smiled brightly at Virgil making him feel good about himself. "Besides I feel like I can trust you, sometimes you make a friend, and instantly you have chemistry, and it feels like you've been friends for years. Right away you know that this is going to be a friend for life...that's kind of how I'm feeling about you," she told him with a shy smile her cheeks blushing slightly.

Virgil felt the same way, he barely knew Alexa and already he felt he could make observations about her as well. She was strong willed, stubborn, funny, caring, and a little on the ridiculous side. He grinned at her letting her know with his eyes and face he felt the same.

"Alright, I'm starving, let's go!" Virgil decided this would be best. They continued talking the whole way back to her home. The further north they traveled the more concerned Virgil became, as the houses were thinning down.

"Where do you live exactly?" Virgil wondered.

"We're almost there," Alexa told Virgil as they walked up a winding gradually sloped path.

They got to the top, there weren't any houses left, Virgil stared ahead realizing they were on the approach to the castle gates.

"Wow, wow, wow!" Virgil said coming to a stop. "Are we going to the castle?" he asked surprised staring up at the towering structure built into the very mountain. "You live at the castle?"

"Yeah," Alexa said not meeting his gaze. Virgil wanted to run right then and there. Alexa looked up at him locking gazes with him seeing his hesitation. "I don't have many friends, people are scared to get close to me because of who I am, and those that aren't usually just want to be close to me to use me. You can go if you want," she said trying to sound indifferent. "I won't hold it against you."

Her words struck Virgil, he felt bad for his momentarily hesitation, she didn't deserve that. "Alexa, who are your parents exactly?" Virgil asked her.

"My mom is Sibylla Diamond, the Grand Hypophetes," Alexa answered. "My dad died several years ago in a battle with some Death Dealers."

"I'm sorry," Virgil said looking down.

"It's okay, my mom and I are close, and I have always had my grandfather. He's been like a second dad to me," Alexa said happily. "He's a little rough around the edges though he's really loving on the inside."

"Okay, but why do you live at the castle?" Virgil asked still not understanding.

Alexa sighed, "Because my grandfather is Aseril Diamond, Grand Prytanis of the Paladins, and King of Alexandros."

Chapter 15
<u>Dinner with the Grand Prytanis</u>

Virgil walked beside Alexa to the castle gates, the guards had some very unfriendly stares for Virgil, greeting Alexa enthusiastically. "Princess Alexa!" They cried out in gleefully campy delight. Virgil noticed these guards were friendlier than the rest he'd met. "So good to see you this evening Princess!" They also had British accents.

"Guys, please! Just Alexa, especially in front of my guest," she pretended to whisper.

"And who is this GUEST, you want to trounce on about all through the castle?" One of the guards asked with an especially snarky and sassy attitude. He popped out a hip placing his hand on his side glaring at Virgil. An aquamarine Devil Arms symbol in the shape of a trident on his hand.

"I'm Virgil Pitcher, from the Upsilon Delta Chapter," he said nervously.

"Never heard of 'em," the other guard with a deeper voice said flatly. A golden symbol in the shape of a staff on his hand.

"We've only been a Chapter for six years now," Virgil responded meekly not surprised.

"Only six years he said," the guard said to his friend.

"Not long at all I reckon," His friend shook his head.

"We got TOP Paladin Chapter award our first year as a Chapter," Virgil snapped.

"That's impressive," the sassy guard said eyebrows rising.

The other guard nodded and saw Virgil's Devil Arms, "Bullocks! Alexa what rabble is this now?" he asked motioning towards Virgil's Devil Arms.

"It's a Devil Arms, everyone in this city has one!" Alexa said stomping her foot.

"We can't exactly let someone into the castle like that without some clearance first," the sassy guard said.

"Look my grandfather is the Oracle, the Second Seraph, and *knows* everything right?" Alexa suggested, and they shared a look and then nodded in agreement. "If he would have seen a dangerous guest coming into the castle, he would have surely sent word to our two favorite loveable guards. I'm just trying to bring a friend home without having him interrogated like a criminal, if grandfather wants him out, he'll do it himself," Alexa offered.

The two guards laughed, "May the Creator have mercy on the fool dumb enough to piss off the 'ol King! He's a one-man army onto himself!"

"I'm telling him you called him old," Alexa teased.

"Please don't!" They looked genuinely fearful.

"Promise to treat my friend good and we're good," Alexa nodded with a large grin, having won.

They allowed Virgil to pass, giving him warning glares, the message was obvious, hands off the princess! Virgil followed Alexa inside and was speechless in the grand foyer of the enormous castle. There were so many halls and staircases in the massive room whose ceiling rose so high staring up at it caused things to start to spin. Alexa led Virgil through the castle straight ahead up a series of grand staircases to a higher floor with less open and more enclosed hallways. Virgil realized he could get lost in a place like this and stayed close to his new friend.

"Alexa!" Virgil heard a woman call out and he thought her voice reminded him of softly sung melodies. Alexa's mother was in her late thirties, she bore a striking resemblance to her daughter, same long gold hair, striking sapphire blue eyes, and warm presence. She had a white Devil Arms symbol on her hand.

"Hey mom!" Alexa said walking up and embracing her mother warmly. Alexa's mother hugged her daughter tightly with a smile that reached her eyes, then turned her attention to Virgil.

"You brought home a guest?" she asked smiling at Virgil so warmly he felt strange.

"Yes!" Alexa was excited. "He's a Paladin from Michigan," Alexa turned, and Virgil walked up to her mother feeling overwhelmingly nervous as he approached her.

"Virgil Pitcher let me introduce you to Sibylla Diamond, Grand Hypophetes of the Paladins," Alexa said proudly.

"Nice to meet you Lady Diamond," Virgil said bowing to Alexa's mother.

"Please! There is no need to bow Virgil," she said kindly placing a hand on the side of his arm. "In my eyes we're all equals here," she said with a soft smile.

"Thank you mi'lady," Virgil nodded.

"You can call me Sibyl," she encouraged Virgil.

"Lady Diamond will do just fine," a deep masculine voice corrected her. The Grand Prytanis came down the hall with three men walking with him, all three were talking to him at once giving reports and details about the upcoming Tournament. He was a man of tremendous stature, at 6'5 he was a wall of muscle. He had the same golden blond hair as Alexa and Sibylla, with grey at his temples going back into his ponytail. He had a long scar that ran along his check up his nose, across the middle of his eyebrows to his forehead. King Aseril had a Creation Devil Arms on his hand it looked like a massive lance. "The boy shouldn't get too comfortable, I think Sibyl is a little familiar, is it not?" the Grand Prytanis asked his daughter.

"Be nice," Sibylla admonished King Aseril.

"I invited my new friend to dinner grandpa, I hope that's okay," Alexa said to her grandfather giving him an innocent look batting her eye lashes.

The Grand Prytanis sighed and walked ahead, "I had already alerted the kitchen we'd have four for dinner hours ago!" he grumbled walking off with his advisors tailing him.

"Is it okay that I stay?" Virgil said feeling unwanted by the Grand Prytanis, he didn't want to get in trouble.

"Of course!" Sibylla replied with force. "My father does not speak for the women of house Diamond. Any friend of Alexa's is welcome here indefinitely," she declared. "Have you gotten to see the castle yet?" she asked him sweetly.

"We just got here," Alexa beamed at her mother happy at her warm welcome to Virgil.

"Dinner will be a few minutes yet, let's take a walk while we wait," Sibylla suggested with a smile, she seemed to be absolutely glowing, Virgil thought.

"You're in a good mood mom," Alexa said noticing her mother's glowing aura, did something happen today? You meet a handsome Nephilim in town?"

"Don't be silly!" Sibylla laughed. "Are you enjoying your stay in Alexandros?" Sybil asked Virgil quickly changing subjects.

"Yes, mam," Virgil responded. "It's unlike anything back in America. All the Nephilim with wings! I never knew there were so many people out there, like my brothers, like me," Virgil remarked softly. "It feels empowering, validation that I'm not so alone," he said with a smile feeling honestly happy.

Sibylla's face looked hurt at his words, her expression darkened like she wanted to cry, she kept her face turned from him.

"So, what's your family like Virgil?" Alexa asked Virgil. "Do you have Nephilim parents as well? I'm sure you do, you seem pretty powerful," she commented honestly.

"I," Virgil was quiet. He didn't know how much he should tell. He felt he could trust Alexa, and her mother seemed extremely kind, but these were powerful people, some of the most influential Nephilim in the Paladin order. Virgil didn't know what they knew about him, and he was guessing from the short interaction with the Grand Prytanis, not much. "I grew up raised by regular people, I had a great childhood, my parents were loving yet strict. I knew I was adopted. My parents were told my biological mother died giving birth to me and my father…no one knew anything about him," Virgil said not wanting to lie, and not wanting to reveal his identity either.

"Your father's probably a Judge!" Alexa cried out. "It would explain why you have such a powerful aura."

"It's not powerful, it's the same as anyone else's," Virgil brushed off her comment.

"No, it's not," Alexa said flatly refusing to agree. "I noticed it right away, Axion and his friends did too which is why they didn't hit first, ask questions later. You're not the kind of Nephilim people can push around," she said with a smile that made Virgil blush.

"In truth I kind of wish I was just a normal Nephilim," Virgil admitted to them.

"Really?" Sibylla asked him with a curious look surprised by his response, "Why?"

"Because then I wouldn't have people looking at me like I'm some sort of freak. All my life I've just wanted a place to belong, a place to call home, where I could be myself and not be judged or have expectations simply because of who I am. I want to be like my brothers, with a normal Devil Arms, and fight for everyone without it being a big deal. Sometimes I wonder what it would be like to have a normal life, and I envy people who get to be regular, like everyone else," Virgil said honestly.

"Most people would love how much power you have, and want even more," Sibylla remarked softly

"I have more than enough," Virgil sighed not wanting anymore.

"Perhaps you are not regular like everyone else," Sibylla suggest to Virgil, "Because the world had a need for you, men who are willing to go against the tide in pursuit of what's right, forgoing the easy path. The Creator seldom gives us more than we can handle, and the Creator always has a plan in place. You've been given gifts and worry that you're not best suited for them, but the Creator knows you, Virgil." Sibylla spoke, and Virgil hung on her every word. He had no response and silently reflected on her words. They went on a small tour of the castle,

Sibylla and Alexa commenting on different paintings, statues, or rooms. Alexa told Virgil they seldom entertained and most of the castle they didn't use and felt more like a museum.

They arrived at the dining hall where a massive formal table was positioned in the center. Virgil was relieved to see a much smaller, more comfortable table, on a landing off to the side surrounded by windows looking out into the clouds and the sky. Virgil pulled out Alexa's chair and then took his seat. The Grand Prytanis stormed into the room within moments, coming over to the table he kissed Alexa's forehead, patted his daughter on the shoulder, sitting across from Virgil, staring him down. Virgil tried to look anywhere except at the Grand Prytanis. King Aseril's gaze bore into him forcing Virgil to return his gaze, it was unfriendly. Virgil quickly broke eye contact, salad was brought out to them by castle staff. Alexa and Sibylla began making small talk doing their best to include Virgil.

A few minutes into salad, King Aseril asked Virgil, "What are your intentions with my granddaughter?" Virgil almost choked on his salad. He coughed hard shooting Alexa a desperate plea for help, a smoke bomb, fire alarm, anything!

"Grandpa!" Alexa admonished King Aseril. "Virgil is my guest, please don't embarrass me," she pleaded.

"I just want to make sure this boy is honorable. You can never trust boys his age!" the Grand Prytanis pointed out. "Virgil what are your intentions with Alexa? Are you interested in courting her? Plenty of more eligible suitors running around, banging at the door, asking for her hand," King Aseril warned him.

"Father!" Sibylla yelled an angry look marring her striking features.

"Maybe I should go," Virgil said rising from his seat. "Alexa it was great meeting you. Lady Diamond," Virgil turned to Alexa's mother, Sibylla, her eyes were sad.

"Sit down!" King Aseril demanded rising and slamming his hands on the table. Virgil instantly sat back down his heart racing in his chest, the girls were silent. "I was asking a question, now kindly answer it," King Aseril ordered Virgil sitting back down and holding his fork over his food.

"I just met Alexa earlier today," Virgil explained, King Aseril looking him in the eyes as he spoke. "I came across a boy who was being beaten up, for no other reason than he was an orphan, like I was. I stopped them, and Alexa came into the confrontation before things got physical. We started talking and things just, clicked between us," Virgil smiled looking at Alexa. If they had met at Bay Valley there was no doubt in his mind, she would have fit in with the Alpha girls becoming one of his best friends. Blair would love her, they had a lot in common. "I like Alexa a lot, but as a friend. I don't have any 'impure' intentions towards your granddaughter sir, I assure you," Virgil told the King of Alexandros. "I didn't even know she was your granddaughter until we arrived at the castle, or I might not have accepted the invitation to dinner. I'm sure you know all of this already though, considering you're the Oracle," Virgil said to King Aseril. "Can't you see into the future? That's the Second Seraph's gift, right? You obviously know who I am."

"I'm sorry Virgil, I didn't mean to deceive you," Alexa said looking like she might cry. "I was having so much fun talking with you I didn't want it to end. I didn't want you to treat me different, things felt so…comfortable between us. So, I didn't tell you who I was."

"Alexa dear, don't cry over this weak man," King Aseril scoffed, "The boy deceived you as well."

"What?" Alexa asked looking at Virgil confused.

King Aseril nodded and said, "I knew you'd come to dinner the moment you left your money at Lady Jeter's home," King Aseril told him. "I also know your intentions towards Alexa are pure. Knowing something and living it are two different things. When a man is tested and pushed to confrontation that is when you see what he is really made of, what truly *will* be, free will means endless choices. Ladies allow me to introduce to you, Virgil Pitcher, son of Fallen Judge Raphael, and wielder of the Devil Arms Soul Reaver and Ragnorak," King Aseril said to his family. "Or as he is known in legends, the Redeemer, or the Reaver."

Alexa turned to Virgil surprised. Virgil figured it was no use hiding anymore, and he took off the glove King Aseril had instructed him to wear. Ragnorak's symbol came into full view and Alexa whistled in envy.

"I knew there was something special about you!" Alexa told Virgil. "You could've told me you were the Redeemer!" she said.

"You're the Sixth Seraph," Sibylla nodded looking down. "It's a great burden to bear, I'm sorry so much has been placed on your shoulders."

"Yes," Virgil admitted, "Sorry for not telling you earlier, we had just met, and I wasn't sure if I should admit who my father is…I don't want to be judged by his actions."

"Every person should be judged on their own character," Sibylla asserted.

"Virgil, it is good to finally meet you, in person," King Aseril said his aggressive tone and attitude alleviated slightly, though Virgil still felt something else beneath the surface. Like King Aseril looked upon him with less than favorable eyes.

"It is an honor to meet you sir, my Chapter Advisor, Professor Ramuh speaks of you in the highest regards," Virgil told him honestly.

At the mention of his name, King Aseril's face lit up, "That old scoundrel! What a Nephilim!" King Aseril laughed. "We've known each other since the days at the Academy, Ramuh's a true friend."

"He comes to visit on occasion," Alexa interjected, "He is one of grandfather's closest friends."

"I've heard about a great deal of you from Ramuh, he seems to think highly of you," King Aseril said. "We have much to discuss," his words sounded like it wasn't going to be pleasant.

"Virgil's our guest!" Sibylla cried out. "It's not fair if you hog him."

"I won't have you treat him unkindly," Alexa warned darkly.

"Virgil is a Seraph, he is going to be a key player in much of what is to come," King Aseril said plainly, "We'll be working closely and there are things we need to go over."

"Father, surely whatever you wish to discuss with Virgil can wait until after the Tournament?" Sibylla offered him. "We get so few visitors these days, can't we just enjoy this time together?" she asked kindly.

"Alright," King Aseril sighed. Two servants cleared their plates and brought out the main course, lots of vegetables, chicken, and rice. "Are you looking forward to the games Virgil?" King Aseril asked.

"I guess," Virgil replied, "Honestly I don't know much about what's going to happen. I'm pretty much doing what the older brothers ask of me."

"You're not from here, so it's to be expected you don't know much about them," Alexa nodded. "Their basically like the Olympics for the Paladins, only the winning Chapter is given the Chalice of Immortals to protect and safeguard."

"Isn't that the Chalice from the Oath of the Paladin?" Virgil asked remembering the story that the Jeweled Officers told new pledges on the night of bid acceptance.

"The one and the same," Alexa said grinned, "Every five years the Tournament is held to decide who the strongest warriors are of our people and they are then tasked with protecting it for the next five years. It is a tradition that has existed almost since the founding of Alexandros."

"Five families were holding out from joining the Death Dealers," King Aseril explained to Virgil. "My great grandmother many times removed, was leading them. She had a vision about this land, where the Ediolon Alexander slumbers on the mountain, watching over the fallen Ediolons below. The power of the Ediolons had infused with the land causing it to float in the sky, away from the reach of mortals. She brought her people here and founded Alexandros, in Eidolon Alexander's name."

"It is said Alexander slumbers at the top of this castle and the mountain, awaiting the day he is called upon to fight for the Creator and justice once more," Sibylla spoke softly not looking at Virgil. She met his gaze, "He is one of the Divine Nine, Eidolon of Light and Justice, patron of the Judges, he taught all of them the ways of blade, including your father."

"Wow!" Virgil exclaimed, "I'd never heard that."

"The five founding family names are still prominent in Alexandros," Alexa sighed. "The Diamonds are one family, and so is Axion's," She rolled her eyes. "Even after all these years, our family has ruled over the people for most of the city's history, mostly by election."

"There have been times when a Diamond hasn't been King or Queen of Alexandros," Sibylla added.

"It's incredible this place exists alongside everything back home," Virgil remarked. "It almost feels like another world up here," he joked.

"You'll have to take me back to college with you and show me around your University!" Alexa said enthusiastically to Virgil.

Virgil swallowed his food slowly, "That would be cool, maybe," he replied carefully. "If it was fine with your folks?"

"Absolutely not!" King Aseril barked.

"I wasn't asking you!" Alexa yelled.

"Absolutely not," Sibylla laughed. Alexa sighed dropping the subject in defeat.

Virgil looked around at the three of them, they were close, and they loved each other greatly. The three of them all had Creation Devil Arms, beautiful white symbols. "Do all three of you have similar Devil Arms?" Virgil asked them.

"Most of the people in the Diamond family have wielded lances," Alexa said proudly, "Like the three of us, the Lady Diamond of legend, our ancestor, she wielded a staff, Divine Light. The second most powerful staff in existence."

"Divine Light is the only Devil Arms that can truly defeat Soul Reaver. Our ancestor proved this when she killed Loiken, Lucifer's son, the man who wielded Soul Reaver before you," King Aseril told Virgil harshly. Virgil raised an eyebrow, okay?

"And all of your family is aligned with Creation?" Virgil asked wanting to talk about something else.

"Our family is strong with spirit," King Aseril nodded a great smile coming over his face, making him appear much kinder.

"You all wield lances?" Virgil asked.

"Not all Diamonds wield lances, but my Alexa takes after me," King Aseril boasted proudly. "She had a beautiful double-bladed polearm. My Devil Arms is the Holy lance, Gae Bolg," Aseril said smugly. "One of the mightiest of all Creation Devil Arms."

"I've heard that name before!" Virgil said remembering. "I think Rasler, wielded a lance by the name when he fought the Arch Demon."

"Rasler and I have sparred, he absorbed my Devil Arms form," King Aseril sighed not seeming thrilled with the idea of someone else using his weapon.

"Who is Rasler's family?" Virgil asked. "Are you related to him? Because I was told being aligned with Creation or Chaos was rare," he said.

"Master Rasler," King Aseril corrected him. "He grew up in the city's orphanage actually. He Awakened on his eighteen birthday and Quicksilver came to his hand, signifying his status as the Third Seraph, the Doppelganger."

"So, he was a low born citizen, who became a high born," Virgil said thinking that made some sense as to how his personality became a little hardened. "How do kids end up in the orphanage anyway?"

"Some are found on Earth or brought here by other Nephilim from all over the world," Sibylla explained. "Others are left here by Judges, Pureborns. Judges seldom claim their children, and so most Pureborns never know their lineage. We created foster families in the community to have less and less children living in an orphanage without parents. There simply aren't enough volunteer foster parents, so some get picked over."

They finished dinner, and everyone continued talking, King Aseril had mellowed out greatly and it felt nice, sitting there just the four of them. Alexa brought up the subject of cards and quickly got out a deck to teach Virgil how to play a common game in Alexandros that Virgil had never heard of. Virgil asked her if they knew how to play Euchre, a popular card game in Michigan. She hadn't, so he told Alexa he'd learn her game if she'd learn his next time. The four of them played cards together and the three Diamonds razed on each other so hard Virgil couldn't stop laughing. Alexa and Sybil liked to gang up on King Aseril, seeing as how they were the only two people brave enough in the entire city to poke fun at him to his face, and it was entertaining. They were all having fun and King Aseril was a surprisingly good sport showing a softer side to himself that Virgil felt drawn to. After several rounds Virgil was beginning to feel tired. It had been a long day and it was sure to be a busy and tiring week. He had a long walk across the city and wasn't looking forward to the trek to his bed.

Rasler choose that moment to walk into the dining room, he walked over to their table. "Evening King Aseril, Lady Sibylla, Lady Alexa," he greeted them. His face turned sour seeing Virgil. "What are you doing here?" he asked Virgil.

"My granddaughter made friends with him and invited him to dinner," King Aseril shrugged. "You need to speak with me?" he asked.

"Yes, if I could have a moment of your time," Rasler nodded.

"I should get heading back to the hotel," Virgil told Alexa deciding it was time.

"Aww already," Alexa whined.

"What time is it even?" Virgil asked.

"Close to midnight," Alexa told him.

"Oh no, there is a curfew for participants, I have to get back!" Virgil panicked.

"I can walk you home," Alexa offered. "The guards won't hassle you with me around."

"It's getting late," King Aseril said. "I don't want you wandering the streets alone at this hour."

"We could just fly there, make the trip super quick," Alexa thought, "You have wings, don't you?"

Virgil thought that over, his wings were so different they were a dead giveaway to his identity. "I have a black wing and a white wing," Virgil admitted looking at the four of them, they wore their wings full time and he admired their uniformity.

"Oh!" Alexa exclaimed, "I didn't think that was possible."

"If Virgil can conceal his identity as the Redeemer, for now that is in his best interest," Sibylla cautioned. "Once people know who Virgil is, where he lives, things, are going to start looking for him," she warned.

"Thanks for that," Virgil laughed nervously.

"We don't want that," Alexa shook her head.

"No," Sibylla agreed with her daughter. "I can walk him home," she offered kindly smiling.

"Are you sure?" Virgil said feeling bad someone important had to baby sit him.

"Of course, I don't mind," Sibylla said cheerfully. "It will give me a reason to walk around. The city is easier to enjoy under the moonlight. It is calmer, you feel like you can actually hear a little of what it is trying to say."

"It was so nice having you over," Alexa said sadly, and they got up and shared a long hug. "Promise we can hang out again," she said still hugging him.

"Of course, we're pals now," Virgil grinned, "I'm loyal to the people I care about," Virgil said honestly.

"I'll be rooting for you in the Tournament," Alexa grinned back at him.

"Virgil," King Aseril grumbled goodbye gruffly at him not bothering to stand or make eye contact.

"Your majesty, it was a pleasure," Virgil told the King slipping on the glove over Ragnorak's symbol.

"Nice to see you again Lord Rasler," Virgil said to the Grand Pylortes.

"Indeed," Lord Rasler said to Virgil, "Perhaps we'll have a chance to talk more during the Tournament. Good luck," he offered halfheartedly. Virgil didn't feel popular with the other Seraphs on his side.

"Let's be off," Sibylla nodded leading Virgil from the dining room.

They walked through the large castle out the front gates, the front guards had been replaced by night staff that were stoic. Virgil looked to the east noticing a massive boulder of blue magicite that he had not seen before, from its surface water flowed, creating a small fresh water lake that spilled down into a river that ran into the eastern edge of the city.

"It's something isn't it?" Sibylla asked pointing out the large crystal gem in the lake's center. "That magicite makes life possible on this floating land," she told him.

"Because of the water it produces?" Virgil guessed.

Sibylla nodded, "That's why the castle was built into the mountain, not only for defensive purposes but also to stay as close to the water source as possible. That magicite is in a very raw pure form, aligned with water, which it produces. Thousands of gallons flow from its surface every day! But like all good things, its power diminishes, supposedly when Alexandros was first built it was many times larger. Someday its energy will fade, and the water will flow no more," Sibylla said sadly.

They walked side by side keeping a steady gait, the night was warm as they tend to be in June in the Midwest. There were guards about, in their silver garb, patrolling the streets trying to keep the rowdiness abated. The city looked like it had really cut loose once the sun had gone down. There were bottles and food scraps laying around that hadn't been there in the daylight. A few bars were still noisy and filled with people.

"This is nothing, every night things will get a little wilder. On the last night the guards usually give up and let the people party until sunrise," Sibylla giggled.

"I bet it is exciting having so many Nephilim from all over the world, gathered together in one city, kind of like an extended family reunion," Virgil thought. Sibylla laughed at that. "Hey, is it just me, or does King Aseril not like me?" he asked. He liked Alexa's mom, and from everything Tarek's mother had said about her, he felt she was trustworthy.

Sibylla looked off into the city, "My father is a complicated man. Imagine constantly being bombarded by visions from the past and the future. The burden of the Oracle is a heavy one to bear. It takes a toll, it is sometimes hard to juggle the responsibility of the Sight, along with trying to have a normal life."

"I get that," Virgil said remembering the Judge Ipos, "But I feel his dislike is more…personal. I mean we're both Seraphs, we're allies, I haven't done anything wrong, or maybe this is about Alexa?" Virgil said thinking out loud.

"My father warms up to new people slowly," Sibylla offered. "Just be patient with him and he'll come around, he doesn't...have a good reason not to like you."

They arrived at Virgil's hotel, "Thank you for walking me home," Virgil said. He liked Sibylla, she seemed like one of those moms that was a mom to all her children's friends. "It was really nice meeting you. Alexa's lucky to have such a great family," he smiled.

Sibylla walked forward and embraced Virgil, he was taken back, and politely hugged her back. She broke contact quickly and gave him a big smile. "It was a pleasure meeting you Virgil. Alexa and I will be cheering for you in the games. I hope to see you again soon," her voice was tight like she was sad.

"Thank you, Lady Diamond, good night," Virgil said turning to the Good Neighbor entrance and walking into the hotel.

"Where have YOU been?" Virgil heard his Big ask him from across the room.

Virgil turned to see the lobby was full of guys playing cards or rolling dice, some of which were his brothers. Vahn, Gabriel, Tarek, Dante, Birdy, Louie, Nev, and Rowan were hanging out in a group. Virgil walked over to them.

"Who was that woman you were with?" Louie asked Virgil and the guys turned to see Lady Diamond walking away.

"Well what do you know?" Gabriel said, "Virgil has a thing for MILF's like his Big Brother," he smirked making himself laugh.

"Knock it off," Virgil sighed, "It is nothing like that!"

"I know her!" Tarek cried out, "That's Lady Diamond, princess of Alexandros!"

Everyone jumped up to get a look at Sibylla. The guys turned to Virgil, "Spill it!" Vahn demanded.

"We thought you'd fallen off the edge of the city and gone tumbling down into Lake Michigan," Dante exclaimed. "Your Big has been worried sick!"

"Shut it Dante," Vahn said with a chuckle, then put on a stern face as he turned to Virgil. "But seriously, I've been worried sick!" He yelled. "Where did you go? We walked around for hours trying to find you, you left your money at Lady Jeter's home," Vahn said tossing Virgil his money.

"Well I was walking back to get my money when I heard some guys beating on a young kid," Virgil said his cheeks flushing.

"Lordie hereeeee we go," Gabriel sighed. "Did you get thrown in jail?" he asked seriously.

"No!" Virgil cried, "Come on give me a little credit."

"So far you're sticking your nose in where it doesn't belong," Vahn said crossing him arms, "Continue," he demanded.

"Well we exchanged a few words, then suddenly Alexa Diamond showed up, and the guys were tripping over themselves to do as she said. Alexa and I started talking and," Virgil recalled.

"Who is Alexa?" Birdy asked.

"Alexa Diamond," Tarek said, "The granddaughter of the Grand Prytanis, Sibylla's daughter, and princess of Alexandros."

"Damn!" Louie exclaimed.

"Well Alexa and I started talking and before I knew it the sun was setting, she invited me back for dinner, so I accepted," Virgil said simply.

"You had dinner, at the castle?" Vahn asked.

"Yeah," Virgil nodded, all eyes boring into him, he checked the elevators.

"With the Grand Prytanis," Gabriel asked.

"Lucky bastard," Dante laughed.

"Here I was worried sick and you're dinning with the Grand Prytanis and his family!" Vahn exclaimed in exasperation.

"I'm sorry Vahn, I wish I had my phone. I would've called and let you know where I was," Virgil said.

"It's okay," Vahn sighed his irritation falling away completely patting his Lil on the back with an obvious look of relief, "You're safe so that's all that matters."

"Some people get all the luck," Nev commented.

"I'm kind of tired," Virgil told his friends, "I'm going to head back to my room to shower and get some rest."

"Good idea," Gabriel said, "Tomorrow is the start of the games and it's going to be a long day, get some rest bud!" The brothers hailed goodbye to Virgil, and he walked back to his room to clean up for bed. The future felt filled with promise, he was restless that night, his mind on the Diamonds.

Chapter 16
<u>The Tournament</u>

The opening ceremony started at 10am, it took place on the eastern edge of the city outside of the Coliseum in an outdoor track and sports arena that was much smaller in scale. It was separated from the residential district by the river that flowed from the giant magicite near the castle. Two large bridges were built over the river connecting the Coliseum with the city. The river flowed past emptying into a reservoir attached to a water treatment plant. The enormous outdoor track and arena had stands capable of holding thousands. The Coliseum was being reserved for the final event. The eight Grand Officers of the Paladins were present, to preside over the opening ceremony. King Aseril gave a moving opening speech and the Chalice of Immortals was presented to the crowds, the Tournament had begun.

Day one was all about physical fitness, endurance, and Devil Arms individual competitions. Races, weight lifting contests, and extreme obstacle courses were some of the events, along with javelin throwing, which only allowed Nephilim with a polearm Devil Arms to compete. Virgil was in one of the earlier events, he ran the mile race for Upsilon Delta, placing twenty-second out of four hundred Chapters. If Virgil had Ascended, his eyes going gold like a Judges, he'd have placed first. He felt proud, it had brought their team a lot of points. The competitions continued throughout the day and the brothers were given their assignments of when they had to be available. They could wander the city throughout the day, as the events went from sun up to sun down, and not everyone from Upsilon Delta had to be there at all times.

The Third Seraph, Rasler, approached Virgil after he'd come back from wandering around with his friends, "Might I have a word with you?" he asked Virgil and they walked to a secluded place where they could speak freely. "I wanted to wish you luck in the competition," Rasler said simply.

"Thank you Grand Pylortes, it is an honor sir," Virgil said trying to be polite.

"You don't have to be so formal," Rasler insisted, "We're both Seraphs. We'll be working together a lot in the future I am sure. It is important we stick together," he smiled.

"I agree," Virgil nodded, "And I want you to know you can count on me to help you out if you ever need anything."

"Good, I was hoping I could ask you for a favor," Rasler's eyes lighting up.

"Sure, what is it?" Virgil asked.

"I was hoping we could train together sometime, being two of the most valuable members of the Paladins, it is important we improve our skills and ability to fight together," Rasler suggested.

"That sounds great!" Virgil nodded. "I could use the practice, I've seen you in action, and I have a lot to learn."

"You'll get there," Rasler grinned. "We all do, growing up just takes time. It was good running into you, good luck again," he said and walked away.

Virgil ran into Alexa not seconds later, they engaged greetings.

"What did Rasler want?" Alexa asked in a sassy tone, and a skeptical glance back.

"Oh, he just wanted to invite me to train with him," Virgil shrugged.

Alexa's face became concerned, "I would be careful if I were you," she said.

"What do you mean?" Virgil asked not getting what she was implying.

"Rasler was overly friendly with my grandfather when he first got Quick Silver, but once he absorbed Gae Bolg's power, he stopped wanting to practice with him. I'm sure Rasler just wants Ragnorak's power," Alexa told Virgil.

Alexa's words rang true, Virgil nodded, "Thanks for the advice," he said making a mental promise to never let Quick Silver touch Ragnorak.

"I watched your race," Alexa told him, "You did really well! My mom and I were cheering for you," she admitted proudly.

"Thanks," Virgil smiled. "I'm a little nervous about the other events though," he nodded.

"What are you nervous about?" Alexa asked.

"Well there are lots of things I still don't know how to do," Virgil said.

"Like what?" Alexa snapped with sassy attitude, "Spit it out."

"Restoration and Bending," Virgil mumbled feeling embarassed. "Those are two categories I think I could get good at," he admitted not feeling she'd think he was arrogant. If he'd admitted that to his brothers, he didn't know if they would have felt the same. "In fact, I think I have used Bending, at least once. I've never used a healing spell, I have tried Ply, but it didn't work."

Alexa laughed, "Yeah! Ply is a water spell, you're not aligned with water, so you can't use any of those spells silly. I can teach you a few things, if you have time," she offered slyly.

"I'd love to!" Virgil grinned. Alexa led the way back into the city. Not far from the gaming area there was a large gym, in it were different sparring rooms, and weight machines. Alexa easily got them a room and they had half a gym's worth of space to themselves.

"Let's start with Bending," Alexa said, "Because it will be easy for you. Close your eyes and clear your mind," she instructed, and he listened. "Bending is about FEELING the world around you, using the matter available, calling out to the fabric of the world and using its strength. Bending doesn't require much energy. A true bender moves the element around, because the element is responding to the Nephilim's mind, doing what it desires because the matter wishes to please the bender."

Virgil snapped his finger and felt a small ball of fire in his hand, he'd used a small amount of his aura. He rolled the flames in his hand, concentrating on its warmth and power. He danced around pretending there was some music on, letting the fire dance with him. The fire flowed around his hand, extending after him to dance beside him, spinning as he spun. Virgil moved the fire through the air, making it move around before it disappeared.

"That was amazing!" Alexa said. "You've got a real talent for it. The elements respond to you, strange you are so proficient in fire and don't have a fire Devil Arms," she added.

"What does it mean?" Virgil asker her.

"You have a secondary affinity for fire after spirit. It is rare for people to be bonded to more than one element, but technically spirit, Chaos and Creation, are one entity," Alexa explained and then giggled, "You're like a walking contradiction," she rolled her eyes.

"Funny," Virgil said flatly. "So, Bending is all about feeling the element and shaping its form with your mind. What about Restoration spells? Can you teach me a few?" he asked. "This isn't so much for the Tournament as I want to be able to protect my friends if they are wounded," he said seriously.

"Of course," Alex said kindly with a big smile. "You're a good friend," she said softly almost envious. "The brothers must feel lucky to have you around."

"Ehh," Virgil shrugged, "I talk a lot, drives some of them crazy," he laughed.

"I'm surprised no one has taught you Creation spells," she wondered.

"Well, none of my brothers have a Creation Devil Arms, I'm the only one in the Chapter," Virgil mussed.

Alexa nodded, "That must have been tough," she remarked. "Trying to master your Devil Arms without a proper tutor. But you seem to be doing well for yourself! You are a Seraph like Grandpa after all. Can use you Chaos spells as well?" she asked interested.

"No," Virgil shook his head, thinking it was best not to learn spells like that. "I've never tried. Fire spells are about all I've been using."

Alexa explained there were four tiers of spells, which Virgil already knew, and six schools of magic, also known to him. Restoration was at once the most simplistic school of magic, and the most complex. Fewer Nephilim could use it than any other branch of spells. It required the user to have a very clear, and focused mind. Someone who was of stable mind and body, someone who had good and pure intentions. You had to want to pour life into a person, to save them, to protect them. There were many supportive spells, the one Alexa taught Virgil was a first-tier healing spell, Cura. It rapidly accelerated regeneration like Ply, working on oneself and up to two other people. It was more powerful than Ply and did not require constant concentration. Once the spell was cast it went to work and one could continue fighting. The downside was Creation healing cost more energy than Water healing spells. Alexa demonstrated the spell, from her Creation Devil Arms an aura of light surrounded her, and the same light shot across the room to Virgil. It surrounded Virgil, he glowed in a warm light feeling his whole-body brimming with life, mending any scraps, wounds, and relieving his fatigue. He felt well rested, like he'd just woken up. Virgil's expression became intrigued smiling at Alexa, this was a powerful spell, if he could just master it. They worked on it for an hour, and Virgil was not able to use Cura once. Alexa suggested it was easiest to learn when it was most needed. Alexa told him the higher forms of the spell were Curada, Curaga, and Curaja.

After practicing they went out to lunch together, Alexa knew of a great place down the road. They ran into Damian a couple blocks over, he was with a Beta Virgil had seen before but never officially met.

"Damian!" Virgil yelled catching his attention. Alex and Virgil walked over to them.

"How are the Games going for you guys?" Virgil asked.

"Pretty good," Damian nodded. "Trent this is Virgil Pitcher, an Omega from back home," he motioned to Virgil. The man raised his eyebrows, he looked at Virgil's Devil Arms looking confused just seeing the one. He stared at Virgil's hidden symbol on his right hand, Virgil nervously touched his glove.

"And, I'm not sure of his companion," Damian said.

"I'm Alexa," She said introducing herself, "A native Alexandrian."

"We were just getting some food would you like to join us?" Virgil asked them.

Damian and his brother exchanged looks and Damian nodded, "Why not?" he smiled.

Together the four of them walked to the restaurant, Alexa leading the way. "So how do you two know each other?" she asked.

"We're rivals," Damian told her.

"We're friends," Virgil responded at the same time. Virgil gave Damian a grimace and shook his head.

"We were roommates freshmen year of college, and joined rival Paladin Chapters," Damian told Alexa.

"Now that is interesting!" Alexa nodded, "You guys managed to stay friends?" she asked in disbelief.

"Virgil kind of insisted upon it," Damian chuckled making it sound like he had no choice. They were seated in a corner booth of the large restaurant. They enjoyed visiting with Damian and Trent, the four of them were laughing often by the end. Trent seemed cool and was one of Damian's closest friends. They liked Alexa, which pleased Virgil, what wasn't to like about her? She was confident, fiery, and had a sassy demeanor, and was sincerely kind hearted. After they were done Virgil parted ways with the group. He had to get back to the stadium to see how his Chapter was doing. Virgil hugged Alexa and she headed back home. Virgil wished Damian, Trent, and the Betas the best of luck in the Games and walked briskly back to the stadium spotting Jace and Mu easily from their tall stature in the crowd.

"How we are doing?" Virgil asked.

"Not bad, but not great," Jace answered. "We're averaging in the top quarter, but not the top twenty," he pointed out. "Tomorrow we need to do better."

"What's tomorrow?" Virgil asked.

"Tomorrow is all about Will, competitions focusing on the power of the mind, the spirit, using spells and manipulating matter," Landon explained.

"And what's the third day?" Louie asked seated close by.

"The third day is when things get heated," Tarek explained, "It is all about Devil Arms. We start having one on one matches between Paladins, in a bracket match up. As you beat out other opponents, you move up, and the closer you get to the top, the more points you earn for your group," Tarek told them. "Because one Chapter can have all their members be at the top of the bracket in the end, if they beat out everyone else. It is the day that can change the ranks the most."

"So, the third day is the most important," Virgil nodded.

"You have to do well the first two days to qualify to compete in the third day," Tarek said. "The Chapters that are in the lower quarter of the scores after day two are cut from the competition. So, we just have to stay above three hundredth place and we'll get a shot."

"So, we have a good shot," Virgil nodded.

"To compete in day three yes," Magnus said sarcastically, "To get to day four, the Finals, you have to be in the top six of all four hundred and some Chapters in points. Every point counts, every competition matters. One higher place in one competition, could be what places us in that next spot. Each time we go out there, we must give it our all, or we will be cheating our team."

Upsilon Delta finished out the day strong ranking as the 39th Chapter overall. Ranked number one was Alpha Chapter, the Chapter of Paladins from the Academy in Alexandros, the equivalent of college or a university in America. They were usually the top contenders every year, losing the previous Tournament to a Chapter from England, but they were determined to win. Axion Whitefeather was their Chapter's Prytanis and he placed first and second in the two competitions he competed in. Some Chapters had Paladins that were college athlete level talent, no wonder their Chapters did better in the physical challenges.

Day Two of the Tournament the fraternity went to the stadium with a winning attitude, Magnus was signing Nev, Nolan, Landon, and himself up for most of the competitions. Birdy was signed up for the Alteration Spell casting competition, he surprised the brothers by being gifted with wards and barriers, but not Virgil. He knew his best friend had potential and was glad he was getting a chance to show it. There was a competition in each of the six schools of magic, Alteration, Conjuration, Destruction, Enchanting, Illusion, and Restoration. On their schedule for the day they were competing in all the competitions except Bending. They hadn't signed anybody up for it because no one in the group could do it.

"Magnus," Virgil said getting his Prytanis attention. "Sign me up for Bending," he said. Magnus gave him a, 'are you stoned' look of disbelief. "I can do it!" Virgil asserted. "I first did it on accident fighting against Vahn, when we did Capture the Flag last week," he said going quiet.

"Okay," Vahn said nodding, "That would make sense. You blasted me with a spell out of nowhere, I'd never seen a spell form like that."

"Good," Magnus nodded, "Even if you can participate, that will put us further ahead with that spot then we were," he added. Virgil smiled nodding, he'd seen the empty spot the day before and had asked about it, it was the first time he'd heard about Bending. Luckily Alexa had helped him gain a little confidence.

Nev and Nolan placed in the top ten of all the competitions they were in. Magnus placed second in the Destruction spelling competition, losing to Alpha Chapter. They had a guy who had a fire staff, who was extremely talented at casting. Birdy placed in tenth in the Alteration spelling competition earing him huge praises from the brothers and especially his Big Lamar, who couldn't stop bragging about him. The Bending competition was the last of the day, everyone was ready for the games to come to close for the night. Virgil was nervous, he'd have to perform on the field in front of thousands, doing something he'd only done a couple times. He told himself he'd just try to do something interesting then end his performance. He watched with his brothers as the competition ranged from pathetic, a guy who could barely make a rock move across the ground, to breath taking. A woman from a China Paladin Chapter stood out most to Virgil. She made water dance through the air, she had dozens of different forms floating around her, some were like dragons which wowed the crowd.

It was Virgil's turn to perform and he took to the stage, nervous but ready to be done. He ran forward and shot from his hand a stream of fire, he grabbed the fire and twirled around spinning it over his head he cracked it like a whip the fire smacking down in front of him. Virgil let go of the fire and it slithered on the ground turning into a snake. Virgil willed more fire from his hand and then swung it around like a whip once more, at the snake, the snaked hissed. The crowd cheered, and Virgil earned some claps from the audience. Virgil didn't have any more ideas, so he moved his hands around and the fire picked up and began to surround him. Virgil closed his hands and spun around in place, feeling the fire, and it began to dance with him of its own accord. Virgil danced, and the fire moved like his partner, he moved with the fire mirroring him, then closed his fists, and knelt to the ground. The fire seeped into the ground dissipating from existence. Virgil got a nice reaction from the audience and earned eleventh overall.

At the end of the second day Upsilon Delta was up to 20th place. The Betas from their university were in 38th place, out of over four hundred groups that put them both in the top ten percent. The Chapter was pleased with their position and no one had any complaints. Everyone had taken notice of their Chapter, and the other Omegas at the Tournament flocked to them, everyone was saying the Upsilon Delta boys were wild! All the other Omegas wanted to party with the Upsilon Delta Chapter, and suddenly the night became full of meeting Omegas from all over the country. It was a thrill a minute for Virgil, each new acquaintance being a brother of his fraternity. After the games all the Omegas got together and partied at the hotel until 2am, when the hotel manager had to come break it up personally.

The third day of the Tournament was the semi-finals. The bottom quarter of the competition Chapters had been cut and the rest of the Chapters had their members signing up for the brackets. The rule was you had to keep the Dull spell on your Devil Arms or be cut from the competition. Spells and Devil Arms were allowed and encouraged, if someone was knocked down a referee began counting, if they couldn't get back up in ten seconds, they lost, or one side could always forfeit. There were officials running the Tournament as judges for disputes that rose. The duels lasted all day, and there were a dozen starting around the same time. They had so many going at once to speed up the process. Virgil's first fight was easy, against a Paladin from Utah, he was too green, not enough of a warrior's spirit in him. He hesitated when he tried to strike Virgil. Virgil easily out maneuvered him and beat him down with Soul Reaver. He quickly forfeited, moving Virgil up. Magnus easily won his first several rounds, then was ominously placed against a towering muscle man from a Germany Chapter. The other Paladin was built like a tank and wielded a massive mace. When the fight started the other Paladin cast Shell, a barrier Alteration spell that for a short period of time, reduces the impact and damage of spells. After this he charged Magnus like a rhino, and savagely beat at him with the mace. Magnus used spells to no avail, and when the mace was in his face, he used his Tempest Staff to fight back. Magnus used the bostaff like it was a second limb, but he got hit once too hard with the mace, and the second attack hit him right in the jaw, knocking him out for twenty seconds flat. Magnus was so enraged he lost he stormed out of the area going back to the hotel for the entire day.

Gabriel took over as the coordinator for their Chapter, making sure people were at their designated spots at the right time. Their Chapter was doing well, maybe it was from all the practice they'd put in, maybe it was all their experience in the field, or maybe it was having Lambda class around to kick their butts constantly, tough opponents bred stronger warriors. Virgil was beat out by a handsome man from Italy, his name was Ezio, and he wielded a flame spatha. Their duel lasted fifteen minutes, and by the end Virgil was exhausted, Ezio had bested him in combat. Gabriel made it into the top tiers, getting beat by Axion Whitefeather at the top. Rowan, Dante, and Tarek all made it to top positions as well, only to get beat out by Alpha Chapter Paladins. Gabriel's older brother Ezkiel was there, he came over to Gabriel after his bitter loss. Ezkiel told him that he was the better man and to not worry about the loss. Gabriel seemed to brighten up whenever his older brother was around, and with his brother's encouragement, Gabriel took the loss well. Virgil was envious, he'd never had siblings, one of the reasons he'd joined the Omegas.

At the end of the day came the announcements of Chapters placements. To no one's surprise Alpha Chapter was announced first place at the start of tomorrow's Finals. Axion Whitefeather and his Chapter of Paladins celebrated as did all the natives of Alexandros. Upsilon Delta had ranked 7th place in the overall Tournament! Out of all the Chapters of Paladins in the world, to be seventh, that was uplifting to Upsilon Delta, most of the guys got a little teary eyed, the Sweethearts were hugging the ones who needed it the most. While that was a great accomplishment, it meant they wouldn't be moving onto the Final event tomorrow in the Coliseum. They were one place off, just one. Magnus took the news the hardest, he blamed his loss against the Russian Paladin, his weakness, for the Chapter's loss of opportunity to shine.

Virgil's brothers were depressed, everyone had retreated to their rooms after the announcement came that their Chapter had placed seventh in the semifinals, only two points behind the sixth place Chapter from England. Virgil's Chapter had lost the opportunity by such a narrow margin. When they'd started this competition just two days earlier, no one was thinking they'd win, they just wanted to do their best and show the world that Upsilon Delta was one of the best Chapters of the Paladins. When they'd made it to the semifinals, their entire Chapter had started to hope, that maybe they had a shot at making it to the Finals. Virgil lay in bed next to Birdy, they were watching a movie on TV, Louie was laying on the other bed asleep, Dante had gone for a walk as he had a hard time sitting still.

A pounding came at their door, Virgil answered it, Jace was standing in the doorway, his face flushed, eyes wild.

"Emergency meeting in Magnus' room!" Jace's speech was rapid the words practically spoken together, he turned and began running down the hall, a few doors down he stopped, pounding on the door. Abe answered it, Jace gave him a similar message. Virgil was standing in the doorway like an idiot.

"Dude who was it?" Birdy asked Virgil.

"Jace, he told us to go to Magnus' room for an emergency meeting or something," Virgil said walking back into the room.

"What for?" Birdy asked.

"Not sure," Virgil replied walking over to Louie to wake him up.

The three friends hurried over to Magnus' room he was sharing with Gabriel, Tarek, and Rowan. All the Omegas who'd came to Alexandros from their Chapter were present, they were talking amongst themselves the energy of the room was starting to rise.

"Alright guys listen up!" Gabriel shouted, and the men grew quiet.

"The Grand Grammateus contacted me thirty minutes ago," Magnus told them. "Apparently the fifth-place team, a Paladin Chapter from Russia was disqualified for using magicite in the matches. The same guy who beat me," he said proudly, glad there was an excuse he could use for his loss. "Bastard hid it in his shoe. It was helping to negate the effects of spells. One of the reasons he was able to come at me, unhindered by the spells that slammed into him," Magnus said. "Magicite made his skin reflect magic like rubber! Can you believe that?" Magnus ranted going off topic.

Gabriel sighed rolling his eyes at Magnus, he took over speaking, "Anyways guys, this bumps the Chapter from the UK into fifth place, and us up to sixth place, which means," but everyone had already started cheering. Virgil rose to his feet and screamed jumping up and down, embracing the men around him, everyone was ecstatic. They'd made it to the Finals!

"The Final event starts tomorrow at noon," Magnus continued once everyone had gotten the initial excitement out and quieted down. "We will be one of six Chapters going into the Coliseum. The Chalice of Immortals will be positioned at the center, the first Chapter to have a member touch the Chalice wins the Tournament. We have to decide who we're sending in, only twelve of us can go," Magnus said and suddenly the room got quiet. That was less than half of their men. "It is imperative we only take our strongest warriors. Every Tournament at least one Paladin dies in the Coliseum. It will be cutthroat in there. Our opponents will fight to the death to stop us from winning. We need brothers who can clash head on with the competition and keep moving forward to the next battle."

Immediately several people started talking at once, saying why they should go, most of the people in the room wanted to participate. The whole room began talking, everyone wanted to be heard and everyone felt they had a right to be one of the twelve. Magnus and Gabriel shared a look.

"QUIET!" Gabriel shouted silencing the men.

"This is not something that will be open for discussion," Magnus told them, "I am the Prytanis, I will be deciding the team."

"That's bullshit!" Lamar shouted out. "We should vote."

Magnus stared Lamar down, "Lamar, one more comment like that and you can go back to your room," Magnus said with a tone that left no room for debate.

"This isn't something we are going to vote on," Magnus explained to his men, "People could die in there. This isn't a game of capture the flag with the local Nephilim women. The people in that arena aren't our friends, they are fighting to win, and willing do what it takes."

"Who is going?" Jace asked angry.

"Gabriel, Vahn, Tarek and myself," Magnus said quickly and easily, "That's four." He looked to Landon and Jagger. "What about the rest of Lambda?" he asked.

"I'm out," Landon said flatly taking off his hat and scratching his head. "Someone else can take my spot."

"He's just a lil guy," Brody said in a high-pitched falsetto tone.

"I love you," Gabriel said to Landon cracking up.

"I'm in," Jagger nodded.

"Five," Magnus crossed his arms swaying in place looking around, his gaze piercing, his mind impossible to read.

"We should take Dante and Louie," Gabriel said speaking up.

"Agreed," Magnus nodded.

"Yes!" Dante shouted unable to hold his excitement in.

"Shiiiiiit," Louie responded sinking into his chair like he was doomed.

"Dante's not even an Active!" Lamar cried out. "He shouldn't be allowed to participate!"

"Screw you!" Dante said his temper flaring, "I'm just as much a brother of this Chapter whether I'm Active or Inactive."

"Inactives shouldn't go over Actives," Lamar said shaking his head.

"Dante is one of the best warriors on our team, the other Chapters have seen this from his sparring match with that Japanese warrior earlier today. We'd be stupid not to take him," Gabriel said in Dante's defense.

"I wanna go," Rowan said speaking up. "I know I'm the new guy in the fraternity, but I hold my own. And I am the only one here with actual military experience, I work well under pressure," he argued.

"Rowan's one of our best," Gabriel said motioning a hand into the air advocating for his Lil.

"Alright, that's eight," Magnus said.

"I want in," Zender said, "You're going to need some brains on this operation besides Magnus," he said.

Magnus chuckled, "Nine."

The room was quiet, Virgil looked around, everyone had the same look in their eye, they all wanted to speak up and say why they should go.

"Well shoot, no one else is speaking up," Brody said, "I want to go!" he said laughing nervously.

"Screw you Brody, you should take me instead," Jace said jokingly.

Magnus nodded thinking to himself, "Brody will make ten," he said.

"The last two?" Vahn asked.

"I'm thinking Lamar and Birdy?" Magnus asked the room.

Virgil's face started to grow hot, he knew he had to speak up or forever hold his peace, "I want to go," Virgil told his brothers.

People got quiet, no one would meet his gaze but Magnus. Magnus looked him in the eyes and said, "Maybe you should sit this one out bud."

Virgil's brow furrowed, WHAT!? His ego and pride enraged. "I should go," Virgil argued. "If it gets dangerous in there, I know I'll be able to summon Ragnorak."

"You're not supposed to," Gabriel pointed out motioning with his hand like it was obvious.

"You said that it is imperative we take only our strongest warriors," Virgil said his cheeks burning with heat. "I am one of the strongest, and when I summon Ragnorak I am THE strongest," Virgil told his brothers hating how arrogant he sounded in part knowing he spoke the truth. "If shit hits the fan tomorrow, I want to be there to protect all of you."

"I'm fine with you coming," Gabriel admitted putting his hands up in defeat not wanting to argue.

"Who doesn't want me to come?" Virgil asked now understanding what was happening. They'd had this conversation already before most of the brothers had arrived. He looked at Magnus, his eyes told Virgil he wasn't the one who had the issue. Virgil looked around the room, spotting Vahn trying hard to disappear into the floor. His Big, of course.

Vahn locked eyes with Virgil and shook his head, "I think you should sit this one out," Vahn told Virgil.

"Why?" Virgil asked angry.

"Can't you just sit this one out?" Vahn pleaded.

"Why not take me?" Virgil asked. "I am a strong asset to this team. Denying me access to the twelve is denying yourselves a better chance of surviving and ultimately winning." No one argued with Virgil though he felt a few angry stares and heard an unkind laugh from someone.

"Our Chapter did just fine before you came, we'll be doing just fine after you're gone," Lamar told Virgil his tone betraying his irritation.

"What the hell is that supposed to mean?" Virgil yelled.

"You think you are top shit because your Devil Arms is some legend and your daddy is a Big Bad? You're not better than the rest of us Pitcher," Lamar said chastising Virgil.

"I have never ONCE said or thought I was better than anyone in this room!" Virgil shouted. "Power does not equate superiority. Those with power should be of service to those without. I never asked to be given Ragnorak! You think I want to be different from you guys? Does Omega want to go into this competition on all cylinders looking to conquer, or do you want to bench me and diminish our odds?"

Lamar laughed at that comment, Virgil clenched his fists, "If you want to go into the Finals with the best chance for success, you will take me," Virgil told them.

"You're so full of yourself," Lamar said shaking his head. Soul Reaver's symbol began to dance with dark light.

"Virgil control your temper!" Magnus demanded.

"The part of me that is your Big Brother doesn't want you to come because I'm worried about you," Vahn admitted. "The part of me that is a brother of Omega knows you are right. If we're going to do this, we shouldn't half ass it. I've seen you wield Ragnorak twice now, we'd be fools not to take you."

"Virgil is the eleventh then," Magnus said. "One spot left."

"I want to go," Lamar, Birdy, and Abe said at once.

"We can only take one more," Magnus said.

"I'm a Jeweled Officer," Abe protested.

"Put their names in a hat and draw one out," Vahn suggested.

"My Lil shouldn't go over me!" Lamar yelled.

"Lamar, quit causing trouble," Gabriel admonished his friend.

"Birdy is better than you all give him credit for," Virgil said with confidence, it was easy to brag about people he cared about and speak with conviction and passion. "His Alteration spells are better than anyone in our Chapter."

"Virgil has a good point," Louie said, "That Birdbrain is a genius with that junk."

"Whatever, it is clear this is just a popularity contest, I'm out," Lamar said storming out of the room. Troy, Agustin, Abe and Mu went after him. Virgil kept his eyes on the floor, he didn't like what he saw in some of his brothers' eyes when he met them as they left.

Once the door had closed focus turned back to Magnus. "This is not a popularity contest," Magnus told them his tone getting heated. "Some of us are treating it like it is. This is going to be dangerous and we need a team of men who can handle themselves, who work well under pressure, and most importantly work well as a team. We DON'T need someone who is going to be causing chaos, arguing every step of the way," Magnus finished clearly ready to be done with the conversation.

"Birdy, you want in?" Gabriel asked him.

"Hell yeah!" Birdy responded.

"We have our team," Magnus nodded ending the emergency meeting.

Chapter 17
The Chalice of Immortals

The Coliseum was overflowing, all the seats were filled, and people were crowded in the walkways. The Coliseum was larger than any sporting arena on Earth, a dome covered the playing field with screens suspended in air, powered by magicite, showing different angles of inside the battle ground. The dome was infused with magic, expanding the size inside, several times over the physical space it took up creating a playing field that stretched for miles. Six teams were competing, in first place the Academy in Alexandros, Alpha Chapter, led by Axion Whitefeather. Second-place was Epsilon-Theta Chapter from Germany, in third place was Rho Chapter from China, fourth place was Gamma-Gamma Chapter from Italy, fifth place was Kappa-Beta Chapter from England, with the sixth-place team being the Omegas, Upsilon Delta Chapter. The teams had separate entrances into the dome, with their destination being the center where the Chalice was waiting, the first team to have a member touch it would be declared the winners.

Virgil was gathered with his brothers in a small locker room underneath the Coliseum, dressed in lightweight battle armor provided by the Capital for each team. The name of their Chapter was on each of their backs, Upsilon Delta, so in the heat of the battle, you could tell who friend or foe was in the pandemonium. The twelve of them were quiet, everyone was nervous and on edge, the crowd above was cheering and stomping. Tournament officials came announcing it was time. They led the Omegas onto the field to stand before their entrance into the magically enhanced dome. Virgil looked up, their team was on one of the screens, as were the five others. He'd seen many of these Nephilim competing, they were the strongest and best their race had to offer. The officials came around placing the Dull spell on each participant, removing it in combat with another Paladin in the dome was grounds for being disqualified. The only real rule other than flight wasn't possible inside the dome, to prevent those with wings from just skipping to the goal. A horn sounded, the first team ran into the dome, a few minutes passed, another horn blast and the second-place team went in. After fifteen minutes, the dome opened in front of the Omegas, the final horn sounded, and they ran through.

The inside was filled with massive trees, clumped together in a dense formation like a jungle that stretched to the very top, it was enchanted to look like the open sky. The door closed behind them, the entrance fading to look like the forest around them. It was impossible to see the Chalice from their position, the center was miles from where they were, thanks to the dome's enchantment.

"Keep a tight formation," Gabriel instructed, "Let's avoid unnecessary conflicts, and make it to the center." Gabriel, Tarek and Dante led the group walking fast, Virgil was at the back with Louie and Magnus. Everyone was vigilant, they had no idea what to expect. Insects began to bite at Virgil's neck and exposed flesh, they weren't allowed any magicite, not even the standard Paladin ring of Dreamstone. It wasn't long before they heard something, up ahead the trees were thinned in a wide clearing, a giant boulder sat around a campfire. Actually, there were three boulders, but they looked like they were moving...or breathing?

"Golems," Magnus whispered, "Elementals, created by powerful Nephilim. Only someone with a strong alignment to their element can use Conjuration magic of this caliber."

"We gotta fight those things?" Louie almost yelled and the brothers told him to shut up.

"I didn't realize there was going to be other stuff in here besides the six Chapters," Birdy whispered nervously ahead of Virgil, his hand was itching to hold his lightning lance.

"Maybe we should go around?" Vahn suggested.

A boulder turned its head, glowing yellow eyes above a mouth, which it opened into a growl, Louie looked like he was ready to faint.

"TO ARMS!" Gabriel shouted, "LIONSHEART!" His longsword coming to his hand he sprinted towards their obstacle. Everyone screamed their soul weapons identity and ran after their fearless leader. Virgil's scythe flew next to him as he charged forward. Gabriel swung his sword smashing it against a tall golem, another swung a fist at Gabriel who dodged the blow narrowly. The golem's fist crashed into the ground creating a small crater. Gabriel stabbed the same golem, sparks flew from the blade's edge as it jammed into the hard rock surface. It raised a mighty arm to squash Gabriel! An ice arrow flew landing in its eye socket. It groaned in pain stumbling.

"Storm ray!" Magnus shouted, and a small strike of lightning crashed down hitting a golem stunning it.

Tarek ran forward using his ice lance he worked with Gabriel assaulting the same golem. Dante, Birdy and Zender attacked another. That golem swung its fist catching Dante in the stomach sending him sailing through the air. Virgil charged a third golem, dropping to the ground, its arm swinging just above his head. Virgil jumped to his feet and sent his scythe to assault the golem, while his scythe struck the golem's face, he snapped his fingers producing a small ball of flame. He willed the flames to spread and using it like a whip cracked it at the golem's legs. The golem's feet were swept from under it, it toppled down. Jagger charged forward, his long polearm had an axe on the end of it. He swung his blade onto the golem's face. Virgil's scythe returned to him and he ran to the rising golem screaming as he swung the blade viciously into its rocky flesh. The golem shuttered under their blows and fell to the ground, the rocks that formed its body crumbling, the life leaving its body.

"We got one!" Jagger yelled out.

The other guys quickly turned the tide against the remaining two golems, and each crumbled into nothingness. They regrouped looking each other over for wounds, Gabriel's left arm hung limply at his side. Tarek quickly applied some healing light from his Devil Arms, mending Gabriel's arm within seconds.

"We wasted too much time on these things," Magnus said frustrated, "We need to move!"

The Omegas turned off their weapons and began jogging through the jungle, Magnus kept them on point as their navigator. The stinging bite of bugs came back, the heat inside the dome was stifling, as an artificial sun hung over the center raising the temperature to uncomfortable levels. The men became sweaty as they trekked through the manufactured jungle. Time crept by slowly only heightening the sense of urgency within the men, they hadn't seen another group yet, being the last team, they had to make up for lost time. Gabriel set the pace, jogging speed for him was near sprinting for Louie.

Unnaturally the jungle came abruptly to an end. Ahead of them loomed a towering maze that seemed to have risen right out of the earthen ground. Far into the maze they saw a step pyramid nestled in the center, presumably the Chalice was at its summit. There was more than one entrance, outside of the maze in the distance near a northern entrance, they could see a group of Paladins fighting each other, the Chapters from Germany and England were engaged in combat.

"What should we do?" Virgil asked his brothers.

"Let them fight each other, we need to head into the maze!" Magnus shouted charging ahead.

Gabriel sprinted towards the maze entrance, Virgil and the others close behind him. The Paladins who were fighting saw them, someone yelled out "Get the Americans!" The two groups ceased fighting and started running for the Omegas.

"Move it!" Gabriel yelled to his men.

A ball of fire blasted towards them, Tarek yelled out, in response a blast of ice shooting out from his Devil Arms colliding with the fire spell, they exploded canceling each other out. More spells rained upon them from their pursuers, Magnus, Gabriel, and Birdy made it into the maze. Virgil watched as a spell narrowly missed Vahn, exploding behind him where his feet had been less than a second earlier. A beam of electricity flashed in front of Virgil, connecting with Dante, he groaned in pain and went tumbling to the dirt. Virgil immediately stopped, struggling to pull him up. Dante was disoriented, being mostly muscle he weighed more than what he looked like.

"Get up Dante!" Virgil grunted. Louie grabbed the other side of Dante, and together they hoisted him to his feet and made it into the long entrance of the maze. Everyone had run in, Dante was still unable to stand on his own.

"Get back!" Magnus commanded summoning his Devil Arms, Tempest Staff. Electricity crackled along its service, Magnus shouted, and a blast of energy surged forward striking the wall. The rock crumbled, and the walls of the maze began to cave in, sealing the entrance they'd used, protecting them from their pursuers. Louie cast Ply on Dante, and after maintaining the spell for fifteen seconds he had mostly recovered.

"How are we holding up?" Vahn asked the group. A chorus of cheeky responses came back, Vahn rolled his eyes.

"That rubble won't hold long," Zender said focusing the group, "We need to move towards the Chalice."

"I'm tired dawg," Louie whined, "Can't we take a breather?" he asked.

"Would you rather sit here and be beaten to death by those Paladins in the next few minutes?" Magnus asked.

"Why are they hating on the Americans?" Birdy asked. "We're the good guys!" he exclaimed.

"Because of arrogant attitudes like that!" Vahn retorted. "Americans have become unpopular in other countries because of our superior attitudes. We as a people need to change how we think and act if we're to wipe away the derogative stereotype that comes with being an American," he told them.

"A topic for another time!" Gabriel cut off his friend clearly irritated, "Magnus, which way?" he asked.

Magnus walked to the end of the lane that came to a t-intersection. Magnus looked both ways lost deep in thought. An explosion came from behind them.

"This way!" Magnus shouted running to the north his brothers close behind him. The Omegas followed their Prytanis who led them towards the heart of the maze, and the pyramid that towered over it. It wasn't long before their progress slowed to a crawl, twice they hit a dead end within a minute of each other. They got so confused they started arguing over which direction they'd come from.

Gabriel knelt and placed his hand over the dirt, light flowed from his Devil Arms moving some of the ground to form an arrow in it. "We'll have to start marking which direction we're coming from so we don't get turned around," Gabriel announced proudly.

"It could lead our pursuers' right to us!" Dante argued.

"We need to do something to keep our bearings!" Gabriel snapped back.

Gabriel's suggestion started helping, especially as the intersections became more convoluted. One area had ten paths leading off from it in different directions, some of those paths splitting into other paths just paces into it. They kept coming back to this big intersection, finding some of the paths lopped together in a circle while others ended abruptly at a dead end. Virgil groaned as they once again found themselves back at the big intersection. Dante grunted and punched a wall, bloodying his knuckles.

"You idiot!" Louie admonished him, "I'm not patching that up," he told his friend, "Waste my energy on your bitch ass," he grumbled to himself.

"You got something to say!" Dante barked at his friend.

"Shut up!" Zender growled at them.

"Please," Tarek sighed frustrated. Everyone was getting annoyed and losing patience.

"Let's try this one," Vahn suggested pointing out a path they had yet to try.

"It's in the opposite direction of the pyramid," Gabriel clipped a short and irritated response.

"Yeah well there are only a few paths left, it is worth a shot," Vahn offered. The group begrudgingly followed him, no one had a better suggestion. The path stretched down, bending to the left after a long walk. They walked a very short distance before the path quickly turned again heading back towards the pyramid. The path continued with the occasional opening in a different direction, they kept walking forward heading in the direction of the looming pyramid. The path eventually opened up into a wide-open courtyard filled with huge bushes that had been trimmed to look like statues.

"Nice work," Magnus said to Vahn as they had now finally made some progress into the maze.

A blast of light went into the air to the south of their position, an Omega sign hung in the sky, the signal to the officials that a Chapter was forfeiting.

"What do you think happened?" Louie asked nervously.

"Better not to dwell on it," Virgil said sadly, "We need to stay focused."

"Virgil's right, we still have a shot at winning this thing," Magnus said resolutely a determined fierce look on his face. "Let's get through this garden and see what's past it."

They tread carefully through the garden, Virgil thought he saw a little red leg stick out of a bush, it quickly disappeared when he blinked. Virgil considered it might be fatigue until he noticed Louie, a deep frown on his face staring bug eyed at the same bush, they locked eyes.

"Umm guys?" Louie hesitantly warned the group.

"What is it now chicken wuss?" Zender asked irritated.

A creature leapt out from a bush onto Zender's head, it began biting at his ear, and scratching his face. Zender screamed grabbing for the creature, which nimbly jumped around on his shoulders. Dozens of similar creatures sprung out from hiding, they stood two feet tall, with red bumpy skin, and long tongues that hung out of their mouths filled with sharp teeth.

"Imps!" Magnus shouted, and the group was swarmed in a sea of small feisty monsters. They were fast, they were mean, and they were ugly. One jumped on Louie's shoulders and licked his face with its long tongue, 'Scrumptious!' it cried. Louie squealed like a school girl frantically trying to dislodge the evasive critter. Virgil summoned Soul Reaver to his hand and started spinning it around him, the dark flames of the blade creating a perimeter of black fire around him. He cut down a few imps while doing so and the rest that had come at him backed off. Virgil went on the offensive screaming as he hacked through the creatures that attacked his friends. Magnus whipped up a wind storm, a small funnel forming like a mini tornado. He controlled the funnel and moved it through the garden sucking up imp after imp until it was full of the dang things howling in protest. Magnus commanded the funnel back the way they'd come, sending the imps hurdling over the walls through the maze. The group took control of the situation, and the imps that were left alive retreated back into hiding, their numbers had dwindled too low to be courageous. Tarek and Louie tended to the wounded and they eagerly left the garden behind.

Past the garden they walked through a fancy archway, the surroundings gave way to dusty barren ground like a desert without all the sand. They were in a massive area, empty except for the large step pyramid that stood in the center, the Chalice of Immortals at its peak.

"We made it boys!" Dante laughed in delight.

A group of ten men and two women emerged from another archway out of the maze all of them had white wings upon their back, Axion was leading them, it was Alpha Chapter!

"Crap!" Louie exclaimed.

"Get to the Chalice!" Gabriel shouted.

Both groups began sprinting for the pyramid, Axion raised his hand into the air and shouted, "Smite!" a blast of white energy rocked the ground in front of the Omegas, knocking Gabriel, Tarek and Dante down, leaving a circular crater where the spell had hit. Louie's ice bow came to his hand, he took aim and shot an arrow at their adversaries. The arrow sailed through the air heading straight for Axion. One of their male members with a staff cast a spell and a cloud of fire burst from his Devil Arms engulfing the arrow and disintegrating it. Axion's crew shifted their direction, they turned from running to the pyramid to heading for the Omegas.

"It is time to show the world who the true Paladins are!" Axion told them. They wanted a fight!

Everyone raised their Devil Arms and charged straight for the Academy Paladins. The twenty-four warriors clashed, and the weathered ground became a battlefield! Gabriel's longsword aligned with Earth met with Axion's mighty broadsword aligned with Creation, the two powerful warriors driving against each other for dominance. Their mage wielded a fire staff he squared off against Magnus and the two began throwing spells at one another. Birdy was attacked by one of the females, she wielded two lightning daggers and used jumps and kicks mixed with her blades that moved with blinding speed. Virgil had no time to worry about his brothers, the other woman came for Virgil, she wielded a chain scythe, and hers was aligned with Wind. Her scythe's blade was much smaller, attached to a long metal chain she used to fling the blade forward like a flail. She was fast, her scythe was hard to block, on her second strike she managed to hit Virgil hard in the shoulder, if not for the Dull spell he'd be gushing blood.

Virgil swatted her attack down, and swung his scythe across her body, she took the blow to the chest and fell to the ground writhing in pain. Virgil turned his attention to the battle, a man charged Virgil taking a swing at him with a metal claw. Virgil barely missed taking the claw to the face scrambling back, Virgil shouted, "Firebolt!" and sent a beam of fire at the clawed warrior, it hit him and sent him rolling. He got back to his feet charging Virgil like a bull, Virgil raised his scythe to swing at him when it stopped in its tracks. Virgil looked back, the woman had wrapped her chain around the scythe's blade and struggled to control Virgil's weapon. He struggled against her, the man with the claw brought an upper cut to Virgil, he screamed in pain, the claw would have gored him right through the stomach. The man assaulted Virgil with impudence, pummeling him until Virgil fell to the ground unable to take anymore. Pain thrived along every nerve ending, he couldn't think straight, Soul Reaver disappeared in a flash, and the man stopped.

The battle wasn't going well for the Omegas, Tarek and Dante, stood back to back surrounded by a team of five Alpha Paladins. Only a few of their members were laying on the ground whereas most of the Omegas had been beaten and were incapacitated. They were too strong. Axion looked down at Gabriel, who lay defeated in the dirt, and over at Virgil shaking his head in disappointment. One of Axion's men came up to him, he had an ice battleaxe, and he healed Axion who looked like he'd taken some beatings from Gabriel before he'd subdued the Omega's best warrior.

"Is this all the Upsilon Delta Chapter has to offer?" Axion taunted them. "You're pathetic!" he shouted kicking Gabriel. "Not even a challenge worthy of our Chapter."

Virgil's body ached, but his mind was fully functioning. *Are you going to lay here and watch our brothers be beaten down?* A familiar voice rang out in his mind, it was the voice of his inner Judge, the part of his unconscious mind that he tapped into when he Ascended. What am I supposed to do, Virgil thought. *Fight! We are better than this, YOU are better than this.* The voice insisted. Virgil knew what it meant, he hadn't fought with his full strength, not even close.

Axion kicked Gabriel again who groaned in pain. "Leave him alone you bastard!" Vahn screamed overcoming his opponent, who wielded a claymore aligned with earth. "You haven't beaten us yet!" Vahn yelled charging Axion. Vahn! Virgil struggled to his feet, he couldn't let his Big take them both on by himself.

"Where do you think you're going?" the man with the claw Devil Arms said kicking Virgil hard sending him back to the ground.

"He cares about that one," the woman said.

"Then let's make sure he watches Axion and Jarione kick his ass," he said forcing Virgil up to his knees grabbing a fistful of his hair and yanking his head up. The woman threw her chain around Virgil's neck pulling it tight choking the air from his lungs.

Vahn fought with a fierceness Virgil had never seen, he took on the two warriors without fear or hesitation, Gabriel was one of his best friends. Even as skilled as Vahn was, their combined strength was too much. Jarione, the warrior with an ice battle axe, landed a blow on Vahn's side doubling him over. Axion slashed his blade across Vahn's chest who screamed in agony.

"Vahn!" Virgil screamed tears coming to his eyes. The chain pulled at his neck and the man yanked on Virgil's hair. Virgil didn't feel like holding back anymore. He felt the power within him bubbling to the service, if he wanted to Ascend, he knew he could. Even though Vahn was going down, they continued striking him unnecessarily, each blow like a needle piercing Virgil's heart.

"Knock it off!" Virgil screamed feeling the power washing over his body, his eyes going gold and his aura expanding. He yelled and threw his arms out pure power hurling the two warriors off him with tremendous force. Virgil rose to his feet, he had Ascended, the superhuman strength and speed of a Judge were his to command. Virgil turned towards the woman with the scythe.

"What the hell is he!" she yelled. Virgil pounded his feet on the ground easily dodging her chain scythe as it flew out to strike him, he leapt into the air kicking out both feet, drop kicking her square in the chest with as much force as he could muster. He heard her ribs crack under the pressure and she fell to the ground. Virgil went into a roll and came to his feet nimbly.

The man with the claw Devil Arms screamed and ran for Virgil. Virgil sprinted towards him, swinging a fist out, landing a solid hit on his right cheekbone. The man took the hit and kept coming swinging wildly with his claw trying to take Virgil down. But his movements were sluggish to Virgil, like the world around him had slowed to a crawl, and Virgil dodged his strikes with lithe grace. Virgil used his fists and pummeled the man, hitting him again, and again. Virgil didn't even need his Devil Arms in this state, he was so fast and strong beating this Alpha Chapter Paladin was effortless. At last Virgil landed an uppercut to his jaw and he went airborne landing hard on his back, not getting up. Virgil clenched his fists and turned his attention to Axion, Axion and his warriors grouped together, staring at Virgil with repulsion. There were six of them still, three of them charged Virgil yelling out battle cries.

Virgil raised his right hand into the air, "Light Surge," he spoke, and dozens of beams of creation energy rained down from the sky, barraging the ground like missile strikes. When the spell ended the three warriors lay injured and defeated. The spell had pulled a great deal of energy from his aura, but he had plenty more to spare.

"He's a freak!" Jarione with the ice axe shouted.

The woman with the twin lightning daggers was at Axion's side as well. "We can take him," she told her comrades. "He's no match for the three of us," she said.

Virgil had no intention of fighting them on his own, "Cura!" Virgil shouted and three warm white energy bursts flew from his right hand, one surrounded him healing his wounds, the other two landed on Vahn and Gabriel. They both began to stir as the spell sped up their cellular regeneration a thousand fold and their wounds began to mend. Thanks to Alexa who'd taught him that spell, he'd been unable to use it when she'd tried to teach him, but in his Ascended state it was easy to cast. Cura was stronger than Ply, capable of restoring more than one person at a time. Virgil ran to his brothers' side.

"Virgil?" Vahn asked blood still in his mouth and on his chin from the beating.

"Help me brothers, help me show these arrogant bastards what Upsilon Delta is capable of!" Virgil shouted standing between Gabriel and Vahn.

"You're sure you want this?" Gabriel asked him. "Everyone will know your secret."

"That doesn't matter anymore," Virgil told him. "What use is having power, if you can't use it to protect the people you care about?"

"I beat them once, I can beat them again!" Axion shouted out confidently.

"No! This time you will face me!" Virgil yelled at Axion. He grabbed the glove covering his right hand and threw it off, revealing his Creation Devil Arms. He stretched his right hand to the sky. "Ragnorak!" Virgil screamed. A bolt of white lightning crashed down from the heavens into his palm, expanding out into the Holy Blade. The aura of light from the sword spread to cover Virgil. Virgil willed his wings from his back, they burst through his clothing spreading out for the world to see.

"He's the Redeemer!" the woman cried out.

"Seraph or not, he's still a Nephilim," Axion said though with less confidence.

"You two handle the others," Virgil said to his brothers taking flight and charging Axion. It felt like a three-hundred-pound weight was on his back, stopping him from ascending much higher than he could stand, he used his wings to propel him towards Axion. Virgil swung Ragnorak at Axion who swung his massive Creation broadsword out, the two swords grinded against each other. Virgil kicked out hard hitting Axion in the chest. He kicked off Axion propelling himself backwards in the air, and landed on his feet in front of him. Axion rushed forward swinging his sword with the deadly precision of an expert warrior. Even with Virgil's heightened senses he struggled to keep up with Axion's blows, there was a reason he was the leader of his Chapter. Virgil clashed with Axion's sword and shoved him back, Axion stumbling, Virgil twirled Ragnorak around rotating his wrist as he walked forward.

Virgil rushed forward stabbing Ragnorak at Axion's chest, he barely managed to deflect the blow almost losing grip of his sword, Virgil used this to his advantage. He savagely struck at him again, and again, bringing Ragnorak down with impudence, showing Axion the same merciless wrath he'd unleashed upon his brothers. As Virgil fought Ragnorak's clear blade began to slowly fill with golden energy. Virgil smashed through Axion's guard and swung Ragnorak hard hitting him full. Axion was flung off his feet to the ground. Virgil swung Ragnorak around and pointed the tip of the blade at Axion.

"Rise!" Virgil commanded, he would not beat on a warrior as he lay on the ground, he was not honor less like these people.

Axion got to his feet, his arrogance marring his handsome features with a look of pure disgust. "You filthy, filthy Lamb!" Axion shouted at Virgil getting to his feet. "How DARE you speak to ME in such a manner! I'm a WHITEFEATHER! My family has lived in Alexandros since its founding! You ARE NOTHING! YOU ARE A NOBODY!" he screamed. "I'll cut you down, then make you watch as I beat every one of your bothers to a pulp!"

Ragnorak let out a howl and it overflowed with golden light, brimming with immense power. Axion stood aghast staring at the blade dumbfounded. "You don't deserve to call yourself a Paladin," Virgil told him. "Ragnorak screams in revulsion at your foul words."

"Devil Arms cannot speak!" Axion laughed. "You're insane!"

Virgil raised Ragnorak into the air and the blade howled for all to hear. Axion screamed out the name of his Devil Arms, "Heaven's Charge!" and his broadsword glowed with white light and he sprinted towards Virgil. "Judgment Bolt!" Virgil yelled and swung his sword towards Axion. A beam of white energy rocketed out from Ragnorak like a giant bolt of lightning, crashing into him and propelling him through the air like a rag doll. He rolled across the ground finally coming to a stop against the pyramid, he didn't get back up. Ragnorak's Soul Scream had emptied its power and the blade returned to its normal appearance. Virgil had reached the end of his Ascended state, he could only maintain the power for so long. His eyes returned to normal as did his aura, the heightened abilities of a Judge leaving his mortal body.

Virgil turned to see Gabriel and Vahn had defeated Axion's comrades, they were tending to their other brothers, everyone looked like crap. Vahn locked eyes with Virgil and he pointed to the Chalice. Virgil looked up at the pyramid.

"Go get it!" Gabriel told him. "It should be you who grabs it."

Virgil began running up the steep stone steps, climbing as fast as he could. It took him almost five minutes to reach the top, the Chalice of Immortals stood on a pedestal at the center of the summit. It was a silver cup that had Angelic runes covering its surface, power emanated from within. Virgil hesitantly reached for the Chalice, his fingers closed around the neck of the cup and he found the metal was warm to the touch. He lifted it into the air and went to the edge of the pyramid raising it in the air for all to see. He heard his brothers cheering and his face spread into a giant grin…they'd done it!

A massive black portal opened above Virgil's head, from the portal poured Nephilim warriors with black wings…Death Dealers! Virgil heard someone shout his name, he ran to the edge of the pyramid and jumped off opening his wings he glided to the ground. As he landed another portal opened in front of him, the Harbinger and the Gatekeeper glad in full black battle armor stepped out, the portal closed behind them.

"Retrieve the Chalice at all costs!" the Harbinger said to his partner turning his attention to the warriors left on the field.

The Gatekeeper nodded and stepped towards Virgil, Virgil backed up. The Gatekeeper extended its hand demanding the Chalice without words. Virgil shook his head, if the Death Dealers wanted the cup, Virgil would do everything in his power to prevent that from happening. The Gatekeeper held out its right hand and a blade materialized into its grasp. The sword was different from others he'd seen, the part after the cross guard looked mechanical, almost like a gun, halfway up its body a blade came out of the demonic looking gun. Virgil took of the Dull spell from both his Devil Arms. The Gatekeeper charged Virgil, a portal opened up in front of the warrior, it ran through, Virgil had started running to meet the Death Dealer and stopped in his tracks. Virgil felt the portal open directly behind him and didn't have time to turn around before a swift kick landed in the small of his back sending him tumbling into the dirt. Virgil quickly got to his feet just in time to raise Ragnorak and catch the Gatekeeper's sword, he struggled against the warrior's might. The Gatekeeper shoved Virgil back breaking the deadlock of their blades. The warrior ran at Virgil right into another portal, Virgil quickly spun around not falling for the same trick again. A portal opened above his head the Gatekeeper came through swiftly kicking at Virgil and going straight into a back-flip landing gracefully on the ground. Virgil breathed heavily, this warrior was one of the seven Seraphs, one of the most powerful Nephilim to ever exist. Virgil was tired from the Tournament; he couldn't hold up long.

Almost sensing his thoughts, the warrior held out its hand motioning for Virgil to give up the Chalice. Virgil gritted his teeth, "Never!" he shouted in defiance. The Gatekeeper raised its sword at Virgil and cocked it back like it was a shotgun, the blade morphed into the weapon disappearing, the end where the blade was began charging with black light. The Gatekeeper pulled a trigger on the weapon, a powerful blast of energy raced towards Virgil. It hit him on the side, Virgil was knocked down rolling along the ground. The entire left side of his body was in agony, like someone had thrown a fireball at his bare flesh, his nerve endings were screaming from the pain of the massive burn he'd incurred.

Virgil heard the Harbinger, Sethos, laughing in the distance, "You've never faced a Nephilim with a gunblade before have you?" he taunted. "The Gatekeeper is beyond your skill level," he mocked Virgil. Virgil saw Sethos was battling what remained of the Paladins, his brothers included, still standing. Sethos wielded a massive sword about the size of an average person, Virgil would have struggled to lift it. The pummel and cross guard were black, the blade of the sword was pure white, he swung it around like it was made of plastic. Some Death Dealers were dragging Paladins' unconscious bodies, the Gatekeeper moved its hand and black portals opened for them, they dragged the Paladins in disappearing as the portals closed. The Gatekeeper walked over to Virgil and picked him up by his shirt. At that moment the Grand Prytanis Aseril, and Rasler came into the arena. Everything inside was being shown on monitors to the people sitting in the Coliseum, they had come to help!

"Virgil!" Aseril yelled his voice panicked, "They mustn't take the Chalice!" he roared.

"Go!" Sethos commanded of his partner, "I will be right behind you." The Gatekeeper held Virgil close creating a portal, Virgil struggled to break free from the warrior's grasp. The Gatekeeper ripped the Chalice from Virgil's grasp, and moved to the portal. Virgil knew what he had to do, Virgil felt the power of Soul Reaver build in his left hand. He didn't want his scythe though, just the flames. Virgil placed his left hand on the Gatekeeper's wrist holding the Chalice and let the dark flames flow from his symbol. The Gatekeeper howled in pain and struggled against Virgil, the Chalice falling from its hand, but Virgil refused to let go. Virgil shoved against the warrior with all his might and the two of them fell through the portal. The uncomfortable sensation battered Virgil about for less than a second of time, and they fell onto the ground in a completely alien and foreign land. Virgil pounded his other fist against the Gatekeeper. Virgil heard someone approaching from behind, he turned to see a fist connect with his face, and he was knocked unconscious instantly.

Chapter 18
<u>Prisoner in Hel</u>

Virgil awoke with a start jumping up from the small bed he'd been laying on, wildly looking around the room. It was a small dank cell, lit by a small piece of magicite that hung on the wall like a lamp. A toilet and sink were directly across from him, with a blue force field at the front of the small room. Virgil swung his feet over the bed and stood up seeing he had a rounded black bracelet looking device on each hand. Virgil walked to the force field, there were two Death Dealers stationed on the sides of his prison cell. Virgil hesitantly touched the barrier with no repercussions, it held him inside, though it didn't hurt. Virgil placed both hands on the force field and tried to look around, there was a walkway leading past his cell presumably to other cells, he couldn't see on either side. He could see across the tower however. The middle of the prison was hollow, with the outsides spiraling around, he saw prison cells like his across the way in the distance, hundreds of them. Virgil was inside a Death Dealer prison.

"What's going on?" Virgil asked the guards outside his cell.

"Shut up!" one of the guards responded.

"Where am I?" Virgil demanded.

The guards laughed, "You're in Hel! Now shut up and get away from the door!" they yelled.

Virgil backed up from the doorway, if he could use Ragnorak he was sure he could destroy the barrier and escape from this place. He concentrated on his Devil Arms and felt…nothing, almost like they weren't there. Virgil examined the devices on his hands, these must be like handcuffs for Nephilim he thought, preventing one from summoning their Devil Arms. Virgil went to the sink and started banging the bracelet against it.

"I wouldn't do that," one of the guards said standing in front of the barrier looking inside. "Rattle those things around too much and they'll explode destroying your hand," he winked at Virgil grinning. Virgil stopped and fell onto his bed, hopelessness sinking into his mind, like he was drowning, gulping down water, and floating slowly away from the surface. What was he going to do?

Time was impossible to measure. Virgil's stomach rumbled painfully, eventually it became too much, Virgil went to the sink, and drank some water. He drank until it felt like he could feel the water slushing around inside him. He lay back down staring up at the dirty ceiling feeling defeated, how did things come to this? Virgil never imagined himself being captured by the enemy, he had no idea what lay in store for him. He was sure they had plans for him, he was the Sixth Seraph, the Redeemer. They'd likely want to turn him to their side, Virgil would sooner die then fight against his brothers.

Eventually someone approached the door, the barrier fell, and Virgil stood up. The two guards had their Devil Arms drawn and a third had a tray with food on it. "No heroics, Paladin," one of the guards said his spear aimed at Virgil. Virgil watched the man place the tray on the ground and he left the cell. One of the Death Dealers pushed something on the outside and the barrier came back on. Virgil walked over to the tray, the food was strange looking, what did they have to eat in the Ever After anyways? Virgil took the tray and sat on the edge of his bed. He doubted it was poisoned, he was too valuable an asset to do away with, so he ate the food. He sat down for a while, then he got tired of sitting, so he got to his feet and decided to exercise. He started doing pushups and sit ups, the best thing to do in a prison situation was bulk up and bide your time. Virgil wouldn't sit idly by forever, there would come a time when he'd have a chance to fight, to make an escape, and he planned to be ready for it.

Virgil worked out until he was sore and couldn't anymore, then he had nothing to do, except sit back in the bed, and stare at the plain dark walls. Time dragged by so slowly, he'd never been good at being bored, he had too active of a mind, and he was the type that liked to always be doing something. Eventually he drifted off into sleep. Virgil dreamed he was back at Bay Valley, it was summer, and he was outside the Omega manor with his brothers, Blair, Helene, TK, and Selene were there as well. They were playing volleyball in the front yard, everyone was laughing and having a good time. Then the skies darkened like the Ever After, a portal opened, the Fourth and Fifth Seraph, the Harbinger and the Gatekeeper, walked through. The Gatekeeper grabbed hold of Blair dragging her through a portal, Virgil screamed, frozen in place, unable to help his friend.

Virgil awoke breathing heavy, he looked around and sighed, he was going to go crazy in this place. Virgil paced the length of the room, tired of this small ugly cell. Virgil's mind went to his brothers, what had happened to them? Virgil remembered seeing Death Dealers dragging people through portals, had his brothers been taken prisoner? Virgil prayed that wasn't the case, he wondered what the rest of the Chapter was doing. He thought about Alexandros and how the Paladin Capital was reacting to this. He remembered seeing King Aseril and Rasler coming into the arena to help them, which had been seconds before he'd gone through the portal with the Gatekeeper. Virgil had done everything he could to stop the Death Dealer from taking the Chalice, even placing himself in this predicament. Virgil hoped that it had been worth the sacrifice. The Chalice of Immortals was the cup originally given to the first Paladins by a group of Judges, signifying their alliance against the dark forces of Diablos. The Chalice is what made it possible for the Paladins to make more of their kind. The Omegas imitation cup was linked to the original Chalice, and it was an important piece of the Oath of the Paladin. Without that Nephilim who had very little Angel blood in their veins couldn't be given the full powers of a Nephilim. Though the Judges could bless them will a new source in theory, the Judges didn't communicate with mortals.

"Is the Redeemer in there?" a powerful masculine voice asked.

"Yes sir," the guards outside Virgil's cell responded.

"You're relieved from duty, give us some privacy," the voice commanded, and Virgil heard the guards walking away. Virgil got up from his bed, the force field dropped, and someone came in. Virgil's heart began to race, his body sensed that something important was going to happen even before his mind understood. The man before him was extremely tall clad in formal and elegant attire. He was incredibly handsome, with long raven hair that hung to his waist, and large black wings folded on his back. He EMANATED power. Virgil didn't need to concentrate to see his aura, it filled the entire room and then some. Just being in its perimeter was overwhelming, making his thoughts foggy and his movements sluggish. Virgil got a better look at his face and he gasped startled, he looked like he could pass for Virgil's older brother! The physical resemblance between them was astounding. His face was perpetually smooth, like every Judge. The only real difference was the Judge had a stronger jaw line than Virgil, and his eyes were sockets of glowing gold light. Virgil looked up at the powerful being feeling out of place, he'd dreamed of meeting his biological father since he was a child, but he never pictured their reunion quite like this.

"Virgil," he said in a surprisingly gentle and heartfelt tone, "How I have dreamed of this day," he said sounding like he was on the verge of tears.

Virgil looked down at the floor, he didn't know what to say, he was scared, he was happy, he was nervous, he was so confused.

"Look at me," he commanded. Virgil hesitantly stared up at this being who was a stranger to him and yet…Virgil felt such a strong pull to him. Virgil was full of contradicting feelings, and it was sensory overload. He felt emotional, and he wished he wasn't. He needed to be strong in this moment and not show weakness. "Do you know who I am?" he asked Virgil.

Virgil nodded, "I have your face," Virgil said looking down, it was hard to meet the Judge's eyes, his gaze pierced Virgil's soul.

"Virgil," he said taking a step towards him reaching out his hand, Virgil instinctively took a step back. The Judge let his hand fall, his expression becoming despondent. "Don't be afraid of me, I would no sooner harm you than myself. Here let me hide my eyes," the Judge offered. The Judge's eyes became less godlike and more human, easier to meet his gaze.

Virgil felt tears coming to his eyes, please don't cry he begged himself. "I don't know what to feel," Virgil said honestly. "I've dreamed of meeting you since I learned I was adopted, this is never what I had imagined," he explained to the Judge trying to let him know how he felt.

"This isn't how I wanted us to meet for the first time," the Judge agreed nodding, "You need to know, there hasn't been a day of your life, that I haven't thought about you. You have always been in my prayers and in my heart son," the Judge told Virgil. Tears fell from Virgil's eyes, he didn't want to cry, he couldn't help it. This man was his enemy, Virgil needed to be careful. "Oh son," the Judge said, and he walked forward. He carefully reached out to Virgil, Virgil didn't pull away, and for the first time in Virgil's life, his father hugged him.

Virgil pulled away and wiped his face dry. "What's going to happen to me?" Virgil asked him.

The Judge looked uncomfortable at that question, which was why Virgil asked. Virgil needed to keep a clear head. "Why don't we go somewhere more comfortable?" the Judge suggested politely to Virgil. "I've missed out on so many things, I want to hear about your life," he exclaimed excitedly.

"More comfortable?" Virgil asked distrusting.

"There are larger rooms further down in the tower, I've had one of them remodeled as to make your time here more amicable," the Judge grinned. "First let's start fresh, I'm former Seraphim Judge Raphael," he said extending his hand out. Virgil arched an eyebrow at him. "I'm told this is a typical greeting for Americans," he remarked casually, a small grin peaking at the corners of his mouth.

Virgil nodded, "I'm Virgil Pitcher," he replied taking his father's hand.

"It is a pleasure to meet you Master Virgil," Raphael was delighted. "Follow me, I'm sure you are tired of this small cell."

Virgil followed his father out of the cell. The tower was colossal, a railing was positioned along the walkway, the tower went down so far that Virgil couldn't see the bottom. The tower spiraled up to a great height, he could see there was no ceiling, the dark stormy clouds that hung perpetually in the Ever After sky could be seen through the distant opening. Virgil quickly looked away from the top of the tower not wanting Raphael to know what he was thinking, a way out of here! Virgil followed his father down into the tower's depths. They passed Death Dealer guards who would occasionally shoot Virgil unkind glares, they remained rigid and silent in Raphael's presence. Virgil knew Raphael was one of the four God Generals, the Fallen Judges in charge of Diablos' forces in the Ever After, seeing Raphael and how the Death Dealers responded to his presence made that knowledge feel more real. Knowing his father was one of the big bad guys and that he was Virgil's enemy was easier having not met him, now…Virgil didn't know how to feel. He didn't get the feeling Raphael was a danger to him, it felt like Raphael cared about him. Virgil looked up at his father walking at his side, could he fight his father? Would he fight him if he had to? Maybe if Raphael was trying to kill one of his brothers, Virgil's mind wouldn't stop racing.

They reached the room Virgil would now be staying in, Raphael pressed a small switch on the side of the wall and the force field lifted. Virgil followed him inside, it was three times the size of the previous room, with a shower behind a small wall for privacy along with a table and chairs, and a more comfortable looking bed with a change of clothes laid out for him.

"Have a seat, let's talk," Raphael said to him.

Virgil sat at the table looking around. "So how long am I supposed to stay here?" Virgil asked looking Raphael head on.

Raphael sighed, "Wouldn't you like to start the conversation in a friendlier way?"

"Perhaps it is best to stay honest with each other," Virgil suggested politely, "I am your prisoner, we are not sitting down for dinner after a day of work and school."

"Are you hungry?" Raphael asked cheerfully. "I can have something brought to you."

"Thank you, Raphael, I'm fine right now," Virgil lied.

"Please, call me dad," Raphael insisted. "I can tell your lying I'll having something brought to you," Virgil bit his lip. That wasn't something he was willing to do, Raphael would have to earn that right from him.

"You said you wanted to talk, what would you like to know?" Virgil asked him.

Raphael's demeanor changed he looked excited and leaned in, "Tell me what your childhood was like. Were you well cared for? Where did you live? Did you have a lot of friends? What did you do for fun?" he asked Virgil.

Virgil raised his eyebrows and chuckled, in a way Raphael reminded Virgil of himself and how he was when interviewing brothers. "I had a great childhood, I was raised by a loving couple who gave me everything I could ever want, and they loved me unconditionally. They raised me to be respectful and to be polite. They were a little strict, but I think that helped me from turning into a spoiled brat like some kids are nowadays," Virgil told him. Virgil started talking and once he got going, he could out talk the best of them. Virgil told Raphael all about life growing up in rural America. He didn't tell him the names of any towns or even the state, he would not put his mother in danger.

After some time of listening, which Raphael did with enthusiasm and good body language and eye contact, he interjected with a question, "Were these people who raised you, were they...human?" Raphael asked.

"Yes," Virgil said, "Just a normal human couple. You didn't know where I was?" Virgil asked.

"No," Raphael said coldly his face going still in an angry scowl.

"How did you meet my mom?" Virgil asked him. Raphael was quiet and looked down, deep in thought. "I was told she died giving birth to me, and that no one knew who my father was."

This peaked Raphael's interest, he looked up at Virgil, wearing an expression of intrigue. "You've never met your mother?" he asked curious.

"No," Virgil said confused, "I thought she died during childbirth, isn't that what happened?" he asked.

Raphael became very hard to read, he stood up and turned away from Virgil. "Virgil, human women, they can't survive the birth of a child sired by a Judge. They don't have Judge blood in their veins and the process is too great for a pure mortal body to handle," Raphael told him still looking away.

"Why did you do it then?" Virgil asked feeling a little angry at him. "If you knew it would kill her, why would you condemn her to such a fate?"

"Sometimes...people fall in love," Raphael said turning around to face Virgil.

"Or lust," Virgil countered.

"Virgil, there is something you need to understand about me," Raphael said seriously sitting down and staring into Virgil's eyes. "For a very long time now, the one thing I have wanted in this world...is a son. Someone I could train, someone who could carry on my legacy, someone I could share my time with, someone I could love. Virgil, you are the one thing in this world that I have always wanted, and I would have done anything, will do anything, to have you in my life," Raphael spoke with such passion Virgil had to look away.

"They say you once wielded Ragnorak," Virgil said still not meeting his father's intimidating gaze, "The same sword I now wield."

"You wield it as a sword?" Raphael asked shell shocked looking at Virgil's Devil Arms. Virgil put his hands on the table and Raphael examined Ragnorak's symbol with great curiosity.

"Yeah didn't you?" Virgil asked surprised by his father's response.

"No, I wielded Ragnorak in its true form. Ragnorak must have taken a form that was more attuned to who you are in order for you to wield it," Raphael reasoned.

"Why did Ragnorak leave you?" Virgil asked his father. "Why did you join Diablos?" at the mention of the Dark Lord's name the light in the room seemed to dim slightly.

"It is unwise to speak his name, especially in the Ever After," Raphael told Virgil.

"Why isn't he sealed away?" Virgil asked.

"He is very much alive," Raphael told him. "His body is sealed like a statue here in the Ever After preventing him from moving or outright speaking, but Lilith can communicate with him. She speaks for him and we frequently visit him to receive orders." Virgil felt shivers go down his spine, alright bringing that up was a bad idea. "It is a long story but let me try to explain. After the creation of man, Judges started laying with mortals, creating the race of Nephilim, something the Creator had not intended. The Creator grew angry at the Judges, as we were not supposed to have offspring, we could not remain impartial protectors of justice if we became so intermingled with the world. Seeing so many of my brethren having children I wanted one of my own, a son in my image," Raphael said looking at Virgil with a smile.

"I went to the Creator one day," Raphael told Virgil, "We often took walks together, in the fields of Nirvana, and I asked for a son." Virgil felt he knew the answer. "The Creator told me my place was to wield Ragnorak, and continue to protect the world righting wrongs and upholding justice. For one cannot wield Ragnorak in its true state without turning ones back on selfish desires such as connections with other people. I wasn't satisfied with this; I had begun to yearn for a child of my own more than anything. It was at that time Lucifer and Beatrix came to me, telling me that the Dark Lord, though he was called something very different in those times, had a proposition for me," Raphael told me.

"What did he want with you?" Virgil asked his father curious.

"Diablos wanted to take over Nirvana, he wanted to break the chains of servitude that bound us all, giving us the gift of free will that he felt had been squandered on humanity. And he needed my help," Raphael said.

"I don't understand," Virgil said with furrowed eyebrows.

"Let me give you a little background then. Eidolons were the first race, great spirits whose entities created the known world, their home is the Feymarch," Raphael explained, "But they were a chaotic race, and the world was unbalanced, so the Creator made the Judges, to bring order into the world and maintain peace. The third race was the Sidhe Fairies, descended from the Eidolons, they were a humanistic race of Ediolons, far less powerful but more individualistic with unique personalities. Their home was the Ever After, a gift from the Eidolons, a land of paradise. Judges were, and to this day still are, jealous of them, for in the Fairies, Eidolons had gained offspring, something Judges were not capable of producing. It wasn't until the creation of man that things went haywire," Raphael sighed.

"What'd they do?" Virgil asked.

"It's not what they did, it is what they were given," Raphael told Virgil. "Before the race of mortals came to be, all races had a specific purpose, a duty to perform in the world. And we were happy with that, we didn't know any different. The time in between the creation of each race spanned billions of years, and by the time the Fairies had lived in the Ever After for billions of years, the Creator grew tired. The Creator created Diablos, to be a Creator himself. It was the dream of the Creator that the Dark Lord would go on to make his own universes and his own races. The Dark Lord was always a solitary being, he would visit with the other races, but he did not make friends, he was distant and indifferent. One day he was summoned by the Creator and all the races gathered," Raphael became quiet.

"The Creator told the Dark Lord the time had come for him to make his first sentient being," Raphael spoke carefully, "The Creator made from dirt the first mortal man, breathing life into his body. This human was different from any of the other self-aware races, it was frail, and in many eyes, pathetic. The heavenly host laughed and mocked the human, wondering why the Creator had given such a weak creature the gift of consciousness. The Creator told everyone present that human was unique in that, its potential, unlike every other race, was limitless. The Creator said that while the other races were immortal, the human had a spirit inside it and when it died it would live on forever, attaining true immortality. Though Judges are immortal, if we are killed in combat we cease to exist forever, we don't have the human soul. The human, the Creator added could dream to be whatever it wanted, do whatever it wanted, limited only by the scope of its imagination. You see, what the Creator had given it was something that none of us realized we hadn't been given...free will. Every other creation until that point had been made with a specific purpose to perform a specific function, but human, he could become whatever he desired."

"I've never heard this before," Virgil said so drawn into his father's story he was on the edge of his seat.

"Well you've probably never spoken with someone who was there before," Raphael smiled. Virgil's eyebrows raised, just how old is my dad? "To finish my story, the Creator asked the Dark Lord to make man's counterpart, a companion to keep him company and to give him happiness. The Dark Lord created Lilith, the first demon, a being that couldn't have been more opposite of man. Man was made with Creation energy, Lilith was made with Chaos energy like all the demons who would come after her. Lilith was full of dark power, magic, and hatred. Lilith begged her master, the Dark Lord, not to force her to be with the human, she despised him for his weakness and vowed she would never be subservient to man. The Dark Lord took her to his side promising her she did not have to stay with the human. The Dark Lord was pleased with his creation, but the Creator was appalled, for it saw in that moment the Dark Lord for what he was, a being with malevolence and darkness in his heart. The Creator agreed to let the Dark Lord keep Lilith as long as he promised never to create another race as long as he lived, making him swear upon the Barfrost. The Dark Lord was enraged but was forced to obey his master, some say that was the day he began to despise our Creator," Raphael said.

"That's incredible," Virgil said speechless from his father's tale.

"It wasn't long after that the Dark Lord planned and executed his revolt, and the Battle of the Fallen took place. The Dark Lord needed me to help him win over warriors, before I joined his cause there were precious few who would turn against the Creator for him. The Dark Lord offered me the one thing that the Creator had refused," Raphael told Virgil.

"He promised you a son," Virgil said understanding his father's motivation.

Raphael nodded, "The Dark Lord made his second and final promise on the Barfrost to me, that if I brought him the warriors he needed, he would reward me with a son," he told Virgil. "Promises on the Barfrost cannot be broken, doing so would destroy the person who made it, even a god. And so in my selfishness I made a pact with him, forever sealing my fate with his own. When I led the charge against the heavenly host, Ragnorak forever left my side," Raphael said with a look of regret.

"But he never fulfilled his side of the bargain," Virgil told his father. "I wasn't made by him," Virgil said, "You turned you're back on your people for nothing?"

"Not nothing," Raphael shook his head, "Virgil you are everything to me. Having you in my life, is all I have ever wanted."

Virgil looked down, his father didn't get the point he was trying to make. Diablos had used Raphael making him a promise he had never fulfilled. This was a lot to take in, Raphael had wanted for so long nothing more than a son, almost fanatically dwelling on it. But Virgil did not sense madness within Raphael, he was surprisingly kind, if not for the black wings on his back Virgil would have said he was a regular Judge.

"Where do we go from here?" Virgil asked his father.

"What do you mean?" Raphael asked.

"It is not that I don't want you in my life, because if I am being honest with myself, I do," Virgil owned.

"I want that more than anything," Raphael smiled a genuinely bright smile that crinkled the corners of his eyes.

"But I am a Paladin," Virgil told his father with conviction. "A warrior who protects humanity from demons, Death Dealers, and Fallen Judges. My brothers…they are family to me. I cannot turn my back on everything that I am," Virgil said wincing as he ended with, "Not even for you Raphael."

"Join me Virgil," Raphael beseeched Virgil, "They may feel like family but I am your TRUE family! The only blood family you have left in this world," he reminded Virgil. "I have longed for the day when you would stand at my side, there is much I can show you, much I can teach you about this world. I know that we would be happy together, as father and son, I have seen a future of us together, and in it you are happy being in my life, and I in yours."

Virgil nodded, "I am sure I would be happy, spending time with my biological father. I don't think there is anything a child wants more than the love and attention of their parents," he said sadly.

"Then why can't we?" Raphael asked Virgil. "We deserve each other Virgil. I have missed out on so much of your life already, I don't want to miss out on any more of it," he said sounding miserable.

"You are asking me to join the Death Dealers," Virgil said shaking his head.

"You don't have to be a Death Dealer if you don't want to," Raphael countered, "If I say it is to be than others will listen. If you don't want to be a part of them you don't have to."

"But I would have to pledge fealty to your Master, wouldn't I?" Virgil asked his father. Raphael went silent, taking on a deadly stillness that no mortal could imitate, like he had suddenly become lifeless. Virgil spoke again, "If I were to join you, your Dark Lord would make me swear fealty to him," Virgil said knowing he spoke the truth, his father's lack of response spoke louder than any words could. "I will never turn my back on humanity. Your Dark Lord seeks to destroy everything in his reawakening, the war of Ragnorak, and all the things that I have come to love. Even if I wasn't a Paladin, even if I wasn't a brother of the Omegas," Virgil paused, how was he supposed to say this? "I grew up with humans, I was raised by them, and I believed I was one until nine months ago. I love them Raphael," Virgil said passion filling his voice, tears at his eyes. "Humans are flawed, they are weak spiteful creatures, they kill without mercy, they hate without reason. But I have seen the good in them, I have seen compassion, empathy, hope and love. People helping others simply because it is the right thing to do. Only when humanity uses its great gift of consciousness in works of compassion and selflessness is it truly worthy of life on Earth. I believe that humanity still has a chance, a chance to show the universe and themselves, that they are more than hate and suffering, that they can have empathy for each other and at last…attain peace as a species. And I will not give up on them, not for anything, not for you," Virgil spoke from his heart feeling like it was breaking in the process.

Raphael had not moved but Virgil knew he had listened intently, he hung his head when Virgil had finished almost in defeat. "Whoever raised you, they did a fantastic job. I wish to commend them someday on loving my son as deeply as they did to give you such hopeful eyes," Raphael told Virgil. "I hear everything you are saying son, but I don't agree with you. Diablos will rise again, and when he does, he will destroy everything in his path. His hatred for humanity cannot be abated, he will crush their race to extinction and anyone who gets in his way. His return is inevitable, all we can hope to do is survive the aftermath of the destruction," he said sadly.

"I won't stand by and watch the world I love be destroyed," Virgil's words were steel. "If he wants our world, he'll have a fight waiting for him when he wakes up."

"Please don't do this," Raphael pleaded, "You have such potential Virgil, so much to give. Your place is at my side son, and I wish you could see that."

"I do Raphael," Virgil said closing his eyes his heart aching. "I think if things had been different, perhaps we would have been the best of friends. I would have been your right hand, and together we would have been happy. There is still a very strong part of me, the part that is Judge, that wants nothing more than to make you happy, to make you proud, and to stand with you." Virgil opened his eyes. "But a stronger part of me, the part of me that is human, loves my world too much to turn my back on it. I can't Raphael, I just can't," Virgil said tears rolling down his cheeks.

Raphael was dejected, "Perhaps you need more time to think things over," Raphael rose up from the table, he looked like he might cry, Virgil wasn't sure if Judges could cry.

"I am sorry Raphael," Virgil said meaning the words more than he had ever meant anything.

"As am I," Raphael replied. "You will not be allowed to leave this place, Hel, the Death Dealer prison. You are a Paladin and an enemy of the Dark Lord. The only way to regain your freedom is to pledge your eternal loyalty to him, and to me," Raphael informed him.

"That doesn't sound like freedom," Virgil said staring into his father's golden eyes, "That sounds like slavery."

"I will be back to see you every day you are here, until you take your rightful place at my side," Raphael offered turning to walk out of the cell his shoulders hunched, defeated, Virgil knew he had wounded his father more than any weapon could.

With a heavy heart Virgil asked him, "What if that day never comes?"

"Then you will spend your life in this prison," Raphael said sadly turning the force field on sealing Virgil in his prison cell.

Chapter 19
The First Seraph, the Avatar, Artreyu

The rest of Virgil's day was spent reflecting on his first visit with his father, he showered and changed his clothes, feeling more relaxed in this cell. The guards could not see him when he was laying in the bed, he was grateful for the privacy. Virgil didn't doubt that Raphael cared for him, in his own way his father loved him deeply. Virgil had a hard time falling asleep that night, the next day his father came in the morning bringing breakfast for him. Raphael was friendly, upbeat, and inquisitive. They easily enjoyed each other's company sticking to conversation that wouldn't ruin the open communication. Raphael told Virgil he would be back in the evening to bring him dinner. Before he left Raphael produced a book from his clothes and set it on the table, Virgil waited until Raphael walked away to examine it. The first Harry Potter novel. Virgil smiled, it was boring as Hel in the prison, pun intended. He sat down and spent his day rereading the classic taking breaks to work out or walk around, feeling the bittersweet joy of the ending as powerfully as he had the first time. Virgil appreciated his father providing him with entertainment, he wondered if he stayed here for decades if the gifts and visits would continue...probably not.

Raphael came back for dinner that evening, bringing foods that Virgil was familiar with, chicken, potatoes, broccoli and black pepper. The food tasted good for the most part, but in the Ever After food never stayed good for long. Virgil and Raphael discussed J.K. Rowling's master piece saga leading them to talk about all their favorite authors. Raphael had similar tastes with Virgil, and he enjoyed listening to his father explain things he'd never heard of before. After Virgil was finished Raphael had a chess board brought in for them to play. Virgil had spent the day being civil because it had felt kind of good, giving into the situation and bonding with his birth father.

Less than ten minutes into the game Virgil realized he didn't have a prayer of making it competitive. He casually asked something he'd been wanting to know since he'd regained consciousness. "When I was captured, I saw some of the other Paladins being taken, are they here too?"

"There was a group of new prisoners brought in from the Tournament," Raphael nodded, "A secondary goal was to remove some of their most promising members from their military," he informed Virgil.

"I would like to see them," Virgil asserted surprising himself.

"I don't think that is a good idea," Raphael shook his head.

"My brothers were on that field with me!" Virgil yelled. "I have been thinking about this since I got here, I need to know if any of my friends were taken hostage," he told his father letting him see how concerned he was. "All I am asking is to meet with the prisoners for a few minutes," Virgil explained. "So I can be at peace of mind, knowing who is in here with me, and who is safely back home." Virgil stared into his father's eyes knowing that he was making him uncomfortable. "Please Raphael," Virgil begged.

"Alright," Raphael nodded. "I can take you there before I leave for the night," he said rising. "Are you ready?" he asked.

"Yes sir," Virgil nodded.

"Easy on the sir," Raphael told him as they left the prison cell together. Raphael led Virgil further down into the tower. It wasn't a long walk, less than five minutes until they came to a cell similar in size to Virgil's current one, maybe a little bigger. There were over a dozen men in each cell, with just one toilet and two beds each. They were treating these people like animals!

"Virgil!" he heard Louie shout out running up to the force field.

"Louie V!" Virgil cried out bursting into a sprint racing past his father to meet his pledge brother.

The Omegas were mixed in with Paladins from Alpha class. The two cells next to each other had a mixture of men and women from the Coliseum, a few from Germany, China, and England had wound up in here as well. Gabriel, Magnus, and Dante approached the force field in the cell next to Louie's. They were far enough away that the people next to each other could not easily have conversations. So many of his brothers were here, only Zender and Brody hadn't been taken of the twelve Omegas in the Coliseum. Virgil could only stand in front of one force field at a time, he ran back and forth to see who was here. The Death Dealer guards grumbled insults, Virgil didn't care paying them no mind, he was too concerned with the wellbeing of his brothers.

"How is everyone holding up? Are they feeding you?" Virgil asked them.

"We've been worried about you," Vahn admitted looking so relieved to see him.

"Where have they been keeping you?" Magnus asked.

"I haven't eaten since I woke up in this place!" Louie cried out chiming in.

Dante sighed, and Virgil made eye contact watching him roll his eyes, "They bring each cell one meal a day, barely enough to go around but everyone gets a little bit."

"Those were snacks!" Louie barked, "I'm starving!"

"We're all hungry Louie, pipe down over there!" Tarek yelled from down the hall.

"I want my daily food rations given to these men," Virgil told Raphael. Raphael gave Virgil a look like, are you kidding, Virgil didn't back down. "This is inhumane, there are not enough places for each man to sleep in here. Not to mention one toilet and no privacy, this is abhorrent and shows how moral less the people who run this tower are!" Virgil yelled. "We passed how many empty cells on the way here!"

"We barely have food to feed ourselves!" One of the Death Dealer guards yelled, "We aren't going to starve so prisoners can eat like pigs," he finished crossing his arms over his chest and going back to staring straight ahead.

"Raphael," Virgil turned to his father asking in the most diplomatic tone he could muster, "Please let me bring some of my brothers back to my cell to share the space. There is more than enough room, and it would make the space more comfortable for the ones left."

"I'll go!" Louie volunteered.

"Me too," Birdy said waving at Virgil. Seeing so many people he cared about in this awful place made Virgil more than frightened, panic was setting in.

"No," Raphael said, "You are receiving special treatment under my direct supervision," Raphael told Virgil. "The boss won't go for large numbers of prisoners getting special treatment, simply because my son wishes it so."

"Then leave me here," Virgil said, "I'd rather stay with my brothers than sit in a cell by myself," he walked over to stand next to Birdy, Louie, Dante, Rowan, and Jagger just on the other side of the barrier to their cell. He wanted to press the button and open the cell, but so far in each other's company, Virgil and his father had shown each other a great deal of respect. Virgil didn't want to ruin whatever they had between them.

"That wasn't what we agreed upon," Raphael said shaking his head, "You asked to come see if your friends, we are here, so speak with them," he put his hands at his side and walked several paces back the way they'd came standing near the guard rail. "I'll give you a few minutes then we're going back," he said aloud.

"Virgil what's going on?" Magnus called from the other force field. Virgil ran over to their prison cell. "I'm being held captive here as well, just a five-minute walk higher into the tower. This place is the Death Dealer prison Hel," he told them.

"Yeah we knew that," Gabriel told him. "He meant what's going on with you and that Judge?" he said motioning to Raphael.

"That's the God General, Fallen Judge Raphael," Virgil told them.

"Third in command," Magnus said.

"Behind Lucifer and Beatrix," Tarek added.

"The only person above the God Generals is the Dark Mother Lilith and the Dark Lord," Magnus said aloud.

"How has it been, meeting your father?" Vahn asked Virgil.

The brothers were quiet, "It has been…overwhelming but exciting as well," he admitted feeling his face warm knowing his brothers, the other Paladins including ones from Alpha Chapter, the Death Dealer guards, and Raphael could hear him.

"You have to stay here too?" Tarek asked him.

"They want me to pledge allegiance to their leader and join their ranks, then I'll be allowed to leave," Virgil explained.

"I knew it!" Virgil heard Axion shout coming up from behind Gabriel and Magnus. "You're a traitor!"

"I have not turned my back on the Paladins, and I never will!" Virgil yelled cutting off Axion, he would not waste his time listening to his nonsense.

"He's a prisoner here too!" Vahn shouted at the other Paladin.

"How do we know that?" Axion said. "We aren't allowed to walk around. Maybe he has come down here to trick us all and make us think he's still fighting for our side. Maybe he's already been to Diablos' Throne and bent the knee."

"You don't know anything about him!" Vahn shouted. "Virgil's not the type to turn his back on people he cares about," Vahn turned to Virgil. "We're doing fine Virgil, hang in there bud, we're going to get through this," Vahn told Virgil wanting him to believe that.

Virgil walked over to his pledge brothers, Rowan, and Jagger, "I'll be back again soon, and I'll try to help as much as I can," Virgil told them.

"We know," Birdy nodded. He looked worn but Virgil saw hope in his eyes, he saw it in all their eyes, they were depending on him. The panic was starting to build, growing to become hopelessness. How was he supposed to save all these people? There were thousands of prisoners in this tower, and hundreds of Death Dealer guards with Fallen Judges apparently checking in.

"It is time son," Raphael told Virgil and he said good-bye to his friends following his father back up to his cell. He walked in and went right to his bed sitting down and pulling his legs up to his chest. Raphael came in and stood near his bed.

"It is not right, having so many men in one cell," Virgil commented staring ahead, "How are they supposed to survive that way?" he asked looking up at his dad.

"They typically don't," Raphael told him. "They usually die off until enough are left that can be sustained in the space," he said simply.

"That's dark," Virgil said looking down.

"I'm sorry about your friends," Raphael told Virgil. "If you are willing to join me, you may have all of them as your personal guard," he told him.

Virgil laughed. "My friends would never join me at your side. They would tell me I'd betrayed them, then hopefully, they would take me down. And I'd want them to," Virgil said looking back at his father. "Because I don't want to be that person."

"You need more time," Raphael nodded doing his best to be non-confrontational. "We have lots of time son," Raphael said, "I will see you again tomorrow."

"How long are you going to put me through this?!" Virgil shouted getting up to stare at his father's retreating back feeling angrier with Raphael than he ever had. "I will not spend my life trapped in this tower, with only your visits to give me companionship, protecting my psyche from isolation and the sweet whispers of insanity! If you truly loved me, you'd set me free!" Virgil yelled at him.

Raphael was quiet, "If I could Virgil, I would take you and all your friends, back to the human world. If I could do so without anyone ever knowing, I would. But I can't. My influence has its limits," Raphael said, "And I offer you the best that I can," he said before leaving Virgil and turning back on the force field.

Virgil lay in bed and willed himself to sleep. Virgil woke realizing where he was and became depressed. Raphael came to visit but he refused to get out of bed. Virgil began to pass his time by sleeping, things were looking more hopeless the longer he was here, what was the point in playing happy camper anymore? After several days of only laying in bed, not moving or eating, his father physically picked him up one morning, putting him under the shower. Virgil was pissed off, but Raphael left him alone, setting out a fresh towel and a change of clothes. Once Virgil had gotten dressed he came to the table where Raphael had food waiting for him, he insisted Virgil sit and eat.

"We are going on a trip today," Raphael told Virgil.

"To see my brothers?" Virgil asked excitedly.

"No, but the man is a prisoner in this tower, he is close to the top, it will be a long walk up to his room so finish your plate," Raphael encouraged. "You'll need your energy. The exercise will be good for you too."

"We could just fly up there," Virgil suggested. Raphael raised an eyebrow at Virgil, like he was trying to play a trick. "I wouldn't try and escape," Virgil sighed, "I wouldn't get far before you caught me," he pointed out.

"It would be faster than walking all the way up," Raphael nodded. "It shall be our first flight together!" he acknowledged with pride.

Virgil finished quickly, and they left his cell walking up to the guard railing. Virgil willed his wings from his back, they burst from his flesh in a flash of magic and pain. They extended out and Raphael looked them over. "Their uniqueness and splendor are unparalleled," he complimented appreciating their stark contrast. Raphael spread his wings from his back and nodded to Virgil running over to the edge and leaping off. Virgil ran after his father climbing into the railing and vaulting off, beating his wings he gained altitude quickly following his father. They flew next to each other and it felt exhilarating to fly at his side. Virgil only used his wings on special occasions, and it felt uplifting. Raphael had a large smile on his face, Virgil looked over smiling as well, just being together had a way of making a moment more special…Virgil looked forward. He needed to protect himself, situations like this had a way of cutting him deep, and how much pain would he keep inflicting on himself in this place?

Raphael landed, and Virgil saw they were closer to the top, the hole in the sky having grown from a speck, to include details such as movement in the storm clouds. These cells all only had one prisoner each, the guard station was not much further up from them. Both walkways from the sides of the tower met in a large open space and there was a guard room that worked the gate. The gate also operated the bridge beyond. Most people here could simply fly about where they needed, including leaving the tower, but some goods including prisoners could not fly hence the long drawbridge built connecting the tower to land. Virgil did not get to see the top, he landed next to his father, the exit from the tower just a few minutes higher.

Raphael approached a prison cell, and he rapped his knuckles against the barrier a few times. An elderly old man rose up from his bed and came over. He had to have been in his late sixties or seventies, his skin and face reflected the ravages of time. His body was gaunt, he was thin and frail walking slow, Virgil doubted he had long to live. A ruby Devil Arms was on his left hand, looking as vibrant and as full of life as any Devil Arms he'd ever seen on a Nephilim. Virgil looked up at Raphael wondering how he knew this man and why he'd been brought here.

"Good morning John," Raphael called to him.

"Morning Judge," John called back to Raphael in a friendly tone.

"I brought my boy here to meet you. He came in almost a week ago now, and has been staying in the lower levels," Raphael told John.

"Is that right?" John nodded looking from Raphael to Virgil. "What's your name boy?" John asked.

"Virgil, Virgil Pitcher," he told John.

"I was hoping you may be able to talk with him, he has been under the weather lately, and I figured you could give him some advice," Raphael said politely to John.

"I would be glad to," John said, and Raphael turned off the force field. Virgil walked into his room taking a seat on a small chair, John sat on his bed.

"How long have you been in here sir?" Virgil asked him.

"John is fine Virgil," John told him, "Over forty years," he sighed.

"That long!" Virgil reacted with concern. "How have you survived?" he asked astonished.

"It's all up here," John said tapping his head. "A mind game, the one's that live long lives in here are all fighters, more resilient than the rest, perhaps we are just too stubborn to die. Or maybe we just can't see giving up fighting, if even it's the fight to retain the freedom to choose to stay in here rather than join their ranks," John spoke with passion.

"I don't know how long I've been here but I'm already starting to lose faith," Virgil told John looking down at his hands.

"That's not true," John said. "If you'd truly have given up faith, you'd have joined your father. You are still hanging in there, same as me," John told Virgil. "There is a lot of fight left in you," he said staring into Virgil's eyes. "Don't sell yourself short kid, you're the type who goes down swinging," he nodded.

"How do you know, we've known each other less than five minutes," Virgil pointed out.

"Takes one to see it in another," John smiled, his teeth were decayed. Life in the prison must be grueling.

"John was my father's name," Virgil told him. "My adopted dad, he raised me, taught me that respect and etiquette were some of the most important qualities in a true gentleman. He died a few years ago, but I still miss him. He was so strong, so fun, so kind," Virgil smiled at John, "John is a strong name," he complimented him. "How did you end up here?" Virgil asked him.

"I was a Paladin once, same as you," John explained. "I was from a Chapter of Omegas in Indiana, one of the first Omega Chapters founded using a fraternity as a Paladin Chapter," he told Virgil.

"I'm an Omega!" Virgil shouted grinning.

"No kidding?" John asked. They stood up and John ushered the challenge to Virgil, Virgil demonstrated the secret handshake for John and they broke their contact. John smiled, Virgil had earned his trust, they were both Omegas, you didn't need to know more than that to know you would stand at each other's side. Suddenly Virgil saw John with renewed respect, he felt the same as the older man.

"It is such an honor to meet a brother of my fraternity," John said sitting down and getting a little misty eyed. "I never thought I'd see an Omega again, before I passed."

"How did you go from being an Omega to being in the Death Dealer prison?" Virgil asked the older frater.

"Our Chapter was on mission; I was in my senior year at my University. We were ambushed by the demons we were hunting, but quickly regained composure and turned the tide. Death Dealers had used the demons to distract us, they quickly overwhelmed us, catching us surprised, weakened from killing the demons. We were brought here, to be held until we turned defector, and joined the ranks of the enemy. Fourteen of my brothers, including myself were thrown into a prison cell, far down into the depths of the tower," John's eyes stared off at the wall, but what he was seeing was from another time. "We were caged like animals, in a space that would have been crowded with four of us. They didn't give us enough food to live on, the men held strong for the first few weeks but...," John hung his head. "Mortal men are weak, the brothers turned on each other. Driven by hunger and being driven mad with no room to move or space to think. Some of the brothers got into a fight, killing a few of our members. A few others died off from starvation. After several months our prison cell of fourteen had fallen to eight, and then two of our men joined the Death Dealers. Unable to handle the conditions, they'd rather join the enemy than continue to live like we were," there was such grief in his words. John did not cry but his face was haunted by the pain of his past.

"How did you make it all this time?" Virgil asked feeling the immense loss and suffering this man had to endure just to cling to the miserable existence that was his life.

"I had a Fallen Judge for a father," John told Virgil. "He came to visit me one day and was infuriated I was living in barbaric conditions. He ordered me placed in a private cell and came to visit me daily, slowly helping me regain strength and vitality," he said with a small smile. Virgil felt worried, was John? Did Raphael? Is that why he wanted Virgil to meet John? How many kids did he have locked away here Virgil thought angrily? John saw the wrong connections being made in his thinking and he waved his hand, "No, no, Raphael is not my father. My father wasn't one of the powerful Judges, just a normal Fallen, but he cared about me," John nodded. "He begged me to join the Death Dealers, telling me a life with them, even if it went against what I believed in, was better than a life of suffering in this prison," John recalled.

"But you never did," Virgil nodded.

"No, I didn't. No matter how bad things were in this prison, I could never become one of them. A murderer, taking innocent lives, Nephilim, mortals, children," John shook his head, "I'd rather stay here and starve than live a life of sin and death. Here I have spent my time in mediation and self-reflection. It wasn't a grand life but when I pass on and approach the golden gates of Nirvana, I can live my eternal peace knowing I lived my life the best way I could," John said. John was a wise and deep man, Virgil felt there was much knowledge he could pass onto him.

"Did your father stop coming to see you?" Virgil asked.

"He comes around every so often," John said, "I haven't seen him in a few years though, he stopped coming daily after we got into a bad fight," he admitted.

"A fight?" Virgil asked.

"At first he came each day, sometimes with gifts," Virgil felt awkward as that was how things had gone with Raphael. "After a few months, one night during dinner, he tried to kill me," John told Virgil calmly. Virgil was stunned silent, his mouth was hanging open a little, such a dark and depressing scenario, a father and son fighting to the death. "The argument was the same argument we'd had every day since he started coming to see me," John told him. "He wanted me to join the Death Dealers, to liberate myself from this fate, from this hell hole. But I refused," he shrugged. "That night he became more upset than I'd ever seen him. He told me he couldn't stand to watch me live my days out in this prison, all my potential wasted as day by day, year by year, my mortal body aged until finally I died in my cell, a prisoner to my last breath. My father told me by killing me he was setting me free, liberating me from a bleak future of living my days in a small cell, never truly living. He attacked me, and he tried to kill me," John said staring down at the table.

Virgil was dead silent, he was trying not to move, not even breath he didn't want to disturb John's story, and Virgil hung on his every word. "What happened next?" Virgil asked.

"The guards came in and stopped him," John shrugged looking at him seeming disappointed. "I was already unconscious, beaten to a bloody pulp, not sure how I survived. I continued on living though," John sighed leaning back in his chair and taking a deep breath.

"Were you mad at him?" Virgil asked. "Did you hate your father for trying to murder you?"

"No," John said simply with no concealed animosity. "My father was trying to protect me. When I wouldn't leave the prison, the only way I was allowed, he tried to save me the pain of having to live my days as a prisoner. He told me he couldn't stand to know I was here, it was eating him up inside, thinking his son, his legacy, was wasting his potential, his life. He loved me too much," John laughed.

"That's crazy," Virgil said shaking his head.

"He came to see me, several months later, to apologize," John told Virgil tears in his eyes. "He told me he was afraid I'd never want to see him again. He was scared I hated him. I told him he was my father, and no matter what came to pass, no matter how much wrong he did me, he would always be my dad, and I would always love him for that," John wiped at his eyes. "He told me that he couldn't come see me much anymore, it hurt him too much to see me here. He hugged me and shook my hand giving me a parting present, leaving, only to return a few more times over the next forty years," John said, his story coming to an end and going quiet.

"That was incredible John," Virgil didn't know what to say, "I'm honored you shared that with me." Virgil thought about what he'd said, "What was the parting present?" he asked John.

John shrugged, "It doesn't matter now," he brushed aside Virgil's comment. "Listen to me boy," John said leaning forward. "My father fought so hard for me to join the Death Dealers because he loved me fiercely. I see how Raphael looks at you, and I see the eyes of a father who worries deeply for his son. Raphael does not want you in this prison. I am sure he is hoping seeing an old man like myself, will show you what is in store if you don't give in," John told him.

Virgil nodded, "It is a harrowing message," Virgil looked down, "I doubt I would live as long as you have though. You're a man of incredible resilience, I have fight in me, but not enough to last a lifetime."

"Good luck to you, Virgil," John said taking Virgil's hand and smiling deeply. "One last thing before you go, your father, he's not all bad." John spoke quietly so Virgil had to lean in. "Most of the things in the Ever After just want to watch the world burn, Raphael is different, classy like an old school gentleman, and he doesn't tolerate senseless violence. The people around here, they like him, for good reason. I'm not saying you should join him, just that things aren't always black and white, we all exist somewhere in the grey."

"Thank you, for everything. Good luck to you, John," Virgil whispered back, "You will be in my thoughts and in my prayers frater." They hugged, and Virgil left his cell, Raphael was waiting for him. Raphael recommended they walk down to his cell to give him more time outside and more exercise. Raphael made small talk with Virgil along the way, trying not to bring up John and his story. Virgil knew what Raphael was trying to say, don't end up like him. Virgil didn't know if he could keep saying no to Raphael, year after year. How long would he last before he cast aside this prison for the life of a Death Dealer? It was easy to say he would spend his life here, and never give in. But forever, is a very long time.

Virgil had dinner with Raphael, he didn't eat, he hadn't eaten or drank anything in the time they'd spent together. Raphael wanted to play chess afterwards, he wanted a rematch, but Virgil didn't want to play, Raphael was far superior, it wasn't much fun. Raphael practically begged him, Virgil felt kind of bad for him, asking so ardently he was starting to sound pathetic. Virgil gave in and Raphael purposefully made several dumb moves to keep the game more even. Raphael still won, but Virgil appreciated what he did. Afterwards Virgil told him he was tired. Virgil had a lot on his mind, and he needed to be alone.

"It was nice, spending time with you today Virgil," Raphael said happily a real smile on his face.

"It was Raphael," Virgil nodded unable to stop himself from smiling with his father. "I enjoyed flying with you."

"I hope you will reflect on John's story," Raphael told Virgil the first time they'd brought him up since they'd left John's cell.

"I will," Virgil nodded looking away from his dad. "I appreciate all you're trying to do for me. I know you care about me Raphael," he told him walking over to his bed. "Goodnight," he called back.

"See you tomorrow," Raphael called walking away, "I love you son," he said softly before he left turning back on the force field.

Virgil rolled onto his side to look at the wall. He read for as long as he could to keep his mind busy before finally giving into his exhaustion, letting sleep take over, passing out. A knocking woke him up. Virgil rubbed his eyes, he sat up, and moved the book off his chest. He swung his feet over the bed and got up. A knock came again, Virgil didn't think it was morning, it didn't feel like he'd gotten much sleep. He turned on the light in his cell and approached the force field. The barrier turned off and a Judge walked in the room. It was Raphael.

"Raphael," Virgil said, "What are you doing back so soon?" he asked yawning.

"I have come to speak with you son," Raphael said sounding off.

Virgil stared at his father intently, "Okayyy, what's going on?" he asked. Virgil concentrated feeling the power of his aura surrounding him. Virgil could now visibly see his own aura, which was comforting, it looked as it always had, a vibrant gold. But the aura surrounding Raphael was all wrong, the first time Virgil had seen Raphael his aura had been so overpowering it had been hard to be in the same room with him. Over time and with Raphael restraining his power, it had become more bearable, that's how dominant a Judge's aura could be. But this person, their aura was not like Raphael's. It was immensely powerful, but different. Aura's were almost like DNA, each person's slightly different, yet a little uniquely their own. Virgil was no fool, he immediately took a large step back narrowing his eyes.

"You're not my father," Virgil told him.

"Son, how can you say that?" Raphael told him, "It's meant so much to me hearing you call me that these days we've spent together," he said.

"Funny," Virgil said crossing his arms, "Considering I've never ONCE called you dad, or father, or anything other than Raphael and sir," Virgil said with confidence and attitude.

The fake Raphael had a look on his face, the startled uh-oh I've been caught, then he smiled coyly, and his appearance rippled. "That surprises me Redeemer, I think better of you now." The appearance of Raphael melted away revealing a man slightly shorter than Virgil. He had tanned skin, almost brown, with stark white hair that hung to his waist. His hair was done in several intricate unique braids, the majority flowed down his back. His clothes were far more elegant then anything Virgil had seen in Alexandros, which in his mind had set the bar for sophisticated attire. Breathtaking wings of irrefutable wonder sprouted from his back, they were nearly the same height as him, white wings but distinctive by the gold tips on every feather. They were as distinctive and unique as his mismatched ones. The man had white gloves over both of his hands. He had a toned and muscled physique, with a striking face, and uniquely stunning grey colored eyes, with a triple layer iris. The outer layer was a darker grey that seemed to move around like thunder clouds. The inner layers of his iris were lighter grey followed by a small layer of lilac. It looked like purple lightning strikes were happening from the outside of his eye into the black pupil. Virgil blinked a few times getting lost in them. He had a deceptively youthful appearance, like that of a teenager, but his body language suggested he was much older.

"It is good to know you're not too naïve," he said to Virgil. "Even if Raphael is your father, calling him that will do neither of you any good."

"Who are you really?" Virgil asked. "You're not a Judge," he pointed out.

"I can't explain everything because we're on a schedule, I apologize for the earlier deception," his voice was soft, his words well pronounced and precise. He gave off a regale and noble air of authority, utmost he was polite and serious to a fault. "That was glamour, a powerful form of Illusion magic most sidhe fairies use like mortals drive cars," he told Virgil. "I'm one of the most gifted in my mother's court, it's the only reason I was able to fool the Death Dealers," he said, "I came in with stealth, and that is how I will escort you out," he explained.

"Wow," Virgil said staring open mouthed and wide eyed, this man was here to rescue him! Virgil's earlier thoughts at having to spend his remaining days in this prison, everything had changed in an instant. And his appearance had looked good enough to fool Virgil! At least...at face value, without careful inspection, it'd been a near flawless impersonation. "You can clearly use powerful magic, but why are you helping me?" Virgil asked him.

"Forgive my rudeness, I should have begun with introductions," he nodded, "I am the son of Andais, Queen of Darkness and Storms, Queen of the Unseelie sidhe fairy court, and son of Judge Odin, King of Judges and Ruler of Nirvana. My name is Artreyu, I am the First Seraph, the Avatar. I was recruited to rescue you from the Ever After."

Chapter 20
<u>Escape and Betrayal</u>

"Who sent you to rescue me?" Virgil wondered skeptical the First Seraph was risking his life out of kindness. "Why haven't I seen you up till now, you weren't at the Paladin Games."

"I'm not a mortal Nephilim," Artreyu shrugged, "My mother doesn't like the UnSeelie Sidhe fairies mingling in mortal affairs. Let's be gone from this cell and take to the air." Artreyu's appearance rippled like the surface of water, morphing once more to reflect the Fallen Judge Raphael.

"Creepy," Virgil nodded following Artreyu out of the cell. Artreyu hit the button to turn the force field back on to Virgil's cell, so it wouldn't draw attention. Artreyu approached the guard rail, his fake black wings rustled, he was anxious to get going.

"My cuffs?" Virgil asked motioning his restraints towards Artreyu, "I can help you fight."

"It'll look more convincing if they stay on until we clear the tower," Artreyu waved off Virgil's suggestion. "Let's start flying to the top."

"Wait!" Virgil exclaimed trying to keep his voice down but needing Artreyu to understand the importance of his words.

"We don't have time to talk everything over," Artreyu said impatiently as if admonishing a child.

"My brothers are in this prison not five-minutes further down," Virgil told him. "I'm not leaving here without them," he said crossing his arms over his chest.

"Virgil, we don't have TIME to rescue your friends," Artreyu said firmly.

"Well then I don't have TIME, to fly with you to the top, DAD," Virgil got huffy and turned towards the path to his friends.

"I can't believe this," he sighed, "Darker more powerful things are sealed here besides Nephilim," Artreyu whispered his confidence cracking to show…fear. Virgil swallowed hard. "If we take too long here, things may be set into motion that would be devastating for the lives of millions," he warned. "We CANNOT allow that to happen. You are asking me to help you save the lives of a few men and endanger those many times over," he said to Virgil.

"Help me get them, and we leave!" he insisted. "Let's get moving!"

"Fine!" Artreyu cut him off. "Stay silent and keep your eyes on the ground," he demanded, "I asked the guards outside your room to go on break, though there are plenty more around. They so much as think I'm not the real Raphael and we'll be swarmed by hundreds of Death Dealers. We're powerful, but even Seraphs have limits," he warned.

"Got it," Virgil responded, and they began power walking the path to his friends. Luckily the real Raphael had put him in an area without neighbors. Within a minute they started passing cells with prisoners and the occasional guard. It was night in the Ever After, which meant it was day light on Earth. The guards were running on a skeleton crew, the few they walked past were tired and not paying them any attention. Virgil's pulse was racing; his adrenaline was pumping at full throttle. For the first time since he'd been in this prison, he had hope of escape. The cells of prisoners he passed, he wondered who they were, how'd they'd gotten here. Should Virgil insist they save them all? Were they capable of saving them all? Virgil selfishly said nothing, staring at the ground, not suggesting the idea as it diminished the chances of him bringing back his Omegas.

They reached the cells of his friends without incident, there were two guards between the two cells, but none on the walkway around them. Artreyu approached the men with confidence, "Morning men," he said in a voice that was noble and strong.

"Good morning Judge Raphael," they replied politely their tone indicating they liked him.

"I have need to speak with these prisoners, please take a half hour off for leisure, and give us some privacy?" the fake Raphael asked the Nephilim guards.

"Of course, Judge Raphael," they answered surprised but unquestioning. "Thank you kindly for the break sir," they bowed slightly and headed back up. They waited for the Death Dealers to leave, and Virgil ran over to Vahn's prison cell first, and lifted the barrier.

"You guys alright?" Virgil asked the men. Most of them were trying to sleep, the entire floor was covered in bodies. Virgil turned the light back on which brought a chorus of complaints. "You want a chance to bust out of Hel, or do you want to go back to cuddling on the dirty floor?" Virgil asked them with sass. The room quickly got to their feet. "I don't have time to explain I need all of you to stay quiet and follow me immediately!"

"How is this happening?" Magnus asked. "Who is helping you?" he wondered looking out to see Raphael standing outside their prison cell.

"Is your dad helping us escape?" Vahn asked disbelieving.

"No," Virgil said, "It's the First Seraph, the Avatar," he told them. That garnered everyone's attention, and even Axion and the other non-Omegas were now very interested.

Virgil quickly went over to the other prison cell and did the same thing. Both groups gathered in the walkway outside, the Chapters who had men that were separated by prison cells quickly reunited and hugged, happy to see their friends and brothers once more.

"We don't have a moment to spare, so let's make precious haste and fly," Artreyu spoke and everyone went still, he had a strange presence that was overpowering to normal mortals.

"Wait, fly out?" Dante asked. "Um news flash, some of us don't have wings," he said laughing like they were idiots his face getting red. "Is that the plan? Those with wings get to go free while the rest of us stay here to rot!" he shouted getting fired up.

"Hush you wanker!" A Paladin from England barked at him, "Your bloody trap's about to get us caught!"

"Those with wings produce them," Artreyu asked the men. Virgil looked around his heart sinking, his pledge brothers, Birdy, Louie, and Dante didn't have wings as well as a Paladin from Germany. Four men…three of them that meant the most to Virgil. They were Omicron, Virgil's best friends, Virgil turned to Artreyu, fearful. He couldn't leave them behind!

"We can't leave them," Virgil said shaking his head.

"We can't run to the top!" Artreyu asserted. "We'll never make it!"

"We need to get leaving," Axion said interjecting, "Let the Lambs rot in the hell fire," he smirked.

"Shut your hole," Virgil snapped pissed off and in no mood. "These are my best friends and I will not be abandoning them any time soon! There has got to be another way," Virgil said desperately.

"You're the Redeemer," Artreyu encouraged Virgil. "If anyone can solve this dilemma, it is you," he smiled.

"What do you mean?" Virgil asked his older, wiser rescuer.

"The Redeemer has the ability to bestow power on others, give your friends Redemption, and let us be on our way." Artreyu was straight forward, Virgil had thought him rude for not wanting to help rescue his brothers, now he just realized he was nervous, and was normally very polite. Virgil sensed a great kindness from Artreyu, of all the Seraphs he'd met, he was the most recognizable force for Creation.

"What?" Virgil asked puzzled. "You mean the ability I'm supposed to use on the Fallen? How is that going to help?"

"Anyone you use that power on, gains access to their Devil Arms' Soul Scream, and for Fallen Judges, they get their Holy wings back. Wingless Nephilim in turn sprout wings like Judges, becoming full-fledged members of their race," Artreyu told Virgil.

Virgil stared down at Ragnorak's symbol. He'd used the power once before, to Redeem the Fallen Judge Ipos…could he really give them wings?

"It is worth a shot," Magnus suggested. "We can't all be standing out here looking like dumbasses. Someone is going to notice this group soon, and when they do, I doubt they'll inquire as to why Raphael is taking so many prisoners out for a stroll," he surmised sarcastically.

"I'll try," Virgil nodded.

"That is out of the question," Axion said speaking up. "Using those powers is forbidden by the Alexandros government. It is not legal for you to take the power of the Creator into your hands, and decide who has wings and who does not," Axion said angrily. "The distinction of the winged over the wingless has been a backbone of our society since we were founded," he pointed out.

Virgil smiled wickedly, "Even better a reason to do this, perhaps if we make it out alive, I should stand in the Alexandros town square, and offer to all the lowborn, wings of their own," he suggested.

"Sacrilege!" Axion shouted pissed off.

"Shut up already," a Paladin from Germany said. "If the Redeemer wants to offer a chance to help my brother flee this wretched dungeon then NO one will stand in his way," he told Axion his ruby red Devil Arms symbol glowing to flex his intention.

"ENOUGH," Artreyu cut across his voice was not loud, yet his very speech held so much power it rolled the minds of mere mortals. "Redeem them or we fly, now!" He commanded with urgency.

"I can't feel my Devil Arms with these things," Virgil told Artreyu motioning to the cuffs on his wrists.

"I'll take them off," Artreyu stated. His glamour fell, and everyone was surprised taking a step away from him. He approached Virgil and raised his gloved hand to the cuffs. A sphere of white light splashed out from where he touched, and the cuffs fell to the floor…destroyed.

"What was that?" Louie commented on the Avatar's mysterious power.

While Artreyu uncuffed the rest of the group Virgil closed his eyes and concentrated on the four men grouped together standing shoulder to shoulder. They'd retreated inside the cell as to not be so conspicuous standing in the walkway. Virgil dug deep within himself feeling for the power, the power that allowed him to Ascend…it was the same power he needed now. The 'other Virgil' the unconscious part of his mind that housed his inner Judge. He felt it awaken and its thoughts merge with his, it was at once familiar and foreign. His power came online his eyes going gold like his father's, with a blaze of life gold ribbons of light extending out from Rangorak, four in all, snaking out to reach for the men in front of him. They were frightened, Virgil smiled gently, and let his aura stretch out comforting them, letting them see in his spirit the purity of his intentions. They opened up their minds to him, Virgil's bands of light connected with their arms and time stopped. Virgil's mind was flooded with images of their lives, playing from the beginning and moving forward.

Virgil saw Birdy using different hearing aid devices as a child and getting bullied by his peers for being different. Birdy was taught how to use sign language, and his written skills increased dramatically even surpassing his peers. Louie grew up in a blended family, his parents didn't work out and he had half siblings on both sides along with multiple step siblings. Louie's natural artistic talent flowed from him like laughter from a child. Virgil watched as Louie created works of art, he felt like he was the one doing the painting. Dante had an older half-brother on his dad's side, he was always envious of how big and strong his brother was, and how his dad seemed to just shine when he came around. Dante pushed himself hard always wanting to do his best to make his parents proud, developing in him an indomitable spirit. The German man's name was Max, he grew up with normal human parents like Virgil. Only when he joined his fraternity did he learn of his Nephilim blood and join the Paladins. He wanted to return home to his human family, his human life more than anything. Four life times in the span of a second, Virgil's thoughts raced from one memory, one image, one conversation to the next, the men's lives intermingling to become one long message, of life, loss, and triumph. They were good people and that inner light shone through clearly as the memories were linked together, and the visions finally came to an end.

The connection broke on its own, the ribbons of light falling away like dust to the ground, Virgil's eye returned to normal. The four men sprouted wings from their backs, they were startled and a little uneasy. But after the shock came grins, they were like little kids wanting to try out new toys. The tower shook, a deep menacing roar echoed through, something deep beneath the tower was stirring from Virgil's power.

"What was that?" Gabriel asked taking a warrior's stance out of habit.

"She awakens," Artreyu whispered horrified, "She has sensed the Redeemer's power! We need to get to the top!" Artreyu shouted to them with a renewed sense of urgency, "If they begin to close the tower, we'll have to land and fight our way out," he told them. "We'll fly as hard as we can until that point, everyone NEEDS to keep up. You fall behind, you get left behind," he finished. His appearance rippled, like a heat wave flaring in front of him, he wavered in place then became Raphael.

"Creepy," Louie commented.

"Right?" Virgil asked.

The men leapt into the air and took flight, the massive empty space in the center giving them plenty of room to spread out. They wanted to whoop and shout out in absolute resounding joy...FREEDOM! The Nephilim were elated to be free from their cell, for most this was the first time they'd left it since they'd arrived. Nothing was as exhilarating as flying on angel wings.

Artreyu stuck to the head of the pack, staring up at the tiny hole reflecting the night sky in the great distance with a look of pure determination. Omicron was doing well, they kept up pace learning to use their new appendages at crash and burn, breakneck speeds.

They started to hear shouting, guards had noticed them, a few took flight, jumping from the tower high above them, diving down to meet the escaping prisoners.

"Don't slow down!" Artreyu cried out, "PUSH FORWARD!" he screamed, "FIRAGA!" Ruby energy flowed from his hands and a Master level fire spell erupted into existence in the air above the group, a lethal explosion the width of the entire tower. The Death Dealers were engulfed entirely in the flames, their limp bodies fell past them, plummeting to the ground below. The spell didn't even phase the Avatar, he kept flight at the head of the pack, his strength and endurance outpacing everyone. Seconds went by, the tower was starting to come alive, other prisoners were awake and some were pounding on their cell barriers crying out to be rescued. They kept flying higher, another batch of Death Dealers took flight from above, circling around preparing to attack.

"THUNDAGA!" Artreyu shouted amethyst energy flowing from his hands towards the approaching pursuers. Lightning bolts zapped down from above, several barrages of energy clapped down fraying out its destructive power. The guards were caught in the storm, each getting struck by the spell, one fell onto a portion of prison walkway further down, the other two kept falling into the darkness.

"He's not even using a staff," Magnus remarked in awe slightly ahead of Virgil. "How is he able to expend so much energy? Those spells take a massive toll on an aura," he said. Virgil stuck to the back looking to keep an eye on their flank while Artreyu speared them through. The tiny dot that had been the sky above was gradually expanding, they were over halfway to the top!

A loud siren began to fill the tower. Below them in the large circular opening that stretched the length of the tower, hatches started to move. There were gates that could lock off the center open area! They began to close, including the ones above them.

"Damn!" Artreyu cursed, "We must land and take the rest of the journey on foot!" he called out diving for the walkway. Artretyu's appearance rippled and he looked himself once more. "We push through to the top! Our fates are now forever intertwined, we must prevail!"

Artreyu landed taking lead, everyone following close behind. Virgil's feet hit the ground and he went right into a brisk jog to keep up with his group. The path curved ascending slowly, up ahead a group of four guards, their Devil Arms drawn and ready to receive them.

"Blizzaga!" Artreyu shouted, pale blue energy leaked from his hands. A gale force blizzard sprang into existence propelling towards the Death Dealers with battering speeds. The ice that flowed around them solidified in seconds becoming a massive glacier. Artreyu snapped his fingers, the ice shattered spraying dusts of ice like shards of glass. When the magic settled the Death Dealers were left on the ground, the group running past them. Virgil was impressed by Artreyu's abilities, so was everyone else. Further up, they came across a group of six guards.

"Help me cut a path!" Artreyu yelled out. Gabriel and Axion formed their Devil Arms and charged forward. The strain of the spells was starting to show, though Artreyu hadn't slowed down, he ran forward to engage in hand combat rather than use precious energy. Artreyu fought with his gloved hands. The moment they touched a Death Dealer, spheres of white light erupted at the point of impact, the person would scream in pain. Artreyu weaved through the warriors like a dancer, striking vital points on the body with powerful blows or karate chops from his hands, taking men down in three to four strikes. Virgil didn't know what kind of Devil Arms he had, or if he was even using one, but it was a sight to behold.

Virgil was standing watching, he looked to his left and saw a young man, no more than a few years older than himself, standing against the barrier of his cell, looking out at them. Virgil locked eyes with the man, his eyes were screaming, shrill at the top of their lungs! CARE! I am here, and I need help! SAVE ME! They shouted for his trembling lips would not, the fight had been beat out of him, he did not dare to ask, to hope, to dream. Virgil punched the button to his barrier, and the man stepped out. Virgil summoned his scythe placing the tip onto the bracelet of his Devil Arms hand. The bracelet was destroyed by Soul Reaver, he stared into Virgil's eyes, and the gratitude in them was almost too much to bear. He silently entered their group.

They took down the Death Dealers and continued the climb. Everyone had their Devil Arms drawn, ready to do their part to earn their freedom. More Death Dealers greeted them in each new area, and Artreyu led the assault, never tiring, never stopping. Gabriel and Axion showed signs of fatigue and fell back into the group, all the prisoners looked gaunt, and their faces shallow from lack of nutrition, sunlight, and proper hygiene. Four more of their group moved forward to take their place supporting Artreyu. The group was working as one, any earlier tension between men from the various Chapters evaporated. They were one team now. They were Paladins against a sea of black winged Nephilim, all working towards the hope of returning home.

Every time they stopped for more than a second to engage in Death Dealer resistance, Virgil ran along the passage, opening as many prison cells as possible before he had to start running to keep up with the moving group. Their throng of fleeing prisoners was increasing with every battle. Artreyu shot Virgil an arched eyebrow with a questioning gaze as they started their climb once more but didn't comment. With each freed prisoner, they were one member stronger, and in this tower the prisoners outnumbered the guards by fifteen to one. Some of the freed prisoners simply could not keep up, they were emaciated, so weak, so little energy to spare, but giving it their all for freedom limping after the group getting left in the dust. Virgil had fallen behind, encouraging the weakest to move faster, physically picking up some that had fallen, dragging them to others who could bear their weight and keep moving. Virgil could no longer see his team. Virgil took flight to catch up to his brothers flying over the fleeing prisoners. His group was halted a minute's flight ahead by a barrier of Death Dealers. A dozen strong, they were more experienced than the others they'd encountered before, and they were concentrating their strikes on taking out warriors helping Artreyu. He was too fast and powerful for them to effectively counter, but the freed prisoners were easy pickings. A few warriors who Virgil had freed received grave injuries falling unable to stand.

"Get your butt up here Redeemer!" Artreyu called back to Virgil once he landed, "You cannot fall behind trying to save everyone! You CAN'T save them all!" he yelled.

Virgil charged into the battle screaming, spinning Soul Reaver like a madman knocking Death Dealers back. With Soul Reaver's deadly flames Virgil quickly weakened and overcame several guards, turning the tide in their favor. They finished off the last Death Dealer and started running once more. The passageways were getting thinner, Virgil was starting to recognize the area, they were close to where he'd visited the Omega John! Virgil focused his attention on the cells they passed, the other prisoners had started helping him free their fellow inmates. He didn't have to stop for each one like he'd done at the beginning. Virgil had to get John out of here, he deserved to see Earth once again, to spend his last days breathing free air and living life by his own choices. Virgil ran up to John's cell as the group ran past, he had to make time for this.

"Virgil!" John shouted seeing him approach. Virgil hit the switch for the barrier, and John stepped out. Virgil used Soul Reaver to break his Devil Arms restraint.

"We are being rescued by the Avatar!" Virgil spoke quickly. "Come with us!" he asked.

"I have waited for this day since the first night I slept in this godforsaken tower," John said overcome with emotion, "I had accepted that I'd spend my final days here."

"I'm not leaving without all the Omegas," Virgil winked at his friend, "We have to catch up to the group, we're making the final push to the bridge!" The two began moving with the stream of freed prisoners that were running far behind his main group.

John spoke to Virgil as they ran side by side. "The bridge will be hard to take," John warned him. "Their strongest Nephilim are posted at the entrance. Warriors will be guarding the exit by the hundreds!"

"By the time we reach them, we'll number the hundreds as well!" Virgil shouted back.

"Their seasoned warriors, we're starved prisoners," another fleeing inmate who was running close by spoke up.

"They are fighting because it is their job! We are fighting for our freedom!" Virgil yelled. "I am the Redeemer, the Sixth Seraph! Wielder of Ragnorak!" Virgil said with confidence, turning heads and gaining the attention from the other fleeing warriors. "I will fight to my last breath to liberate us from this hell or die trying!" he screamed. The prisoners let out a chorus of cheers, chanting Redeemer as they ran rallying behind Virgil's fierce determination. John held his spear in his hand once more, the first time he'd been allowed to hold his Devil Arms since he was a young man. Virgil was proud to fight at the old warrior's side.

They arrived at the top of the tower, and the passageway opened onto a large semicircular area. Artreyu and the others were blocked from the exit by hundreds of Death Dealers forming a wall of living flesh between them and their freedom. Their small team of warriors ran forward fighting fiercely, there were no Dull spells in the battles of this prison, the two forces fought with savagery. Artreyu was the most powerful being in the room, showering spells down upon the mob of guards, taking out handfuls at a time. Jumping fearlessly at the phalanx of soldiers he used his fists to take down enemies with Devil Arms. But they were hopelessly outnumbered, even with Artreyu fighting like an unstoppable maniac through the crowds.

Virgil's large team of freed prisoners ran forward jumping into the battle. Their numbers were much needed, and they helped revitalize the spirt of those warriors at the front. Virgil fiercely charged forward with Soul Reaver, his scythe cutting through each Death Dealer with a savageness that he'd never shown on the battlefield. Virgil kept close to John maneuvering him up the field, protecting him with all he had. They were getting close to his friends, everyone looked so tired, pushing to give everything they had.

"Virgil!" John cried out. Virgil turned unable to stop the attack in time. A Death Dealer threw his spear at Virgil's back, things slowed down. John close to Virgil's side, leapt into Virgil using his body as a living shield, taking the death blow meant for the Redeemer. John was flung back knocking Virgil and him over. Virgil knelt over John's impaled body his blood quickly saturating the ground he was open mouthed and in shock. Soul Reaver faded from existence, he had too much pain in his soul to hold onto the anger needed to fuel its power. Two prisoners attacked the Death Dealer who'd thrown his spear and took his attention off Virgil and John.

"I can help you," Virgil kept muttering to himself, his hands shaking covered in the man's blood. He reached out to the power of his aura, if he used enough energy, he could possibly close John's wound. If he used Cura enough times he might live, even though it'd take most of his aura he had to try!

"Virgil, stop," John said putting his hand over Virgil's. "You must move on, these people need you," he told him.

"I can help you!" Virgil cried out tears trembling down his cheeks. "Please let me help you!" He'd wanted so badly to bring John back to his home, to bring some measure of happiness to a man who'd lived a life of hardship and suffering.

"My friend," John smiled clasping Virgil's hand tightly looking deep into his eyes, "You already have." His words sank into Virgil's spirit. He hadn't felt like he'd done a thing. "I would rather die fighting to protect a noble warrior like you Redeemer, then have spent another ten years in that cell. Here," he said placing something in Virgil's hand. Virgil looked down at the yellow gem in his hand, it was Optimum! The same magicite he'd examined while browsing in a shop in Alexandros. Virgil could feel the energy stored inside; it was tenfold the amount of energy that was held in his own aura! "The next time my father visited me after he tried to kill me," John coughed, he was losing focus, "He told me that if he couldn't convince me to leave the suffering of my cell behind by joining him, he wanted me to have a fighting chance, if I ever had to opportunity to break free," he told Virgil. "Give 'em hell boy! Was what he said to me," John remembered with a smile. "I've siphoned energy from my aura into that magicite every day since, use it. Use it to lead these men to freedom! Give 'em hell boy!" John yelled with a look of fierce determination, settling back with a smile on his face.

"Thank you, frater John," Virgil whispered to John. He was gone, having died with a smile on his face. Virgil stood disoriented trying to focus once more on the fight. There were so many Death Dealers left, and the prisoners just didn't have the energy to match their strength. Virgil felt the Optimum in his hand, it burned with energy, John had packed the thing so full it couldn't hold a single drop of more power. Virgil hadn't known John more than a day, but the man's story had moved him. He'd been an Omega from another time, robbed of his mortality in a war of violence and hate. Virgil picked through his thoughts thinking how he could best save them, to lead them to freedom. Virgil felt the power in his hand, and the answer came to him. He'd never used the spell outside of his Ascended state, but he felt confident in this moment, he knew if he spoke the words his Will would make it happen.

Virgil raised his right hand to the sky aiming at the sea of Death Dealers opposing them, holding the Optimum the spell drained its cost from the stone. "Light Surge!" Virgil screamed. A barrage of Creation energy rained down like missiles upon the Death Dealers. "Light Surge!" Virgil yelled again drinking more energy from the magicite, the spell raining down again even before the first had finished. "Light Surge!" he yelled fiercely for the fallen men who had died for their freedom. "Light Surge!" Beams of white energy hailed down from the dark sky like lightning strikes. "LIGHT SURGE!" Virgil screamed using the spell again. "LIGHT SURGE!" He screamed the spell's name again and again into the night, screaming with rage, anger, and despair. Everyone on the battlefield turned to stare in fear and awe, as he rained the fury of heaven upon his enemies.

Virgil's sight was blinded by the sheer volume of blinding white lights crashing down around them shaking the whole tower. A huge cloud of smoke hung in the air, and with it the sounds of battle had stopped completely. Virgil stood breathing heavy staring ahead of him. Hundreds of Death Dealers lay decimated, the entire army of guards who'd been blocking their path lay motionless, and there were no more warriors to oppose them. The magicite in Virgil's hand still had some energy, enough to power several more spells, John had truly given him a generous gift. The few Death Dealers who'd been in the fray of battle and not been grouped together were quickly dealt with. Virgil stared at the bodies harrowed by the vision of death; he'd done this. He'd slaughtered men by the hundreds to protect his friends and fellow prisoners, he'd never had to kill before tonight…

"That was impressive Virgil!" Artreyu came to his side showing genuine excitement and praise. "You single handedly cleared us a path and saved these men!" Artreyu's elation fell as he investigated the face of his comrade, seeing the mental toll it had taken on him to cause so much death. Virgil stood still staring blankly ahead, numb, still processing what he had done. "It is over now Virgil. You do not need to carry the burden of their deaths with you. Let us be gone from this place and only carry life forth," he said gently steering Virgil towards the bridge. Virgil was in a daze, he let Artreyu lead him, pocketing the magicite as they approached the exit. Some of the prisoners were heading for the bridge, a large group stuck back, they were older, more worn, these were the prisoners who'd weathered long years in this tower.

"You coming?" Artreyu shouted out.

"We're staying," a prisoner in the group said. "There shouldn't be many Death Dealers left, we're going to free all the prisoners, and then make our escape, together," he said getting several nods from his comrades.

"May the Goddess guide you," Artreyu said and the two groups of men parted ways.

Virgil and his group of a hundred strong ran out onto the draw bridge. Virgil could see for the first time what lay between the tower and the land of the Ever After up close. A sea of nothingness, a blackness so deep that to fall into its infinite depths was to be swallowed into oblivion. The tower stood at the very limits of the Ever After! The dark black storm raged around them, the bridge the only path from the tower to the larger landmass of the Ever After.

"We should use the bridge!" Artreyu yelled, the power of the storm making it hard for his voice to carry. "The air here is hard to fly in, until we get the land underneath our feet," he led them across the bridge leaving the tower behind. The fierce winds battered them to a sluggish gait, and the bridge flailed in the darkness beneath their feet feeling like it'd give way at any moment.

The air was foggy, a warrior with wings was walking towards them. Virgil's heart raced, he prayed it was not his father, could the group of them even hope to stand against him?

"My, my, it seems I came just in time," Rasler said approaching them.

"Rasler?" Axion asked shocked to see the Paladin's Grand Pylortes, "Thank goodness the Paladins have sent you to rescues us! We're making our escape now, lead the way!"

"Making your escape?" Rasler asked surprised, "Shouldn't you be locked inside a prison cell at the bottom of Hel?" he suggested coldly. "Why don't you turn around little Axion, the world is a better place without you in it."

Axion was confused but Artreyu was not, he stared Rasler down, his eyes narrowing. "You've betrayed the Paladins," Artreyu accused him. "You serve Diablos!" he shouted.

"The Avatar," Rasler said looking him over. "I was wondering when you'd show your girlish face. You've been hiding from us, though it seems at long last the Seven Seraphs are beginning to gather. The War of Ragnorak is quickly approaching."

He apparently hit a sore subject with Artreyu, "My race ages slowly, I am still considered a child among my people!" he defended his youthful appearance. Virgil had thought he looked like a teenager, even younger than Virgil, when he'd first seen him.

"You're over a hundred! Grow up already!" Rasler mocked Artreyu.

Virgil stared at Rasler, stunned. He'd never been fond of his superior attitude, his cold and calculated way of thinking. But Rasler was the Doppelganger, one of the Seven Seraphs, an important ally…

"How could you turn on your own people?!" Virgil asked horrified. "You are one of the Grand Jeweled Officers of the Paladins!"

"Save me the morally righteous rant, Redeemer, it really is overplayed," Rasler sighed. "I grew up in Alexandros, the lowest of the low. Everyone treated me like dirt, a Lamb they called me. Even though I'd never spent a day anywhere else, I was treated as nothing because I didn't have a family name. It wasn't until I got wings that I got treated like a real person. Alexandros is a city of lies, betrayal, and pompous idiots who see themselves above all others. They aren't worth saving! They aren't worth protecting! I was approached by Sethos some time ago. I would rather be on the winning side of the coming war. I gladly agreed to help him take the Chalice at this year's Tournament," Rasler told them. "If not for Virgil's intervening, it wouldn't still be in Paladin custody!" He spat clearly angry.

"What a weak, weak man," Virgil shook his head in disgust at Rasler's explanation for his betrayal.

"You're an insult to Paladins everywhere," Magnus told him.

"I grow tired of this exchange," Rasler growled, "Get back into Hel! More Death Dealers are on their way as we speak, it won't be long before they arrive to take back control of the tower."

"We're not going back," Virgil left no room for arguing Ragnorak's symbol coming to life.

"We must make it to the portal," Artreyu's tone holding urgency. "It won't be long before She awakens and begins hunting for the Redeemer."

"You're not going anywhere," Rasler said his white Devil Arms symbol glowing, the silver rapier, Quick Silver, flowing into his hand. "If I capture the Avatar and the Redeemer, I'm sure to be promoted to First Lieutenant of the Death Dealers," he smiled wickedly.

"Virgil, you must face him," Artreyu said to Virgil still staring ahead at their ally turned enemy.

"Me?" Virgil exclaimed. "You're stronger, faster, and way more powerful," he laughed like this was insane.

"You are better suited to fight the Doppelganger," Artreyu insisted, "He is a Devil Arms specialist, capable of changing his weapon to another form at will, deadly to someone who doesn't have a Devil Arms and has to fight up close and personal…like me."

"You don't have a Devil Arms?" Virgil asked bewildered. Wasn't he the First Seraph? Didn't all Nephilim have Devil Arms?

"You are the wielder of Ragnorak," Artreyu asserted. "The most powerful Devil Arms in existence, you can take him," Artreyu said confidently. "You have to believe that you can though."

"Come Redeemer, I have longed to claim the power of your Devil Arms for my own!" Rasler spoke with feverish passion. "Once I have the power of Ragnorak, I will be greatest of all Nephilim!" he cried out. Virgil didn't want him to absorb Ragnorak's power.

"Get the men to the portal," Virgil told Artreyu, "I'll keep him busy, just promise you will get them home!" he demanded.

"We're not leaving without you," Dante said looking angry. "You're the only reason we made it out!"

"I came to rescue you, Virgil," Artreyu said looking at Virgil with look of surprise and sadness.

"And I'll be right behind you, my people's needs come before my own!" he demanded. "Ragnorak!" Virgil cried out, a bolt of white lightning illuminating the darkness splitting the sky open, crashing down into his hand, the Holy Blade took shape once more. Its power washed over Virgil, surrounding him in a veil of protection and healing energy. Virgil beat his wings and flew into the air, "You want Ragnorak's power?!" Virgil taunted him.

Rasler leapt into the air his Devil Arms flashing, becoming a large amethyst bow, Virgil had seen him use the weapon before. Rasler fired large lightning blasts from the weapon, Virgil dodged the first one, but the second blast he couldn't shake off, he spun around to swing Ragnorak at the attack. The sword collided with the lightning destroying the blast, protecting Virgil. The winds battered them about, it was dangerous flying in this dead zone, the wind was beyond strong. Virgil struggled to maintain control. Artreyu led the group across the long bridge, Virgil had to buy them enough time. Rasler dived from Virgil, heading back towards the fleeing group. Virgil chased after him, he'd not let him slaughter the men he'd worked so hard to save! Ragnorak pulsed in his hand and he swung the blade in a wide arc, a wave of energy leaping from the blade's surface. Rasler turned around and his Devil Arms flashed changing into a massive shield, he held it in front of him and the wave crashed into him.

Rasler was knocked down to the bridge and remained relatively unharmed thanks to his Devil Arms. It flashed again becoming a glowing Holy lance, Gae Bolg, Aseril's Devil Arms! Rasler charged ahead of their group slamming down onto the bridge blocking the group from getting past him. He spun his holy lance around challenging someone to step forward. Virgil dived to the bridge landing hard, placing himself between Rasler and the group.

Rasler swung the lance around, the glow of its power intensifying. Virgil charged forward clashing Ragnorak against Gae Bolg, Rasler was swift, his arms moved the heavy weapon with poise and precision like a surgeon. Virgil's sword struggled to hold back Gae Bolg, he broke the block and stabbed Ragnorak forward, Rasler knocked the blow to Virgil's right. Virgil summoned his scythe to his hand throwing it with his mind, blocking Rasler's counter strike. Virgil used his two Devil Arms in tandem, blocking and striking, he fought with everything he had to give. Rasler fluidly changed his Devil Arms to his original form, the rapier clashed against Ragnorak.

"No!" Virgil cried out. Quick Silver glowed humming with power, its surface began to ripple with silver like boiling metal. Its power pushed Virgil back and he stumbled to keep his balance. Quick Silver was transforming, changing shape. A mirror image of Ragnorak formed in Rasler's hand, he held an exact replica of the Holy Blade!

"Yes, yes…YES!" Rasler laughed manically holding the sword in the air, it radiated with power. "The power of the Holy Blade is mine! I am the most powerful Nephilim in the world!" He shouted. "All mortals will bow before my power! All who oppose me will be crushed by the might of my wrath and scorched by my vengeance!"

He swung Ragnorak around to face Virgil, preparing to send a wave of energy at him, he raised the blade in the air. The Ragnorak that was in Virgil's hand began to howl, its cry was different from any other time, it sounded…angry! Ragnorak, the true Ragnorak, began to glow gold filling with power, howling for all to hear its fury. The Ragnorak that was in Rasler's hands began to glow with the same power, and Rasler's face fell. He began screaming waving the sword through the air trying to let go but the sword clung to him. The sword burst into blue flames, Angel fire; the most powerful fire in existence. The flames burned Rasler and he writhed in pain falling to the ground, screaming as the flames burned his hand, punishing him for touching the Holy Blade.

"Only one whom Ragnorak deems worthy may wield its power," Artreyu said for all to hear. "The Creator laid a powerful curse on the Holy Blade, if whoever touches it is unworthy, they shall be punished with Holy fire."

In response to Ragnorak's howling, a deep roar like the sound of mountains colliding shook the bridge. Deep at the base of the tower it began shaking, flames coming out of the openings.

"She is freed!" Artreyu yelled, "We must go!" and the group began running.

Virgil turned away from Rasler's limp body to look at the tower, what was coming to the surface? Rasler rose up silently from the ground. His right arm was completely burned but his Devil Arms symbol remained unaffected. He had his rapier in his hand and a murderous look in his eye.

"Virgil!" Dante yelled running forward raising his double-bladed earth axe in the air. "You can't take him!" Dante screamed and his axe, Gaia's Wrath, began to howl! It's Soul Scream! "Gaia's Wrath!" Dante yelled. "Earth Scar!" and he smashed his axe into the bridge, three waves of power rose up from the surface clawing across the ground, slashing through Rasler. Rasler screamed as the Soul Scream had been so powerful it ripped deep jagged lines through where it touched. Rasler lay bloodied and badly wounded on the bridge. They could see the end of the bridge! The edge of the Ever After was a small mountain range.

"Dante," Virgil said in awe.

The top of the tower exploded, a giant dragon emerging from its destroyed surface. "Redeemer!" The dragon yelled. "I want MY Redemption!" she yelled.

"Fly! Fly for your lives!" Artreyu cried out in panic, taking to the air flying to the mountains beyond the bridge. Those who couldn't fly were quickly outpaced. There was a small cave not far from the bridge, Artreyu was leading them to the entrance. What sounded like thunder blasted the air, the dragon had beat its wings! Her form seemed to keep flowing from the tower, how had she fit inside? She leapt from the tower and started to fly to the mountains.

Artreyu was beyond fearful, he flew like a madman whispering to himself in a language Virgil had never heard. "Don't look back!" He screamed, "Don't slow down!" They flew to the entrance of the cave, not far inside there was a black portal hanging in the air, who was helping him on the other side keeping it open? The men who were running were almost to the cave, running up the steep incline to its entrance.

"Go!" Artreyu commanded and the ones with wings started flowing through the portal. Virgil's brothers nodded to Virgil and ran through, Virgil hung back near the entrance, screaming at the freed Nephilim to move faster. The dragon was getting close…

"You need to go through!" Artreyu said grabbing Virgil by the arm. "We need to close this portal now!

"Not until they've all made it!" he insisted.

"We may not have time for them!" Artreyu snapped, "I'm never going on another operation with you! You create too many problems!"

The men had reached the cave and they barreled inside running right into the portal, it took them almost a full minute to run through, there were so many.

"REDEEMER!" The dragon screamed. "YOU WILL GIVE ME WHAT I WANT!" she yelled, her voice shaking Virgil to the core, he turned away from the opening. Together Artreyu and Virgil ran through the portal, they were the last ones through.

Chapter 21
The Mother of Eidolons, Queen of Dragons, Tiamat

Virgil burst through the portal back into human world, they were outside the city of Alexandros in the grassy fields. Some of their group ran into the city, Virgil's brothers were waiting for him. Virgil let go of Ragnorak, the blade fading in a ray of gold light. It was close to sunset back on Earth, the opposite of the Ever After. Colorful oranges stretched out from the west, as the darkness of night crept in from the east. The group breathed heavily, everyone had pushed themselves hard to make it, a few of the people bent over and threw up, combination of fear and fatigue. Virgil was shaking, he'd been scared too, he'd battled an Arch Demon and a fellow Seraph, but neither had filled him with the same dread and sense of doom as the dragon.

"Are we safe?" Louie asked them panic still etched in his face.

"Why is the portal still open?" Dante asked. Virgil and the others immediately turned around, the portal still hung in the air ominously.

"Close it!" Vahn shouted.

"It should have already closed!" Artreyu yelled running across the grass to the portal. He raised both of his hands before the portal, and began to chant, his palms glowing with light. The portal pulsed, and Artreyu was flung back, he landed gracefully on his feet.

"Goddess help us," Artreyu whispered fear upon the mighty warrior's face.

"What's happening?!" Virgil asked. The portal pulsed again, the normal black spiral with purple blue energy running through it began to expand rapidly.

"She is forcing her way through!" Artreyu shouted. "We must move!" he ordered turning from the portal he ran to Virgil's side. "Now Virgil!" he demanded. Virgil and the others ran into the city, there were no guards at the gate, and made it several blocks in coming to the large circular open area, with shops surrounding the perimeter, and the dazzling fountain at the center. A roar echoed out into the morning air, so mighty it shook the houses and shops around them.

"She has come!" Artreyu told them. The ground began to quake, as the booming footsteps of the dragon came from just outside the city.

"Redeemer!" the menacing and powerful voice called out. It could be heard from everywhere in the city, including the castle. "I will have my Redemption!" she cried. It sounded like thunder blasted their ears, the dragon beat its mighty wings, and took to the sky. Artreyu quickly shouted out a spell, slamming his palms into the ground, a small white dome of light rose up to cover the group, preventing the dragon from detecting Virgil's presence. The gargantuan form of the dragon flew overhead, the shadow it cast on the ground almost as large as the circular area they were in. The dragon opened its maw and a beam of energy shot out running across a portion of the city, a shockwave of fire and energy blasting up from the ground destroying everything in its path. The dragon began to spit fire into the city spreading her malice and anger. Panic set in the populace, the city became chaos, families fled from their homes flooding the city streets, unsure of what was happening around them.

"My family!" one of the Nephilim they had rescued screamed and he ran outside of the dome further into the heart of the city.

"Thank you for saving us, but we have to make sure our families escape!" Another Nephilim told Virgil and the others. The men and woman they had saved quickly fled in different directions, including the Paladins from the Coliseum. Axion gave Virgil a thankful last glance and started heading home. The group fell into the crowds of people that had taken to the streets running wildly about in sheer panic. It was just the Omegas and Virgil standing together now inside the safety of the small dome of light Artreyu had cast.

"What are we going to do!" Dante screamed. "She'll destroy the city in less than an hour at this rate!"

"There is nothing we can do!" Artreyu spat, "Don't you get it? She is the mother of Eidolons, the most powerful beings ever created. Not even the God Generals could hope to tame or defeat her, which is why she was sealed in Hel! She was never supposed to be set free. She will ravage this world, and level humanity to extinction," Artreyu spoke forlornly as if it had already happened.

"NO!" Virgil yelled. "We have to stop her!" Virgil looked into Artreyu's stormy triple colored iris eyes. "How do we stop her Artreyu?" Virgil asked him.

Artreyu met Virgil's gaze, a sad expression overcoming his face, "We don't," he spoke gently. "We are powerless in the face of such ancient might," Artreyu said solemnly looking away from Virgil's pleading expression.

"There must be a way!" Virgil cried desperately. He grabbed Artreyu's fancy clothing with both hands forcing him to look back at Virgil. "Please tell me!" Virgil demanded.

"Virgil," Artreyu said calmly staring him directly on, "I warned you that we had to escape the Ever After quickly, I told you that we didn't have time to save your friends. For every action there are consequences. Not every life can be saved Virgil, a lesson you should have learned by now. In trying to protect the lives of a few, you have doomed the lives of billions," Artreyu said solemnly.

Virgil let go of Artreyu his words weighing heavy upon his conscience. I am to blame for this, he thought to himself, this monster wouldn't be unleashed upon the world if I had just listened to him.

"Hey!" Dante said getting angry with Artreyu, "What the hell kind of talk is that, like Virgil needs that right now."

"I speak the truth," Artreyu responded unapologetic, "Virgil must learn that not every life can be saved. This is a cruel and unforgiving world, and one must weigh the outcomes before running blindly into decisions. Leaders are faced with these choices, sacrifice a few for the good of the many, it is an inconvenient truth of a dark world."

"That's awful!" Louie shouted taken aback.

"Is it?" Artreyu asked Louie turning to look at him. "Look at the devastation Virgil has wrought upon this world!" Arteryu yelled. "In saving a small group, he has doomed this Nephilim city to fall! Would you have wanted Virgil to save you, if you knew it would mean the deaths of thousands of children, millions of people?" Louie looked down not having a response worth saying. "This city is lost, we must flee Virgil, as long as we remain alive, we will be able to fight another day. This world needs us now, more than ever. The Seven Seraphs are all that stands between the free peoples of this world and utter destruction."

"What are we supposed to do!" Virgil shouted clenching his fists, anger boiling inside of his mind, he hated himself in that moment. "Run like cowards and leave the people of this city to the mercy of the dragon!"

"Yes," Artreyu nodded. "You are the Redeemer, as long as you live, there will be hope for this world. Dying here would accomplish nothing, and only doom countless more lives to the same fate!"

"Look!" Birdy shouted. Paladins had taken flight, wearing the garb of the Capital, they were highly trained warriors, the same ones who guarded the city and worked in the castle, some of the most powerful Nephilim in existence. They formed aerial units and began an assault on the menacing form of the giant dragon destroying their city. "Their fighting back!" Birdy raised a fist.

"Fools," Artreyu said shaking his head, "They fly to their deaths."

"At least they are trying to do something about this!" Dante said. "We should join them!"

They watched as two units of warriors began to attack the dragon in the air. She became infuriated, turning her attention from the city to the warriors. She inhaled deeply and breathed a beam of energy from her maw sweeping it across their paths. Some were able to dodge her powerful blast, others were caught in the blast and screamed as their bodies were destroyed, they fell to the city below already dead. More Nephilim took to the skies, some fleeing the city others trying to help fight the dragon. They watched in horror, as every single Nephilim who fought died horribly. Some were able to land blows on her body, or throw spells against her. However, her scales were thicker than the mightiest armor, and dragon hide seemed resistant to spells. She killed dozens of warriors, and they were able to do little more than scratch her.

"It is futile to fight Tiamat," Artreyu told them. "Dragons are one of the mightiest races ever born, their skin is thick and naturally resistant to magic. But Tiamat is no ordinary dragon, she is an Eidolon who has taken a dragon's form, an old god from the beginning of time when the universe had just been born. Mortals are no match for a god." Virgil's friends quickly realized taking flight to fight the monster in the sky was pointless, everyone who approached her was killed swiftly, and mercilessly.

"Redeemer!" The dragon's voice boomed across the city. "Come out and face me!" she demanded.

"We must flee the city!" Artreyu said once more. "Quickly follow me! We can use the transporters near the Colosseum. I can create a portal there in a matter of seconds." Artreyu broke the spell that had shielded them and ran east, towards the tall structure of the sports arena Coliseum that towered over the eastern edge of the city. He looked back noticing Virgil and his friends hadn't followed him.

"Come on!" Artreyu demanded. Virgil and his friends shared a look.

"What about the city, what about the Grand Prytanis?" Virgil asked silently thinking about Alexa, and her mother Sybil, would they be safe?

"They will have to save themselves!" Artreyu yelled. "If we don't move, we will eventually be found! I do not have the power to protect you from Tiamat, Virgil! We will both die if it comes to that!" Artreyu told them.

Virgil and his brothers ran after Artreyu, the guy was unbelievably fast, they could barely keep up. He weaved through the people with the lithe grace of a dancer. They made it several blocks east, rubble littered the streets, homes were destroyed, and had collapsed into the road. Pandemonium had gripped the city, and still warriors took to the sky to face the dragon, to protect their beloved home and people. It touched Virgil's heart every time he saw another brave soul take flight towards her, to love this place, and your family so much, you'd be willing to face something like that…knowing you had no hope. Virgil's eyes became misted, it should be him making that sacrifice.

"Why do they keep fighting?" Louie yelled to the others. "It is suicide to fight that thing!" his voice dripping with fear.

"Because Louie!" Gabriel barked at his friend, "They aren't worried about dying or thinking about being afraid. They love this city, it's their home! And to some people dying protecting what they love is more important than living another day as a fleeing coward!"

"I'm okay with being a coward!" Louie added happily, "Arch demons are the line for Louie V!"

"Hmp!" Dante huffed, "Never expected you to in the first place Louie!"

Virgil's heart hammered in his chest, they didn't slow down, climbing over debris and barreling through the crowds. Virgil was lost in his thoughts, his body following his friends, not processing what he was doing. How can I leave these people? They are paying for my mistake with their lives! This city, Virgil looked around him, I love this city, he realized. It was a haven for his kind, a place where Nephilim could live freely as themselves without persecution from mortals.

The sound of a child crying brought Virgil's attention back to reality, they were passing by a small residential street, and a boy lay in the road sobbing. A destroyed building was leaning over, its support giving out. A loud crack rent the air, the building started to topple over, it was so large that it would squash the child completely. Virgil didn't have time to think, only react, he spread his wings and took flight flying close to the ground, he beat his wings forcefully demanding they move faster. The child looked up in the air as the broken structure of a house began to fall on him, he screamed at the top of his lungs. Virgil reached out, snatching the child into his arms, the house crashing right behind him. He quickly came to a stop landing on the ground setting the child down.

The child couldn't be older than ten, he looked up at Virgil with fearful eyes, fresh tears still on his cheeks. "Thank you," he told Virgil.

"You're welcome," Virgil replied casually with a smile.

"Adrian!" a woman cried out. She came from around corner of another street with a man, and ran over to the boy, he ran into her arms, and the three embraced fiercely. "We've been looking all over for you, where have you been!" she screamed at him.

"I didn't know where you were! I went home to find you! He saved me," he told his parents. They turned their attention to Virgil.

"You?" the boy's father said looking at Virgil with contempt. "I recognize you, you're that Nephilim from the tournament, the one who wields Ragnorak!"

"Look at his wings," the woman pointed out, "He's the Redeemer!"

"You!" the father spat anger overcoming him. "You're the one that monster wants! You're the only reason it is attacking our city!"

Virgil hung his head, his body feeling hot all over, unable to look them in the eyes.

"You coward!" The man yelled at Virgil. "Because of you our home is gone! Countless people are dead! How dare you stand there while innocent people are dying all around you! We should offer YOU to the dragon and be done with it!" he yelled in rage spittle spraying from his mouth.

"Dad! Stop it!" the boy yelled at his father giving him a shove, startling the man. "He saved me!"

"Joseph, please," the woman said trying to still her husband's anger.

"No," Virgil said looking up, "He is right." The three people became quiet and looked at Virgil. "It is my fault the dragon is here; it is me she wants." Virgil turned to look north; the dragon was flying over the city blasts of fire raining down upon the homes of the people. There were no more warriors fighting her, those that were brave or foolish enough to try had already perished.

"I can't stand by while innocent lives are paid for my mistake!" Virgil said passionately, his eyes filling with tears. "While people are dying around me, how am I supposed to run? How can I turn my back on this?" he asked. Virgil made a step away from them his gaze fixed on Tiamat…he knew what he had to do.

"No!" Virgil heard the boy cry out and he grabbed Virgil's hand stopping him. "Please, don't go!" the boy begged Virgil. "I don't think you're evil," he told Virgil. "I saw you in the tournament, you were my favorite Paladin! Those guys were hurting your friends, and you summoned Ragnorak, and protected them, you're a hero!" he told Virgil. Virgil stared down into the boy's eyes, where once they'd been filled with fear, now they only contained hope. Virgil hated how people gave him that look, it tightened his chest made his eyes misty. So many hopes rested on his one heart, it made failing impossible, with so many souls depending on him, how could he possibly ever fail? It was a lot of pressure, and Virgil was only mortal. "Come with us Redeemer!" the boy told him fiercely holding onto his hand. "We can escape the city together!"

"Adrian!" the boy's mother said shocked.

Virgil knelt to look the boy straight on, "Thank you, Adrian," Virgil whispered honored by his fierce compassion. "I'd come with you but, I want to protect this beautiful city. I can't run, I have to take responsibility for what I have done," Virgil said with passion. "I need to make this place safe for you again." Virgil stood up letting go of the boy's hand. "Ragnorak choose me, hoping that I would use its power to protect the innocent," Virgil spoke his truth. It was the only reason he'd been entrusted with it. Virgil stared up at the monstrous form of the dragon that terrorized the city from above, he felt afraid, so very afraid. He clenched his fists and gritted his teeth. He couldn't afford to be afraid! This boy, these people, this city needed him! Good people get hurt by bad people every day, for no reason. If those good people of the world, don't stand up against the senseless hate of the bad people, civilization falls into chaos.

"Redeemer!" the boy's father called out. Virgil stopped, "Be safe," he told Virgil. His words were genuine and heartfelt, his earlier anger evaporated. "You don't have to face it for us. Forget what I said earlier. You saved my son; I couldn't ask for a greater favor. No man should have to face that monster alone, especially one so young."

"My husband's right, you're not much older than my brother, certainly not old enough to be fighting dragons," she spoke with concern, her eyes showing him her gratitude for saving her son. Virgil's heart hurt, and his eyes filled with tears. He felt power build in him, the power of Ascending, the part of him that was Judge, his godhood, was at his fingertips. Like a mental flood gate, all he had to do was allow the power to come online. Virgil opened himself to that power, his eyes became gold light, his aura expanded, and he radiated with power, his senses heightened, he was given superhuman strength and speed once more.

"The dragon wants me to use my power on her, make her stronger," Virgil explained his voice filled with power, keeping his gaze from them, "I will lead it away from the city."

"No!" the boy cried out.

Virgil turned to look at them and the three of them gasped at Virgil's eye sockets, now glowing gold his eyes seemingly disappeared. "Forgive me," he humbly asked. He stretched his hand towards the heavens, "Ragnorak!" he screamed. A bolt of white lightning shot down into the palm of his hand growing out into his sword. The golden light that surrounded the sword spread to surround him, if he held Ragnorak, it would slowly heal physical wounds he endured. Virgil extended his wings and looked to the dragon.

"You'll come back right?" the boy asked Virgil.

Virgil did not want to lie and say everything was going to be alright. It was too cliché and giving either of them false hope was wrong. "Get to safety," Virgil said with concern. "Ragnorak," Virgil said to his sword swinging it to face the dragon, Tiamat. "Take me to the dragon!" he commanded. The blade howled and its power surged Virgil forward lifting him off the ground. His wings streamed dusts of magic behind him as he rocketed through the air to his target. Virgil flew faster than he ever had, the power of Ragnorak leading him with such force and propulsion he looked like a ray of gold light streaking through the air. Virgil narrowed his eyes, the dragon looming closer, having made its way to the northern end of the city near the castle. I must protect this place, Virgil demanded of himself.

Virgil came to a halting stop above the dragon at a safe distance, it sensed his presence and began to turn its focus to Virgil. Virgil raised his sword straight up in the air, "Howling Blade!" Virgil screamed and the sword Ragnorak began to howl. The glass like blade filled with golden light, charging up its immense power.

"There you are," the dragon's deep rumbling voice called out. "I thought I'd have to devour the city before you'd show your cowardly face," it taunted him.

"Begone from our world, slave of darkness!" Virgil yelled feeling in his heart the pain and suffering of all the men and women who had died fighting and fleeing from the dragon's wrath. "Judgment Bolt!" he screamed and swung his sword to point it at Tiamat. Ragnorak released the power of its Soul Scream, like it had against the Arch Demon, Abdanon. The sound of a sonic boom rent the air and a beam of golden energy rocketed out from the tip of Ragnorak like lightning tearing into Tiamat. The dragon cried out in pain as the beam shot her downwards, knocking her out of the air, and slamming her into the ground with its power. Tiamat hit the ground with such force it created a small crater where she landed, obliterating everything underneath her. Dust and smoke rose up, and the sky was cloudy in a haze of debris. Virgil shielded his eyes with his left hand, his wings beating steadily keeping him afloat. Ragnorak returned to its normal state once more.

As the dust settled Virgil could see the dragon's form, and remains of homes that she had landed on. Virgil breathed deeply, grateful to Ragnorak for its power, at last the dragon's wrath had quelled! The dragon began to move getting to its feet, and Virgil's heart sank. Even Ragnorak's great power wasn't enough to fell this creature!

Tiamat had dark purplish black skin covered in thick scales. Her body was covered in grotesque scars from past battles, her wings were tattered with small holes throughout. She had a long powerful neck attached to a long lizard like body, which had four legs, her front two more like arms. She stirred and opened her yellow eyes turning her head to look up at Virgil.

"You fool!" She yelled at him. "You think yourself a match for the great Tiamat! I was born eons before the first Judge walked the hills of Nirvana, I am the mother of Eidolons! I cannot be killed by a mortal! I am immortal!" she howled.

Virgil knew at that moment fighting the dragon was futile, he had used his strongest attack against her, and all it had done was wound her. Virgil did not have the power to use Ragnorak's Soul Scream again, it could take hours or a whole day. I'm screwed, Virgil thought panic and hysteria setting in, rattling his focus. *Stay strong!* Virgil heard the presence of his inner Judge yell at him, *you cannot lose hope or she will have already won!* Virgil knew that it was right, he couldn't give in to fear or hopelessness. The people of this city were counting on him!

"You want your Redemption?" Virgil asked Tiamat. "Come and claim it!" he demanded. Turning from the dragon he surged forward flying away from the floating city of Alexandros.

"There is no where you can run that I can't follow," Tiamat's voice boomed. "I am lord of the skies!" Virgil heard her wings beat, like the sound of thunder behind him, taking to the air hot on his heels.

I must lead her away from city! Virgil beat his wings with as much force as he could muster, flying around the castle and the mountain it had been built into. The very air around him became distorted as the dragon gained on him with incredible speed, the force of its wing beats shaking Virgil around. Virgil fought through the power of the wind she created willing himself to fly further, he had to clear the city before she fell upon him! He couldn't let her destroy any more of Alexandros or take another life. Please just a little more, Virgil begged his body, his wings already beginning to tire from the equivalent of what sprinting does to one's legs. His wings couldn't maintain this pace, he felt himself slowing down. He passed over the mountain, behind it was a small ruined area that housed what looked like a field of grave stones next to a small forest. In the middle of the forest was a decrepit old building that looked like a church. Virgil flew past the small area of land behind the mountain and finally cleared the floating landmass. Now just the wide expanse of beautiful Lake Michigan lay below him, he'd made it.

The dragon descended upon Virgil having caught up, reaching out with its front claws, it made a grab for him. Virgil swiftly turned around, "Soul Reaver!" he yelled summoning his scythe to his left hand. Virgil threw his scythe at her approaching claw, the metal grinding against her thick talons keeping Virgil out of her clutches. The dragon lashed out with her other claw with more force and anger this time. Virgil used Ragnorak to slash at her hand fighting desperately to keep himself free. He willed his scythe back to him, making it spin in circles around his body, using it as a shield. The dragon was growing impatient with Virgil, its neck stretched down to tear at him. Virgil didn't want to be anywhere near her mouth, he'd seen what she was capable of, her most powerful attacks came in the form of dragon fire and powerful blasts of energy. Virgil tucked his wings in and she went sailing over him, Virgil flying underneath her belly. Virgil came to her chest and pushed himself towards her with a burst of speed from his wings, landing on her soft underside. He raised Ragnorak and began to hammer away at her scales with his sword. His first blow hit her hard, Virgil's sword clanged against her flesh like it was pure metal, she shook her body in irritation as if the blow had caused her some discomfort. She reached towards him with her claws with renewed vigor, raking her claws in the air and against her belly seeking to gore Virgil. Virgil used his scythe as a shield sending it against her claws, spinning with vicious speed, the metal and flames worked to protect Virgil, but it required him to concentrate his mind to maneuver it. He didn't know how long he could keep her off him this way. He used the precious few seconds he earned himself to swing Ragnorak again, and again against her flesh. His last blow cleaved a chunk of her flesh away, revealing softer more tender muscle, she roared in shock. Virgil plunged his blade into the wound he'd created and desperately worked the blade back and forth seeking to work it in deeper.

Tiamat unexpectedly went into a barrel roll, knocking Virgil off balance he clung to Ragnorak impaled in her flesh hanging on for dear life as the world began to spin, the massive fresh lake and the sky spinning round and round. Virgil lost sight of Soul Reaver and commanded it to dematerialize, the black symbol on his hand dying down in response. The dragon went from rolling over again and again in the air into a straight dive towards the water below. The wind began to whip against Virgil pushing against him with such force the sword was ripped from her flesh and he went flying back. He quickly regained composure using his wings to level himself out. The dragon was far below him, she pulled out of her dive, began to turn around, and ascended higher in the air. She rose up higher above the water working to come back to Virgil's level, then she came to a slow stop, using her wings to hover in place. She opened her mouth and energy began to gather in her maw. She's going to blast me out of the sky!

Virgil became panicked, he couldn't get hit with her powerful breath attack. He pointed Ragnorak down at her, *take me to her*, he commanded, and the blade howled. His sword shot forward like a rocket, he held on tight racing against time to get closer to her, he was safest close to her body. He was a gold streak through the air, like a shooting star, aiming to get underneath her once more. A great sphere of energy was gathered in her jaws, she exhaled, and the sphere turned into an all-powerful beam of purple energy. Tiamat swept the beam through the air trying to catch Virgil, he flew under it as it came down in blinding speed, and he could feel its heat, the energy mere yards away from him. The blast of energy came closer every second and Ragnorak worked tirelessly to keep him propelled forward. Virgil went flying underneath Tiamat and past her, the blast dying down and then stopping altogether. Virgil quickly circled around and shot forward towards her underside.

Virgil approached her chest near the front of her underside once more. Her hind legs reached out almost snatching him from the air as he flew past them. He twirled through the air spinning through her grasp missing her claws by inches. He could see the wound he'd created, it was oozing a dark colored blood. She began to roll through the air once more to keep him off her. Virgil slammed into her chest clinging against her as they spun through the air. She went right into a dive. Virgil struggled to raise himself against the tremendous pressure as they fell straight towards the water below with blinding speed. Virgil raised Ragnorak in the air and swung it against her wound with all the force he could muster screaming as he did. Tiamat howled in pain, a deafening roar that chilled Virgil to his core. He couldn't stop, he had to give it everything he had! Virgil raised the Holy Blade once more and brought it down onto her wound, like a hammer on an anvil. The point of the blade stuck into her flesh and he viciously tore into her, she screamed in pain. A massive chunk of flesh ripped off her and went flying back, underneath Virgil saw muscle, flesh, lots of blood, and lodged deep in her chest, perhaps near where her heart was…a dark purple black gem. It was massive in size, and only a small piece of it was exposed. Tiamat's actions suddenly changed; she began to swipe at him with her front claws with an urgency that wasn't there before. Virgil swung his sword at her first claw, trying hard to keep her back, her other claw grabbed him forcefully, wrapping her long fingers around his body as she squeezed tight. Virgil cried out as the bones in his wings snapped and his biceps were crushed in her mighty grip. Virgil's sword fell from his grip, and vanished in a ray of gold light.

Tiamat moved her closed claw up to her face, Virgil struggled against her but that only made her squeeze harder, he heard the bones in his arm snap. He felt his power fading, his Ascended state only lasted so long, the power left his body, the gold of his eyes receding, his aura calming back down. The last of his power faded, the presence of his inner Judge going back to his unconscious mind, and Virgil became just himself once more. Tears involuntarily began running down his face, the pain was overwhelming, she was squeezing him so hard black spots began to dot his vision. She stopped diving and hovered in the air, the lake was closer, still a ways down though. Alexandros could be seen to the south, at a much higher altitude. She brought him close to her face, her yellow eyes fixed on him, an anger and all-consuming greed emanated from her.

"You fought well Judge Spawn," Tiamat spoke in her menacing deep voice that somehow maintained a touch of femininity. "But you are only mortal, you were foolish to try and defy me." Virgil met her gaze unflinching, his brain was flooded with signals from his body telling him he was pain, but he tried hard not to let her see how much he hurt. "I have waited long enough to be returned to my former glory, I will not be denied Redemption," she told him.

"I can only Redeem those who are worthy," Virgil told her his words coming out pressured, it was hard for him to breath.

"There is no one worthier than I!" Tiamat yelled. "I am the mother of Eidolons, second born of all the Creator's children!"

"You must seek forgiveness for all the wrongs you have committed, for every sin you bare. Only if you truly feel remorse, deep within, can I give you what you seek," Virgil told her.

The dragon growled, her eyes narrowing, her sharp teeth that were longer than Virgil's legs were exposed as her lips opened slightly. "You dare to play games with me Redeemer?" Tiamat asked.

"No!" Virgil shouted. "I can only give you, what you deserve! If you have no remorse for your actions, your crimes against all life, and for turning your back on the Light and our Creator, than I cannot Redeem you! It is not within me to give power to those who do not deserve it!" He yelled at her.

She squeezed harder earning a painful cry from Virgil. "Chose your next words carefully mortal," she gritted out through clenched fangs. "Or I may tear you apart in my anger!"

Virgil knew she was not worthy of Redemption, he didn't have to use his power to touch her mind, the malice and hate within her was almost palpable. He'd only used his power twice, once on the Fallen Judge Ipos back in January, and a second time in the Death Dealer prison earlier this same morning. Virgil had used his power to give his friends wings so they could escape with him, but they had deserved the power he'd bestowed them. Their memories and lives still swam through his mind. When his mind touched theirs, he'd seen every memory of his friends, felt every emotion, they were not perfect, but no being in this world was. They were good people though, and more than worthy of receiving the power he'd been tasked with safe guarding. This ability to give others power, it was too great a responsibility for him, he was just one man! But Virgil understood in that moment, perhaps an inkling of why the Creator had chosen him for this. Even if it meant being ripped apart and slowly consumed by this dragon, Virgil would not dishonor the Creator by giving the power of Redemption to one who did not deserve it. He would rather die protecting the world from a corrupt being, than give in, and relinquish even greater power unto an evil spirit.

"Redeem me!" Tiamat commanded.

Virgil's eyes never left hers, "I cannot," he told her, "There is too much hate in your heart. If I returned you to your former self, you'd only use your power to destroy. I will not be responsible for creating a tyrant," he spoke with every word knowing it could be his last. "I love this world too much," he said passionately, "If only you could move past your own grief and anger, if only you could want to help heal this world, to help it become what it once was. That is the Tiamat that I would Redeem," Virgil finished.

The dragon growled, "I will burn every mortal city to the ground and enslave what little of your race survives. All who live will know that they suffer because you refused to return me to original form!" Tiamat shouted.

Virgil screamed Soul Reaver's name in his mind, the scythe materialized in his hand, Virgil fell from her grasp and went tumbling towards the vast fresh water of Lake Michigan below.

Chapter 22
<u>Holy</u>

Virgil fell through the air, his body tumbling over itself, his wings were broken and could not save him, and his arms were crushed, and could barely move. The lake grew closer as he rapidly approached the massive freshwater sea below. Virgil doubted he'd survive the impact; at the height he'd fallen hitting the water's surface would be the same as it he was falling on concrete. Virgil thought about his brothers, he prayed they were safe and had escaped the Nephilim Capital. Virgil thought of all his brothers, but especially his best friends, Birdy, Dante, Louie V and Blair, he wished he'd had more time to spend with them. Virgil's thoughts came to his mother and his chest hurt, she'd never know what happened to him. She'd probably be told a fabricated story about his death, like they told to Boyd and Darius' parents. She'd be all alone in the world with him gone, Virgil closed his eyes as his lips trembled. He loved his mom so much, he wished in that moment he could tell her how grateful he was that'd she'd adopted him, and raised him with as much love as if he was her own. He couldn't have asked for a more loving and accepting family, they were always encouraging him to dream, to strive to be whoever he felt he was inside. He wanted to tell her that he wouldn't be half the man he'd become without her unconditional love. She'd taught him the most valuable lessons in life, to love freely and live without hate in one's heart. Love had been the thing Virgil cherished the most, always love, and he'd lived a life full of it.

Virgil opened his eyes the waves rolling below him, so close now he could smell the water. The wind was knocked out of him as it felt like he was slammed in the side by a speeding car. Virgil looked wildly about unsure of what happened, he wasn't falling anymore, he was speeding along vertically then started ascending into the air once more. Virgil looked and saw that he was in the left arm of a warrior, she was clad in full battle armor, which gleamed a majestic silver, with a helmet covering her face. Her hair was hidden up in her helmet, two dazzling white wings spread out from her back propelling them through the air.

"You foolish boy!" She admonished him. "What were you thinking challenging Tiamat alone!" she yelled at him.

"Who are you?" Virgil asked.

"An ally," she told him, "Why did you go after the dragon?" she asked angrily.

Virgil felt defensive, what business was it of hers to question his motives? But considering she'd just saved him from imminent death he chose to answer her. "I couldn't, I couldn't let that monster take another life," Virgil said tears welling up. "All that destruction, all those people's lives forever changed, and it is all my fault. I'M the reason Tiamat was able to come over to this world. I had to take responsibility for what I'd done," Virgil told her.

"By throwing your life away!" she yelled at him.

"I wasn't trying to die!" Virgil yelled back. "I just wanted to lead her away from the city, I didn't have a plan more than that," he admitted going silent.

The warrior was quiet for a moment, "Oh Virgil," she said as if she had tears in her eyes.

"How do you know my name?" Virgil asked her, "Who are you?" he asked once more.

A dragon's roar echoed through the air, Tiamat had seen them, she was off in the distance but quickly put herself on a path to intercept them.

"We need to reach land!" the woman yelled. "Divine Light!" Her Devil Arms flashed and a long white staff came into her right hand. It radiated Creation energy, warm white light pulsed within it. A flawless diamond was adorned at the top of the staff, it caught the light of the sun reflecting dazzling colors from its crystal surface. "Curaga!" she said and the diamond crystal at the top of her staff became filled with a mix of white and sea green light, she touched the staff to Virgil's arm and the energy of her spell moved to him. Virgil felt his body being reshaped, the bones in his arms were being mended, and he felt the delicate tendons of his wings being knitted together. His vitality had been completely restored, he felt rejuvenated and refreshed, more then he'd felt since his capture. Virgil looked into the warrior's masked face with a questioning look.

"I need you in peak condition!" she told him, "I cannot face Tiamat alone."

Tiamat was almost upon them, the warrior clung protectively to Virgil her wings fiercely working to keep them out of the dragon's clutches. Tiamat was gaining on them, every second she drew closer, hopelessly outpacing them. The warrior swung around in the air flying backwards and facing the oncoming dragon. She raised her staff in the air, she spoke a spell and spheres of light began to gather around her staff in a circular formation.

"The boy is mine!" the dragon yelled at her.

"I'll never let you have him!" the warrior fiercely told Tiamat. The dragon made a lunge forward to them. "Phantasm's Prism!" the warrior yelled. The spheres of light shot forward spinning around maintaining a circle, the dragon approached. The spheres began to shoot beams of Creation energy at the dragon's face, the dragon recoiled in pain swiping with her claws at the spheres. The small spheres of light were impossibly fast, they followed the dragon's face, a barrage of beams flying from their centers attacking the dragon's face with an unrelenting assault. The warrior used the opportunity to gain distance from Tiamat turning her focus towards Alexandros continent, flying towards the floating landmass. They were approaching the backside of Alexandros behind the mountain, there was a large area of stone structures that looked like grave markers, trees dotted the land, growing thicker at the eastern end where a decaying building sat. The mountain loomed over the small area closing it off from the rest of the small floating island.

"I was trying to take her away from Alexandros!" Virgil told the warrior. "Why lead her back?"

"Fighting Tiamat in the air is suicide, we need to get to land!" the warrior said.

The hairs on Virgil's arm began to stand up. He turned his head and Tiamat descended on them from above, stealthily dropping down on them.

"Watch out!" Virgil yelled. The warrior began a series of aerial maneuvers to keep the dragon off them, Tiamat chased them with narrowed focus, she was so close Virgil could feel the heat of her breath. Tiamat opened her mouth stretching out to swallow them whole, the warrior giving it everything she had, but Tiamat's speed was superior. Virgil started screaming, the dragon had won.

"Thundaja!" a powerful voice rang out. The sky exploded in a shower of lightning bolts as an Ultimate Level spell took form and assaulted the form of the dragon. She was overwhelmed by the spell, giving the woman holding onto Virgil time to push forward. Artreyu came flying up next to them.

"Damn you Virgil!" Artreyu said, "You couldn't listen to me and flee when you had the chance. What were you thinking challenging her? We are no match for Tiamat!" Artreyu told Virgil.

"I had to do something!" Virgil said defending himself.

"She's coming back!" the warrior told Artreyu.

"Get to the Eidolon Graveyard," Artreyu told them, "I will slow her down!"

Artreyu's eyes lit up like lightning was striking around his pupil. Artreyu spoke to the sky moving his hands and the clouds began to blacken. The air became stormy and all around them the calm morning turned into a raging tempest. Funnels began to spiral down from clouds. Tiamat was ascending once more and Artreyu commanded dozens of tornadoes to descend down, the air around them turned into a scene unlike any Virgil had witnessed. Like the worst storm in history, massive destructive funnels speared from the sky raging through the air. If they had formed near land, they would have ripped apart everything in their path. Even Tiamat's mighty body could not resist the power of the storm, she fought to escape their power, but she was sucked into the storm and assaulted by the powerful winds, her form disappearing from view as each funnel sprang into a new storm cloud.

The woman landed on solid ground near the wooded forest and Virgil stood on his own, his body completely healed from her spell. They looked on to the north as Artreyu's storm effectively halted Tiamat's advance. Artreyu hovered in the air not far from the island, he shouted to the storm and a crack of lightning shot through the funnels crashing into Tiamat's body lighting up her shadow through the dozens of funnels. Virgil looked on at Artreyu's incredible power with awe, the Avatar was truly the greatest of the Seven Seraphs.

The great Titan of darkness fought on, wreathing through the great tornados her body taking the damage, but so great was her power she slowly moved through.

"Blizzaja!" Artreyu cried out casting an Ultimate Spell. A wave of ice shards flying from his palms toward the dragon. An ice storm spread out, massive spears and glaciers of ice flying into the dragon, the greatest ice spell in existence. She became pelted with the very element she was weakest against. A massive block of ice formed from the many pieces, stabbing through her body at half her size, it shattered out in a blast of power, sending a shockwave of ice and water at fatal speeds. Finally, Tiamat's strength gave in and she plummeted from the air, not beaten but momentarily too weakened to sustain combat. She began to sink through the air to the Great Lake below.

Artreyu flew over to them, his waist length white hair tied back, wildly blowing around, he landed near them looking as powerful and well rested as he had when they first met. His stamina was perhaps his greatest strength; Virgil had never seen an aura's like his. He had the largest Will pool of any warrior, capable of using more spells before his aura finally shrank to the point it barely hovered above his flesh. For most of Virgil's brothers that was a couple of spells, for Virgil maybe a few more than that.

"We need a strategy," Artreyu spoke looking towards the warrior with the powerful staff Devil Arms clad in battle armor. "Immediately," he added after a short blink.

"She'll be back in the air in less than five minutes," the battle maiden told Artreyu.

"You seemed more than capable of handling Tiamat," Virgil pointed out hoping he could keep up his devastating power, he'd effectively immobilized her and from a safe distance.

"I don't have enough energy to defeat her with spells alone, Ultimate Spells are powerful but even I have my limits. I won't last casting like that for long," he said. "There's a reason I was using Master Spells while we fought to escape Hel, their cost is great but far less than the final tier."

"I can attack her again, but she nearly killed me last time," Virgil admitted. "I don't know how much damage I really did. I'd have to repeat what happened a hundred times over before I'd start to see results," he said hopelessly. "Where is the Grand Prytanis? He's a Seraph, he should be here helping us!" Virgil yelled.

"He is likely having his hands full evacuating the city," Artreyu commented. "It must be the three of us working in precision," Artreyu commented walking forward then he began to pace. "What do you think?" he asked the armor glad warrior again. "This is a tangled mess you have roped me into," he said to her. She went to say something, then turned to look at Virgil and stopped. Did they…know each other? Virgil wondered.

"Artreyu who is this woman?" Virgil asked.

Artreyu crossed his arms and looked hard at the battle maiden, seemingly ignoring Virgil and his question all together. Neither of them spoke.

"What the hell is going on!?" Virgil yelled.

"Battle strategy," Artreyu spoke turning to join Virgil in the conversation.

"We cannot hope to take it head on, it will tear us apart and we will fail every time," the Battle Maiden said. They were quiet for a moment, Virgil looked around raking his brain, freaking out inside willing himself to think of a brilliant plan that could save them. He felt lost, hopeless…

"What is this place?" Virgil asked.

"This is what the city of Alexandros is built on," Artreyu said, "A holy land of corpses," his solemn tone reflected how much of what he said meant to him. Virgil thought of Artreyu as stoic, reserved, hard to read, and stern. True emotion shown through now, and it was sorrow, Artreyu continued, "After the Battle of the Fallen over half of the world's Eidolons had been slain, the world was crippled, fractured to its core. Eidolons are the very essence of the world, that which makes life possible. Great Spirits that willed themselves to manifest physical forms at the dawn of time," Artreyu spoke of them with the utmost reverence. "Since their death, the worlds lost much of their magic and vibrancy."

"Tiamat had divided her kind," the Battle Maiden said, "Her mate, the King of the Eidolons, the Hallowed Father and Firstborn of the Creator, would not bend to Diablos' side. Tiamat took half of their race and fought for Diablos in the battle, the Eidolons that turned to Diablos' power became corrupted by malevolence, the power of Chaos. After Diablos fell, those dark Eidolons were thrown into the Ever After with the Fallen, but Tiamat was too powerful," the Battle Maiden said. "She was sealed in Hel so she would not destroy the Ever After in her rage."

Artreyu looked at the vast field of monuments, "The bodies of the slain Eidolons were laid to rest on this piece of land, their bodies forever changing it. Blessing it, that is why this landmass floats. Even in death, the deep magic, that is Creation itself, is within the very ground of this land. But here more than anywhere else," Artreyu noted.

Virgil looked out onto the vast field, with hundreds of stone grave markers, some were more like shrines, and there were six small temple buildings, each representing one of the six elements and a great Eidolon that had passed in the Battle. "This is where they were buried," Virgil said looking out in renewed awe and wonder.

"The first Paladins settled this land under Lady Diamond, they loved it for its seclusion from the human race. My people were offended by the "halfling" mortals desecrating one of our most sacred lands. The Sidhe fairies, are direct descendants of the Eidolons. The first of the Great races to be born from another. My Grandfather the King of the UnSeelie Sidhe Court at the time, told Lady Diamond the Paladins had to leave, they refused of course. To this day relations remain sour between Nephilim and fairies," Artreyu explained sadly.

"It was a miscommunication," the Battle Madien nodded in agreement, "Like most stories of conflict, it could have been resolved if either side would have looked past their own pride to mend the wound that had formed."

A fierce roar echoed in the air, Tiamat was getting her strength back…

"We still don't have a plan," Artreyu said looking to the edge of the land and the forbidding empty swath of clouds floating past.

"Something is happening here," the Battle Maiden said her head inclined slightly as if in deep thought, "A choice," she turned to Virgil. "You wounded her earlier didn't you?" she asked Virgil.

"Barely," Virgil shrugged. "Like I said, I'd have to make a wound like I had, a hundred times over to see some sort of progress."

"Tiamat may be one of the most powerful Eidolons of all time, but she is still just a dragon," the Battle Maiden said. "Tell us what you did exactly," she asked Virgil.

They turned to Virgil, Artreyu wore a curious expression, "Um," Virgil didn't know what this woman wanted, "I knew I had to stay away from its mouth, her neck is quick and flexible, and her jaws are where her most powerful attacks start. I tried to attack her underside, it was less thick than the top, so I just…smashed Ragnorak as hard as I could against her. I tore off a piece of her flesh, even saw a weird dragon organ inside, it looked like a gem almost," Virgil said.

"What!?" Artreyu exclaimed, "You saw her Dragoon Stone?" he asked suddenly excited about Virgil's story.

"I don't know, it looked like magicite I guess, was probably so big I couldn't carry it in my hands," Virgil said trying to remember. "She started attacking me with a ferociousness when I cut deep enough, she snatched me up within seconds of seeing it," he said looking down not wanting to remember, a chill went down his spine, he didn't want to go back to that.

"Every dragon is born with a Dragoon Stone inside, they grow as the dragon ages, but once expelled the dragon and stone cease to grow again. As long as that stone survives, so does the dragon, even if the dragon's body is destroyed, its spirit, mind, and magical essence or aura is still alive," Artreyu explained speaking rapidly.

"Destroy the Stone, kill the dragon?" Virgil asked wanting to get to the punch line.

"Yes," Artreyu nodded.

"She will never let any of us near it," the Battle Maiden told them. "She knows Virgil saw it, she is going to be overly protective of her weak spot."

"Then what do you suggest?" Virgil said annoyed.

"Destroying the Dragoon Stone is the only way we can hope to stop Tiamat," the Battle Maiden said. The Battle Maiden swayed almost falling over, Artreyu ran over to her side catching her in his arms. "Lady!" Artreyu said passionately with concern.

"I am fine," she said getting back to her feet with his help.

"What is it?" he asked her, still standing close. Virgil arched an eyebrow, did Artreyu have a thing for this Judge or Nephilim, whoever she was.

"There is a spell that will work," she told Artreyu. "But you are the only one who can hope to cast it and survive," she warned.

"What?" Artreyu asked suddenly disdainful and unapprovingly, "that spell has been lost since the Battle of the Fallen," he told her. "And I don't think I'm powerful enough to cast it," he mentioned uncharacteristically humble.

"You're the Avatar, you are capable of casting ANY spell. I will help you with the incantation, but it must be you who channels the spell," the Battle Maiden told him.

"Even if I am able to cast it, the cost of that magic could destroy me," Artreyu told her.

"We won't be using our energy," the Battle Maiden told Artreyu, "We'll use the Eidolons'," she said looking out at the graves.

"You mean to cast a circle, and channel their auras?" Artreyu asked surprised.

"It will work," the Battle Maiden assured him, "But we don't have much time. Tiamat will know that we mean to cast the greatest spell of Creation and use her ultimate attack, Dark

Flare, on us," the Battle Maiden spoke, her words tight. "We have to get a circle cast and start the incantation, we will need someone to keep Tiamat off us while we get the spell ready," the Battle Maiden said heavily not looking towards Virgil when she did.

"You're talking about me?" Virgil asked them.

"Circle casting is one of the most basic forms of spelling," Artreyu said, "You just need to create a perimeter of spells or even a physical one. When joined it forms a sphere, or circle, most that practice magic utilize this, like witches."

"I've helped do one before, I placed a barrier spell around my mother's house in the winter," Virgil said, "I can do this. Where is the circle going?" he asked them.

"It needs to completely encompass the six temples, each represents an element and a patron Eidolon, with the power of the six elements, we can cast the spell with ease," the Battle Maiden said.

Artreyu flew in a circle, landing at each temple, and casting a ruin on the building, when all six had been completed he came to land in front of the graveyard, a massive circle formed on the ground glowing with power. The various grave markers began to glow as did the six temples he'd cast on. Artreyu stood at the head of circle, and the Battle Madien joined hands with him. She began reciting a spell, and Artreyu repeated after her. Tiamat flew up past the land from below flying high above, descending in a glide as she approached them. Tiamat opened her maw.

Virgil screamed, "Ragnorak!" and a lightning bolt snaked into his hand stretching out into the Holy Blade. His wings climbed him through the air, to face the dragon, and protect his allies from her wrath. Tiamat expelled a blast of fire at Artreyu and the Battle Maiden. Virgil's blade pulsed with energy and he swung it at the ball of dragon fire, a gold wave of energy swam out to meet the fire colliding and dissipating both harmlessly.

"Out of my way, mortal!" Tiamat commanded coming at Virgil with her jaws and claws.

Virgil charged Tiamat summoning Soul Reaver to his side to act as his shield. She aimed her face straight for Virgil, looking to tear him apart. Soul Reaver kept her from swallowing him whole. He kept the dark blade of fire in constant motion. Virgil brought his sword down on her face and she yelled out in pain. Her claws came up to tear at him, Soul Reaver swatted her limbs away, moving to counter each incoming blow. He stabbed Ragnorak again piercing the underside of her jaw. She thrashed her head yanking his blade clean, and rounded on him with savagery! Virgil wielded both Devil Arms with desperation as she fiercely attempted to shred him to pieces.

A large glyph appeared in front of Artreyu with six empty slots, the spell!

"NO!" Tiamat said forgetting Virgil. She moved into a backflip in the air, coming to hover in the skies looking down at the graveyard. She opened her jaws and energy began gathering.

"Virgil!" the battle maiden shouted. "The spell is not complete!" she yelled. "We need more time!" One of the slots on the glyph filled in, representing the element fire, five more to go.

Tiamat's ultimate attack, Dark Flare, was almost charged the dark power of her mega flare rippled out from her jaws, with the force of a super nova, the energy gathered exploded out into a beam of dark purple fire aimed straight at Artreyu and the Battle Maiden. They'd be destroyed! Virgil flew straight into its path aiming Ragnorak at the approaching destructive energy. He had to buy them time, he had to protect them! Ragnorak howled radiating with gold energy.

"Judgment Bolt!" Virgil screamed unleashing Ragnorak's Soul Scream. Tiamat's Dark Flare collided with the Ragnorak's power. The two forces pushed against one another, Tiamat exhaled a long deep breath, Dark Flare continuing in full force. The dark energy pushed against Ragnorak's light, Ragnorak's power began to shake and weaken, and once it gave way it began to give out quickly. Virgil would be consumed in seconds, he wasn't strong enough! Virgil felt the power spread through his body, out of self-preservation, he involuntarily Ascended. The gold light of a Judge radiating from him. It powered Ragnorak's Soul Scream and helped begin to push the might of Dark Flare back. Virgil's arm began to waver, it was consuming his energy maintaining Ragnorak's power and he wouldn't last much longer. *Push yourself!* The Voice of his inner Judge demanded. *You cannot give up on them, their lives are in your hands!* It screamed at him. Virgil screamed his arm shaking, the power of Dark Flare straining everything in his mortal body. He'd destroy himself if he kept this up! Virgil remembered the magicite in his pocket, the Optimum, John's gift still had a great deal of energy. He reached for it with his left hand gripping it. A spell came to his lips, not of his own mind but that of his spirit's, his inner Judge. An Ultimate spell, greater in power and cost than anything Virgil had attempted. He didn't have a choice but to cast it before his strength gave out.

Using the energy in the magicite to fuel his words, Virgil screamed, "Heaven's Wrath!" A beam of light pierced the heavens crashing down through Tiamat into Alexandros. The beam moved swiftly across the ground through Tiamat, a shockwave of fire and energy rose up from where the beam cut engulfing Tiamat. Tiamat lost her focus and her breath attack was expended. Ragnorak's Soul Scream shot forward unhindered exploding into her chest where Virgil had wounded her. Virgil's strength gave out seconds later, and he literally dropped from the sky, his body no longer even having the strength to move his wings.

"HOLY!" Artreyu shouted. The glyph filled in with the power of the six elements opened a massive portal that shot, like a cannon, a ray of Creation energy so large it consumed Tiamat. She screamed as the spell Holy, burned away her flesh, her exposed Dragoon Stone was destroyed. Tiamat let out a mighty last roar and fell to the ground. Virgil crashed into a small tree, hitting a few branches and then the earth below. He couldn't move himself, his body was in so much pain it had gone numb. Virgil couldn't feel his hands, his legs, he started to panic, his world spinning out of focus.

The Battle Maiden cried out kneeling down next to him. "Curaga!" She chanted, and the Master level healing spell flowed to Virgil. Virgil's consciousness began to fade, his eyes fluttered shut, too tired to keep them open.

"Will he be alright?" Artreyu asked her.

"Yes," she said with relief.

"It doesn't feel real that we beat her," Artreyu said in shock. "I didn't think we'd live through it."

"Neither did I!" she laughed still riding the high of narrowing having escaped death. "But we did, because Virgil gave it everything he had, he never gives up when he sets his mind to something," she said lovingly.

"He doesn't know," Artreyu acknowledged.

"He's not ready," she choked out sadly, and Virgil drifted out of reality.

Chapter 23
<u>Guardians of the Chalice</u>

Virgil dreamed he was in a beautiful garden, with fountains, flowers, and exotic plants. He heard a familiar lullaby being sung, the same one he heard as a child some nights when he was half awake. Virgil was running through the large garden; he knew he had to find who was singing. He'd always wanted to know who it was, who was watching over him. He knew that if he found the person who was singing, he'd find answers to questions that plagued his unconscious mind. He was so close to finding them, he knew in his heart that they were important, so important to both his past and his future. Virgil woke up and looked around, he was in a large bedchamber with expensive decorations and lavish trimmings.

"You're awake!" Alexa exclaimed happily getting up from her chair and jumping into Virgil's bed.

"What's going on?" Virgil asked sleepily.

"You're the hero of the city!" Alexa laughed. "I'm really glad you're okay," she added softly.

"Where am I?" Virgil asked looking around.

"Inside the castle, your safe," Alexa declared proudly. "The Avatar brought you here, unconscious. He told us you had killed Tiamat, effectively saving Alexandros from destruction! The townspeople are singing your praises, apparently almost a hundred citizens returned from the Ever After who'd been missing for a few years to a few decades. Everyone wants to meet the legendary Sixth Seraph, the Redeemer, slayer of Tiamat!" Alex cried.

"I'm not the one who defeated her," Virgil admitted, "It was Artreyu and a Battle Maiden."

"Who?" Alexa asked curiously.

"She wielded a Creation Devil Arms in the form of a powerful staff," Virgil recalled. "She reminded me of a Valkyrie," he said.

"She could be," Alexa nodded. "Some Valkyrie choose Nephilim from birth to guard and guide, kind of like a guardian angel for our race. My great grandfather had a guardian Valkyrie that saved his life twice," she told Virgil. "I've never heard of a Valkyrie wielding a staff," she added.

"That must be it though," Virgil nodded. "She's a Judge! A Judge saved me and helped Artreyu destroy Tiamat."

Alexa shrugged. "Only a handful of people even know the Avatar's identity. This was the first time I had seen or known of him, grandfather talked to him with great respect, like he knew him well," she remarked.

"I'm sure he does," Virgil sighed. The Oracle had sent the Avatar to rescue the Redeemer, and they were betrayed by the Doppelganger...Rasler! "Alexa! Rasler's a traitor!" Virgil shouted.

"Grandpa knows," Alexa told Virgil. "Artreyu told him, he didn't seem surprised, like he had known or at least suspected."

"How could he not know Rasler was working for the Death Dealers?" Virgil asked. "Isn't he the Oracle? I thought he was supposed to have visions of the future?"

"He does, it's not as simple as you think. Sometimes visions don't come, he must concentrate really hard, on people or events. The visions show choices, and paths those choices lead to, or at least that's how Grandpa explained it," Alexa said.

"He's not all seeing then," Virgil nodded.

"Nope," Alexa grinned, "He likes to make people think he knows everything, that's just not true."

There came a knock at the door, Lady Sibylla came into the room. "Master Virgil!" Lady Sibylla said with a happy expression that lit up her eyes. "It is so good to see you awake. You must be hungry; I'll have some food brought to your room immediately."

"Thank you, milady," Virgil said relieved to see she was safe.

"Alexa has barely left your side a moment since you got here," Sibylla winked at Virgil. "She's been praying for you to wake up for three days now."

"That long?" Virgil sighed. "What day is it anyway?" he asked.

"It is July 4th," Alexa told him.

"Independence Day!" Virgil nodded.

"An American holiday?" Alexa asked.

"You've never heard of the 4th of July?" Virgil asked.

"Oh yeah, the humans below light off fireworks every year on that day," Alexa nodded.

"It is to celebrate the birth of America's ideals, its principles, that laid the foundation for the country," Virgil told them.

"Your brothers have been concerned for you," Sibylla mentioned when he'd finished. "They are waiting a few floors down, after you've eaten something, I'll take you to them. You can shower and change in the bathroom."

"We'll talk more later," Alexa gave Virgil a hug. Virgil got up and used the bathroom, getting cleaned and changed. Sibylla came back fifteen minutes later with a home cooked breakfast. Virgil ate it all hungrily at a small table while Sibylla caught him up on current events, and they exchanged small talk. Afterwards he smiled feeling full and lazy.

"Thank you so much," he sighed having inhaled his food, "I don't deserve to be pampered this good!" he jokingly said with a laugh. Sibylla sighed and rolled her eyes at him. "Can I see my brothers now?" Virgil asked her.

"Of course," Sibylla nodded, and they left his room.

Virgil saw that his quarters were the guest rooms in the residential suite of the royal chambers, where Aseril, Sibylla, and Alexa lived! He'd been kept in the safest most secluded part of the castle. Sibylla lead Virgil down several floors to a less guarded and more accessible floor. A large living space had been given to the brothers to stay. Virgil walked into the Omega's temporary living space, the room erupted into cheers and people calling out his name. A grin spread across Virgil's face, he was relieved and thrilled to see all the people he cared about.

"We are so glad your awake homes," Louie said giving him a quick hug.

"How have things been?" Virgil asked the brothers.

"Things have been so crazy since you guys got captured," Jace took his cap off frowning in deep thought. "We didn't think we were ever going to see any of you again."

"That's twice now you've gone into the Ever After, and come out the other side alive," Magnus told Virgil. "You are the luckiest man I've ever met."

"That's not luck, its skill," Virgil said pulling up an imaginary collar earning some laughs and eye rolls. The group broke up some, people going back to doing what they were doing.

"Things are going to be so different this year," Gabriel said to Vahn.

"Why is that?" Virgil asked.

"We won the Tournament, or did you forget?" Gabriel asked.

"Oh yeah!" Virgil exclaimed. Things had gotten so crazy from the moment he had touched the Chalice. He had gotten captured and lived in the Ever After for over a week! Met his father, met the Avatar, and had escaped Hel. So much had happened it felt like the Tournament was years ago.

"The winners of the Tournament become the new Guardians of the Chalice," Gabriel explained. "The Chalice of Immortals will be brought to Bay Valley soon and be kept there until the next Tournament."

"Rasler said Sethos is after the Chalice!" Virgil exclaimed. "That is why they ambushed the Tournament, to steal the Chalice!"

"Correct," Gabriel said.

"Which is why a garrison of Paladins will be stationed at our University for the next five years," Magnus said, "Per as usual when the Chalice moves location."

"Oh," Virgil nodded not liking the idea of so many people from Internationals poking around their Chapter business.

"Exactly," Magnus nodded, "It will suck for us."

"Well maybe having all the extra protection will be worth it," Vahn added. "I can't imagine the Death Dealers just sitting around, I'm sure they'll come for it again.

"Why do they want it so badly?" Virgil asked.

"It may be the Chalice is used in the Oath of the Paladin," Magnus mused.

"Wouldn't it be best to just leave it where it is?" Virgil asked.

"It was in England as one of their Chapters beat out Alpha class by a small margin the Tournament before ours, but it is currently in the castle," Magnus said. "The protection of the Chalice is something that is a part of the very fabric of Paladin society. We are honor bound to bring it to the Omega house, to say we are too scared to accept the duty would make us look weak," he spat as if the very words were too much.

"Then let us look weak!" Lamar cried out. "We need to stop getting involved with this Internationals stuff and concentrate on our own Chapter. It is safest here, for us, for everyone we know," Lamar warned. "I don't want that thing in our home, it will bring nothing but misfortune," he spoke genuine words with fear filled eyes.

Virgil weighed what Lamar said, maybe it would be best to let it stay here. "All the Alumni are pumped that we won," Gabriel said. "They are throwing our Chapter a huge party this year at Retreat to honor our victory at the Paladin Games. They think we're Billy Badasses, and told Magnus our Chapter has never looked so good," Gabriel sighed. "I think the Grand

Prytanis should decide where the Chalice goes. We can express the group's doubts and leave it on his shoulders," Gabriel told them.

"Agreed," Magnus said, "Our Grand Prytanis is probably the wisest Nephilim in our race, with his power, he can see what will be best for the Chalice, and for us," Magnus told them ending the discussion.

There was a clear division in the line of thinking across the Chapter...like in most topics. Men were so different, and everyone had their unique perspectives and viewpoints. Virgil caught up with his friends, this was the first time he had a chance to sit down and talk with them since the Tournament first began. The brothers who had been prisoners in the Ever After were easy to spot in the room. The ten of them seemed, distant, sullen, and more serious. Perhaps because they had seen what was really out there in this world. The peace that existed in America was so frail, on the brink of toppling over into complete anarchy, and humanity was oblivious to it all. Virgil felt determined now more than ever to continue to serve the Paladins, whether that was where his Chapter was headed or not. He had to help his race, and humanity, and the best way he could do that was developing strong allies with the other Seraphs and Nephilim who opposed Diablos.

The brotherhood was called to a meeting with the Grand Prytanis in the throne room, a large gathering of officials and townspeople. Not all the Jeweled Officers were present, Rasler had yet to be replaced and his absence did not go unnoticed. Grand Hypophetes, Sibylla Diamond, was at her father's side, his closest confidant. The Grand Prytanis officially announced the Upsilon Delta Chapter the winners of the Games, and ceremoniously Magnus was handed the Chalice by the Grand Prytanis, Aseril. King Aseril addressed Rasler's absence announcing he had joined the Death Dealers and played a part in helping them enter the Tournament in an attempt to steal the Chalice. The crowd was surprised but Aseril asserted they'd overcome this betrayal and loss. The ceremony was over and the group retired to their chamber. Gabriel and Magnus were called on by a few guards for a short audience with the Grand Prytanis to state their case for having the Chalice remain in Alexandros. They came back in twenty minutes, King Aseril told them it was tradition, and that it was best for the Paladins for the Upsilon Delta Chapter to take the Chalice. They had no choice but to agree with the Grand Prytanis...

That evening the group was headed home to Bay City, Michigan. A small party was thrown for the brothers by Alexa and her mother in the same dinning room Virgil had first ate with them. The brothers had a fun night eating and drinking with the royal family. King Aseril joined them and the brothers flocked to him, he turned out to have a good sense of humor and had the guys laughing so hard they egged him on for more stories. Alexa talked Virgil's ear off, she was sad he was leaving, and wanted him to come back and visit. Virgil promised her he'd come to visit a weekend in the fall, if it was okay with Grandpa Oracle, Virgil joked earning a laugh from Alexa and a raised eyebrow from the King. Did he hear me? Virgil wondered like a dog caught on the kitchen table eating the family dinner. Virgil spent his time talking with Alexa and Sibylla. He lived with his brothers and saw them every day, and his new friends he wouldn't be seeing again for some time. Alexandros was as much another continent as it was another world. Though with a jump through a portal, travel time was less than a minute so there wasn't really much excuse. Alexa gave Virgil a special gift when they parted, an ornate hand mirror that she had spelled to act as a communication device. She had a similar mirror linked to it, so they could have weekly face to face chats and stay in touch. He gave her a big hug.

They had so much fun they didn't want to leave, but Magnus rounded up the group once the sun was setting, Virgil had a tearful hug goodbye with Alexa. Sibylla hugged Virgil tightly and told him he was always welcome in their home. King Aseril was distant from Virgil, colder to him than any of his brothers. Virgil and his friends walked down from the castle to the transporters near the Coliseum. Magnus spelled a small archway and a portal opened, they walked through as a group stepping into their temple just a short walk from their fraternity house. Virgil walked the familiar worn path back to their house, he remembered tripping over a log in the path smiling to himself, no wait, that was Birdy's memory. As the Omega manor came into view Virgil sighed, he was finally home! The trip had changed him, Virgil didn't feel like the same naïve country boy who'd left to visit the big city. Prison has a way of making you appreciate all the little things, like fresh air, and the ability to do what you wanted, when you wanted. Virgil went up to his room and jumped in his bed laughing as he thought he'd never see it again. It felt surreal being back here.

Virgil laid on his bed staring up at the ceiling, his bedroom was smaller than his second prison cell, and the cell had its own shower. Virgil sat up, but he could leave this room any time he wanted. Virgil wondered how his father reacted to him escaping. Virgil wondered if he'd be able to find him and drag him back to the Ever After. Would he do that? Virgil didn't get the sense that Raphael wanted him in Hel, but he didn't have the authority to release him either. Virgil had killed while he was in the Ever After, he'd killed mortals for the first time. The scariest thing about it was, Virgil didn't think he was a monster for having done it. That was the slippery slope. Perspective was everything, and it could blind men and turn them into murdering monsters. Virgil knew he wouldn't kill again unless forced to, but he discerned now that he could kill, he would kill mercilessly to protect people he loved. It was unsettling, learning the darker truths of the mortal mind, having to bear the sin of murder upon one's psyche.

All the bad had brought something good as well though, Virgil was more confident in himself now. He no longer wished he'd never been given power, he had grown passed such childish fancies. This was his world, he needed to accept it and move on. He accepted that he was given this power, he had no control over his environment. But he did have control of how he used his power. And Virgil knew he had to use it to stand against the Death Dealers, against the Fallen...against his father. Virgil wondered if the reason the Creator had finally bestowed a son onto Raphael was to correct an imbalance his father had created in the world. Virgil was the answer to his father's sins, meant to tip the scales of Justice.

Virgil still had three maybe four years of college left. He planned on finishing his education and then joining King Aseril in Alexandros to help him against the Death Dealers. With the Doppelganger now with the Death Dealers, each side in the war had three Seraphs, if the Paladins included Artreyu on their side. Virgil wondered when the next time he'd meet the Avatar was. He had been a mysterious and powerful man. They'd never had a chance to have a real conversation. The entire time they'd been together had been filled with running, fighting, and killing. Virgil knew they could count on him as their ally. Virgil thought about it and he realized he'd never really said thank you to Artreyu, for everything he'd done for his friends and him. He would make sure to do so the next time their paths crossed.

"Hey Virg," Dante came into his room with Birdy and Louie.

"Hey guys," Virgil smiled getting up from his bed. "What's up?"

"The guys are going flying during the fireworks," Birdy said, "Apparently the brothers do it every year. Bay City has the biggest fireworks in the State of Michigan, and the display can be seen from far away," he told Virgil.

"We're all going out for, a fly, I guess?" Dante laughed, "Whatever you want to call a group of guys with angel wings flying together. I guess it's awesome to be in the air and watch in the distance, the brothers all try to outperform each other and show off," he told Virgil.

"Oh, Rowan and you should shine at this then," Virgil told Dante.

"Watch it," Dante quipped with a smirk.

"This reminds me of the," Virgil said.

"Please don't say the first time you went to see the fireworks," Louie said.

"And you got so bored you fell asleep," Birdy added.

"And when you woke up you were bored so you practiced signing your name on a pad of notebook paper from your grandma," Dante finished.

"Weird," Virgil drawled the word out. "How did you guys know what?"

"When you used your power on us," Birdy said, "I seen your whole life flash before my eyes."

"Same for me," Virgil said, "It was like I was living all of your lives simultaneously," he told them.

"That's wrong!" Louie cried out. "Good god, I'm worried what you seen!" he joked laughing hysterically.

"Let's go!" Dante swirled his finger in the air and headed out the door. The rest of Omicron headed out, Nev and Nolan came out of their rooms and tagged along. The six of them headed over the Alpha sister's house. They were having a 4th of July party. When the brothers got there the sisters had a large cake made that said, 'Welcome Home Omegas.' The party was in the Omegas honor, for winning the Tournament…and making it home safely. TK had been on the verge of a mental breakdown while Gabriel was a prisoner in Hel.

Virgil saw Helene first she zipped over to him for a quick hug, "I'm glad you're back!" Helene said to him. "We've been worried about you. Blair has been sick to her stomach and not sleeping, but don't tell her I told you that," she told him. Virgil ran into Blair not a minute later.

"I've been so worried about your punk ass," Blair said punching Virgil first then hugging him.

Virgil started getting teary eyed, "I never thought, I was going to see you again," he said getting emotional.

"I'm here for you guy," Blair said holding him close. "Always know that." They broke contact and Virgil wiped at his eyes laughing.

"I'm sorry," Virgil said, "Didn't mean to get emotional."

"You have a right to cry if you want," Blair whispered, "We're all so happy you boys made it home safely. I didn't know what I was going to do without meathead, birdbrain, and Louie to hassle," Blair told him.

"Virgil!" TK said running up to him for a hug. "I've missed you boy!"

"It's good to see you again TK!" Virgil told her happily.

"Thank you for bringing Gabriel home," TK whispered to Virgil with shiny eyes trying hard to keep it together. "You've truly been a blessing to me. I know the Creator's brought you to us for a reason. Things wouldn't be the same around here without ya," she admitted whole heartedly.

"I appreciate that TK," Virgil managed to get out, moved by her words.

The guys and gals mingled, having some food and drinks. Once the fireworks began those with wings hurried out back. Virgil saw Birdy, Louie, and Dante join the group, they had wings now thanks to him. Blair looked sad watching everyone go.

"Blair come with me for a second, there is something I need to ask you," Virgil said with a small smile. It didn't take much convincing, Virgil used his power once more and gave the gift of Redemption to Blair. Her life flashed before his eyes, surprising him, her life had more pain, sadness, and loss that he had expected. She carried herself with such strength, he had no idea, the amount that she had suffered. When he regained focus, and the visions subsided, they were both crying. Blair had seen his life as well, and they ran into each other's arms hugging fiercely. Wings sprouted from Blair's back and she was overcome with emotion. She jumped into the air squealing with delight.

Virgil and Blair went out into the woods to catch up with the others. Everyone produced their angel wings flying up into the night sky. As they flew around they headed out over Lake Huron to watch the fireworks from the water. The combination of the lake below with fireworks in sky around them was awe inspiring. Virgil laughed so hard, doing flips and playing in the air with everyone else. This is what life is worth living for, he thought, the short happy moments that you get out of the drudge of normal days. The time you got to spend with the people who mattered most and just enjoying those moments of laughter and happiness. Virgil raced his friends, having the most fun racing Vahn as he got overly competitive with Virgil, playfully pushing him around to make him lose. It was good to see his Big doing well and having fun. He would never forget the time Raphael had taken him to see his imprisoned brothers, the living conditions they were subjected to, the looks on their faces and his when they'd realized each other were alive and well. Virgil valued his time with the brothers now more than ever. Each day they had together was a gift with no certainty as to how many more they'd have to come. That was why it was important to live in the moment, to let go and enjoy yourself during special times like the one they were experiencing.

That night celebrating with friends and family was one of the most fun days Virgil could ever remember having. The next few days after, Virgil worked on trying to get his life back together. He applied for some jobs and with Magnus' help, got a job on campus working at one of the front desks of the gym. Virgil could bring his homework and study while he worked, getting twenty to twenty-five hours a week at minimum wage. He started a week before Freshmen move in.

Virgil called his mom to tell her the good news. Sue was extremely worried when she heard from her son, telling him she was ready to call the police. Sue had tried to reach Virgil through the fraternity and had gotten the run around on his location. Virgil felt bad he had made her so upset and did his best to lie convincingly about what had happened. His mother was relieved he was well, though she yelled at him that he could never disappear without notice like that again. She was proud that he'd gotten a job. Virgil went and stayed a week with his mom shortly after getting back home. He needed an escape from everything, and his mom was really missing him. There was such a huge part of his life that he wanted to share with her, so many things she didn't know about him anymore. Virgil felt guilty. If she knew all of what had happened, she might see him as a stranger, and he needed her. Sue Pitcher was his rock.

Summer Retreat came a few weeks later and ended up being one of the best they'd had in a few years. They went away to a cabin owned by Tarek's mother up north a few hours from Bay City. Apparently, people in Alexandros had different vacation homes around the world. Dozens of Alumni came to Retreat and Virgil got to meet brothers from their Chapter he'd never met before. It was a great bonding experience for the Chapter and brought everyone closer together. This Retreat no demons attacked, and the brothers had three days filled with lazy misadventures with no responsibilities except to bond as a family.

The Chalice of Immortals was brought to the Omega house after Retreat, escorted by an army of Paladin warriors. The Chalice was stored on the top floor, locked in a safe in Professor Ramuh's office. The fraternity house was respelled along with the entire campus. The campus was protected by a powerful barrier, like all colleges, to keep the demons out. The barrier was fortified, to help protect against any impending Death Dealer attacks. If any Death Dealers came to the Omega house, they wouldn't even be able to see it, let alone make it far onto the grounds without being repelled. A group of twenty-four Paladins ranging from Alpha to Gamma rank were stationed at Bay Valley with the ability to call in hundreds more. The Betas were still a part of the Paladins, no matter how shady their Prytanis, Malachi, seemed. That gave them three Paladin Chapters on campus, protection of the Chalice would fall to all three organizations if the time came when they had to defend it. Luckily it was still summer! Summer happened to be the best time in Michigan, when the State not only came alive, it thrived! Virgil and his friends spent their last weeks of summer vacation going to the campus beach and doing some well-deserved relaxing before the stress of a college semester took over their lives once more.

About the author:

Christiano Prime, born and raised in Michigan, by age 10 was an avid reader and developed a passion for storytelling. His dream since he was a child was to become an author and captivate readers' imaginations. When Christiano isn't playing RPG video games, or daydreaming about his next story, he is saving lives as a social worker/counselor in a hospital ER doing crisis interventions and mental health evaluations. Christiano dreams of the day he can live on the West coast and return to Michigan each year for its beautiful summers, and his three dads, two moms, and seven sisters.

This is the second of a seven-book series, the third and fourth novels are completed, and I'm currently seeking representation from a literary agent or a publishing company. If you liked this book and would like more like it, please rate my novel amazon.com/author/christianoprime and leave a review. Your support and feedback allow me to keep working hard on the next installment of the series. Thank you for taking the time to read my story, by doing so you've helped me fulfill a lifelong dream, and I couldn't be happier to share more! Those interested in being added to my mail list to receive information about upcoming releases send your email address to primechristiano@gmail.com.